Praise for *The Great Reclamation*:

"An epic, staggering story . . . In Heng's masterful hands, the tale morphs as it spans, challenging our concepts of love, change, and possession. The ultimate revelation is as heartbreaking as it is honest about what lies at the core of many cultural and human transformations."
—New American Voices Award Judges' Citation

"Epic for the reasons life itself is epic. *The Great Reclamation* asks the reader to confront the big things, like love and identity and loss, but it allows us to revel in the little things, too, from the buttery taste of steamed fish to the smooth surface of a rubber seed. It is a pleasure to simply live alongside these characters."
—The New York Times

"[*The Great Reclamation*] illustrates the unsteadiness of both the physical environment and personal and political allegiances during a time of overwhelming historical change."
—The New Yorker

"Original and moving . . . In *The Great Reclamation*, Singapore is given the complexity it deserves."
—The Boston Globe

"Stupendous . . . a masterful work of historical fiction that makes the larger sweep of history intimate."
—Town & Country

"A love story about both heart and home."
—Time

"Precisely and elegantly rendered."
—Vanity Fair

"[A] lush, capacious novel."
—Oprah Daily

"An exquisitely written, heartbreakingly beautiful tale of love and war."
—Ms. magazine

"Defies easy genre categorization, with elements of historical fiction, magical realism, and a sweeping, captivating love story at its heart."
—Harper's Bazaar

Lee Ah Boon and Siok Mei, and the heartbreaking way history can tear apart a family. I'm grateful to Rachel Heng for writing this gorgeous novel."

—Ann Napolitano, author of *Hello Beautiful*

"So beautifully written and perfectly imagined that you follow its characters out to sea, through city streets, into the corners of villages, through every strange quirk of life, until they get under your skin and into your dreams. How does Rachel Heng write about the imaginary and the historical in a way that they are both equally believable and moving and strange? I don't know how she does it, but this book is a marvel."

—Elizabeth McCracken, author of *Bowlaway*

"In telling the story of one country confronting the forces of change . . . Rachel Heng has written one of the most extraordinary novels I have read in some time."

—Cristina Henríquez, author of *The Book of Unknown Americans*

"A monumental epic. A story of an entire nation reckoning with its past combined with a heart-wrenching love story."

—Nathan Harris, author of *The Sweetness of Water*

"Arresting and haunting . . . Rachel Heng asks us to consider the tensions between homeland and nationhood, and whether progress can be made without sacrifice. This is a powerful, expansive book that made my heart ache."

—Crystal Hana Kim, author of *If You Leave Me*

The

Great Reclamation

RACHEL HENG

RIVERHEAD BOOKS
New York

RIVERHEAD BOOKS
An imprint of Penguin Random House LLC
penguinrandomhouse.com

The Library of Congress has catalogued the Riverhead hardcover edition as follows:
Names: Heng, Rachel, author.
Title: The great reclamation / Rachel Heng.
Description: New York: Riverhead Book, 2023.
Identifiers: LCCN 2022001223 (print) | LCCN 2022001224 (ebook) |
ISBN 9780593420119 (hardcover) | ISBN 9780593420133 (ebook)
Classification: LCC PS3608.E548 G74 2023 (print) |
LCC PS3608.E548 (ebook) | DDC 813/.6—dc23
LC record available at https://lccn.loc.gov/2022001223
LC ebook record available at https://lccn.loc.gov/2022001224

First Riverhead hardcover edition: March 2023
First Riverhead trade paperback edition: March 2024
Riverhead trade paperback ISBN: 9780593420126

Printed in the United States of America
1st Printing

Book design by Cassandra Garruzzo Mueller

For my mother

We do not lay undue stress on the past.
We do not see nation-building and modernization as
primarily an exercise in reuniting the present generation
with a past generation and its values and glories.

S. Rajaratnam, Speech at the opening of the
Sixth Asian Advertising Congress at the
Singapore Conference Hall, July 1, 1968

CONTENTS

PART I

A Small Island

Chapter One

Decades later, the kampong would trace it all back to this very hour, waves draining the light from this slim, hungry moon. Decades later, they would wonder what could have been had the Lees simply turned back, had some sickness come upon the father manning the outboard motor, or some screaming fit befallen the youngest, forcing them to abandon the day's work and steer their small wooden craft home. Decades later, they would wonder if any difference could have been made at all.

Or would past still coalesce into present: The uncle dying the way he did, an outcast burned to blackened bone in a house some said was never his anyway. The kampong still destroyed, not swallowed whole by the waves in accordance with some angry god's decree, as the villagers had always feared, but taken to pieces and sold for parts by the inhabitants themselves. If the little boy, the sweetest, most sensitive boy in the kampong, would nevertheless have become a man who so easily bent the future to his will.

Perhaps he would have; perhaps this had nothing to do with the hour, the boat, the sea, and everything to do with the boy. But these questions could only be asked after the wars had been fought and the nation born and the sea—once thought of as dependable, eternal—stopped with ton upon ton of sand. These questions would not occur to anyone until the events had fully passed them by, until there was nothing to be done, all were fossils, all was calcified history.

For now, though, the year was still 1941, the territory of Singapore still governed by the Ang Mohs as it had been for the past century, and the boy, very little, very afraid, still crouched in the back of his father's fishing boat.

Lee Ah Boon was seven, already a year late, as Hia liked to remind him. Hia, now nine, had taken *his* first trip on his sixth birthday. But while Hia at six had been a boy with plump, tanned arms and strong calves like springs that could propel him over the low wooden fence at the perimeter of the kampong, Ah Boon at seven was still cave-chested, with the scrawny limbs and delicate hands of a girl. Despite as much time spent in the sun as his brother, Ah Boon's skin retained its milky pallor, as fine as the white flesh of an expensive fish steamed to perfection. Hence his nickname.

"Bawal!"

At the sound of his brother's voice, Ah Boon sprang away from the boat's side. In the weak moonlight the sea around them appeared as viscous black oil, roiling gently in the breeze. He shuddered to think what could be waiting beneath its pleated surface.

"Scared, ah, Bawal?"

Hia clambered toward Ah Boon, stepping over the ropes and nets that littered the floor of the small boat. He moved with a careless, threatening ease, like the foot-long monitor lizards that scuttled through the tall grass around the kampong. Hia grabbed Ah Boon's shoulders, turning his torso out toward the sea.

"Wah, so brave!"

Hia pushed his brother suddenly, as if to tip him out of the boat. The sea lurched up toward Ah Boon's face and he clawed at the side, letting out a small whimper.

"You know," Hia said. "Pa never tell you everything about your first trip out. He never tell you about the night swim, hor?"

Hia went on to say that it was a tradition that every fisherman's son went through on his first trip. That soon, Pa would stop the boat in the middle of the empty sea and tell Ah Boon to get out into the water.

All around them pulsed the ocean. And up above, blank and starless, was the unending sky. A cloud scraped the thin moon; the darkness deepened.

Ah Boon thought of the fish. Bright-eyed creatures with silver bodies of pure, spasming muscle. For the past year it had been his terrible job to help sort them, still alive in the nets when his father came home. Horrified by gasping, desperate mouths and manic shiny eyes, he had run away crying at first, but the jeers of his brother and the stern, clicking tongue of his father eventually reconciled him to his task.

Thus Ah Boon had learned to present a blank face, to control his expression even when he stepped by accident on a slimy, stingless jellyfish on the beach and the wet alive matter oozed between his toes. He had perfected the containment of his distaste for the unruly water that so dominated the life around him, felt in the pit of his belly like a cold glass marble he'd accidentally swallowed. But what Hia was suggesting now—to plunge his small self into the wide black sea—this he could not bear.

"Don't want" was all he said.

"Don't want?" Hia cried, almost gleefully. "You got no choice! You must swim away, far, far away, until you hear us call you back. It's the tradition. You know what is tradition?"

Tradition was the glue that bound everyone else so naturally, but failed, somehow, to adhere to Ah Boon. Sweeping his grandmother's weeded grave as cicadas screamed like demons in the bushes; visiting the crowded houses of neighbors during the New Year to have his scrawny frame prodded and commented upon; the assumption that he would one day, like his father, be a fisherman. Tradition was the stick against which he was constantly measured, against which, time and time again, he came up short.

"Tradition means: Pa did it, I did it, no choice, you must do also." Hia grinned, his teeth flashing white in the dark.

The arches of Ah Boon's feet tensed up as they always did when he was nervous. He bit his lip. He would not cry.

The boat began to slow.

"Oh, here we go," Hia said. "Ready, Boon? Ready for your long, cold, swim in the dark?"

The engine fell silent, and all Ah Boon could hear was the thrum of the waves. They were louder now, as if crashing onto something. It was so dark. He could almost feel the cold water closing in, the sting of salt in his eyes, the burn at the back of his nose. Movement in the water around him; something invisible and large, or small, it didn't matter. What mattered was that it would touch him. Brush him with its slimy skin when he least expected it, on the sole of a foot, on a cheek, the back of his neck. There was no way to know.

The boat had come to a stop. Ah Boon felt his father stand up from where he was sitting behind them, next to the engine. Any time now Pa would tell him to get up, stop crying, and get into the water. Ah Boon squeezed his eyes shut. He felt Pa's hand on the top of his head. But instead of running his fingers through his hair affectionately as he often did, Pa simply left it resting there.

No one said anything. The boat was rocking gently, and still there was that noise of the crashing waves, louder than they should have been.

"How can?" Pa said. He spoke quietly, as if afraid to disturb the air.

"Don't know," Hia said. "Did we go a different way?"

"Can't be. We always go the same way."

Ah Boon opened his eyes. Neither Pa nor Hia was looking at him. Instead, they were staring at something ahead of the boat, some enormous shape.

It was an island. There was a shoreline, not unlike the one they lived by, rocky in some parts, sandy in others. That was the reason for the sound of the waves; they were in the harbor of this landmass. Unlike the flat shore they lived on, however, this island rose up from the sea, a giant humpbacked monster. Ah Boon had never seen cliffs that high.

The tide was drawing them closer now, rocking the boat gently toward the shore. Ah Boon turned to look at Pa and Hia. Hia's mouth was open, and his thick bottom lip glistened, a dew-soaked slug. His already large nostrils flared, like the gills of a fish gasping on land. Pa's face was the opposite; everything was closed, mouth pinched, eyebrows pulled tight.

From their faces, Ah Boon knew something was wrong. They were both very still, as if afraid of waking the looming shape before them.

But Ah Boon himself felt no fear, only prickling curiosity along with a strange, soft ache. He wished it were day so he could see the shape of the land before him. He wanted to know if its haunches were covered with rocks or trees, if seagulls dotted its shores, whether the ground was sand or mud. If the cliffs gave way to jungle, if there were trails left by animals or people that one could follow. A faint breeze lifted the little hairs on Ah Boon's arm. There was an odd quality to the air now; it seemed to vibrate, as if the island itself were humming.

P a had plied these waters for more than twenty years, a good half of his life. He knew every square kilometer of the coast his kampong was built on, could recognize every swirling, glittering gyre of seaweed and trash, every glossy, jutting rock, the ones favored by seabirds singing their adamant songs, the ones shunned for whatever reason. Certainly he would be familiar with any islands, had there been any in this area, and he knew categorically that there were not.

How, then, to explain this, here, now? Was it a mirage? But the waves proved otherwise—Pa could tell from the rocking of his boat how far they were from land, and its movement tallied with what he was seeing. For a moment Pa had the mad thought of driving the boat straight into the shore, to see if it would go right through.

"Can we go there?" Ah Boon said, as if reading his mind.

Pa shook himself. "Don't be silly, Boon. We don't know anything about this—this place."

He meant to say they didn't know if the harbor was deep or shallow, whether sharp rocks lay beneath, and so on, logical reasons why they ought not to go there, but the words stuck in his throat. A slow dread began to take hold of him. Pa was not a superstitious man, and yet.

"How come we never see this before, Pa?" Hia asked.

Pa was silent. Finally, he turned away from the island. "Come, go home now."

"But we haven't put the nets out yet," Hia protested.

"We will put them out on the way back," Pa said.

"On the way back got no fish. Why we don't put the nets out here? Here close enough to the usual place, right?"

The older boy's voice was insistent but respectful. He knew not to appear to be questioning his father's authority. Still, Pa's frown deepened. He did not want to have to explain himself.

"We catch something that's not a fish here, then how?" Ah Boon said.

Pa's hand was swift, cuffing Ah Boon's right ear in one hard blow. The boy's head bounced to the side, and he brought his arms up to shield himself. But no further blows fell; Pa regretted it as soon as he'd lifted his arm.

"Don't talk nonsense," Pa said.

But a part of him feared the very thing that Ah Boon had voiced. Who knew what lurked in the waters of an impossible island?

"Come, go home," he repeated firmly.

Ah Boon's ear was still smarting from Pa's slap when the wind picked up, a violent howl sweeping across the waves. Again the air seemed to hum. He had the feeling that they were being watched from the darkness. Not by people, or even animals. Inexplicably he was certain they were being watched by the island itself.

Pa pulled the cord that started the engine, and its mechanical roar ripped through the quiet. Ah Boon felt the island flinch at the noise, as if the shore were shying away. But this time he kept his mouth shut.

Pa turned the boat around. Both Ah Boon and Hia scrambled to face the back of the boat, so they could watch the island as they sped away. Despite their traveling at top speed, the looming mass didn't seem to be growing smaller, only larger. It seemed to be chasing them. He wondered if Hia felt the same, and turned to look at his brother.

But Hia wasn't looking at the island anymore. He was lowering the nets at Pa's instruction.

"Come, Bawal, try to be useful," Hia said, handing Ah Boon a corner of a net and showing him where to anchor it on the boat's side.

So Ah Boon turned his attention away from the island. The tasks were straightforward; he was to hold one rope here, tie two knots there, keep an eye on the drift of the net to make sure it didn't get caught in the rudder. They absorbed him momentarily, and for the first time, the life of a fisherman seemed less terrifying, reduced to the simple maneuvering of a net as the wind rushed across one's cheeks. Ah Boon gave himself over to the work at hand.

It was only when Hia asked Pa whom he planned to tell that Ah Boon looked back again. The island was tiny now, visible only if you knew where to look. He squinted at the bump in the distance, watching as it shrank smaller, smaller, and then disappeared. Only the horizon remained.

Chapter Two

When they returned to land, Uncle was already waiting. He stood in the shallows, feet planted in the shifting sand, wooden wheelbarrows parked by his side. His singlet was graying, his shorts of rough canvas pulled high on the waist.

Uncle was Ma's brother, not Pa's, but somehow the two men looked more alike than the actual siblings. Both Uncle and Pa had short, skinny builds, frames lined with wiry muscles, like weathered trees with boughs both thin and flexible. They had the same interrogative, beak-like noses with elongated nostrils, cracked disapproving lips, and skin hardened into the same liver-spotted shell.

The real difference was to be found in their breath: Pa's strong and steady, Uncle's slow, wheezing, a reminder of the long illness he had barely recovered from six months ago. Ah Boon shuddered to think of the sour, metallic smell, nights kept awake by terrible hacking. The fine spray of blood that would emerge from Uncle's mouth with a particularly painful cough, the steaming water in Ma's laundry buckets turned pink when they soaked his sheets the next morning.

Pa stopped the boat where the water was knee-deep for the adults, which meant it would come up to Ah Boon's chest. Hia leaped out of the boat, splashing seawater into Ah Boon's face.

"Come on, you want to stay inside forever is it?"

"Leave him alone." Their father's voice was stern.

Hia made a face at Ah Boon when Pa turned his attention to the nets, but fell silent. He swam around the back of the boat to join his father.

"Come, Boon."

It was Uncle. Ah Boon wrapped his arms around Uncle's neck, trying not to touch the knobbly protrusions of the man's spine. They had grown pronounced and grotesque during his illness and filled Ah Boon with a sick feeling. Still, it was Uncle with whom Ah Boon had always felt most at ease, quiet, patient Uncle. He gently lifted Ah Boon out of the boat, one arm under his buttocks, and carried him to shore.

"Thank you," Ah Boon said, dropping to the wet sand, grateful but also a little resentful. If Uncle had left him for just a minute longer, he thought he might have summoned the courage to swing one leg over the boat's edge and slide into the water. How was he ever going to change if no one ever thought him capable of it?

Pa was staring at the nets. He turned to Hia, asking him a question Ah Boon couldn't hear. Hia shook his head and threw his palms up. Staring at them from the shore, Ah Boon longed for Pa to speak to him as he did to Hia. To be scolded, taken in hand and told what to do. When Pa ran his hand through Ah Boon's hair as he passed, he did it as one might pet a tame animal of whom one did not expect very much.

Uncle and Hia were coming back, each dragging a net filled with fish. Ah Boon couldn't see their faces, but their backs heaved with effort. He pushed the wheelbarrows down the shore toward them, and saw now that the nets were bursting with fish. The fish were large and small, some flashing silver, others shimmering pink. Many were round and flat, the kind that would sell for good money at the market. Mixed among them were several fat, glistening prawns, long whiskers twitching. Ah Boon's eyes widened.

"How come today so good?" he said to Hia. The nets were never even half this full when Pa and Hia returned from a trip.

Hia shook his head. "Don't know," he said. He seemed too amazed to be snide, pointing out the grouper, the black bawal, the catfish the size of his forearm. "Maybe can keep one to steam for tonight!"

Ah Boon's mouth thickened with saliva. The catfish's sticky skin, steamed taut, would yield a buttery white flesh when prodded open with a chopstick. Usually they kept only the smallest of fish for themselves, scrawny creatures filled with pin-like bones, made edible only by frying to a crisp.

"Wah! You think can, Hia? Did you ask Pa?" Ah Boon said.

"Not yet, but look, so much fish. Sure can keep at least one big one, to celebrate!"

Ah Boon nodded happily at his brother. When Hia was kind to him, he could not help but adore him. He gazed at Hia's tanned, plump face, his sparkling black eyes and long fine hair that flopped over his forehead just so. His brother was surely the strongest, the funniest, the handsomest of all the boys in the village. It was natural that Pa should be closest to him, it was the order of things.

Pa called to the boys. He wanted them to run to the houses of his closest friends and fellow fishermen—Ghim Huat, Ah Kee, and Ah Tong—and pass the message that the men should meet at the Lees' house after market hours.

"Is it because we're going to cook a big fish for dinner tonight? Because we caught so much?" Ah Boon asked.

Pa shook his head. He squatted so that his face was level with Ah Boon's.

"Boon, be a good boy and don't tell anyone about today's trip. Not the island, not the fish. Okay?"

"But why?" he asked. "Catch so much fish is good, right?"

"Be a good boy, don't tell anyone," Pa repeated.

Hia grabbed Ah Boon's hand, pulling him away from Pa. "We won't tell anyone. Come, Boon, let's go."

"But why?" Ah Boon asked again. "Why?"

He was tired now. It had been his first trip, after all, and they had risen at three thirty in the morning. Behind them, the sun was beginning to rise, the thin moon fading. The sky was growing brighter. It was the kind of blue that reminded Ah Boon of egg yolks, even though egg yolks were yellow. Pa's face was flushed orange, the cliffs of his cheekbones dusted with fine white specks. Ah Boon knew that if he were to lick Pa's skin, it would be salty, just like the back of his own arm. For as long as he could remember, his skin had always been salty, sweat mingling with seawater. Grains of sand on the soles of his slippers chafed the bottoms of his feet, his eyes stung.

"Why?" he said again.

"Shut up," Hia hissed as he dragged Ah Boon up the beach.

All morning at the market, Pa and Uncle were silent and tense, terrified that someone would notice their unusual catch and start asking questions. They had sold a good deal of it to a middleman before heading to the market themselves, to minimize attention.

It was only now, sitting in the house with Ghim Huat, Ah Tong, and Ah Kee, that the pair began to relax. Cigarettes hung from the corners of all mouths except Pa's and Uncle's. Uncle had, with great difficulty, stopped smoking because of his illness, and Pa had never taken it up to begin with.

Men like them were to be found throughout the kampong, the coast, and the city beyond. Settled in groups of three, four, five, on stools, stoops, pandan mats, wooden floors. Muscles aching sweetly after a long day's work—the location of the ache depending on the cargo hauled, be it fish, brick, rice, trishaws—they permitted themselves coffee, oil black or softened with condensed milk, sipped quietly as they rubbed their knuckles into the hard gnarls of their bodies. Topics of conversation varied by group, tended toward gossip with the occasional foray into politics. Who had won big at chap ji kee, whose son had been matchmade with whose daughter, how the war effort in the homeland was faring, where the most generous servings of nasi lemak might be had. Conversation unspooled languidly, words given up as offerings to the stultifying afternoon heat. Talk softened the knots in their minds, dulled the edges of their aches and pains.

Pa, Uncle, and the three men had engaged in such talk on such golden afternoons many times before. But today their voices were urgent, furtive. There was the matter of a mysterious apparition, an entire solid landmass, an island.

"What you mean cliffs? Here where got cliffs! Eh, Huat, you wake up too early is it, still dreaming on your boat . . ." This was Ah Tong, the most boisterous of the group, a man whose thick palms were as smooth and shiny as the inside of a seashell.

"You mean like Kota Tinggi?" Ah Kee said, thoughtful. He was a quiet man, known for his ability to haul sacks of dirt as large as a pig. Born in a town in northern Malaya, he had moved to the kampong with his parents as a boy and had lived here ever since.

Pa had never been to Kota Tinggi, and said as much.

"Is it you go too far? Go until Sakijang Pelepah? Or Kusu?"

"No," Pa said impatiently. He had fished there his entire life. He knew where those landmasses were, and this was not that.

"Got ask Pak Hassan, Pak Suleh?"

Pa shook his head. He had told no one except those in this room.

"How can suddenly got island appear out of nowhere?" This skepticism came from Ghim Huat, the oldest of the group and a veteran fisherman.

"I know what I saw," Pa said.

"And you all saw the fish, right?" Uncle added.

There was silence except for the nervous tapping of someone's fingernail on the side of his stool.

Ghim Huat conceded that he had seen the fish, and he had never seen such a thing in all his forty years of fishing. The other men nodded along. It was decided that they would all head out together that afternoon, so that they could see the island for themselves.

Ah Boon and Hia ran down to the beach when they heard the engine roaring to a start. How strange to see that many grown men crammed into one small boat. Pa was perched at his usual spot by the motor, while the other four sat two by two, each leaning against the side of the boat to make sure the weight was evenly distributed. They all had their knees pulled into their chests, like children.

The boys watched the boat speed away across the gray waves until it was no more than a speck on the gentle curve of the horizon. What would the men find? Perhaps the island was a secret pirate den, or the habitat of a million colorful songbirds. Despite the fierce afternoon sun beating down on their backs, they stayed until Ma began calling for them.

Booooon! Yaaaaam! Her distant voice stretched from their house to the shore. The boys leaped up and raced toward her, slippers sinking into soft sand. As usual, Hia dashed ahead and when Ah Boon got to the house, he was already sitting on the grass out front, helping Ma arrange the fish in rows on the newspapers laid out on the ground.

"Aiyo, Boon," Ma said. "How many times must I call you boys? Deaf, is it?"

She patted the ground next to her, and Ah Boon joined her in a squat. His job was to take the fish from the bucket, pat them dry with an old cloth, and pass them one by one to Ma, who would lay them out on the newspapers. Hia sat across from them, making neat rows of fish at the other end.

The Lees' home was a modest attap house on the edge of the kampong, facing the sea. A thick strip of burping soil formed their part of the beach. It was more swamp than beach, really, dense with twisting mangroves whose roots reached up through the mud like so many tiny arms. Millions of camouflaged little crabs plied the mud flats, outnumbered only by the tiny, perfect balls of earth they rolled while digging their homes. No larger than a thumbnail and a translucent gray-brown, they gave the impression that the ground itself was skittering and shifting.

The occasional mudskipper could also be seen hopping between the mangrove roots, eyes flashing in the shade. Ah Boon and Hia had often made a game of who could spot the first mudskipper when they were younger. Unlike Hia, whose eyes darted impatiently across the swamp, Ah Boon scanned methodically, inspecting every moss-covered rock, every piece of rotting bark, every blackened root for a frilled fin, a glinting eye. But he would hold his tongue even if he spotted a mudskipper right away, for Hia got frustrated and refused to play if he lost too often.

There were clearings in the swamp, such as the one Pa and the men had departed from this afternoon, where the mangroves gave way to flat and sandy beach. Here, boats could easily be pushed down into the water. The houses closest to these clearings were coveted and rare, lived in by the wealthier families such as Ghim Huat's. The Lees' house did not face such a clearing. It was up against an especially thick area of mangroves where the screech of cicadas was deafening this time of day, when the noon sun seemed determined to scorch everything within its reach.

"This morning the trip how?" Ma asked, without looking up from the drying fish.

"Boon almost cry, he so scared of the water," Hia said, grinning.

But it wasn't a nasty grin. The morning had created an understanding between them. Now they shared a secret, and even if Ma or Uncle or the other fishermen had been told about it, the eerie wonder of those dark hours belonged to them alone.

"You better get used to it, boy," Ma said. "The sea is not going away. So big already, still scared?"

She poked Ah Boon's side, tickling his ribs through his thin singlet. Ah Boon giggled and twisted his torso away.

"I not scared! I not scared!" he said.

And the memory of those moments when he'd thought he was about to be tipped out of the boat for the "night swim" did seem distant now.

"Pa and Hia also scared when they saw the island. Both of them never close mouth like monkey, like this." Ah Boon let his lower lip drop into a gape.

Ma's laugh was rich and bright, a streamer unfurling in the wind. Hia's chin began to jut in annoyance, but then he laughed too.

"Very clever to imitate your pa, huh? Better not let him catch you," she said, tickling Ah Boon again.

He writhed and lost his balance, falling onto his back. Ma took the opportunity to poke his exposed belly, making him laugh even more, kicking his feet up and sending a slipper flying.

"Watch out!" Hia yelled. "The fish!"

Ah Boon lay on his back, sticky with sweat, staring up at the blazing

sky. He thought of the island. Perhaps Pa, Uncle, and the other fishermen were there now. He imagined a coastline fringed with mangroves
leaking into muddy sea, not unlike their own. Broad expanses of sparkling white sand that would burn the soles of bare feet but not the hardened paws of the monkeys who lived there, who would come curiously to
Pa and the other men as they pulled their boat onto the island's shore.
Or perhaps those that would meet them would be Orang Laut, the original boat people of these lands, many of whom the Ang Mohs had since
forced to move to Johor.

The Lees lived on an island too, albeit a much larger one. It had many
names: Temasek, Pulau Ujong, Nanyang, Sin Chew, Singapura, Singapore, depending on who and when you asked.

When put to the question of how large their island was, Ma always
answered vaguely. Sometimes it was ten times the size of the kampong,
other times large enough that you could spend a day cycling from one
end and not reach the other. Never did it occur to Ah Boon that perhaps
Ma didn't know.

He did know this much: Their kampong was on the southeastern
shore of the territory they called Singapore, and was one of four clustered along the best fishing areas of the coast. Two of the kampongs were
Chinese, populated mostly by Hokkien immigrants who had settled at
the turn of the century. The other two were Malay, and were much older.
There lived the fishermen who had taught the first Chinese settlers how
to build boats from mangrove wood, to trap crabs in woven rattan cages,
make sun-dried belacan out of crushed and fermented shrimp. It was out
of respect for their neighbors that very few in Ah Boon's kampong kept
pigs, and those who did made sure to confine them to pens.

Nearly everyone in their kampong today had been born in Singapore;
both Ma and Pa had grown up here. Pa's parents had too, as had Ma's
father, though her mother had come on a ship from the Mainland, driven

by drought and poverty. All were dead now. Pa's mother was the only one Ah Boon had ever met, though he'd been too young to remember it.

Ah Boon hoarded these facts carefully, although he did not know what drought was, or what the adults meant by "the Mainland," though he gathered it was somewhere very far away, a place where everyone was Chinese and looked like them. He had the sense that it was important to remember things. It gave him comfort to be able to recall, exactly a year ago, his mother telling him that he must never marry a woman who was not Hokkien, and preferably not someone who had come from the Mainland, but rather someone who had, like him, grown up in Nanyang. He'd been only six at the time of this pronouncement, but Ah Boon carefully stored it in the corner of his mind that was concerned with the future.

It was late when the boat came back, the sun just barely suspended over the horizon.

What would the men say? They had been gone for the whole afternoon. Ah Boon's stomach twisted with excitement as he raced down the beach, the sun-warmed sand delicious beneath his bare feet. He watched Hia, far ahead of him as usual, white singlet bathed in the dusky light as he splashed into the surf, waving his arms above his head. But the men on the boat did not wave back.

Pa steered the boat toward the shore slowly, just as he had earlier that morning. How strange to think that it had been the same day. Hia called out to them, but Ah Boon was too far away to make out Pa's reply.

Finally Ah Boon was at Hia's side. Something was wrong. The men were wrapped in a thick silence, speaking only the occasional monosyllable as they dragged the boat onto the shore.

"What happened?" Ah Boon whispered to Hia.

"Shut up," Hia said, pushing him away.

The raw edge in Hia's voice suggested he had been scolded by Pa, so Ah Boon did not ask again. Ma was here now too, speaking to Uncle in a low voice on the beach. As soon as the boat was out of the water, the men gathered in a circle.

"What you mean, nothing?" Ma said.

"Nothing," Uncle said. "No island. We went around for hours."

Ah Kee was shaking his head. Ghim Huat scratched the silvery stubble that lined his chin. Ah Tong clicked his tongue over and over again.

Pa was silent too. Folds raked the skin of his neck, stretched like thin rubber bands around his throat. His long earlobes sagged. Ah Boon realized, for the first time, that Pa was old.

They stood there in silence for a long while. Then Pa shook his head, shaking off the whole befuddling day, and said: "No point worrying. Come, go home."

The men exchanged skeptical glances, and Ah Boon saw how it seemed to them.

"It was there!" he blurted. "I saw also. The island was there."

The men stared at him; Ah Boon's cheeks burned. They shook their heads.

"Keep quiet, Boon," Pa said.

"But I saw it," he whined.

"Quiet!"

How could the men not believe what he had seen with his own eyes? It was unbearable to feel them doubting Pa, to feel Pa's own creeping doubt.

"Enough for today," Ghim Huat said. "Everyone is tired. Come, go home."

Chapter Three

Without a word the family went back to their regular routine. Pa and Hia doing the morning trip, Uncle and Pa taking the fish to the market, Ah Boon staying to help Ma around the house. Ah Boon had not cared for fishing before, yet he now longed to return to the boat. But the regular routine meant he was banished from the sea.

Ah Boon shared a bed with his brother and couldn't help but wake up every morning when Pa came to get Hia. Each time he would lie still, keeping his eyes closed, hot with envy and shame. Ah Boon was sure he had fared so poorly on his one trip out that his father now disdained him—what else could be the reason for his no longer being allowed on the boat? He tormented himself by imagining Hia at sea with Pa, the wind whipping through his hair as he faced the black, unknown water.

It had been decided, it seemed, that Hia would be Pa's son, and Ah Boon, Ma's. And so Ah Boon drew water from the well, hung laundry, turned salted fish on sun-warmed mats. What he had previously taken pleasure in now felt like punishment. He tried to remind himself how happy he'd always been to stay by his mother's side on dry land, trapping red ants with matchboxes in the shade of a coconut tree. It was he, after all, who had not wanted anything to do with fish. He who hated the way his skin grew clammy after seawater had dried on it, disliked how sand gave way beneath his feet in a receding surf.

And yet—the island. High cliffs, verdant shores. As dark and implacable as the sea itself. The island made the sea comprehensible, less boundless, more known.

But it had disappeared.

The mystery of it nagged at him as he went about his chores, and he dreaded the day that Pa and Hia would return exuberant, having found it again. Then the island would be a secret that they alone shared, and Ah Boon's exclusion would be complete.

It was not unusual, in the kampong, for adult siblings to throw plates as readily as they would trade insults, wives to chase husbands out of open doors, grandparents to make loud pronouncements regretting their children's birth for minor disobediences. The Lees' house, however, was one of silences. A different quality to each silence: some stiff and crackling, air turned to ice; others thick as ghee, seeming to leave oily smudges on the skin.

The silence around the subject of the island, however, was like nothing Ah Boon had ever encountered. Everything at home seemed fine, other than the apparent amnesia. Ma and Pa had stopped arguing about Uncle going back to work, Uncle no longer fretted about money for the sinseh, Hia even refrained from making fun of Ah Boon for not being let back on the boat. The silence was becoming something physical to Ah Boon, a weight bearing down on his small shoulders.

Finally, one morning, he could not take it any longer. Ah Boon waited until Pa had gone to the market. Hia was bathing himself behind the house. He could hear the distant sound of water sloshing over his brother's body, trickling into the earth, a comforting sound that repeated itself over and over again. Perhaps he shouldn't make a fuss when everyone else seemed happy to forget. But there it was again: the island, looming in his mind, towering, inscrutable.

And so when Hia came in with a faded pink towel wrapped around his waist, water falling from his dark hair, Ah Boon asked him in a small voice if they had seen the island again.

Hia frowned.

"Don't talk about the island," he said. "It's bad luck. Pa say is unclean, some dirty spirit at work."

"So if I tell Pa I won't talk about it, then can I come back on the boat?" Ah Boon asked.

Hia's frown turned to a smirk. He wet his lips.

"Bawal, use your brain. Pa and I do the morning trip together for so many years already. But the island only appear when you're there," Hia said slowly.

"So what?"

"Means if got spirit, it's you the spirit likes. Anyway, last week Pa told me himself, he said you can never be a good fisherman."

Before he knew what he was doing, Ah Boon lunged at his brother with all his strength. Hia fell to the floor with a loud thump. He wrapped his hands around Ah Boon's wrists, fending off his slaps and scratches.

They'd been much younger the last time they'd fought, and now the gap between them had narrowed. All those years of carrying heavy buckets from the well and pushing wheelbarrows up the beach had made Ah Boon's muscles hard and flexible, despite his scrawny frame. Evenly matched, the brothers rolled around the floor making a terrible noise, knocking over stools and getting tangled in the towel Hia had wrapped around his waist.

"What are you doing? Aiyo! Stop it! Stop!"

The boys paused, and in that pause Ma grabbed each by the ear, dragging them apart.

"Boon started it," Hia said.

"Don't bluff, Yam," Ma said.

"I never bluff! We were just talking, then he went crazy," Hia protested.

"What happen, Boon?" Ma said. "Come, stop crying, sit up." She pulled down his singlet where it had ridden up during the fight, smoothing the fabric with her broad palm.

Ah Boon wiped his face. Then, in a small voice, he told her everything: his question to Hia, Hia's assertion that Pa didn't want him on the boat because the island was his fault, the fact that he would never be a fisherman.

There was silence. Then Ma began to laugh.

"He said that? Oh, Yam. You little demon. Talk so much nonsense."

Hia's arms were tightly folded. "It's what Pa said," he repeated.

"Nonsense." Ma ruffled Ah Boon's hair affectionately. "You are not fishing anymore because Pa and I decided you will go to school."

Hia was silent. Ma went on to say that Ah Boon had been enrolled in the school in the neighboring kampong, and that class would start in two weeks.

Ah Boon didn't know what to think. Some boys in the kampong did go to school, it was true. But it was a great luxury, so rarely was this the case for families like their own. He'd always believed he would follow the same path as Hia, helping Pa out with the boat as soon as he was able, eventually saving enough money for a boat of his own. What was the point of school?

"But why must I go, Ma? Why can't I help Pa and Hia, or stay at home with you?" he said. Hia's pronouncements still echoed: *Because you won't make a good fisherman. Because you're cursed.*

"Pa doesn't need more help," Ma said simply. She stood up. "Enough nonsense. Come eat lunch. And put some clothes on, Yam."

Pa had gone to school briefly, for two years, before leaving to help his mother take care of the family. Like most women, of course, Ma had never gone. Uncle was the only one who had completed all of primary school and even part of junior middle, and so it was he who read the newspapers to Ma each morning as they sipped coffee on the porch.

The distant horizon on the steely sea, the chafing of cicadas in the bushes, the echo of the koel bird in the early mornings—*ouh-ouuuh, ouh-ouuuh*. Ah Boon's world had always seemed vast and unbounded, terrifyingly so, and yet he saw now that it had also been limited, circumscribed to the kampong and the family and the sea.

Now the idea of school replaced the island in Ah Boon's daydreams. Sitting out on the grass in front of their house, watching the salted fish dry in the sun, he contemplated the future. School; the mere idea of it cast a light on how little he knew of life outside his home. Ah Boon knew the kampong contained thirty-four families, in twenty-nine houses. The poorer families shared residences and it was to these—the Chans, the Lims, the Kohs—that Pa pointed whenever he wanted to drive home a point about how illusory any stability at all was; all it took was one prolonged illness or deceitful relative for an entire family to be plunged into poverty. Few in the kampong owned their houses; most paid rent to the towkay, a trim man of sixty with two wives and a brood of nine children who lived in a brick house with a large white staircase that led to its front door. The staircase was a popular backdrop for the daughters of other wealthy businessmen to have their pictures taken.

On one such occasion, Ah Boon had gone with the other children in the kampong to watch. How dazzled he'd been by the young lady's embroidered cheongsam of purple silk, her dainty umbrella of glowing wax paper, and on her feet, those small shoes, the color of a dove. Not a speck of dirt could be seen on them. And the photographer, an intimidatingly wrinkled Eurasian man, his shirt soaked translucent, carrying a large black box of metal and glass. The lightbulb that flashed, the spindly tripod legs sinking into mud—all of it hinted at the mysterious, wide world outside the kampong, a place where expensive photographs were taken for leisure and complex technology could be employed for frivolous tasks.

Other things Ah Boon knew: All families with able-bodied men were fishing families. Those households that did not contain a man, such as the Tans next door, were dependent on the women's labor for their livelihoods—laundry and selling sweet cakes. Women were not allowed on boats, this was another thing he knew. It was bad luck. Also a reason why his banishment from his father's boat stung.

The kampong had changed little in his years on this earth, but Ah Boon gathered that this was beginning to shift. The towkay's youngest three children, those in the kampong gossiped, had been sent not to the Chinese-medium school that the towkay himself had helped fund, but rather to the English-medium schools run by nuns in a wealthy neighborhood farther down the coast. Also a subject of discussion was the eldest son of the Lims, who had decided not to take over his father's boat but instead was working at a dried-foods store in the city. More and more young people were opting for jobs and lives outside the kampong, a fact that Uncle and Pa attributed to the softness of a new generation unaccustomed to the hardship that their elders had grown up with.

Was this why Pa had decided Ah Boon should go to school? Did he see his light-skinned son, all soft hands and wispy, girlish hair, as a child of this newly frail generation? Yet this thought did not pierce him quite as much as it used to, now that it meant he would learn to read and write as Uncle could.

The old newspapers they laid the salted fish out upon were suddenly interesting. Ah Boon had always looked at the pictures, usually of Ang Mohs—the translucent-skinned, light-eyed men who ruled the island of Nanyang and the rest of the Malayan territory—cutting ribbons, presiding over meetings, making announcements in front of white fluted columns. He'd only ever seen Ang Mohs on his few trips into the city with Ma; they never came out to the kampong.

More interesting to him were the local men, those with round black glasses perched on shiny noses, hair slicked back with gel or put up in neat turbans. Some Malay, others Indian, many Chinese. These men wore shirts and pants like the Ang Mohs did, except while the Ang Mohs were photographed smiling politely or sitting behind orderly tables, the local men were on stages before large crowds, foreheads scrunched, teeth bared as they shouted into megaphones. They were men of Pa's and Uncle's age, but they looked different, their shapes softer and more rounded, their skin fairer. These were not men who worked in the sun.

Would that be the kind of man he could be? Would he be more than Uncle, who used his schooling only for counting money at the market and reading the newspaper to groups of bored housewives? Suddenly the words on the page glowed with significance, and Ah Boon yearned to discern their meaning.

Chapter Four

Skirting the horizon was a faint lip of sun, dark sky softened by the promise of morning. On the first day of school, Ma and Ah Boon followed the dirt road out of the kampong, the same road that Pa and Uncle traveled by lorry each morning to go to the market. All around them were sprawling ferns and bowed rain trees, crowded by smaller plants growing in every possible space, and despite the brightening sky, the path felt dark and hemmed in. It had rained the day before, so Ah Boon and Ma treaded carefully. But every now and then one would misjudge, sinking a slipper into the soft wet mud, releasing a loud squelch as they pulled free.

Ma walked tall in her good clothes. A simple set, neat top with a high collar and a bottom of matching green cloth, patterned with little white flowers. Ah Boon thought it made her look very fine, like a wealthy tai tai, but he didn't tell her, for they didn't say such things in their family. She walked a short way ahead of him, pointing out puddles and places where blackened coconuts lay rotting in the mud.

"What is school like, Ma?" Ah Boon asked.

The question had been trapped inside him for the past two weeks. But the darkness and Ma's back being turned to him made it easier to ask. She didn't respond at first, and his ears grew hot. Hia would never ask what school was *like*. He would simply have gone, and been good at it.

"You will see soon," Ma said. To Ah Boon's relief, her tone was gentle.

"How come you never go school?" he ventured.

Ma laughed. There was never any chance that she could have gone, she said. So much work to do at home, so many younger siblings to clean and feed. Then she married young, and had children of her own.

"But you want to go?" Ah Boon asked.

Ma fell silent. She gathered up her pants and carefully stepped over a large puddle. Something moved in the puddle and Ah Boon leaped back. A thin snake, blue and black, slid out of the murky water.

"Cannot always want things, Boon," Ma said. It was not the life he had been born to, she went on, and the sooner he understood that, the better.

Ah Boon turned her words over carefully in his mind. What was the life he was born to? To work the boats? And yet here he was, going to school. Did his parents believe he was born to a different life from theirs?

From the trees came the coiled song of a man's voice. Azan. They were passing the kampong that neighbored their own, and through the shifting vegetation he glimpsed the village mosque, a wide, graceful building on sturdy stilts. Sandals and slippers would be amassed neatly outside, the fishermen in their kain pelikat filing quietly into the building. The call to prayer wound through the still morning, a low, haunting sound that seemed to touch every uncertain place in Ah Boon's soul.

The muezzin's melodious call summoned to Ma's mind all the children she had lost, the most recent only a year ago, on a pale dawn not unlike this one. How the birds had shrieked, how the distant baritone had echoed. Mournful and consoling all at once.

A total of four miscarriages. The first was terrible, late enough in the term that a midwife had to be involved, late enough she'd had to push out the small, silent ball of flesh as one would a live child. Ma spent the entirety of her next pregnancy gripped with fear that it would happen again, and had not believed Ah Yam would live until he'd been set on her chest, screaming into her skin. For the first year of his life she'd held fast to the thought that he might die. Eventually the fear had faded; eventually Ah Boon had come along. Life seemed to settle into its prescribed rhythm. She believed herself well on her way to bearing seven, eight children, like her mother and her sisters. The first unfortunate incident had simply been bad luck. She had worked too hard, her blood had been thin, they had not had enough meat. With two children safely delivered—boys, nonetheless!—she was deemed normal and healthy, more fortunate than most.

Then three losses followed. All early, and yet she had felt such grief for the shiny clots and slippery tissue that filled the chamber pot. Pa had been with her then, rubbing her back. Yet she wished him gone, so she could reach down and touch the silken lumps of blood, so like the smooth pieces of liver she might buy from a butcher. Eventually he left, and she did. It disintegrated to thin dark liquid between her fingers, like vinegar or wine. What made blood harden into life, what made it fail?

After the final loss last year, Ma decided she would not allow this to happen again. She would cherish her two existing children, pour herself into raising them, give them all that she could not give to the unborn ones.

As the muezzin's voice faded into the darkness, Ma snuck a glance at her Ah Boon. As he picked his way carefully through the muddy trail, his dear small face was furrowed in concentration. How serious he looked; always she felt he had a grown man's soul crammed into a little boy's body.

He would go to school. She would make sure of it, even if it was difficult, even if Pa disagreed. Pa had Ah Yam to concern himself with. Ah Boon was hers, and under her guidance, he would learn to read and write, he would become more than anyone expected of a fisherman's son.

They walked in silence the rest of the way. From time to time, lorries would rumble past, wheels flinging up mud. Ah Boon realized he could not hear the sea. It unsettled him. But then the silence began to make a space in his mind, a delicious expansiveness he'd never felt before. He was almost disappointed when they reached the other Chinese kampong and the sounds of morning activity began to fill the air.

The school was housed in a simple wooden building with a zinc sheet roof. Over swinging ropes jumped groups of girls; around a brightly feathered chapteh, floating in the air, gathered kicking, shouting boys.

Ah Boon grabbed Ma's leg.

"What?" she said.

He didn't answer. Ah Boon's meager social life had always been dictated by Hia, and he felt his lack sorely now.

Ma squatted down so that they were eye to eye.

"Be good, okay, Boon? Study hard, do well. Make Ma proud."

Her words took hold of him, made him take hold of himself. He thought of the moment in the boat when he believed himself about to be tipped into the water. If he could face the opaque sea, he could face this too.

Ah Boon let go of Ma's leg.

"Good," she said. She handed him a newspaper-wrapped bundle. It was warm, a single steamed bun for a snack at recess.

Suddenly her arms were around him and the smell of her soapy hair was everywhere. It had been a long time since Ma had hugged him. And then it was over. She stood up and pulled her blouse straight, and with a little sniff, gave his shoulder a push toward the school.

It was said that their teacher had an elongated face and the brutish features of an eel. He wore silver-rimmed glasses that, despite being perched on a flat nose bridge, miraculously did not budge. Yet every few minutes, he would flick his hand up toward his face and touch the thin metal wire that joined the two bulging lenses, as if to forestall their sliding. There was never any sliding. He did it so often that rather than saying his name, the students mimicked that characteristic hand motion instead.

"I hear"—then, a hand flick—"used to be a middle school teacher in the city. But the Ang Mohs made the school fire him!"

A hand flick from another student. "Is very ugly, hor. His voice so soft, you think he can be union?"

The children understood little of the unions, of the divided loyalties of the Malayan Chinese between the Communists and the Kuomintang, the colonial government's particular suspicion of the former and grudging forbearance of the latter. They were too young to know of the Kreta Ayer incident, when a scuffle between those carrying Kuomintang flags and wealthy Cantonese merchants at a Sun Yat Sen memorial service grew agitated, ending in the Ang Mohs firing on the whole Chinese crowd. The children were too young to understand the rage and sorrow in the wake of the six shot dead, the fourteen maimed.

Too young to know this, but they, too, lived in its aftermath: handbills appearing from time to time even in the kampong, calling on the workers of the world to unite against their colonial rulers; a group of city outsiders attacking the local provision shop for selling English rather than Chinese cigarettes; the Overseas Chinese Relief Fund volunteers knocking on doors to raise money to defend the Mainland against the

Jipunlang invasion. Tangled webs of patriotism and nationalist alliances might elude them, but the children understood the disappearances; the head shots in the newspapers announcing who had been jailed and when; the night schools being raided and shut down, unions suspended, printing presses and cyclostyles confiscated. And so a teacher who had been fired from his job at the behest of the Ang Mohs was an exciting character indeed.

"Teacher Chia is our teacher, we should respect him," said one girl, her voice ringing clear as a bell.

It was a fearless voice, Ah Boon thought, and yet not the kind that he associated with Hia, one that depended on the fear of others.

The other students booed. "He's not Teacher Chia, he's—" Hand flick. "Do it right, Mei."

The girl pursed her lips. The boys whooped and cheered, but she refused to indulge them. Hands flicked all around her and still she maintained her steadfast glare.

Through the crowd, Ah Boon watched. He was afraid for her, surrounded by all those laughing faces. Groups had always frightened him. A single fish was powerless, but a shoal could be a driving force of muscle capable of capsizing a boat. And how unpredictable such shoals could be, turned this way and that by the whims of light, temperature, and tide.

And yet the girl—*Mei*, he stored this name carefully in his mind— did not flinch. Her face, smooth and bright, was like a fixed pebble on the shore, winking in the sun between each crashing wave. Looking at her, Ah Boon seemed to feel something tighten in his belly. Only much later would he recognize it for what it was.

One of the boys reached out to Mei's face, presumably to flick the pair of imaginary glasses sliding down her nose. Without missing a beat, she grabbed his wrist. The boy chuckled, but when she didn't let go, his laughter turned nervous. The other boys were jeering now.

"Fight!"

"Ah Gau, scared of a girl?"

"Fight! Fight!"

Ah Boon knew what someone like Hia would do. He braced himself for violence, but under his breath, he whispered: "Don't."

A pause, then miraculously, Mei dropped the boy's wrist. Her face softened, and she patted the boy on the shoulders with a kind of teacherly indulgence. Slowly, the tension drained from his brow and he sat back down at his desk. From the other boys came groans of disappointment, but the heckling was good-natured now.

A confusing warmth came over Ah Boon. Who was this girl?

"Good morning, students."

Teacher Chia stood in the classroom doorway. The class scrambled to their desks, and in the bustle of activity, Ah Boon found himself sitting at the desk next to Mei's.

"When I say 'Good morning,' you say 'Good morning, Teacher Chia,'" he said. "And you bow, like this."

He bent over neatly, arms at his sides. As soon as he straightened up, his fingers flicked up toward his face, brushing the bridge of his glasses.

But the students didn't make a sound, not even the boys who'd made fun of him earlier. There was an aura about Teacher Chia. He looked at the children in a way that no other adult did: as if he really saw them, and would hold them responsible for their actions.

"So, let's try again. Good morning, students."

"Good morning, Teacher Chia," the class chorused, bowing in unison.

"Good. Please sit."

The class was silent. Teacher Chia spoke a refined Mandarin, one that sounded better suited to a radio newscaster than a kampong schoolteacher. Ah Boon struggled to understand; he had learned some Mandarin from Uncle, but Teacher Chia spoke fast and high, the tight vowels coming cleanly from the back of his throat, consonants rolling neatly as tiny balls of food in the center of his tongue. A far cry from the harsh edges of the Hokkien that Ah Boon was used to. He thought of what his classmate had said earlier, that Teacher Chia used to work at a prestigious middle school in the city. It must be true, then. His words seemed to lend the simple interior of the classroom—wooden desks with their corners worn to off-white nubs; a gray, scratched blackboard; walls covered in scraps of paper from the corners of posters long torn down—a certain gravity.

From a sheet of paper, Teacher Chia called out their names one by one, ticking them off as they answered.

"Ng Siok Mei," he called at last.

"Here," said Mei.

Ah Boon's hands grew warm beneath his desk. When his own name was called he answered "Yes" distractedly, aware only of how Siok Mei turned her head slightly at the sound of his voice.

She gave him a small, close-lipped smile. It was a smile that seemed to say they understood each other and would talk later, but for now they must pretend to be like everyone else. Ah Boon stared at his desk, the back of his neck prickling. He recalled the way she'd stood up to the boys earlier, the hard thump of her small palm on the desk as she made her point, the coldness she could inject into her voice. Here she was, smiling at him.

When he was done calling their names, Teacher Chia told them he would be in charge of teaching them to read and write, while there was another teacher, Teacher Wu, who would teach them math, geography, and science. He held up a book with a flag on the cover, red and blue, the white stencil of a sun. This would be their textbook. They were to bring in money for their books tomorrow, and he would order them for the children. Since they didn't have books yet today, he would read to them.

Ah Boon, typically attentive to all forms of instruction, was only half listening and would thus forget to bring the money the next day. All he could think of was the half a meter of empty space between his desk and Siok Mei's. It was unbearable, this space. He wished for a wall to spring up and separate them, so the sharp tingling at the back of his skull would cease.

But then Teacher Chia began reading from the book. His voice changed when he was reading; it became louder, more sonorous, quavering with emotion. The story was about a pair of lovers separated by an angry god, one lover on earth, the other banished to the moon. Despite the many Mandarin words that Ah Boon struggled to understand, he now found himself transfixed. Teacher Chia's low, melodious voice soothed him, allowed him to come back to himself.

He snuck a glance at Siok Mei. She sat with her elbows splayed on the desk, chin propped up with the heels of her palms. Beneath the desk her legs were crossed in an adult manner. Her wide eyes were shining, dark and bright as those of a live fish. Ah Boon wondered if, like him, she was imagining herself trapped on the desolate surface of the moon.

Chapter Five

Where the springy moss climbed over every rock were buried three generations of Lees: Pa's parents, his paternal grandparents, a great-grandfather. Their family plot was deep in the cemetery, beside an old bent tree that grew—propped up with a carved stake—nearly horizontal to the ground. The simple tablets bore only names and years, no pictures, no proverbs, none of the flourishes of the wealthy. Still, the rough-hewn stone was always free of cobwebs, the carved grooves cleaned with a rag and toothpick that Pa brought with him for this purpose.

Few visited the cemetery outside of Cheng Meng and other significant dates, and Pa was no exception. But he found himself here regularly in the weeks that followed the encounter with the island. He knew the others in the kampong mocked him for his strange pronouncement, for their futile, maddening trip. Their disbelief stung, yes, and his pride was not unhurt by the whispers that followed him at the market or the provision store. People talked to him slowly, kindly, as if he were stupid or mad. Any man would find it humiliating.

But Pa was a man firm in the belief in his own senses, and he knew what he had seen. The more his obsession with the island grew, the less he found himself able to speak of it. How to talk of the moment where the seas he'd known all his life suddenly conspired against him, throwing up not just unusual weather or odd currents, but an entire looming landmass where there should have been none?

It was more than the simple matter of its appearance and disappearance. He did not voice this to Ma or Uncle, but it had to do with the bountiful catch that had appeared in their nets that morning. It was strange, yes, everyone agreed. What they had not seen—what his sons, in their youthful distraction, had not seen—was the rippling of water that started off in the distance when they put their nets out, a rippling that came closer and closer toward the wall of the drift net. The schools of fish had been swimming *toward* them.

Pa was not a man who believed in luck. Yet he had been named for prosperity—Lee Ah *Huat*. A gambling man, Pa's father had been addicted to mahjong, chap ji kee, and all the vices they came with: drinking, sloth, infidelity. Pa himself had been an accident; he'd come late in his father's life, when the latter had been fifty-three and, in his own words, was pleased he was "still able to shoot." Pa was named for the riches his father hoped he would bring, for at the time of his birth, the family was in dire financial straits. His father had gambled almost everything away, including their fishing boat. He would gamble away all that his long-suffering wife and daughters brought home from the odd jobs people gave them out of charity, if they didn't immediately hide it in the biscuit tin they kept buried beneath a large pile of dirty laundry.

His father had hoped that Pa would be his lucky star. An heir to his name at last, after an endless string of daughters. But Pa had raged against him from a young age, taking the side of his mother and sisters. Never would Pa forget the worst beating he'd ever received. He had been nine. His parents were arguing about money, again.

"You want your son to pay off your debts for the rest of his life? Is that what you want?" his mother shouted.

His father looked at him, eyes yellow and red-rimmed, nose bulbous and shiny. "Ah Huat don't mind, right? Ah Huat loves his father, he'll support him like a good son."

Pa remembered the sudden flash of hatred, the way the skin on his arms grew hot and prickly, as if he had been out in the sun for too long.

"I'll take care of Ma, but I won't have anything to do with you," he said, calmly and without heat.

His father usually used the cane, but that night he had no time to stop and look for it. For weeks after, Pa could not open his right eye.

He turned out to be anything but his father's lucky star. The family's situation only got worse, their finances more precarious, until one night, his father had not come home. The next morning his body was found lying facedown in the surf, a halo of vomit lapping serenely at his temples. Returning from a drunken card game, he had made a detour to the beach. It seemed he had somehow tripped and fallen face-first, and too drunk to hoist himself up, he had drowned in less than two inches of seawater.

After the habitual mourning period, the family removed the white squares of cloth pinned to their sleeves and got on with it. They cleaned the house from top to bottom, making a pile of his father's clothes: worn singlets, tattered khaki shorts, several pairs of graying underclothes. Pa remembered how small and sad that pile of clothes was. Was that the sum of a man? Was that what one amounted to—a worn shirt here, a chipped enamel mug there? The pile was like the old shed skin of a snake, but instead of emerging anew, his father was gone forever.

Aside from this brief sadness, their life got much better after the patriarch died. Gone were the drunken late-night storms when his father would tear into everyone around him after losing money at some fellow gambler's house; gone were the panicked scrambles for the biscuit tin when his mother forgot she'd changed the hiding place and became certain her husband had gotten into it; gone were the beatings, the screaming, the vague undirected fury.

Pa's eldest sister married shortly after their father died, and her new husband started taking Pa out on his boat. He would never forget the first time. Motor engines were rare back then, and it was a boat of the old sort, a perfectly honed construction used by the Malay fishermen. The boat had a narrow prowless body and a single large sail that his brother-in-law maneuvered with deft grace. Pa had been mesmerized by that sail, by its power to capture the fickle wind and make it a solid, driving thing; by the sudden jerk, the way it went from limp to taut within seconds. He was never happier than when the wind was strong and the waves stronger, when the body of the boat cut through the jeweled sea like an enormous flying fish. Years later, when he'd paid off his father's debts and bought a motored fishing boat of his own, he still found himself thinking of that old sailboat. But times had changed; all the Chinese fishermen used fuel engines these days, and it would be foolish to purchase a sailboat on a sentimental whim.

So now he was a man with a business and a family of his own, an existence that moved in rhythms as reliable as the receding tide. Nothing of note had ever happened to trouble the surface of his life, nothing, that is, until now.

Pa might dedicate regular prayers to Tua Pek Gong and Ma Chio, burn joss sticks at their altar and offer cooked meals to their ancestors to keep their little seacraft safe. But the material manifestations of the supernatural—corporeal ghosts, pontianaks, and sitting spirits—he left to the fearful minds of others. So this island, the strange, undeniable behavior of fish swimming into his net as if it were filled with bait, everything about it was at odds with his understanding of the world.

And yet he longed for nothing more than to find it again. Worse still, he thought he knew how. Thus he found himself before the ancestors: to ask for permission, perhaps forgiveness.

It was his wife who first put the notion into his head. From her he learned of the fighting between their sons that had taken place weeks before and that the older had told the younger that the whole island business was his fault.

"Yam said Boon was bad luck," Ma went on. "Cursed, and that's why you don't want him back on your boat."

Pa had laughed at first. What a son, the older boy, always coming up with ingenious ways to torture his brother. Then he paused.

It had been, after all, the first time he'd taken Ah Boon on the boat. That had been the only thing that was different.

The island was out there. And Ah Boon was the one who could show him where it was.

But was it prudent, was it fair? Ah Boon was meant to be in school now, that was what he had promised his wife. Would he be inviting trouble upon the family if he made the boy do it?

Pa began to clean the same headstone that he'd cleaned when he'd come here yesterday. His mother's. Wrap the blunt end of the toothpick with the rag, ease the soft fabric into the carved grooves in the stone. The rag came away only slightly gray, a tiny red ant struggling in its folds.

A sign, perhaps, but of what? Pa contemplated the ant. The sun was setting, mosquitoes sliding in and out of earshot as the orange rays drew deep shadows from the headstones. He touched the ant with his finger and it straightened, scuttling toward his knuckle in a crooked line.

Pak Hassan was not home when Pa arrived.

"Fishing," one of his six daughters, Aminah, told Pa, shaking her head as if the head fisherman were a naughty child. On her lap squirmed a baby with the face of a plum. The dark lick of hair plastered to its forehead reminded Pa of Hia when he'd first been born, with his full head of wispy curls.

"Boy or girl?" Pa asked in his marketplace Malay.

"Girl," Aminah said, a little indignant, as if it should have been obvious. "My daughter's first."

"Pak Hassan a great-grandfather, and still out fishing?"

Aminah smiled, brushing the back of her hand against the child's sticky chest. "You know him."

Pa did. It was the great mystery of the four kampongs, how old exactly Hassan Bin Dengkel was. From a distance he could easily be mistaken for one of his sons, with his confident, lingering gait. Close up, however, one saw that the skin of Pak Hassan's cheeks clung to his bones, that whiskers of pure white sprang from his chin. But nothing escaped his quick eyes, renowned for being able to spot a shoal from hundreds of meters away. For his unrivaled knowledge of the sea around their home, Pak Hassan was often consulted by wealthy towkays from as far as the northern coast for his skills as a pawang in selecting the best hunting grounds to build expensive offshore fishing structures. He was no magical expert, Pak Hassan would say, tapping his temple. He simply knew how to use his eyes and his brain.

Pa waited with Aminah on the porch, making faces at the baby and exchanging comments about the lack of rain.

In this kampong were many of the same sights as in their own: wide nets strung out, shrimp paste on rattan trays drying red in the sun, boats pushed up against the foundations of houses. But these houses were older, larger, and gave a greater impression of permanence. While many of the houses in Pa's kampong sat on the ground, with walls of zinc sheets thrown and nailed together, the ones here were skilled wooden constructions, many painted white and topped with elegantly pitched attap roofs. It was said this kampong had been here for almost two centuries now, the first of the four to be founded by Sumatran fishermen generations ago. It had been named for the word gelap—*darkness that conceals*—a reference to the solar eclipse that was said to have occurred when the first fishermen set foot on these shores.

For the most part, the men of each kampong kept to themselves. The Malay fishermen, besides, used different methods than the Chinese, choosing to cast their nets in shallower waters near shore or to use hand lines from their koleks. The Ang Mohs had been trying to meddle in their ways for years now, recruiting the sons of fishermen to training programs on handling power craft and new types of nets, but the Malay fishermen preferred the methods they'd relied on for generations. The Chinese, with their new immigrants' hunger for accumulation, had switched to boats with motor engines once they saw how much more money could be made. Seeking out deeper waters to ply with large nets requiring multiple men to operate, they did not often run into their Malay neighbors while out at sea.

Even if he chose to stay close to shore, Pak Hassan had been one of the first to show many of the older Chinese fishermen which deep-sea areas were safe and which were not, where the best fishing grounds might be found. If someone knew about a vanishing island far out at sea, Pa thought, it would be Pak Hassan.

And here he came now, green kain pelikat wrapped around his waist, bare-chested, the bones of his ribs shifting beneath creased tan skin.

"Pak Hassan." Pa rose from his seat.

Aminah took her father's hand and kissed it lightly.

"What brings you here so late, Lee?" Pak Hassan said.

"I—" Pa found he was at a loss for words. How to explain what he had seen, what he wanted to know?

In the silence that followed, Aminah left discreetly with the baby, going to talk to a neighbor on a nearby porch.

"Is this about Lim and Razia? Because Lim can come talk to me about it himself, if he dares, the little snake—"

"No, no, nothing to do with Razia," Pa said. A young fisherman from their kampong was said to be in love with one of Pak Hassan's granddaughters—a doomed affair from the start, as he'd seen fit to approach her while she'd been on her own, trapping crabs in the estuary.

"Then what?" Pak Hassan eyed Pa carefully.

"You ever see—maybe seven kilometers out, east of the white bird rock—you see before, I don't know, anything?"

"Anything?"

"Anything—anything unusual," Pa said.

Pak Hassan clicked his tongue. "Lee," he said, "I see many unusual things in my life. You don't know about the shark I catch with hand line? Fifteen feet long, two piculs heavy!"

"Not a fish," Pa said. "Or yes, fish also—" He stopped, thinking of the enormous shoals rushing toward them, backs riffling the waves.

"You want to tell me what you see, or not?"

A sudden possessiveness came over Pa. Perhaps it was true that only they, only his son, could find this island. If so, it was theirs. And if he told Pak Hassan, and Pak Hassan did not believe him, he would be the laughingstock not only in his kampong but here as well.

"So?" Pak Hassan said.

"Yes, fish," Pa lied. "Big like a dugong, silver like mackerel."

Pak Hassan perked up. "Shark ah?"

"Maybe," Pa said. *Island*, he thought, swallowing the word down. "Maybe shark. Don't know, my son got a better look."

"You got see the fin? Black tip?"

"Don't remember. So shocked, never see."

"You young fishermen." Pak Hassan laughed. "See anything, also scared. Shark or no shark, all kinds of unusual fish can find in the sea, if only you stop to open your eyes."

Pa gave a self-effacing smile. They were on familiar ground now; Pak Hassan loved to chide the Chinese fishermen, especially, for their haste, their loud motorboats and clumsy drift nets.

"Better teach your son," Pak Hassan said. "You don't disturb the shark, the shark don't disturb you."

At dinner each night, Pa watched Ah Boon separate the strands of steamed bean sprouts in his bowl before placing them into his mouth one at a time, each accompanied by a carefully measured sip of congee. He watched the younger boy open his mouth to speak, only to get talked over by the older.

Pa knew how painfully Ah Boon felt every intrusion of the world, knew how his ears burned at every perceived snub, how his stomach churned as he trailed his father, too nervous to say what he wanted. Throughout the boy's young life, many in the kampong had expressed surprise that he—pale-skinned, skittish, doe-eyed—was Pa's son, and yet Pa, too, had been this way when he was a boy. It hadn't lasted. His father's beatings had put an end to it. Pa'd swallowed his pride, a bitter pill, and it had made him strong.

He could not bring himself to do this to his own son. Instead he avoided the boy. With his older son, Pa felt like a good father raising a good man. Ah Yam would move through the world without hesitation. If he ever broke anything, they would be small things, by accident, easily put back together again. He had none of Ah Boon's brooding energy. The younger boy, however, hoarded his pain, and Pa did not know what he would do with it.

Thus Pa hesitated about the islands. Ah Boon was unpredictable, as easily set on a course as a paper boat on the receding tide. And so Pa fretted day and night, unable to decide, until one day the decision was made for him.

Uncle's coughing came back. A wet, hollow cough, one that Pa recognized from the worst days of his brother-in-law's illness. Ma heard it too, he knew, and went about with a pinched look on her face. There was no money for another sinseh's visit; they already owed much to Swee Hong, the owner of the local provision shop, whose offers of credit would not last forever.

The fish they'd caught on the day they found the island had paid for the family's food for nearly a week, along with Ah Boon's textbooks, but Uncle's tonics would soon put them back into debt. And then there was the cost of chicken meat for nourishing broths, and shoes for Ah Boon, now that he was going to school.

Uncle tried to hide his cough, muffling it in his pillow at night so he wouldn't wake anyone. Everyone knew he was getting worse again, and yet no one said anything. Without money, there was nothing to be done. Even the boys, usually oblivious to the adults' woes, tiptoed around the house, bringing cups of water to their uncle as he lay in his darkened room. The tight, small smile on Ma's face was immovable during the day, but at night she would often get up from bed to pace on the porch.

Pa put aside questions of luck and fate. He would do what was necessary.

The next afternoon, he waited for his son to get home from school. He spotted Ah Boon some way off, walking down the path toward their house, neighbors waving as he passed, calling out greetings, making jokes. Ah Boon would wave back shyly and cast his gaze firmly to the ground. Despite his reserved nature, Ah Boon was clearly well loved, particularly by the women of the kampong.

"Boon," Pa said. "Come, let's go to the boat."

"Oh. Now?"

"Yes. I want to show you something," Pa said. It was a lie, but he didn't know how else to explain.

"Okay." Ah Boon cracked a wide smile. His front teeth were small and even, his mother's teeth. "I put my books in the house first."

He ran into the house and in a few seconds came back out. They walked over to where the boat lay, overturned in the shade, and Pa had his first misgivings. How would they even carry it down to the beach? But he could not ask his brother-in-law, or Ah Yam, or he would have to explain why he was taking the boat out in the afternoon with his younger son.

"Use both hands. Hold that side," he said. "Bend your legs. Back straight."

Ah Boon scrambled over to the far end of the boat. He wedged his hands under its edge, scrawny arms straining. For a moment Pa was worried that his knobbly shoulders would pop, but then with perfect posture, Ah Boon straightened his knees and the boat lifted off the ground.

"Oh. Good," Pa said.

He picked up his end lightly, and they made the walk without incident down the path to the beach. At the edge of the surf, he told his son to remain where he was as Pa pivoted around him, so that the engine side would be in the water. His son sucked in his lower lip, nostrils flared in concentration. A red mosquito bite swelled under his left eye.

Pa felt a sudden rush of pained love. He ought not to be so harsh on the boy. But if he wasn't, surely the world would be, surely it would chew him up and spit him out.

"Okay, put down," he said gruffly.

Pa pushed the boat out. The water that sloshed around his calves was warmer than he was used to, warmed by the sun to a temperature that felt to him like that of freshly passed urine.

His son didn't move. "Are we going out, Pa?" he asked.

"Of course lah, why else I ask you to bring the boat down?" Pa replied irritably.

Ah Boon's mouth widened into an O, but he didn't say anything more. He climbed into the boat, sitting in its wide middle.

"Move up," Pa said. "Up to the front. Where Yam sits."

Ah Boon hesitated again, looking back at his father. Pa remained stone-faced. On days like these, when the waves were choppy and the wind strong, it was in the front of the boat that you felt as though you were flying. Most boys would rush at the opportunity. But Ah Boon wanted to sit as far away from the vast expanse of water as possible, close to his father. Pa would make him sit near the front.

Once Ah Boon had settled into position, Pa pushed the boat out. He took his usual seat next to the engine and they set off.

"Where are we going, Pa?" Ah Boon asked from the front of the boat. He had to shout over the engine to make himself heard.

Pa didn't answer. He would carry out his experiment—if the island appeared, then he would be proven right. If it didn't, then Ah Boon would be none the wiser.

The little boat skimmed the water's surface, bouncing lightly and sending a spray out on each side. In the dark of the predawn mornings, the waves would glitter black under the moonlight, the scales of some gelatinous beast. But all mystique was stripped by the unforgiving afternoon sun, the sea revealed to be a murky, insipid brown. A film of perspiration gathered on the back of Pa's neck. He pulled his singlet up. The sight of Ah Boon's small shoulders turning pink in the sun made something twist inside him, a painful, wrenching love. The boy would not sleep well tonight.

They rode in silence for ten minutes. The horizon seemed to taunt Pa. No island. Nothing but sea. His frustration grew. This was how it had been when he'd gone out with Uncle and the other men.

He remembered the way Ah Kee had looked at him—a sideways, skeptical glance, half-humorous. Perhaps he had been right to look at him that way. Perhaps it *had* been a hallucination.

He stared at Ah Boon's small form at the front of the boat, his hands gripping his seat so hard that the tendons stood out against his pale skin.

Pa stopped the boat.

"What is it, Pa?" Ah Boon asked. Behind it, other questions, like what they were doing out there in the first place.

"Boon," Pa said. "Do you remember that day you came with me and Yam—"

"—And we saw the island?" Ah Boon said.

"You saw it too, right?"

"Yes, yes, I saw!" Ah Boon nearly stood up with excitement, but the boat rocked and he grabbed his seat once again.

"You remember . . . you remember where?" Pa said, aware of how ridiculous the question was. The island was meant to be right here. This was where they had seen it, and yet there was nothing, again, just as all the other days of all the weeks before.

But Ah Boon didn't laugh or look skeptical at all. The boy simply stared into the water as he considered the question. Then he looked up, sweeping his gaze across the emptiness ahead of them, and pointed in the two o'clock direction.

"There," he said.

So calm was his conviction, and such was the irregularity of the entire mission, that Pa did not question his statement. He nodded and started the engine again.

Five minutes later, Ah Boon twisted his body around and shouted over the engine. "More that way!" Now to the right.

Pa turned the boat. They kept going. Five minutes passed, then ten. The doubt came back, along with it a helpless fury.

Pa killed the engine.

"We going where?" he shouted.

He considered now the possibility that Ah Boon, unused to being asked to direct anything, was simply pointing in random directions because he did not dare disappoint his father.

"To the island," Ah Boon said seriously. "Look!"

He pointed to their left, into the sun. The glare bouncing off the waves dazzled Pa's eyes as he turned, but a few seconds later, once they had adjusted, he finally saw it. Just as before. A dark, humped shape looming in the distance.

"Oh. Oh!" Pa started the engine again.

He stroked the side of the boat distractedly, as if urging a horse. Ah Boon was right. There it was! A black patch on the horizon, unmistakably land. It grew larger as they approached, but it looked different this time, smaller and broader. Could it be a trick of the light? But no—he remembered the way the cliffs had loomed, the exposed limestone had glowed in the moonlight.

This island was more or less flat, though a slight hill undulated across its length. The topography was similar to that of their own beach, except here the mangroves formed a thick and formidable barrier to the land. You could not dock a boat on that shore. Why would you want to? It was enough to be here.

"How can?" he murmured to himself.

"Look! Pa!" Ah Boon shouted from the front of the boat. His small face was bright with excitement.

Pa thought of Ah Kee's sneer, Ghim Huat's doubtful frown. They'd thought he was crazy. For a brief moment he, too, had doubted what he'd seen. But the kampong was wrong; he was right. Here was the island.

They lowered the nets—here would be the fish. There would be money for the sinseh, for food, for school.

"Good job, Boon," Pa said.

Ah Boon flushed even redder than he already was. He burst into a rare, sloppy, teeth-baring grin. In that moment, Pa himself felt like a young man again, and as the island drew nearer, he resolved to make more of an effort with his son. The sun beat down; the sea rippled like a sheet of shining muscle, promising, for the first time, a bright future. Slowly, the nets began to fill with the silver bodies of fish.

Chapter Six

There was a new shape to Ah Boon's days. Or perhaps it was he who was newly shaped, his edges solidifying, his body gaining mass. Previously it had been possible to pass unseen through the world, for his father's hand to lightly graze his hair and his eyes to go right through him, but now he felt the eyes of his family on him all the time. Ma's love was nothing new—Ah Boon knew well the enfolding warmth of its deep pockets, the darkness he could disappear into. But this new Pa, who waited for him on the porch and called to him affectionately as he came home from school, this new Hia, his jealousy overcome by his childish excitement over the discovery of the islands and his urge to discuss them, Ah Boon was not used to.

A closeness had sprung up, especially, between him and Uncle. That first afternoon, after their triumphant rediscovery of the islands, Ah Boon himself had run up from the beach to tell Uncle the news. He burst into the bedroom where his dear uncle lay shivering in a cloud of stale smells and told him in a rush: they'd found the islands again, the nets were groaning under the weight of all the fish they'd caught, they would have money now, the sinseh could come back. Uncle broke into a wide smile, and for a moment the dark hollows under his eyes seemed to vanish, his cheeks seemed to fill out, and he was his old, strong self again.

"Knew you could do it, boy," he said, clapping one thin hand on Ah Boon's shoulder, and Ah Boon glowed with pride.

The sinseh they could now afford came back at regular intervals, and Uncle was nursed back to robust health. In a few months, he could comfortably push a full wheelbarrow of fish from the surf to the top of the beach without panting. A new playfulness came over him, and he got into the habit of picking up Ah Boon and carrying him around on his shoulders—his daily exercise, he called it. Ah Boon loved being high up on Uncle's back. Often they would walk through the forest that way, Ah Boon plucking mangosteens and guavas from low branches, peeling them and sharing the juicy flesh with Uncle. The world seemed less terrifying from up on Uncle's shoulders, more open and friendlier than Ah Boon had previously felt.

He'd even grown to enjoy the fishing trips themselves, and found himself staring at the squeaky progress of the overhead fan at the end of a long math period with a new restlessness. The ocean came to him often and at unexpected times. At sea, he felt himself to be peering through a window once covered entirely by a threatening mold, now wiped clean. Yet at the window's edges the darkness lingered. Even in his most pleasurable moments at sea, when the wind whipping through his hair finally became something exhilarating, he remained balanced on the knifepoint between joy and terror.

Then there was school. The thrill of school turned out to be not the books or lessons, but one particular classmate. For months now, Ah Boon had sat in the desk next to Siok Mei's without daring to speak a word to her. If she ever looked his way, he kept his eyes carefully averted, cheeks burning so hot he was sure she could feel them. Sometimes he was certain she was on the cusp of speaking to him, but always, he would duck his head and pretend to rummage in his bag for a pencil, or pretend to break into a coughing fit. Other times he did his best to behave as if she were not there at all.

School had become hours of quiet anguish, sitting silently at Siok Mei's side. Ah Boon was no closer to understanding the pages of the old newspapers they used to dry fish. He'd learned to identify a few simple characters, mastered the right way to grasp a pencil in his fist, to fill the green boxes in his exercise books with the strokes that would one day allow him to write full words. He did his writing homework dutifully, but he was not a natural student. His strokes could not be confined to their boxes; he often broke the tip of his pencil. He could see the shape he wanted to make so clearly in his mind: perfect, regular, yet when he actually touched the pencil to the page, what came out was ugly and broken.

Ah Boon had grown to loathe the writing exercises. In each inadequate character he saw his failure to do what he really wanted: to speak to Siok Mei.

Of course, he'd known other girls his age. Often he felt more comfortable with them than with the boys, Hia's loud, rowdy friends. There was graceful Aisyah, the grandniece of Pak Hassan, who often came around to pick guavas from the tall trees behind the Lees' house. There was Ah Hui, daughter to the neighboring Chan family, who once bet Hia she could hold her breath longer than him underwater and won. And Siok Mei was just one of the three girls in their class of twenty, the kampong being too small to support two schools—one for boys, one for girls—and few families wanting their girls to read and write anyway.

But with other girls Ah Boon had never felt this confusing mix of fear and longing; had never felt that they opened up a window to some other wide world. The girls he knew fit neatly into the rubric of the kampong. They sorted fish as he did, played hopscotch and marbles, alluded with easy smiles to futures spent married to fishermen like their fathers. Siok Mei, on the other hand, did not play at recess. Most often she could be seen sitting in the shade of a coconut tree, reading some pamphlet or another that she had borrowed from Teacher Chia. Ah Boon knew from his classmates that she lived with an uncle. It was unclear what had happened to her parents. Some said they were dead, others that Siok Mei had never had parents to begin with. Most credible were the whispers of them "going abroad," which meant they were "political," though Ah Boon did not know what this meant either.

He cared little for the rumors. What absorbed him was the stern look that furrowed her brow as she read, the way she never hesitated to correct anyone, not even Teacher Chia, at times. She lived her life with a seriousness he'd never encountered before, as if she was preparing for some larger destiny. How could someone be so utterly apart, so completely and naturally themselves?

It seemed he would never talk to her. But finally it was his handwriting that brought him to Siok Mei.

One interminable afternoon, the class had been kept back for misbehaving, and as their punishment the children were made to copy out a long and dense passage from their textbook. As each student completed the mind-numbing exercise, they handed their workbook in to the class monitor and skipped gleefully out into the golden afternoon light. Ah Boon, of course, was one of the last. Only he and a handful of others were left when Siok Mei returned to the classroom to retrieve a book from her desk.

"It's not easy," Siok Mei said to him casually, as if they were in the habit of speaking to each other. "I found it hard at first also. You want to show me?"

Ah Boon flushed violently. She was looking at the exercise book in front of him, at the pages half-filled with his crooked, badly formed strokes. He closed the exercise book, retrieved the broken pencil from the floor.

"No," he said. He would not humiliate himself in front of her.

"Okay." She turned away.

The word filled Ah Boon with remorse.

"You live with your uncle, right?" he blurted. Immediately he regretted it. Why remind her of her missing parents?

But Siok Mei only nodded.

"And you live near the old well?" she said. "At the end of the last kampong? You want to walk together?"

Ah Boon hesitated. The walk was a good twenty minutes; they would be obliged to talk for twenty minutes. He wanted it and did not want it. Finally he shook his head.

"Need to finish," he said, gesturing to the exercise book.

"I wait for you," Siok Mei replied easily.

"No, I need to walk fast, Pa is waiting for me." A lie.

"I also can walk fast," Siok Mei said. She could run faster than many of the boys in class, she went on.

Ah Boon couldn't deny this. What could he say? "Okay."

She nodded, then settled into her seat to read while she waited.

Never had writing been such a joy. His pencil seemed to take on a life of its own, flying from box to box, each character fully, if messily, formed. It was not so difficult after all. Soon he was done, and, handing in his exercise book to the grouchy class monitor ("Wah, finally!"), he set off with Siok Mei.

Outside the school, Ah Boon broke into a run. Past the noodle cart, past the houses with aunties sitting on their front steps, past the little temple with its charred joss stick smell. He took a shortcut, pushing through the undergrowth, lalang slicing at his shins for a good five minutes before he emerged onto the main path that connected all the kampongs. The whole time he heard Siok Mei several paces behind him, so close her breath seemed to tickle his neck.

He paused, throat and lungs straining for air. Siok Mei stopped beside him, completely unflustered.

"Ready?" she said, poised to take off again.

Ah Boon stared down at the path ahead of them. The same bowed trees pressing in from both sides, the same loud insect screech ricocheting through the dim, humid passage, somehow no longer as frightening as that first morning when he'd walked the path with Ma. Now he noticed the shards of light that pierced the canopy, the conversational rustle of leaves and insects.

Siok Mei took up the stance of a competitive runner, the way they'd been taught in physical education class.

"Who cannot keep up?" she said, grinning.

Her damp fringe clung to her forehead, and her face was pink with exertion. Cockily she dusted off a shoulder.

Ah Boon laughed, but his lungs were still heaving and he began to hiccup. Siok Mei thumped him on his back; the touch of her hard, small hand made the blood rush to his face. To avoid her eyes he began running again, ducking under low branches, leaping over tree roots. His chest felt as though it would burst, but there was a satisfaction to the pain, a joyful wringing out. He kept going, no longer trying to outrun Siok Mei, wanting to stay in the burn of his calves, the wind on his face. She was right beside him. He had the impression she was holding back to stay by his side, but he didn't mind.

Finally they stopped at a bend in the road. Ah Boon looked around— in their haste they'd gone right past the Malay kampong, past their own, and were now far beyond the turn that led to his house. So they began to walk back. The awkwardness gone, they talked as they strolled. Siok Mei asked him what his parents did, if he had siblings, whether he liked

school and Teacher Chia. She received each answer with a certain gravity, as if the trivialities that Ah Boon uttered were precious stones with
which she'd been entrusted. She was especially excited to hear that Ah
Boon helped his father with fishing, and wanted to know if he could take
her out on their boat one day.

"Women cannot go," he said.

"Why not?" Siok Mei asked.

Could she really not know? He reminded himself that her parents
were not fishing people. He explained gravely that it was bad luck.

"And why?"

He was at a loss. It angered the spirits of the sea, he went on.

"But why?"

"I don't know," he said, and laughed. For some reason he felt no shame
admitting ignorance in front of Siok Mei. It was almost a pleasant thing,
to puzzle over their lack of knowledge together.

At this pause, Ah Boon was overcome by self-consciousness. He'd
been talking too much! No one ever asked him anything, and now that
someone had, he'd spent almost fifteen minutes going on about the most
boring details of his life. He struggled to recover.

"You? What about your siblings?" he found himself asking.

A long silence ensued, in which he had time to kick himself mentally.
Again, her family, a topic to be avoided. And yet he could think of nothing else to ask. Siok Mei lowered her eyes.

"I have Hia," Ah Boon blurted, to fill the silence.

"Two sisters, three brothers," Siok Mei said at last. "My brothers went
with my parents, my sisters are staying with an auntie in the city."

The city. Twice he had taken the hour-long bus trip into town with
Ma when she'd had to buy something for a special birthday or the Lunar
New Year. On those trips the countryside seemed to roll by forever, end-
less swaths of old spreading trees with parasitic ferns perched in their

joints, the occasional clusters of roadside vendors, houses of attap and zinc roofs. Then all of a sudden the emptiness would give way to the noise and crowds of the city—row after row of wooden houses; children spilling out of open doors chasing bedraggled chickens; lone dogs rummaging in heaps of trash; tanned, wizened old men gliding gracefully on bicycles over potholes. Out where the Lees lived, there were mostly Chinese and Malay villagers, but in the city it felt to Ah Boon as though every country was represented, every language spoken. Indian moneylenders sat behind dusty shophouse counters, freckled Eurasian girls skipped rope in their pleated convent school uniforms, Javanese workers carried woven baskets of bricks, pale, devilish Ang Mohs, the rulers of the island, strolled self-importantly in strange, stiff outfits not made for the heat.

Confronted with so many buildings leaning into one another, so many people talking all at once, Ah Boon would bury his face in his mother's side, sticking close to her as they navigated the crowded streets to get to whatever store she needed to visit. The city always filled him with a terrible, awe-struck sense of how many lives there were being lived every single day. And always he returned to the kampong with a feeling of troubled relief.

But now the city loomed with new intrigue. Now the city contained Siok Mei's past, Siok Mei's siblings.

"You miss them?" he asked.

"Sometimes," Siok Mei said. "Ma, a lot."

"What do you miss?"

She paused.

"Her smell. Her telling me what to do." She stared at her feet. "Aiya!"

The white canvas of her school shoes was now caked in mud, and she squatted to scrape it off. Ah Boon found a large dry leaf and began to help her, working on her left foot as she worked on the right. They fell silent, engrossed in their task. After a while Siok Mei straightened up. She examined her shoes sadly.

"If you wash them they'll be okay," Ah Boon said.

"Maybe," she said with a faraway look, and he knew it wasn't the shoes she was sad about.

"I can show you the boat one day, if you want," he said. "Even if we can't take it out, you can sit in it."

Siok Mei lifted her eyes. Dark marbles that seemed to absorb all the light that fell through the canopy. It seemed to Ah Boon that Siok Mei was in those eyes, a tiny, miniature Siok Mei trapped within cold, curved walls. He imagined stepping inside to meet her.

"Okay," she said, then thought for a moment. "I can help you with your writing homework. If you want."

This time Ah Boon said yes. He stuck his hand out, she shook it seriously. Here were the insects shrieking in their bushes, here was the crushed light falling through the trees. The faint sound of the ocean washing back and forth, back and forth, or perhaps that was only in his head. Ah Boon had the feeling, with this handshake, that he was entering into a contract that would last a long time, though what he was agreeing to, he could not yet understand.

Chapter Seven

For the fourth month in a row, Ma bid low at tontine. She snuck glances at the other women sitting around the table as she scribbled the number onto the scrap of paper, making sure no one was watching. The eight women would place their folded-up slips into the little biscuit carton and Sor Hong, the tontine manager, would shake them up before she drew out the slips and read them. Only the one who bid the highest interest would step forward and take control of the fund for the month. So there was no way the others could be aware that the Lee family, previously known for their precarious financial situation, had in the past months found their fortunes entirely changed, such that Ma no longer needed the tontine loans to get by.

When all the slips of paper were in, Sor Hong shook the box with her long, thin fingers. The rustling was like a snake in the undergrowth, and instinctively Ma looked to the ground. But beneath the table there were only her bare feet, the clean wood floors of Sor Hong's large, prosperous house. It was the only house of its kind in the kampong, built on raised concrete columns, with space enough for a living room, three bedrooms, dining room, kitchen, bathroom, and toilet. It was in the dining room they now sat, around an oval table with a clean cloth of cheerful yellow laid upon it. The smells of Sor Hong's family's lunch still lingered; Ma could detect the sweet scent of charred sambal, a tinge of rice wine on the air.

Sor Hong unfolded each note, read the bid, and placed the piece of paper on the table according to how high or low it had been. Fingers tapped nervously on the table, straw fans moved through the air. Ma could always tell who needed money that month; even if they kept a straight face, their bodies betrayed them. She herself tried to sit up straighter, to clasp her hands nervously, bite a fingernail.

But something strange was happening. As Sor Hong opened each slip of paper, Ma realized that each bid was lower than hers, lower than ever happened. She'd bid two dollars on the hundred-dollar pool, but every bid that Sor Hong opened was one-fifty or one.

"Wah," Sor Hong said. "Everyone feeling rich this month ah?"

The women laughed.

Two dollars was the highest, Sor Hong said. At this point, normally, she'd ask who it was. But all seven women were looking straight at Ma.

"Me," she said lightly. "So lucky this week! All give chance is it?"

She could tell from their meaningful glances, however, that what had happened was not a fluke.

"Ah Bee," Sor Hong said, and paused.

"What?" Ma clasped her hands together under the table. Her heart knocked in her chest. Stupid, stupid. She'd been discovered. She should have performed their need better, bid high and paid the price to take the pool.

"When are you going to tell us? Your husband win big at mahjong is it?" Swee Poh said.

Her voice was loud, braying. Dumpy-shouldered Swee Poh knew that Ma's husband didn't gamble, everyone knew that, and so this was her idea of a joke. She was the neighbor who rushed to console you on any misfortune and congratulate you on any success, all with the sly eagerness of one who was looking you up and down, gathering details on your demeanor, your tone of voice, so as to better share them with the rest of the kampong later.

Ma had always been the sort of woman who roused an ugly hunger in neighbors like Swee Poh. Though she sat dutifully with the other women at the coffee stall, smiling along and fanning herself just like anyone else, her participation had the air of forbearance about it. She did everything right: laughed at the women's bawdy jokes, clicked her tongue at the way certain children were allowed to run around half naked and shrieking. Yet she never actively censured, never pronounced her opinions frankly, as the others did. One felt she was holding something back, and like a bloodhound, Swee Poh longed to sniff it out.

"Sor Hong and I noticed someone bid low every month, always two dollars, always same handwriting," she said.

They thought it looked like Ma's handwriting, and so they asked everyone else to bid below two dollars to see if it was really her.

Ma flushed. There was no need for the whole charade of bidding, then, since they'd already recognized her handwriting, and if they'd already asked everyone else—a clear violation of the anonymity of tontine—then why bother drawing the notes this month? Swee Poh simply wanted to put her on the spot in front of everyone. This Ma understood from Swee Poh, but Sor Hong, the wife of the most senior fisherman in town, Ghim Huat, Pa's good friend? Leong Ho, the plump sister of the provision shop owner, who always slipped Ma a little extra rice when she knew they were going through a tough time? Ma looked around the circle of women now, and perhaps there was an accusatory jut to her chin, for some of them would not meet her eyes.

"Ah Huat's catch has been very good lately," Sor Hong said.

A blunt statement, but not one that was cruel. Sor Hong's face was soft with mild concern. As if she could sense the weight on Ma's mind. Looking into the older woman's wide, sun-browned face, Ma longed to tell her everything.

That Pa had been visiting the island's waters for four months now, each time coming back with straining nets after just ten, fifteen minutes of work. That somehow Ah Boon was the only one who could divine the island's location. That over this time, they had discovered there was not only one island, but an indeterminate, ever-changing number, though how this could be, she did not understand.

Pa described them to her in a feverish voice. Some were flat and ringed by brilliant white sands, he said. Others jagged with limestone cliffs, like the very first island they'd found, the one they called Batu. Some were large, taking a full twenty minutes to circle with the boat, others no bigger than wide sandbars, several paces across. What they all had in common was the richness of their waters, their teeming schools of fish.

Ma didn't know what to say. The quiet, slow man she'd known all her life had taken on an unfamiliar sheen.

"What will you do?" she'd asked.

"Don't know," he'd replied. "But we don't tell anyone for now."

"Why?"

His face had hardened. "They won't believe me. Like last time."

"But you know where they are now, you can show them."

Pa's chin jutted stubbornly. "No," he said. "They think I'm crazy. Let them."

And so they kept it to themselves. Uncle knew, of course, they'd had to tell him to ease his mounting worries about the cost of doctors and food. But they hadn't told anyone else, not Ah Kee, not Ghim Huat, not Ah Tong, not Pak Hassan. A nervous shine had settled in her husband's eyes. When she touched his shoulder, she seemed to feel a new energy vibrating through him. His laughter came in violent bursts, fading quickly into an inscrutable brooding.

Ma was worried for her husband, and as she looked into Sor Hong's calm, accepting face now, she felt a sudden relief. She would tell Ah Huat that the women had guessed themselves; that their husbands had noticed the unusually good catch over the months. The secret would finally be out, and it would not be her fault.

Ma's hand lay open on the table. Gently, with the ridges of her knuckles, Sor Hong brushed Ma's open palm, as if coaxing a child.

"Tell me," she said, and Ma began to talk.

Later, Ma hurried home. While the thick vegetation provided some shelter from the afternoon sun, damp heat rose from the red earth itself, from the flat blades of waxy cow grass, the sharp bowed lalang, the rubber fruit scattered over the ground. Ma pulled the collar of her blouse away from her neck.

Pa would be taking his afternoon nap now. She could picture him lying on the futon in the living room, the windiest spot in the house and his favorite place to sleep in the day. He would be curled on his side, the singlet riding up, revealing skin that was still pale for never seeing the sun. It was a body more familiar to Ma than her own. The precise curvature of his knobbly spine roused an aching tenderness in her. When he was sleeping like that, she'd often had the urge to touch her fingers to those bumps, to let her hands find his neck in a caress. But that was not the kind of relationship that they had.

Her husband was not an unreasonable man. She would tell him the women had confronted her outright. She would cite Sor Hong herself—Ah Huat respected her greatly—Sor Hong had said there was no room for secrets in a kampong as small as theirs, that lies and half truths would only poison the ties that bound them together. Such talk of values and communities would appeal to Pa, she knew. It was why she had always loved him, though love was not a thing they spoke of.

Her own mother had been sold, at nine years old, by her impoverished parents to a wealthy merchant family. She lived as a servant in their house, betrothed to their adult son, though marrying him as his third wife when she turned thirteen did little to raise her status. She remained, effectively, a servant, and the fact that she'd borne nothing but daughter after daughter—Ma being the fourth, unlucky girl, Uncle coming only later—did not help.

It meant that when Ma turned sixteen, and it was *her* turn to marry, she had little more choice in the matter than her own mother had. Her older sisters had been married off to, respectively, a cripple; an ill-clothed Mainland man, newly arrived and with an aggressive glint in the eye; and a night-soil collector, whose hands always smelled of excrement. And so Ma had resigned herself to a life like her sisters', one of endless work and fighting for scraps. When her mother had told her about Ah Huat, the youngest son of a gambler and drunk who'd bankrupted his family with his habits, Ma had pressed her lips together and said nothing.

She had taken the small photograph and pretended to study it, giving herself time to compose herself. She examined the long, sorrowful eyebrows, sharp cheekbones and nose, the slight crinkling of the eyes that suggested laughter. This was to be her future. She struggled to understand, but all she could think was that the man in the picture looked like a man, like any man.

"He seems kind," she said at last, meeting her mother's gaze.

"High nose, like your brother," her mother had said. She took the photo back from Ma and touched one steady finger to the paper. "Face of a good man."

Her mother seemed satisfied then. Gone was the tremble in her voice, the dangerous shine of her eyes. One of the biggest sorrows of Ma's life was that her mother never made it to her wedding. Some months before, her mother had been riding on the back of a cousin's bicycle when a bus swerved into them. She'd died on the spot, the bag of white rice balanced on her lap bursting open on the dirt road. When Ma's elder sister arrived at the sorry scene, she'd held in her tears and carefully swept the rice back into the bag, even though it was brown with dirt. She would wash it when she got home. It was what her mother would have done.

Ma missed her mother dearly at the simple wedding, but what truly made her ache was that her mother would never know she'd been right. Ah Huat turned out to be a good man, the best of men. There were the obvious things: the fact that he was never violent or loud, he didn't gamble or drink, no one worked harder than he. But beyond that, beyond the things she could have put into words for her mother, there was the look Pa gave her on their wedding day, when he took her hand for the first time. One of neither ownership nor wonder—the only two aspects of men she'd known till now. The former was vastly more common, playing itself out in the everyday dramas of so many households, and the latter she had seen just once, when, as a child, she'd spied on a cousin and her lover. The boyfriend had cupped her cousin's face between his hands, his whole body keening toward her, as if capturing some precious liquid that might trickle away.

Ma had never given much thought to how she wanted to be looked at by men, though if she had, she would not have wanted to be a precious liquid. Such an attitude would turn her fragile even if she were not. But with Ah Huat the negotiations of power were somehow absent; he neither imposed his will nor subjugated it to hers. Together they were two trees planted some unbreachable distance apart, whose shadows were gently intertwined.

Ma was almost home now. From the bushes around the house emerged an unfamiliar voice, shrill with laughter. Then a shout, this time a voice she knew well.

Ah Boon was darting about the vegetation, sending the birds scattering from their low perches in the trees. A girl emerged into the clearing. Even from a distance, Ma could make out the many places where her light blue samfu had been patched. The girl laughed as she held something up in her hand. Ah Boon stopped, making the same gesture. He, too, held something small between his fingers. Like two kittens about to pounce, they faced each other. Then, on some invisible signal, both dashed toward the front of the house.

When Ma got to the house, Ah Boon and the girl were standing near the old well. Now she understood. Each held a rubber seed in their hands. If rubbed hard and fast enough against the brick wall of the well, the seed would grow scalding hot, and pressed against an arm, it could be used as a weapon.

Ah Boon had a friend! Her younger son had always been the child she ached for, fretted over, the one for whom she wanted to make everything right. The reclusive, quiet boy with still eyes, who never played with the other boys in the kampong as his brother did. It was one of the reasons for sending him to school.

So occupied were they in their game that both jumped when she called Ah Boon's name. They turned to her with vaguely guilty looks on their faces, as if losing themselves in so much fun must somehow be against the rules.

"Ma," Ah Boon said. "I come help with the washing soon." He turned the rubber seed in his hand, like a ball he was about to throw.

"Who's your friend?" Ma turned to the girl.

"Hello, Auntie," the girl said, bobbing her head.

Her voice was strong, her teeth small and white. Ma liked her right away.

"What's your name?"

"Ng Siok Mei, Auntie, I go to school with Ah Boon. I live with my second uncle, not too far from the provision shop."

Ma noticed the small white square pinned to Siok Mei's sleeve. So, this was the daughter of the Ngs, the parents so patriotic they'd returned to the Mainland to join in the war effort against the invading Jipunlang, leaving their children scattered among relatives. The father, she'd heard, had been recently killed—hence the mourning patch. The mother, it was said, remained in hiding near the southwest border, protecting the convoy of vehicles that brought ammunition and supplies to troops via treacherous mountain roads.

Ma was sure it was all very admirable, to have such conviction in one's beliefs, but how they could leave a daughter she did not know. A wave of pity went over her, and she felt the urge to gather this small, strong girl in her arms, to stroke her hair and tell her things would be okay. But the girl's face was bright, her posture tall. There was no air of tragedy about her. She did not need to be comforted.

"You want to eat dinner here tonight?" Ma said.

Ah Boon's face twisted in embarrassment. "Ma, Siok Mei got her own—"

"Thank you, Auntie," Siok Mei said. "Don't want to disturb you."

But Ma wouldn't hear of it. There would be more than enough for all of them. A tall girl like Siok Mei, even taller than their Ah Boon here—Ma was sure she had a good appetite.

Ah Boon's face was a deep purple. Siok Mei smiled her bright, certain smile and nodded happily.

"Good. I call you when dinner is ready," Ma said.

She went into the house, suddenly remembering she still had to talk to Pa about what happened at tontine. But the worry was gone now. Ah Boon had made a new friend, she would steam a beautiful fish with freshly cut chilis. Ah Huat would agree with her. Sharing with the kampong was the right thing to do, and Ah Huat was a man who did things right.

Chapter Eight

The next day, Ah Boon and Siok Mei returned from school to find a small crowd assembled in front of the Lees' home. All the faces were familiar: Swee Poh, Ah Tong, Ghim Huat, Sor Hong, and so on. But here, too, was old Pak Hassan, the most senior fisherman from the neighboring kampong, who seemed to Ah Boon as tall and wise as a banyan, along with two of his sons. They looked at each other meaningfully as he approached, but no one spoke. A creeping dread came over Ah Boon as he neared the crowd.

"Eh, Boon," Uncle said, stepping out.

Ah Boon ran and pressed himself to Uncle's side, burying his face in the damp fabric of his singlet.

"Hello, Uncle Leong," Siok Mei said.

Uncle nodded to her. "Call auntie, uncle," he said to Ah Boon, gesturing at the crowd.

Ah Boon addressed each one of them—*Hello Auntie Swee Poh, Hello Uncle Ah Tong, Hello Uncle Ghim Huat, Hello Pak Hassan*—in a small, respectful voice. They watched him carefully, as if expecting him to take flight or burst into flames. Once he finished greeting everyone he stared resolutely at his feet and imagined curling into a tight ball on the ground until they all went away.

Then a warm, sticky hand slipped into his. The clammy feeling receded. He looked up; Siok Mei stood firmly next to him, certain, compact, completely and utterly herself. She caught his eye, as if to say she wasn't going anywhere, and he felt as if a warm, glowing coal had been placed very gently into the base of his stomach.

Ah Boon turned to Uncle. "Where's Pa?" he asked.

"He will be here soon," Uncle said.

That was who they were waiting for, then. Ah Boon had more questions, but the thick silence didn't allow for them. Siok Mei, too, was quiet. She'd lowered her chin, allowing her heavy hair to fall across her face. Bright eyes peeking out from between the strands, she observed the crowd like a forest creature newly among human beings. They stood like this for what felt like a long time. Every now and then, someone would remark on how hot it was or speculate uninterestedly on when it would rain. It was strange to see so much of the kampong at their house, something that only ever happened at the Lunar New Year, when people came visiting in stiff new clothes, bearing oranges in little net sacks. This association gave the unusual gathering now an oddly festive, nightmarish air.

Finally Ah Boon glimpsed his father coming up from behind the house. He held up the front of their boat, Hia the back, and they were moving toward the beach. The crowd began murmuring and made to follow the men.

"Come on," Uncle said, pulling Ah Boon by the shoulder.

Ah Boon in turn led Siok Mei. It was the wrong time to go out to sea—just past noon, the air still and their shadows stunted in the glaring light—but on went the crowd down the wooded path, past the belt of mangroves that looked naked and ordinary in the midday sun, onto the dry, hot sand. A strange funereal procession, the boat that Pa and Hia carried up front the coffin, and the whole trailing lot of them mourners.

When they got to the beach, Ah Boon saw there were two other boats waiting. The men who stood by them were all fishing men from the neighboring kampongs, Chinese and Malay alike, and though Ah Boon recognized their faces from the market and kolek racing festivals, he didn't know them well. They nodded at Pa, Hia, Uncle, but their attention skittered past Ah Boon, circled the air around his being before landing squarely in the spot above his head.

It became clear to Ah Boon what this was about. There was a tickle in his chest—self-importance or fear, he couldn't tell. Dropping Siok Mei's hand, he ran toward Pa and Hia, grabbing the side of the boat. The smooth warm wood that felt like skin beneath his hands was comforting in its solidity. He helped them guide the boat into the water. Ah Boon thought back to when the lapping waves at his bare thighs would have sent him running back to the shore. Who was that boy? Who was this boy?

Finally Pa turned to Ah Boon. "We go to the islands," he said. "Okay?"

A tremor went through the crowd at the word *islands*. Ah Boon nodded, understanding that the silence of the past months had been broken. He scanned the men's faces for any hint of skepticism or mockery. But there was none; only a faint trepidation, a kind of fearful awe.

The men were already in their boats when Sor Hong stepped forward. Though nearly sixty, she did not have that stretched, sun-worn look of most women of the kampong. No bones were visible beneath her skin, no places on her scalp where hair grew thin. Ample and prosperous, she had the air of someone who'd had an easy life, although this was far from the case. Her arms, hefty as barrels, always comforted Ah Boon to behold. She held one arm out toward Pa now.

"I go also," she said. "I want to see myself."

A murmuring arose. The men exchanged glances among themselves, then looked to Ghim Huat, her milky-eyed husband, who stood now leaning on a cane. His fishing days over, he was still the oldest fisherman in the kampong. They waited for him to tell his wife that of course, she could not go.

But Ghim Huat nodded. "Sor Hong will go for me," he said, addressing himself directly to Pa.

There was a note of warning in his voice and he held Pa's gaze as if to say: *Do not deny me.* After a long silence, Pa nodded. Though the men continued to mutter under their breaths, no one protested. Sor Hong hiked up her samfu bottoms and waded into the sea. Pa helped her into the boat.

"Ah Bee, you also come," Sor Hong said. "Since you told us about it."

Ma flushed, glanced at Pa, then shook her head. Pa didn't disagree. So it was Ma who had told the kampong, Ah Boon thought, looking at his mother with a new curiosity. She looked the same as she always did, her face a soft, inscrutable collection of lines and kindness. He had never heard her disagree with his father before, let alone go against his wishes.

"Wait!" Siok Mei ran out onto the sand. "I want to come."

Her small fists balled as if ready to fight. Siok Mei's fists were often balled, Ah Boon realized, even though he had never seen her in a situation where fighting was necessary. He wondered if she balled them in her sleep. There she stood, stout and strong as a lone shrub on the sand. Again, here was the skin of his arms tingling, as if brushed by the wings of a thousand tiny insects.

Pa raised a weary hand to his forehead. No one wanted to tell the orphaned girl she couldn't come. People were used to treating Siok Mei with kindly forbearance.

Ah Boon knew the right thing to say. She was his friend; it was up to him to tell her that of course she could not go with them. In the pause, he watched a mosquito attach itself to the skin of his knee. He smacked it, his palm coming away with a tiny smear of blood.

"Siok Mei—" Pa began.

But she was looking at Ah Boon, not at Pa. *Please*, her gaze seemed to say. *You said we might.* And he had, after all. It was only fair.

Or this was what Ah Boon told himself; the truth was simpler.

"I want her to come," he said abruptly.

Instantly his cheeks burned. He knew he ought not to want, and yet he did. Ma had taught that life was not about wanting. But what if it couldn't be helped? He wanted Siok Mei to go wherever he went. He felt the whole crowd to be staring at him, felt they could see straight into his soft, yearning heart. But Siok Mei's face lit up, and that was enough.

"Shut up," Hia hissed. For once, the scorn on his face held no power.

Ah Boon ignored him. "She can sit with me. Please, Pa? Can she come?"

Pa's eyebrows lifted in surprise. Ah Boon had never asked anything of him before. Hia was the one who did the asking, the wheedling, the sulking. Perhaps it was the surprise that made Pa nod.

"Okay," he said. "She can sit in front with you."

Siok Mei ran into the surf, splashing water everywhere. The crowd on the shore shook their heads, and Ghim Huat knocked his cane against the ground, perturbed. But he couldn't object now, not when he was the one who first gave his blessing to a woman boarding a boat.

And so Siok Mei clambered up. Ah Boon pressed himself as far into the side as he could to make room for her. But the boat was small, and the two of them were wedged together so tightly that Ah Boon felt his thighs begin to go numb. Siok Mei whispered her thanks with such joy that he didn't care.

The engines ripped through the quiet: one, two, three. Ah Boon felt the vibration at the back of his skull, where it always went, and he wondered if Siok Mei felt it too. Their boat set out first, the other two following behind.

Ah Boon closed his eyes. He felt himself drop into that dark, empty space where the roar of the engine receded and the motion of the waves—up, down, up, down—became a kind of heartbeat. That space had scared him once, and it was this initial fear, the old dread, that pulled him to the islands. Now it was no longer fear but a kind of loneliness he could dip in and out of whenever necessary, grip onto like a slippery rope. He went to his loneliness now. It required a focus; focus that made the engine quiet, made Pa disappear, made the boat itself ghostly and insubstantial. He forgot the purpose of this trip, the expectant faces of his neighbors, even Siok Mei herself, sitting wedged so tightly against his side. When he opened his eyes, he pointed, and his father changed course accordingly. After they'd gone in that direction for several minutes, he pointed again, and they turned again.

"Where are we going?" Siok Mei said.

Ah Boon winced. He became aware again of the boats behind them. Ah Tong was at the engine of the first, Ah Kee at the other. Four more men sat in one boat, five in the other, their knees knocking against one another whenever they took a sharp turn. Eleven faces. Plus Hia, Pa, Sor Hong, and Siok Mei, fifteen then. All fifteen faces were looking straight at Ah Boon, filled with anticipation. A lump formed in his throat.

He turned back to the sea, screwing up his eyes again and concentrating. But he couldn't sense anything, only emptiness. The islands were gone. A slow panic began to take hold of him, and he tried harder, tried to visualize the soaring white cliffs, the flat, rolling meadow. Still there was nothing.

He stayed like that for several minutes, eyes closed, tears beginning to gather hot beneath his eyelids. He could already feel Hia's contempt, Siok Mei's disappointment. All fifteen of them staring straight at his small, skinny back, the force of their skepticism like the afternoon sun searing the exposed skin of his neck. Siok Mei's weight against his side now seemed reproachful, and he kicked himself for insisting that she come. He could already see them turning back to the shore, could hear the sneer in their voices as they told everyone on the beach that the whole thing was a hoax.

Then the boat turned. This was it, Ah Boon thought, Pa had caught on. They were going back. He braced himself for the scolding, the shame. He couldn't look at Siok Mei.

But the boat wasn't turning around. They were simply headed out in a different direction. What was Pa doing? After five minutes, the boat turned again. Then another five minutes, another slight turn. Ah Boon snuck a glance at Pa. His face was set in a look of complete absorption as he stared out into the open sea.

Ah Boon watched Pa steer, not understanding. Then the faces of those in the boats behind them changed. Siok Mei sat up in excitement, Sor Hong and Ah Tong let out loud whoops. It was impossible. He turned back to the front of the boat. There it was: a sinuous coast cloaked in deep green; high white cliffs, jagged and magnificent in the sun. It was the first island they had found, the one they nicknamed Batu because of how its cliffs resembled the famous caves up north. They had names for all the islands now.

Pa tilted his chin toward Ah Boon as if to say: *Did you see what happened?* Ah Boon had seen. It wasn't he who had directed them to the islands this time, but Pa. Even if the others had noticed, none would understand the significance of this. They didn't know yet that the islands were unreliable entities that appeared and disappeared at will. How could they? For here the island was, dry and solid as their own bodies. They did not know that up till now, only Ah Boon could find them.

Ah Boon leaned over the edge of the boat and plunged his hot hands into the sea. Siok Mei laughed, a sound as clear and bright as a brand-new glass marble. Her face shone pink in the sun.

"Beautiful," she said. "I wish we can live there."

He thought of living with Siok Mei, building a house in a tree, roasting line-caught fish over open fires. Suddenly he longed to tip himself out of the boat, to spread his sticky limbs wide in those mysterious, teeming waters, regardless of the jellied forms or feathery fins that they might contain. He wanted to feel the cool water fill the seams behind his knees.

A loud splash came from behind them. Apparently feeling the same desire, Ah Tong had flung himself over the side of his boat. The men laughed and shouted at the sight of his singlet billowing up around him, the clouds of trapped air much like a woman's breasts. Ah Tong began swimming toward the island.

"Tong, what you doing?" Pa called.

Ah Tong didn't reply, only waved an arm midstroke, asking them to join.

The adults looked at one another.

No way she would go in there, Sor Hong said. Who knew what dirty things lurked in those trees?

Pa's face was a mask. What was he thinking? He and Ah Boon had never talked about spirits or magic. Their daily trips had taken on the appearance of the mundane: Each day they took the boat out. Ah Boon directed, Pa steered. They let down the nets, reeled them back in again. Then they went home, taking with them whatever bounty the islands saw fit to give. That was all there had been to it. While on the boat they either sat in silence or spoke of other things: school, Ma, the heat. Never of where they were or what they were doing.

They all watched as Ah Tong waded up to the short, bright beach. The sight of him standing in the spot that Ah Boon had been watching for so many months felt like a violation. He'd never quite believed it was real, solid land. Yet Ah Tong's boat was landing on it now, steered by the remaining men, who jumped out and raced up the beach like little boys.

Pa, however, was smiling. He sat at the engine like a king on his throne, surveying his kingdom with pleasure. He watched the men on the beach with an indulgent look, one that Ah Boon had seen when he and Hia chased mudskippers down by the swamp.

Ah Kee's boat revved past them. "Come on, Huat!" he shouted at Pa.

And so Pa guided their boat to shore. They pulled up to the beach and got out, first Hia, then Pa, then Ah Boon and Siok Mei. All except Sor Hong, who was still worried about "dirty things" and said she would watch the boats. The four walked up the beach after the other men, heading for the jungle at the base of the cliffs.

Chapter Nine

The rest of the afternoon slipped by in dreamlike exploration. The men walked in silence, sometimes in single file, other times in pairs. Hia stuck close to Pa's side, and Ah Boon stayed with Siok Mei, behind them.

The interior of the island trilled with insects. Everywhere wide-trunked casuarinas spilled their tiny pine cones, putat laut shed fluffy pink buds from their waxy crowns. There were no trails to follow. Their bare calves were tickled by the fronds of sprawling ferns, their arms scratched by spiky jeruju as they went. On more than one occasion, Ah Boon held out his hand to help Siok Mei climb a boulder or a fallen tree, thrilling to the weight of her leaning into him. There were moments when he felt he was back home, exploring an unfamiliar part of the shore with Hia, but the silence here was more complete. No human voices except for their own, no distant noise of a rattling lorry or bus. The chorus of insects seemed gentler, the calls of the birds less insistent.

"Look," Siok Mei said.

She turned to Ah Boon with a small, sly smile and thrust her hand out. It was this Ah Boon would remember most, after everything was done. Not the chase that followed, not the shape of this day or all the weeks that would come after, not the arduous journey his heart would take over the years, forming and breaking and forming again. The image he held was this: Siok Mei, no revolutionary yet, under no threat of death or imprisonment, leading no groups of impassioned workers or underground spies, just a child like himself, in the middle of an untouched forest on a mysterious island, holding her hand out to him. Siok Mei offering him something. In her open palm: a rubber seed. Small, round, as suggestive as a tiny egg.

The men were a little way ahead of them, beating a noisy path through the trees. To their right, Ah Boon spotted a large boulder, red and smooth, like the back of large, muddy pig.

With glee he snatched the rubber seed from her palm and made a dash for the boulder. Now he paid no mind to the ferns he crushed underfoot, the jeruju branches that tore little scratches in his arms. He could hear Siok Mei following close behind him, laughing her low, melodious laugh. They crashed through the forest, rubber soles of their slippers slapping the leaf-strewn ground, sending birds flying and shiny beetles scuttling. It occurred to Ah Boon that they should be careful of snakes. Still he ran; he was almost at the boulder now. Here it was, large, red, and looming. He stretched out his arm, rubber seed in hand, ready to rub it against the rock face—

Something crashed into his back and he tumbled to the ground. He lay facedown, arms pinned, Siok Mei sitting on the small of his back.

"Let go!" he said.

He did not mean it. When he fell he seemed to feel his heart fall too, dropping from where it had sat for most of his life, safely, in a cage of bones, through some trapdoor that led to an altogether more dangerous place. He felt it beating a fierce rhythm in his ears, throbbing in his fingertips. Siok Mei's warm hands held his forearms down. Her thighs pinned his waist, her bony behind nestled in the small of his back as if he were a mule. He was stronger than she, he knew, and yet her weight felt impossible to shift.

When she laughed he felt it leave her body and pass into his. His body seemed to laugh too. Siok Mei leaned forward and plucked the rubber seed from between his fingers.

"Never steal from me again," she said.

He grinned nervously. She rolled off and helped him to his feet. Then he watched as she rubbed the seed against the boulder. She was avoiding his gaze too, he noticed, and his heart seemed to return to its home in his chest. He observed the slight flush to her cheeks, the studied focus on the business of the rubber seed and the boulder.

Finally she stopped. She turned to him suddenly, face scrunched up as if angered by something.

"Promise we'll always be friends," she said.

He had the feeling that her statement demanded a response stronger than a simple yes, that she wanted some grand action on his part, for him to—like the romantic heroes in the radio dramas Ma listened to—wrap his arms around her, or worse still, offer himself up for a kiss.

Instead he took the rubber seed from her palm. Then he threaded his fingers through hers, until their hands were clasped together as tightly as the two halves of a clam. She did not pull away.

"Promise," he said.

"And you'll never leave," she said.

"Why would I leave?"

Siok Mei grew quiet then.

"Never mind," she said instead. "You don't have to promise."

"I promise," Ah Boon said quickly. "I'll never leave you."

"We'll see," she said.

"I won't," he insisted. "If you want me. I won't ever."

"Okay," she said quietly.

Now that the pact had been made, a silence hung between them. He was all too aware of her small, sweaty hand clasped in his, the warm smell of her breath. What could be said? Both seemed paralyzed. He had the thought that the island had claimed them now, that they were as bound to it as the large red boulder beside them was.

Then a shout. "Ah Boon!" Pa's voice breaking the spell.

"Come, better go find them," Siok Mei said.

She tugged on his hand, and the moment was over. They headed back toward the adults.

On they went with their exploration. The island was small, and the group circled it in less than forty minutes. The little beach at which they had landed was the only one of its sort, and the rest of the coastline was blanketed in enormous rocks. All the men agreed the top of the beach would be a good place to build a house, for the mangrove belt was slim and much of the earth dry and flat. An enormous old casuarina tree, its branches bowed low with age, provided the perfect shelter. They made jokes about running away from their wives to settle on this island. They would live off what they caught in nets by the shore, build their own houses from the wood of the untouched forest. At this Ah Boon looked, shyly, at Siok Mei.

Pa didn't say much all day, but Ah Boon had never seen him so happy. He'd picked up a piece of narrow driftwood from the beach and was swinging it in his hand as they walked through the vegetation. Sometimes he used it to point to a tree laden with coconuts, other times to a hornbill hiding in the canopy, but mostly he just had it in his hand, swinging back and forth, back and forth.

When the party finally returned to the beach, Sor Hong was waving to them excitedly from the boat. She had not moved from her seat.

"Look! Look!" she shouted, pointing at the sea.

They looked. The boat was rocking from side to side, but they saw now that its movement was erratic and out of sync with the gentle waves lapping the shore. Silver and white flashed at the boat's flank, and Ah Boon was reminded of one wet night when he had seen lightning arcing through the water. But it was day, and the sky so blue it hurt their eyes to look at. As they drew closer they saw that the bright movement was made up of many small parts, twitching and squirming in the sun.

It was fish. More fish than Ah Boon and Pa had ever seen before. They were throwing their bodies against the boat, thrashing wildly in the shallows as if begging to be caught. There were so many that the boat was being jostled from side to side like some fairground ride, Sor Hong still sitting calmly inside with a broad smile plastered across her face.

The men ran to their boats, wading through the teeming water with some difficulty.

"Boon, faster come, what are you doing?" Pa said.

The waves churned with flashing scales. Ah Boon stood frozen at the shore, gripped by his old fear. He and Pa had hauled up full nets many times before in those past few months, but they had never seen anything like this. The fish had always appeared silently and suddenly, the ropes that attached the nets to their boats growing taut without warning. It was a process that he had grown comfortable with, whose reliability he had begun to take for granted.

He'd believed he had completely overcome his fear of the ocean, but the scene that lay before him shattered this illusion. It was straight out of his worst nightmares, a sea come alive with invisible beings that would pull him into unknown depths.

"Come on, Boon," Siok Mei said.

She stepped into the water, fish thrashing at her ankles. She didn't seem to mind; like the others, her face was filled with delight. The intimacy between them suddenly seemed to fade, and Ah Boon was alone in his terror again.

Hia shouted to him from the boat: "What, scared ah, Bawal?"

That old nickname—which had not been used for months—now being used in front of Siok Mei filled Ah Boon with rage. He stepped into the sea. A single fish squirmed under the arch of his foot, trapped against the shifting sand. Ah Boon gritted his teeth and ground his heel down against the muscular flesh of the fish. A wave of nausea rose as tiny fins brushed the exposed skin of his calves. But he continued, taking one step after another toward the boat. Over the sound of the water, he seemed to hear the heat itself: a high, ringing noise.

Then it was over. He was clambering up the side of the boat, landing wet and pale next to Siok Mei.

"Boon? You okay?" Siok Mei said.

Ah Boon nodded blankly. The sky spun above him, sliding in and out of view. He felt Pa's cool palms on his shoulders. Water was trickling down his forehead, stinging his eyes. The world came back into focus.

"Just the heat," Pa said. "Long afternoon."

Ah Boon didn't contradict this. When everyone saw that he was all right, they soon forgot about him and set about wrestling with the bursting nets. Ah Boon sat at the front of the boat, his head nestled between his knees, arms blocking out the light. Siok Mei was wedged in her spot next to him; she gripped his hand tightly but the joy of it was gone now. All Ah Boon could think about was how she had witnessed his humiliation.

The men's chatter seemed like it came from somewhere far, far away. Someone began to sing a made-up song—Ah Tong, maybe, driven by the same exuberance that had propelled him out of his boat and into the sea—and the others laughed and heckled. Ah Boon could feel Hia moving about the boat, could hear Pa's quiet instructions to his brother. Everyone was in a celebratory mood, everyone except for Ah Boon. He felt that they were laughing at him. The butt of all jokes, the fisherman's son who was so afraid of the sea.

More shouts and whistles. The engines fired up, the boat began to move. They were done hauling the fish and were heading home. Ah Boon peeked out from over his arms. The sea was quiet now, its surface ruffled only by the boats cutting through even waves.

When they reached the shore, some of the people who had been waiting outside their house earlier were still gathered at the top of the beach. As they ran down to meet the boats, Ah Boon thought bitterly about how he would be ridiculed yet again for almost fainting at the mere sight of fish. Ma was waiting on the damp sand with the wheelbarrows, her eyes narrowed to a squint in the afternoon glare.

Those onshore gasped at the sight of all the fish that had been caught. "How can?" they asked over and over. "How can?"

Everyone on the boats answering all at once.

"... Full of huge trees, taller than here ..."

"One of our nets broke, even ..."

"Cliffs!"

"A hornbill land on Ah Tong's head, lucky never shit in his hair ..."

"When Ah Tong jumped out I almost got heart attack!" This, from Sor Hong, sent the women into spasms of laughter.

"But where did all the fish come from?" one of the aunties asked.

The men on the boat fell silent.

"Very hard to explain," Sor Hong said. "But Ah Boon here ..."

Ah Boon turned his eyes to the horizon and braced himself. Ah Boon here had been to the islands for months, he said to himself, yet he still couldn't set foot in the water. Ah Boon here fainted, like a girl, you should have seen him!

". . . He led us there. He and Ah Huat. Don't know how they know where to go, but somehow they did. It's a miracle," she said.

The people on the shore were nodding.

"But how you know where the island is?" someone asked.

Ah Boon looked at Pa, who indicated that he should answer.

"I . . . I don't know. I can feel it," he said, blushing. He had never had so many adults listen to him so attentively before.

"And the fish always there? At the island?"

Ah Boon nodded.

"*Islands*. Got more than one. We found six so far," he mumbled.

The hushed whispers grew louder.

Finally, a man in the crowd asked: "Means that we need you on the boat every time we want to find them?"

He spoke dismissively, as if the whole thing were a hoax. It seemed to pain him to have to address his question to a child.

"Ah Boon can show us how to find them ourselves," Pa said. "He showed me."

Ah Boon flushed an even deeper red as the other fishermen murmured approvingly. Even Hia was silent, and when Ah Boon turned to him, Hia gave him a small, slow nod. Ma, too, was looking at Ah Boon as if seeing her son for the first time. So as not to betray the pleasure he felt, Ah Boon stood up to get out of the boat, but everyone continued watching him, as if he were some mystical being. Ah Boon stopped in his tracks. He was tempted to jump in the air or fling his arms out just to see his action mirrored in the gazes of all those people watching. But all he did was stand there, buoyed gently by the wash of waves, the afternoon sun waning behind him at a violent orange slant. A moment of peace. It

was only years later that the memory of this peace would become inextricably mixed with that of the squirming fish beneath the arch of his foot,
that the emotion of joy, for Ah Boon, would become tainted with a fugi-
tive, simmering horror lying dormant beneath the surface of things.

For now, though, the sun was setting, the sea was calm, and he stood
surrounded. His family loved him, and so did the kampong.

Chapter Ten

A period of prosperity followed for the kampong and their neighbors. Daily, Ah Boon and Pa went out to sea with the other men following close behind, and at their instigation explored not just Batu but the other islands as well. Over the following months, the men made a concerted effort to track the elusive landmasses. But it was difficult, for the islands often appeared in different configurations, some vanishing for weeks at a time, others so similar and undistinguished the men couldn't even tell which they were. It was hard enough to ascertain how many islands there were, let alone the patterns of their manifestation.

It was Pa, finally, who figured it out. One especially warm night, Ah Boon lay restless on the floor, tossing and turning to find a comfortable spot for his head. A fly looped loud circles around his ear, its whiny buzz slowly melding with Ah Boon's dreams. Just as he was about to fall asleep, someone shook him by the shoulder.

"Boon. You awake? Boon." It was Pa, teeth gleaming in the dark.

Ah Boon nodded. "What is it?" he whispered, careful not to wake Hia, whose slumbering form lay a few meters from him.

"It's the moon," Pa said.

For a moment Ah Boon was afraid. Who was this new Pa, who roamed the silent house at night, who said things like *It's the moon?*

"The islands," Pa went on impatiently. "They follow the moon."

Something rustled. Ah Boon looked down; Pa was holding a sheaf of paper in his hands, but it was too dark to read. They went out to the porch, where a gas lamp burned on a wooden chair. The air was damp and heavy with the scent of earth.

Pa showed Ah Boon his drawings, crude sketches depicting the approximate location of each island found on each day of the month. Ah Boon had never seen Pa doing any drawings. Now he imagined him sitting outside the house each night, drawing feverishly from memory.

Pa was shuffling the papers excitedly, pointing first to one notation then another, all the while whispering: "See? See?"

As the sleep cleared from Ah Boon's mind, he started to follow what his father was saying. On a full moon, all the islands vanished. As the moon waned again, the islands began to appear, the largest proliferation of them occurring when it was reduced to a sliver. As it filled out again, the islands correspondingly disappeared, one by one. He'd tracked them for nearly a year now, and though there were minor variations, the pattern was unmistakable.

Pa fell silent. "Wait, Pa," Ah Boon said, and scrambled to his feet.

He went back to the room he shared with Hia. His brother lay on his back, mouth wide in a snore. Ah Boon tiptoed around him, gently lifted his own pillow, and drew something out from beneath it. A worn, flattened matchbox. With it gripped tightly in his palm, he returned to Pa.

"I took this from Batu," Ah Boon said.

He slid the box open. In it was a collection of sand, scraps of leaves, and a small twig. Pa looked at him, uncomprehending.

"It doesn't disappear," Ah Boon said.

He'd inadvertently collected the sand and leaves from Batu on one of their trips out, while trying to trap an especially large red ant. The ant was long dead, but the rest of the matter had persisted. It occurred to him that he'd collected part of the island, a small piece of land, really. So he checked the box night after night, to see if the sand would disappear, the way the islands did on a regular basis. But it was always there. It was as if once removed from the sea where it had stood, the land lost its fickle properties and turned to plain matter.

He told this to Pa now, one discovery in exchange for another. They talked late into the night, Pa's calloused hand resting on Ah Boon's shoulder. Ah Boon saw that his father's thick black hair was growing thin; he was filled with tenderness by the places where the skin of his father's scalp showed, and wanted to kiss them. Of course he didn't. They stayed that way: the small of Ah Boon's back pressed into the wall of their house, his mind teeming with lunar charts and unreliable maps. The weight of his father's hand on his shoulder was like an anchor in shifting sands.

After they went to sleep that night, it rained, a thunderous downpour that continued through the next day. They placed buckets in the usual places where water dripped from holes in the roof, and then they waited. A thick gray sheet of damp settled over the outside world, obscuring everything. They could no longer see the shimmering sea from their house. Only the dark forms of looming mangroves marked where land turned to water.

Late in the year as it was, this was no ordinary rain but the beginning of the monsoon season. The monsoons typically marked a lean time, for the boats couldn't go out as often. But this year, from every house came the smell of cooking fish: steamed, fried, salted. The new grounds were so plentiful that the kampong had more fish than it knew what to do with. The families could only sell so much at the market. So while previously they'd subsisted on thin gruel with sweet potato, stringy bean sprouts, and the occasional scrawny chicken, now they feasted, day and night, on fish. They steamed them with ginger and freshly cut chilies; they chopped them up and sautéed the pieces with fragrant sambal, they fried them till the fins grew crispy, a delicious treat for the children. Fish porridge at breakfast, fish bee hoon at lunch, steamed fish over rice for dinner.

Despite the damp that blackened new bread with creeping mold, despite the howling wind, the rain's relentless roar, the mud that found its way into the house no matter how carefully one scrubbed one's feet, a festive atmosphere arose in the kampong. People ran carelessly from one house to another, newspapers tented over their heads, arriving soaked but smiling. The kampong's main dirt road was turned to a pool of wet sludge that the children had great fun splashing around in. Frogs and snails were everywhere. Shins were more often muddy than not.

With the monsoons came the approach of the Lunar New Year. It was still three months away, but as the skies began to brighten, families began preparing. They would normally have made do with what they could find in the local shops, but this year mothers took long bus rides into the city center, where they splurged on expensive fabrics for new clothes. And while in previous years only the towkay's family could afford firecrackers, this year every single household bought crates upon crates of them. They stocked up on bottled fizzy drinks, sodas that left tongues bright orange or purple, usually only offered to guests on special occasions.

When the rains finally eased, the kampong set about cleaning the dried mud that caked front stairs, patching holes in roofs, and cutting back the ferns that encroached onto footpaths and old graves. This year's New Year would be like no other in the kampong's history—never had such abundance been enjoyed.

Like everyone else, the Lees were swept up in the buoyant mood. Ma bustled about, holding strips of cloth up against their shoulders to measure out what she would need for new shirts. Hia proudly brought home a pair of fighting fish that he'd saved up his pocket money to buy, their red fins furling and magnificent. Uncle no longer coughed. Pa went about humming an old tune from a Cantonese opera, a haunting sound that came not from the throat but from inside his chest.

And then there was Siok Mei, who cast a glow over everything that was good in Ah Boon's life and made it even better. They saw each other every afternoon, walking home from school together, playing in the rain among the guava trees and the mangroves. Siok Mei helped him with his homework, and his writing improved. Ah Boon could read and write now, if not with ease, at least with a competence born of studious exertion.

There was school, and then there was outside of school. With Siok Mei he learned what blood looked like when it flowed from a cut, so often had they fallen on some sharp rock or another while chasing each other through the trees. In morbid fascination they had smeared their blood together in their palms—*We're brother and sister now*, Siok Mei had said—watching the mixture grow brown and crusty in the humid air. Together they roamed the kampong, peeking into people's kitchens and bedrooms, stealing, once, fried prawn fritters that lay out cooling on a neighbor's back porch; watching silently through a window, another time, the mysterious athleticism of Ah Tong and his wife tumbling pants-free around their sleeping mat one rainy afternoon.

It was Siok Mei who put the idea of middle school into Ah Boon's head. He'd dismissed her initially; there was no middle school near their kampong, so they would have to commute into the city, an unthinkable thought. Also impractical, given that he had to help Pa on the boat. Besides, they were still children; middle school was years away, an entire lifetime.

And yet Siok Mei was so certain in her own desires that it planted something in Ah Boon, some seed of want. Siok Mei lingered by the provision shop each day, befriending the owner so that she could leaf through the *Sin Chew Jit Poh* without buying it. Under Teacher Chia's guidance, she began writing nationalist poems to submit to the student columns of the Chinese dailies. None was ever published, yet she persisted, reasoning that being only in Standard One, she was at a great disadvantage but would one day make it.

Her mind was like a lightning storm. She was interested in the Jipunlang war in the Mainland, the role of overseas Chinese in the fight for a strong republic, whether their loyalties should lie with the Malayan peninsula they found themselves on or with their ancestral home. Moreover she hated the Ang Mohs who controlled the country; they were clumsy, barbaric, unfit to rule. Even worse were the English-speaking Chinese, the soft-bellied middle classes with their teatimes and music lessons. They had forgotten themselves, capitulated to the Ang Moh devils, as she saw it. These were ideas Siok Mei had heard her parents espouse from a young age, for they had taken great care with cultivating her mind in preparation for revolutionary action.

But Siok Mei was still a child, understanding little of these matters, except to parrot and paraphrase that which she had been taught. Now, whenever she read or wrote or spoke of such things, it was her dead father she thought of, her vanished mother. She still clung to the secret hope that the latter would return. When she did, Siok Mei would recite

her poems, sing her songs. She would present her with the finely polished jewel that was her mind, say, *Look, Ma, look what I did for you.*

In the absence of her parents, Siok Mei found a mentor in Teacher Chia.
If the Mainland were to become the powerful republic it was destined to
be, Teacher Chia believed, then its women must be equal to the men, an
idea that was not uncommon among Chinese vernacular schools of the
time. Their students may have known only Singapore all their lives, but
many educators believed they were Chinese first, Singaporean second, a
philosophy looked upon with great suspicion by the Ang Moh rulers.

Teacher Chia himself had been taken in for questioning by the Ang
Mohs in his time at a prominent middle school in the city, held in a light-
less cell for just over two weeks as the milky-skinned foreigners probed
his loyalties. Was it illegal to love one's homeland? This was the question
he posed to the interrogator accusing him of being an agitator, a partici-
pant in a Kuomintang conspiracy to overturn the Ang Mohs' divine rule.
It was the only thing Teacher Chia would say in the two weeks he'd been
detained. Was it illegal? Was it?

It was not. Some years from now, all pretenses to legality would be
abandoned, but at the time of Teacher Chia's detention, the Ang Mohs
still clung to a certain veneer of civilization. They had no proof of Teacher
Chia's conspiracist culpability, and so he was let go with a warning and a
ban against teaching at any school with a student population greater
than fifty. This was how Teacher Chia, a local-born Cantonese whose
merchant parents had sent him to university in the Mainland at great
expense, ended up teaching at a tiny kampong school with barely an electric bulb in each classroom.

It was humiliating. Yet perhaps even more might be done by awaken-
ing the children of these rural populations. So he set about his educating.

The main benefactor of the school was the local towkay, and Teacher Chia had free rein. In some ways it was better than being at the prestigious middle school, Teacher Chia told himself, free from the rivalries and performative nature of certain revolutionary types. Here he could do the good, honest work of shaping young minds.

Students like Ng Siok Mei made up for the sting of bitterness that still struck him from time to time. The daughter of true patriots who had returned to the Mainland several years before to join the struggle against the Jipunlang invaders, she possessed a natural virtue, a fiery sense of justice. The kampong, the sleepy fishing village, was not prone to politics. No portraits of Sun Yat Sen nor Kuomintang flags were to be found in any household, with the Ngs' being the exception. Teacher Chia himself had not had the pleasure of meeting Siok Mei's parents before they left, but heard about them in great detail from the second uncle to whose care she had been entrusted.

It was testament to Siok Mei's character, Teacher Chia thought, that she did not complain about the unfairness of having to stay back after school to supervise the remedial students, and instead went about her duties with cheerful zeal. Teacher Chia believed she would do great things one day.

And this Lee Ah Boon, of whom she seemed so fond, well, he might be capable of something too. Teacher Chia had not had high hopes for the boy, with his poor handwriting and shy demeanor. When called on in class, Ah Boon had a way of swallowing his words that would try the patience of all but the most tolerant of teachers. Teacher Chia had fully expected the boy to disappear from the classroom a few months in, returning to fishing as so many of his would-be students did once they realized how much toil was required by literacy.

But unexpectedly Ah Boon had persevered. He had grown brighter in class, and now listened alertly, asking the occasional question. His writing had vastly improved. He was even showing interest in the pamphlets that Teacher Chia lent Siok Mei, and had stayed back after class to ask the meaning of some word or another. Teacher Chia had heard the pair discussing middle school at recess once.

Some hidden spark smoldering within the reticent boy, some ambition or longing, had been fanned into flames by Siok Mei. Teacher Chia had thought, at first, that Ah Boon would only hold Siok Mei back. But watching them at recess, he saw how she'd blossomed, how her manner, once severe—and who would not be severe, having lost their family at such a young age—had softened into an easy charisma. Their friendship balanced her, gave her some comfort that Teacher Chia, as much of a mentor as he tried to be, could not provide.

And so he would encourage them to go to middle school together. Middle school was a different world altogether, and its pressures could be overwhelming, exceptional a student as Siok Mei was. With Ah Boon, she would not lose her way. And as for Ah Boon—with Siok Mei's direction, her strength—that hard glint Teacher Chia detected in the boy's eye might bode success for him yet. He gradually came to expand the scope of his expectations to include Ah Boon. Together, he thought, they might do great things.

And so, as 1942 approached, the year of the snake would give way to the year of the horse. What with the kampong's newfound wealth, New Year preparations, and the heavy clouds finally giving way to brighter skies, one could not fault the villagers—a careworn people prone to cynicism—for allowing themselves to finally believe that life was on an upward trajectory. No one would say it lest they spoil their luck. But they felt their good fortune in the plumpness of their fish-fattened limbs, the solidity of their newly repaired houses. Even the forest seemed to recede a little, the cloistered road that led out from the kampong appearing wider, brighter, more blessed with dappled light.

It was only after the last gas lamps had been turned out, after the last restless child had finally drifted off to sleep, that the planes came. Had anyone in the kampong been awake, they would have heard the distant drone of the seventeen naval bombers that circled over the island in those early hours. Having no streetlights or motor vehicles, the kampong was not a target. The bombers went for the city and the harbor, some eight kilometers from where Ah Boon and his family were sleeping. The destruction was far enough away that they did not wake, not even when several buildings collapsed in flames, not even when the air raid sirens finally went off too late, a full fifteen minutes after the planes had done their worst.

The certainty of the war would be put off until they awoke, several hours later. That morning, the Lee family rose with the anticipation and good cheer of the days before. Ma was going to finish up a new sleeping shirt for Hia that he could wear to bed on the night before the New Year, a true luxury. Pa was going to sand and polish the boat; Hia would help him. And Ah Boon, Ah Boon was going to school, to see Siok Mei. After school they had planned to go down to the estuary, where Hia's friends had said they'd seen a dugong.

The family was still washing their faces and putting on their clothes when there came a loud thumping at the door. The noise seemed to reach their very chests. Everyone stopped what they were doing, turning toward the door. No one moved to open it. Then came the inexplicable shout: "Jipunlang! Jipunlang! Jipunlang!"

Chapter Eleven

The kampong had heard about the war, of course, but it was a distant, black-and-white thing, taking place in the cold, far-away lands from which the Ang Mohs hailed. They spoke of it increasingly often, the Ang Mohs, pontificating in English newspapers about their latest victory or the mistakes their enemies had made. The kampong did not know who these enemies were, nor did the kampong read the English newspapers. But they had heard the stories at the wet market, or at the provision store, where Swee Hong regularly listened to the wireless. His English was poor but sufficient to piece together the gist of the bulletins that now came more and more regularly.

Even after the Jipunlang had entered the fray the year before, storming through Malayan swamps north of the island, rolling tanks through villages and cities, the stories had still seemed like just that: stories. Alongside the tanks the Jipunlang soldiers were said to travel from battlefield to battlefield on bicycle, a comical image that the kampong could not quite take seriously.

Now, despite the constant bombings over the next two months, despite the curfew in the city, the kampong found it hard to believe the

island was really at war. Though the drone of planes overhead was a fearsome sound, the bombs never fell near the kampong. They'd heard the
reports, of course, the hundreds of deaths that could happen in one
night. They saw the pictures of the two majestic warships sunk by Jipunlang planes. They saw the distant searchlights scanning the dark skies
each night for the slightest hint of metal.

When the first strangers arrived, it became harder to ignore. Furtive
families pushing wheelbarrows containing sacks of clothes and pots,
children shoeless and crying. They came down the main road, either on
the bus that grew less and less regular, or on foot. Their homes had been
lost. They sought safety in the countryside. The kampong tolerated these
strangers, allowed them to draw water from their wells, to rest their feet
in the shade of their trees. Eventually they always moved on.

The kampong didn't talk about the war, except to exchange bare facts
every now and then, when a particularly bad bombing had occurred the
night before. Two hundred and fifty, someone would say. No, no, it was
three hundred, someone else would retort. That was the limit of the conversation. The villagers wrapped themselves in silence, a thick gauze to
protect against whatever was to come.

The preparations for the Lunar New Year continued at a subdued
pace. The earlier exuberance had been imprudent. Some ancestor or god
must have been offended, to threaten them with this war. Yet it would not
do to halt preparations altogether, for that would be bad luck, akin to
planning for a death that had not yet happened. And so they carried on
with it. No longer did the women heckle their children cheerfully as they
swept out the kitchens, but instead went about their chores with quiet
deliberation. The children ceased their noisy antics, avoided puddles, did
not go into the mangroves. Fathers resumed their silent, fatalist fronts.

Though the fishing grounds around the islands continued to provide, the kampong now steadfastly ignored its good fortune. The lavish fish dishes became a thing of the past. They stuck to simple steaming, or salting and drying, only cooking elaborate meals once a month to offer to the gods. Everywhere there was the feeling of joy being suspended, of breath being held.

As the New Year approached, the bombs came thicker, faster. The kampong received news one night that nearly a thousand people in the city had been killed. They doubled their offerings of chicken and fish, burned joss sticks multiple times a day, made visits to the large temple by the pig-farming kampongs up north, since it was no longer safe to go into the city.

Some wondered if they should continue visiting the islands. After all, they had thought for a long time it was too good to be true, and perhaps it was. Such seeming magic could not come without a price—had they tempted some malevolent spirit by indulging as they had? Fewer and fewer men followed Pa and Ah Boon out each day.

The common wisdom was that Singapore was a fortress. The Gibraltar of the East, the Ang Mohs called it, and so even as the Jipunlang advanced down the Malayan jungle, no one considered the possibility that the war might become more than shortages and air raids.

But two weeks before the New Year, the kampong heard that the causeway that joined Singapore to the Malayan peninsula had been blown up. Not by the Jipunlang, but by the Ang Mohs, the Ang Mohs who had repeated again and again that there was no making it past natural barriers of jungle and sea. Now the causeway had been blown up. Could it be that the Jipunlang were so close? They'd seen pictures in newspapers of kampongs razed, bayoneted villagers lying in the mud. It occurred to them that only a narrow strait separated them from these razed kampongs, bayoneted villagers. A strait that could be crossed by something as simple as a causeway.

Some, like Ma and Sor Hong, argued they should not jump to conclusions. The blowing up of the causeway was said to be precautionary. It implied nothing about the Jipunlang's proximity and they could all agree it was better to be safe than sorry. Others, like Ah Tong, began stocking up on rice, canned goods, and candles. Pa was silent about his views but one day returned home with two large crates filled with tinned luncheon meat and canned vegetables floating in salty water.

"Not in the kitchen," Pa said when Ma moved to unpack.

The boys went behind the house to help Pa dig. When they came back into the kitchen, hands brown with dirt, Ma was standing in the same place they'd left her, worrying the loose knots of skin on her elbows.

"Don't get the boys involved in this," she said. "Don't scare them with your nonsense."

But with each passing day, it seemed less and less like nonsense. The villagers now dropped into the provisions store even if they had nothing to buy, just to ask Swee Hong for news. When he began joking that he ought to charge a fee for the public service he was providing, people got the hint. Soon it became customary to bring him little gifts of steamed cakes and hand-pounded shrimp paste, which he would accept gracefully before dispensing the latest.

Shortly after Pa came home with the crates, Teacher Chia disappeared, and the school was shut down. Now there was nothing for Ah Boon to do but linger in the house with his family, all of them restlessly knocking about, waiting for some new disaster.

When the Jipunlang crossed over the northern straits and started advancing from the north and west, Pa brought home another crate, this one filled with tinned biscuits, matchboxes, a single heavy bag of rice. This time Ma didn't protest, only told him they should wrap the rice tightly in an old tarp before burying it, to protect it from weevils.

The news that reached them was contradictory and confusing. The Ang Mohs had an air advantage, all airstrips were unusable. The Jipunlang were twenty miles away, they were swarming the north coast. The Ang Mohs set the mangroves on fire. The defense line was falling back. The Jipunlang were short of fuel and supplies. Shortages notwithstanding, their tanks were rolling into the western regions of the island. The naval bases had been bombed, clouds of thick black smoke visible even from the kampong. They had been bombed by the Ang Mohs themselves, to prevent them from falling into Jipunlang hands. It was conceivable that things would fall into Jipunlang hands. The guns were pointing the wrong way. The right way, but they were the wrong guns. It didn't matter.

The Jipunlang crossed over into the island a week before the New Year. Still the kampong hung their customary red swaths of cloth above their front doors, not knowing what else they should do. When news came that the Jipunlang were mere miles from the city center, Uncle returned home with a large piece of white fabric. Ma cut a circle of red from their New Year decorations and sewed it onto the white rectangle. It was now a flag. Pa protested—how could they even think of flying the flag of those who had killed so many of their own?—but nevertheless Ma folded it and placed it in a cooking pot. A precaution, she said, and Pa was quiet.

Finally New Year's Day arrived. The mood in the kampong was somber. The night before had been filled with the noise of distant planes, the imagined screams of city folk crushed in rubble. The stream of refugees coming from other parts of the island had intensified, bringing stories of violent looting and chaotic streets.

Reunion dinners had not been had. Likewise, there was no visiting on the day itself. They knew the situation was dire: the island's reservoirs were in enemy hands, the city had been shelled mercilessly overnight, the defense line was crumbling. The kampong went about their daily work with tight smiles on their faces, occasionally muttering "Happy New Year" to each other if their paths happened to cross. No firecrackers were let off, no sweets put out, no fizzy drinks sipped.

In the early evening, a shout came from Swee Hong's shop, and quickly a crowd gathered before it. They were silent, listening intently to the words that streamed from the wireless. "Can make louder?" a new arrival asked, only to be shushed by the rest. The question had already been asked; the wireless was at its loudest.

It was official. On the first day of the Lunar New Year, the Ang Mohs surrendered control of the island they had ruled over for more than a hundred years.

Pa hurried home from Swee Hong's shop. Dinner was already on the table, and he could smell the braised pork trotters that Ma had made, her one concession to the festive period. As Pa stepped into the house, into the circle of his family sitting around the dinner table, familiar, beloved faces turning to greet him, he smiled and said nothing about the surrender.

He let his wife spoon gravy onto his rice, pick out choice pieces of fatty meat for him. He listened to Hia chatter on about a dragonfly he'd caught in his net earlier that day; it was electric green and as long as his palm was wide. He smiled when Uncle told him he'd patched the tiny hole at the bottom of the boat that had been giving them trouble. He patted Ah Boon's head absently, feeling the younger boy's eyes on him.

Pa took a bite of the braised pork. The sauce was thick and oily, the meat as soft as the inside of his own cheek. Ma had made white rice, and each mouthful was so fluffy and sweet it brought a tear to his eye. The family ate quietly, and only the sounds of their chewing and the occasional ping of chopsticks could be heard.

Sitting there, in his dry, comfortable house, as outside the sun began its daily work of filling the sky with color before taking it away, life seemed full of beauty and promise. Here it was: the solidity of the home he had built for his family, who were gathered around him now, filling their bellies with warm, delicious meat. A dangerous pressure began to build behind his eyes.

It was Ah Boon who first asked the question.

"How, Pa?" The younger boy's eyes intent on his father's face.

The family fell silent. Pa looked around at the faces he loved. He knew the things the Jipunlang were rumored to have done in other countries. War was the same everywhere. Pa was grateful not to have a daughter, then felt guilty about all the other daughters in the kampong. He thought of Ah Boon's school friend, Siok Mei, with her bright cheer and clear eyes, and felt sick.

Pa broke the news. Ma caught her face in her palms. A deep frown formed on Hia's face, one that took root that night and would never entirely go away. Uncle said nothing, remained as still as salt. Ah Boon was still watching Pa with anxious eyes.

There was no use delaying; preparations had to be made. Pa cleared the dishes away. He frowned but did not protest when Ma and Uncle got the Jipunlang flag from the pot and hung it outside. Of that night, Ah Boon would always remember the harsh staccato of those nails being hammered into the door.

The island would be renamed Syonan-To, Light of the South Island. Said quickly, the words became Shou Nan Dao, Mandarin for *Island of Pain*.

Word was going around that the kampong might be in particular danger, thanks to the villagers' support of a war fund that had been collecting donations for the struggle in the Mainland against the Jipunlang several years back. Worse still, Teacher Chia's name was rumored to be on the list of the Jipunlang's wanted men—individuals with strong ties to Chinese nationalist movements—which explained his disappearance some weeks earlier. There were whispers that he'd escaped on a fishing boat, was hiding in the city, had fled into the thick jungle up north. But the kampong did not wonder too long about Teacher Chia's whereabouts, for more pressing matters quickly presented themselves.

Through Swee Hong's wireless came the announcement that all Chinese men between the ages of eighteen and fifty were to report to designated registration centers the next day. Here, at last, was something that reached out over the airwaves and touched their lives. The villagers who were in Swee Hong's shop when the announcement was made looked at each other in disbelief. Many of them were between the ages of eighteen and fifty. Swee Hong himself was forty-nine. The straw fan he was holding stopped midair, and with the sudden stillness, houseflies started to settle on his cheek. At last, the war had truly begun.

Pa was not in the shop. He was out fishing with Ah Boon, for in the past weeks, they had been catching as much as they could. The wet market had been shut down and there was nowhere to sell, but outside their house was row upon row of salted fish drying in the sun. They'd used up all the tarps and newspapers they had, and were drying the fish on old clothes now. Pa didn't say what they would do with all the dried fish; all he would say, over and over, was that it was important that they *prepare*.

Uncle was waiting on the beach when they returned. He told Pa the news as they unloaded the fish. Pa didn't say anything for a long while, breaking his silence only to tell Ah Boon to stop dragging the nets on the ground, for they would wear out more quickly that way. When they reached the top of the beach, he turned to Uncle.

"And you think we go?"

Uncle paused, then nodded. "We go, we put our names, come back, keep our heads down."

"You see what the Jipunlang have done?" Pa said. "Children. Babies—"

"Huat."

"How can just—go? Give up like that?"

"This is bigger than us," Uncle said. "Even the Ang Mohs also must surrender."

Pa was silent.

"What's important," Uncle went on, "is we survive. Best way to do that is do what they want, lie low, wait until this is over. We got no choice. You see how strong they are."

"And we cannot do anything. Cannot fight, run, something, anything?"

The anger in Pa's voice made Ah Boon afraid. He had never heard Pa like this before, helpless and bitter.

Back and forth the two men went the whole way home. Pa felt it was cowardice to do as the Jipunlang wanted. Uncle repeated his point that there was nothing they could do, they were fishermen, not soldiers, they were simple people caught in the clash of two greater powers, and the real cowards were the Ang Mohs who had deserted them. Pa talked about massacres in the Mainland, children shot dead in villages up north. How could they cooperate with the perpetrators of those brutalities? Uncle did not see it as cooperation, he saw it as survival. Quietly he asked Pa to think about what the Jipunlang might be capable of here, should the men not do as they wished. He asked Pa to think of his own children.

"We can just not go," Pa said. "How will they know whether we go or not?"

"And if we don't go, and they come looking for us. Then how?" Uncle said.

Pa had no answer for this. Eventually he turned away, a hand to his eyes.

Ah Boon realized Pa was crying, and the realization made him shut his own eyes. Filled with a deep awkwardness, he stepped quickly into the house. He stood by the doorway for a long time, listening to the lowered voices of his father and uncle. Ah Boon wanted to run to Ma and tell her to stop the men, but she had been laid low by food poisoning and was asleep in her room. He had strict instructions not to bother her. Soon Ah Boon could no longer make out what they were saying. Eventually, silence fell.

Pa came in. His expression was inscrutable. Ah Boon wanted to fling himself into his father's arms.

But all he said was: "How, Pa?"

Pa squatted down, taking Ah Boon by the shoulders. His hands were still sticky with brine. Ah Boon breathed in deeply, taking in the familiar, comforting smell of his father, storing it up.

"Ah Boon, listen carefully," Pa said.

Ah Boon swallowed, nodded.

"Tomorrow, I go with Uncle to see the Jipunlang. We go early in the morning, before Ma wakes up."

The heavy feeling in Ah Boon's arms intensified. *Before Ma wakes up.*

Pa went on to say that when Ma did wake up, she'd think he'd gone out on the boat or to run some errands with Uncle. He didn't want Ah Boon telling her about their conversation earlier. And if she did ask, he was to say Pa went out fishing.

Ah Boon didn't nod, but he didn't shake his head either.

"Uncle is right. Ma's sick, no use worrying her. I go with Uncle, we take care of it. We will be back before she even notices."

Pa was asking him to lie to Ma. Ma, who was lying just meters from them in her bedroom, clutching her troublesome stomach.

"Boon, understand or not?" Pa said, more urgently now.

Ah Boon looked into his father's creased face. The whites of his eyes were more yellow and bloodshot than white, the dark pupils wide and dilated. Ah Boon's chest squeezed painfully, and he nodded. He would do it. He would do anything his father asked.

Pa smiled grimly, satisfied. "Don't tell Hia also, okay?"

"Okay," Ah Boon said.

They went back outside to finish sorting the fish. Briefly, life seemed to return to how it always had been, always would be. Here was the sun, relentless behind matted clouds; here was the vast gray sea, glimmering so beautifully it hurt to look at. Here were the crabs scuttling over the mud, the mangroves reaching and bowing, creaking and sighing. As Ah Boon worked, a cloud of chittering birds rose from the canopy. Against the blazing sky they swooped and swirled, one cloud, one vision, like the sardines in a shoal swimming through fire.

Chapter Twelve

The next morning, Ah Boon awoke to find the sun already risen and Pa already gone. He'd hoped to catch him before he left, but they had fished longer than usual yesterday and his weary body had betrayed him.

The table was set with Pa's daily breakfast. A little blue bowl, in which Ah Boon knew were three soft-boiled eggs. Sitting next to it was the small stone gourd that contained thick black soy sauce and a dented tin of fine white pepper.

"Your pa ah, go out so early never tell me," Ma said. She'd made breakfast for him anyway, but he still hadn't come home.

Ah Boon avoided his mother's eyes, the feeling of lead in him.

"You help your father eat, boy. Quick, cold already," Ma said, beckoning him to sit down.

He could almost see his father sitting there in his graying singlet and heavy canvas pants. Ankle hooked over knee, bony shoulder blades making sharp angles as he leaned forward to eat. Pa would be back soon, Ah Boon reminded himself. He had only gone to the city with Uncle to put their names down. It was a formality, nothing more.

Ah Boon sat down at the table. Perfect spheres of yolks in translucent whites, tiny suns suspended peacefully in outer space. It felt inauspicious to break them. But Ma was watching, so he nudged them open with his chopsticks. Slowly they yielded their yellow to the watery fluid. He added the dark soy sauce and pepper, then swirled it all with his chopsticks to make a slimy, frothing mixture. This he slurped. Salty and sweet, they tasted, somehow, human. His eyes prickled, and he pretended to cough, so that Ma would not see.

That morning was a gaping yawn. Usually, when there was no school, Ah Boon passed the time by helping Ma with laundry or Uncle with fixing nets. Sometimes he followed Hia out to the shallows, or made the walk to Siok Mei's uncle's house to see if she wanted to work on writing together.

Today, however, he could not imagine going to see Siok Mei. He wanted to be here when Pa's footsteps sounded down the trail, when his low voice calling a greeting bounced through the trees. So he sat outside, anxiously turning the fish that was drying in the sun.

"Aiyo, what's wrong with you today, boy?" Ma scolded.

Ah Boon would not budge from his place on the porch, and Ma gave up, going back into the house to rest. There he sat, scratching the itchy welts the mosquitoes planted on his ankles, eyes fixed on the path. Eventually he gave up the pretense of doing anything at all and simply sat. Hands tucked under thighs, legs dangling off the porch. The heat swelled as the morning went on, raising the cicadas' song to a manic pitch. The empty space where the path darkened and entered the jungle stayed empty. Ah Boon willed the familiar lanky form of his father to appear.

Time became strange that morning. When asked years later, he would be vague about how long he sat there, staring at the empty path.

He had not felt it to be that long, but Ma and Uncle would tell him it was almost noon when he finally leaped up from his seat, hearing the distant footsteps of someone running down the trail.

The shape of a man appeared in the distance.

Pa! He had returned. His skinny shoulders, angular head, familiar loping gait; Ah Boon would recognize them anywhere. He jumped down from the porch and ran out onto the path to meet his father.

But as the figure came into the light, he saw the shoulders were not as skinny as he had thought, the head less angular, the figure more squat. The man running toward him was Uncle, not Pa. Ah Boon stopped, blinking in the morning sun. Perhaps Pa was behind him? But he saw now that Uncle was alone. Uncle was alone, Uncle was running toward them, panting, shouting, his face red and shiny.

"Boon! Boon!" Uncle cried. "Where's Ma. Call Ma!"

Sweat trickled down the lines in his face, dripping into his eyes. His cheeks were purple and the tendons in his neck stuck out so far that Ah Boon was afraid they would snap.

"Where's Pa, Uncle?" Ah Boon said.

Uncle stopped. He stared at Ah Boon for a long time, unblinking, seeming almost to tremble. A terrible calm came over him. He pressed his lips together and pushed past Ah Boon.

"Ah Bee!" he shouted.

Ah Boon ran after him, the words stuck in his throat. Where was Pa? Panic rose in his chest as he realized that if Pa was just a little way behind Uncle, if Pa had gone to run an errand before coming home, if Pa was anyplace good, anyplace safe, Uncle would say so right away.

Ma came out of the house with Hia beside her. "Aiyo, why shout until like that?" she said.

"I'm sorry," Uncle said. He repeated it over and over. He collapsed on the staircase that led up to the porch.

A stricken look came over Ma. "What are you talking about? Where's Huat?"

Uncle mumbled incomprehensibly, head in his hands. A sudden contempt came into Ma's face, a coldness. As if she had already grasped the terrible truth of whatever had happened, accepted the hardship that was to come, and had no patience for anyone who could not do the same.

She gripped Uncle's wrist and yanked him to his feet as though he were a small child. Hia shrank back.

"Now, talk properly. What happened?" Ma spoke sternly into Uncle's face.

Uncle blinked. He took a deep breath, then he told them.

The first part Ah Boon already knew: Uncle and Pa had set off early, hours before dawn, riding the bus into the city. The closest screening center was a police station that had been taken over by the Jipunlang. When they got there, the building was still closed. A number of Chinese men, young and old, milled about outside. Waiting, like them, to be screened. Whatever that meant. They waited for nearly an hour.

As the sun began to rise, the first Jipunlang soldiers arrived. They were mainly young men with straight, proud backs and eyes like sharks. It was then Uncle began to have second thoughts. Was this a good idea, ought they to slip away? But now that the decision had been made, now that they were there, Pa remained firm. He would do things properly, follow the laws of the new regime, arbitrary or brutal as they may be. It was his way, Ma knew, Uncle pleaded, as if to absolve himself of blame.

The soldiers began to shout orders in their language. Pa and Uncle didn't understand what they were saying, nor did anyone else, and so they just stood there, rooted to the spot. The soldiers were getting angry. One in particular, Uncle noticed, was repeatedly hitting his rifle butt against the ground.

Finally a translator arrived, and in halting Malay ordered the men to form a line to enter the building. They shuffled into a large hall. Tables had been set up at the far end of the room, and they were made to form several lines in front of each table. Behind the tables sat Jipunlang officers accompanied by kowtowing men, some in dark hoods. It seemed they were translators, though why they saw fit to cover their faces Uncle could not understand.

If anyone spoke too loudly or dared to laugh, as some did, nervously, they were shouted at. The officer at Uncle and Pa's table could not be older than thirty-five. His skin was stretched tight over his face like a smooth mask, broken only by a tea-colored birthmark at the corner of his left eye, which gave him an oddly smiling appearance.

When each man was called up to the table, he would be asked a few questions by the translator who stood next to the officer. Their answers would be reported back. Sometimes the officer would speak right away; other times, he would tilt his gaze to the ceiling, press the tips of his fingers together, let the silence unspool in long, slow threads before pronouncing his verdict. On each table lay two rubber stamps and an ink pad. After the officer spoke, the soldiers would stamp the man's arms: one stamp produced a black square, the other a triangle.

The men given squares were waved out of the building. The men with the triangles were led away to some room deeper inside the building. This, it seemed, was the nature of the "registration." Uncle tried to discern a pattern to those who were taken away—age, appearance, occupation?—but there was no rhyme or reason to it. At times boys who looked too young to be eighteen were given triangles, other times men closer to

Uncle's age. Sometimes pale-faced city men with soft hands and black glasses, others wire-thin laborers in their singlets and flip-flops.

The line moved slowly. Uncle did not dare whisper about leaving anymore, there were so many soldiers standing about, watching them with lips curled contemptuously. It was fine, he told himself. Put their names down, go home, lie low. It would be fine.

A commotion broke out at the far end of the room. A man had been stamped with triangles, but when the soldiers started to lead him away, he wrestled himself free and tried to make a run for it. Two swift kicks to the knee from a soldier nearby quickly brought him to the ground. The soldiers surrounded him. The room fell deadly silent except for the man's sharp cries, the sickening thuds as boots met flesh and bone. The cries turned to whimpering, then awful, wet gasps, until finally the man was quiet. Eventually an officer shouted at the soldiers, apparently annoyed by the chaos, and they dragged the man to his feet. This time he let himself be led away.

Pa didn't say a word, but Uncle sensed that the scene had disturbed him. Now he stared at the space in front of him with a deliberate focus, as if fixated on some future moment when they were done with the screening and could leave the building.

"Let me go first," Uncle whispered. He had always been the more charismatic of the two, and figured he would have a better chance of softening the officer up, ensuring they both got square stamps. Not that a triangle meant anything bad, Uncle reminded himself. They did not know what it meant.

Slowly, they progressed to the front of the line, until it was Uncle's turn. He stepped up to the table with his features carefully arranged into earnest humility, a slight stoop in his posture. He gauged it better not to smile.

Name, the translator barked at him. Uncle gave his name. Age, he barked again. Profession. Place of residence. Family members. Uncle named Pa, and Pa's family.

The translator relayed the information to the officer. The officer paused, staring into Uncle's face. Uncle did not raise his eyes, focusing instead on the red rectangle patch on the officer's starched khaki collar. A lucky color, a good omen, he thought. Uncle became very aware of a particular ceiling fan overhead, one that must have been lopsided or damaged in some way, for with every rotation it made a high squeaking noise. Finally the officer said something to the translator, and the translator picked up the stamp closest to him. Uncle held out his forearms. Two squares, two wet patches of ink that dried cold on his arms as he stepped away from the table.

He found an empty spot close to the wall and bent over, pretending to scratch his ankle. He watched the translator ask the same questions of Pa, watched Pa answer slowly, carefully, in the same way that Uncle had. Pa, too, had the reflex not to look into the officer's eyes; Pa, too, held his hands clasped over his stomach, his head bowed.

The soldier took Pa's arms and pressed the wooden blocks against them. Soon, Uncle thought. Soon they would be out of this place and could go home.

Just then, something pushed into his ribs, sending him to the floor. It was one of the young soldiers, shaking his rifle butt. He shouted at Uncle, pointing to the door. Uncle looked back to Pa, straining to see his arms, but from the floor he could only glimpse Pa's outline through the crowd. The soldier shouted again.

Uncle got to his feet and was pushed by the soldier toward the door. As he left, he turned back again, but another man had now taken Pa's place at the table. Where was Pa? Uncle's heart thudded wildly in his chest. The overhead fan squeaked, over and over, like a small animal being slowly devoured. The soldier rammed his rifle butt between

Uncle's shoulders, sending him stumbling. Uncle turned one last time, straining to see over the crowd, and there Pa was: behind the tables, being led away through the door in the back.

The heat left his body. Uncle opened his mouth to shout Pa's name, but no sound came out, and before he knew it Pa had disappeared through the doorway. Without thinking, Uncle grabbed the man closest to him. It was the same soldier who'd hit him with the rifle butt.

"Where are they taking him? What's the triangle for? Where do they go?" he shouted.

The soldier's face darkened. Uncle flinched, for it looked as if the soldier was about to hit him. But then the man relaxed. He hoisted his pants up and looked at Uncle appraisingly. Then he made a universal sign, one fat thumb rubbing against two fingers: *money*. It took Uncle a few seconds to realize the man was asking for a bribe. He had money; Pa had thought they might need to pay to be "registered" and had made sure that Uncle brought a sizable sum. Uncle pulled out several bills from his pocket now and thrust them toward the soldier.

The soldier counted the bills, then looked around furtively. They were standing close to the entrance, and while no other soldiers were nearby, some of the men in the line were staring at them curiously. He grabbed Uncle by the elbow and pulled him outside. Uncle followed reluctantly, asking over and over: "Where are they taking him? Where are they taking my brother?"

Once outside, the soldier dropped Uncle's elbow as if it were filthy. He pulled a spotless handkerchief from his pocket and wiped his hand on it slowly. Then he gestured at Uncle, indicating that he should follow him.

They went around the police station. As they walked, the soldier dragged the butt of his rifle against the building's painted brick wall, leaving a faint line of gray on the dirty white. They turned the corner into an alleyway, one so narrow that Uncle could touch both walls with his elbows bent.

As the street behind them receded, giving way to the quiet, suspended air of the alleyway, Uncle's legs grew heavy. Each step became more difficult—he did not want to reach the end of the passage, where the shouts of rickshaw pullers mingled with the rumbling of cars, browned, tired necks glistened in the morning heat. The soldier's heels crunched into the dry dirt. Uncle imagined him shining his boots with annoyance that night, to get them back to their spotless condition. He felt as though he was being led to his execution, and had the urge to turn around and run back toward where he came.

But they emerged from the alley into the light; the soldier gestured to a large blue lorry parked by the side of the road, a short distance away from them. Men sat in the back of the lorry, thirteen in total, Uncle counted. Their hands were cuffed in their laps, faces drawn and anxious. None was Pa.

He saw now that they were at the back of the building. A door in the wall opened, and another three men were led out by Jipunlang soldiers, herded onto the lorry. The soldiers shouted at the men who were already in the back to make room. They shuffled over slowly—it was difficult with their hands cuffed—eliciting shouts and jabs from the soldier's rifles. Finally space was made.

From where Uncle stood, he could see only the men's profiles, but as they took their places in the lorry, the last figure turned briefly, and his stomach leaped. It was Pa. Uncle began to shout, but a hand clamped down on his mouth. The soldier dragged him back into the shadows of the alleyway.

Then the engine started, a loud, rattling noise, and the lorry pulled away from the curb, entering the busy flow of traffic. Uncle struggled as hard as he could, but the soldier's grip was strong, his nails digging sharp into Uncle's cheek. His hand smelled of soap and kerosene. The soldiers who had led Pa onto the lorry disappeared back into the police station. The lorry vanished as well, swallowed into the distant stream of cars, trishaws, and bicycles. Only then did the soldier release Uncle.

Uncle stood there, in the shade of the police station, hands loose, limbs free, suddenly confused. What was he to do now? What was there to be done?

The soldier looked satisfied. "Brother?" he said in Malay, with a smirk.

His teeth were large and white. Uncle marveled at them, even as he took in the cruel lips that framed them.

Uncle nodded. Brother-in-law, but he had long thought of him, of course, as his brother.

"Where are they taking him?" Uncle asked again. This time without heat, full of a slow, cold dread.

The soldier's smile broadened. His thin lips were cracked; a single black hair protruded from his left nostril. He didn't say anything more, but in one grotesque gesture raised a forefinger to his temple, cocked his thumb, and pretended to fire.

At this point in the story, Ma began letting out little gasps. Uncle sped up, the events that followed spilling out of him with a crazed urgency, as if he was afraid that he wouldn't get them out, that they would be trapped within him forever. Hia wrapped his arms around Ma.

Ah Boon could not feel his hands. He thought of the islands, their lush green slopes, the hornbills that rose in a cloud from the trees. They disappeared, but always came back. They disappeared, but he could always find them again.

It seemed impossible that Pa was gone forever.

Uncle was still speaking. He told them about how he thought the soldier would kill him there and then, so sick was the expression on his face, but that finally, instead, he had let out a braying laugh, then went back into the police station. He told them how he'd seized upon a group of coolies sitting in front of a half-built shophouse across the street. He'd gone to them, asking how many lorries they had seen leave that day. The answer was three that morning alone. They'd counted six or seven yesterday.

Had any of the lorries come back, Uncle had asked. They looked at him with such pity that he covered his face. It was rumored they took them to the beaches, one of the coolies offered, all the way in the east, and then—the man stopped talking. Go home, he'd said to Uncle kindly. See, you're safe now, like us. The coolies showed Uncle the black squares on their arms, as if he ought to be comforted by the shapes.

"The beach," Ah Boon said dumbly.

"What?" Ma said.

Ah Boon took off down the path, toward the shore. The sand was hot and rough beneath his feet. When he reached the surf he jumped straight in and swam out with strong, vigorous kicks.

The seafloor fell away beneath his feet. He treaded water as the waves crashed over his head and the salt stung his nose. Turning his head wildly, Ah Boon scanned the length of the shore as far as he could see. But there was nothing. Only the usual mute vegetation, the kelongs balanced on wooden stilts, boats rocking quietly in the shallows. There were miles and miles of beaches, Ah Boon thought helplessly. Pa could be anywhere. All the way in the east, the coolies had said, far, far from here. Ah Boon would never get to him in time.

And even if he did, what would he do? What could he do?

The waves crashed over his small, helpless self. He was crying. Slowly, he began to swim again, following the curve of the shore. He swam till his calves burned, till his shoulders stiffened with the effort. On the beach his family stood, little dark figures against the sand, getting smaller and smaller as he swam away.

PART II

Only Dogs Have
Licenses and Numbers

Chapter Thirteen

And so the years of Syonan-To began. "Asia for Asians!" the Jipunlang proclaimed, before bayoneting Chinese babies, beheading Indian soldiers, filling Malay guts with water until they splattered and burst. The Greater East Asia Co-Prosperity Sphere would be wrung from the necks of the island's inhabitants, built of its flesh, nourished by its blood.

What happened to Pa, it turned out, was only one small sacrifice that the Co-Prosperity Sphere demanded. Of course dai kensho—*the great inspection*—was a tragedy. Later, historians would argue over how many Chinese men had been rounded up arbitrarily, taken to distant beaches and summarily shot. Thousands? Tens of thousands? What was true and what was fabricated in the name of postwar Sinocentric nationalism? Nevertheless, spirits leaked into surf, their bodies tossed into shallow graves, never to be found or mourned by their families.

And yet it was just one of the many footnotes to an interminable four years. There was the river transformed into a fiery vision of hell, flooded with burning oil from bombed-out godowns; there were the blackened heads of looters displayed in crude cages outside the city cinema; the hopeful Malay soldiers lured out of hiding by the Jipunlang's promise of money and a free ticket home, only to be lined up and shot; the thousands of once-mighty Ang Mohs, paraded like bedraggled ghosts through the streets to the jails; the Javanese laborers suffering slow starvations, living corpses crumpled in doorways after days of backbreaking work.

As if to prove that time was a malleable thing, clocks were moved forward by an hour and a half. Streets and buildings renamed, rededicated, English words replaced by Jipunlang ones. Language lessons appeared in the newspapers and over the radio. Office hours were shortened to encourage upstanding Syonan citizens to spend more time practicing mastery of their newly attained civilized tongue.

Spines acquired discipline during those years, reacting to the sight of a uniformed Jipunlang soldier with a spasm, a twitch that began in the hips and extended quickly to fold the body into a deep bow.

Chinese schools were shut down, suspected, quite rightly, of being breeding grounds of the resistance. Children now spent their days singing Jipunlang anthems, sewing flags, practicing calisthenics routines. As time went on and famine deepened, gardening lessons became mandatory, scruffy patches of dirt in front of crumbling school buildings pressed into service as well, forced to yield misshapen sweet potatoes and stumpy ginger roots.

Then the Jipunlang newspapers began to take on the same hollow tone of victory that the Ang Mohs' had right before the island had fallen, dispensing frantic declarations of glory that rang increasingly false to the war-hardened population. Word spread of the unthinkable bombs that had fallen in the Jipunlang homeland, annihilating two entire cities. In those weeks the soldiers were more dangerous than ever before. Despair drove them to brutality, and many seemed keen to test the limits of their sadism before they were brought to account. People shut themselves in their houses, drew the blinds, hid under beds when the soldiers came knocking. Eventually the Jipunlang wore themselves out with bloodlust and sake parties became common: one final toast followed by a self-detonated explosion of grenades.

Finally, one rainy evening in September 1945, almost four years after they had been humiliated and chased from the island's shores, the Ang Mohs returned. The Jipunlang's surrender was finally complete. That evening the clocks were wound back, the Union Jack flew over the same cinema where the Jipunlang had once displayed severed heads, and the amusement parks rollicked with the surreal sounds of American jazz.

But many found it hard to shake the habits they had acquired. People continued shoving their daughters into closets when an unfamiliar knock sounded at the door. Spines continued to bend at the sight of any uniformed individual, be they Ang Moh or local. Jipunlang flags were folded up and stored carefully in biscuit tins, lest the tides of history should shift and loyalties had to be proven once again. Even after people moved on—resurrecting houses, dismantling altars to dead children, wearing long sleeves to cover scars and burns—the memory of those four years did not fade away, but rather became an indelible stain upon the island's landscape. Even as they raced to rebuild in the wake of so much destruction, tried to move forward and forget, always there was the lingering, ghostly call of the dead. For their blood had seeped into the fertile red earth, earth that was laid bare whenever a shovel cracked the ground for the foundation of a new building, or when a child's hands scrabbled about seeking earthworms after the rain.

As for Ah Boon—like others of his generation, he grew up quickly, becoming a man at the age of eight. Once Pa was gone, Hia was technically the head of the household, but the reality of Hia's temperament meant he was far less suited to being useful to Uncle or Ma in the daily running of their home. The war did not bring out his best qualities, and during that time Hia turned bitter and violent, like an angry dog chained and kenneled. He frequently picked fights with Jipunlang soldiers in the streets and came home with broken bones. Ma cried often, certain that he would one day court his own death, but against all odds, Hia survived.

Ah Boon, on the other hand, returned to his old seriousness, his brooding silence, though this silence was now channeled into action. It was he who sat with Ma while she lamented Hia's itinerant comings and goings, he who stayed up late into the night, helping Uncle patch a hole in the boat that threatened to ruin their livelihood. It was he who answered in a clear voice when the Jipunlang soldiers who ransacked their house, taking Ma's jewelry and Pa's old watch, asked him where his father was.

"Dead, sir," Ah Boon said without flinching, as the rest of his family cowered on the ground.

The soldiers seemed baffled by this young boy, so scrawny he had the appearance of being halfway dead himself, unsure if his stoicism was defiance or dull-mindedness. Finally deciding it was the latter, they left the ransacked house, laughing. *Dead, sir*, they chanted all the way out the door. *Dead, sir, dead.*

Spooked, perhaps, by military trucks rattling down coastal roads, rifles pointing out as if the vegetation itself posed a threat, the islands became erratic. Landmasses appeared and disappeared at will, forming spontaneously behind Uncle and Ah Boon's boat even as it sped in one direction or another, fading behind thick mists and vanishing entirely. The fish, too, turned strange. In their nets they found purple bruised snappers, three-tailed prawns, squid overgrown with tentacles. Never would Ah Boon forget one nightmarish haul of squirming catfish, ordinary-seeming at first, then revealed on closer inspection to have neither eyes nor mouths.

Perhaps it was the smell of fear, emanating from the fishermen's skin, that so changed things. Perhaps it was the blood of so many shot and killed on beaches, washing out to sea.

Still Uncle and Ah Boon continued to ply their waters. The famine meant they had to work thrice as hard, even if the islands provided, since they never knew whether they'd be able to sell their fish at the market or the Jipunlang truck would roll up and requisition their catch. Like many in the kampong, Ah Boon grew gaunt and sallow, hunger becoming an intimate friend. He welcomed its gnawing demands, its tenacious hooks and spells of dizziness. In those early days after Pa's death, for which Ah Boon blamed himself—he ought to have stopped Pa; he ought to have told Ma, who would have stopped Pa; he ought to have been bigger, stronger, able to protect his family—he felt he deserved to suffer. Often he gave his meager share of congee to Hia, claiming not to be hungry even as his belly gurgled.

Uncle, too, would not eat. An ominous quiet had come over him ever since Pa's death; he moved slowly, as if sleepwalking, and often would not hear when his name was called. Relentlessly he turned over those fateful days leading to Pa's death in his mind. It was he who ought to have died, he often thought. Pa had not wanted to go. Pa did not trust the Jipunlang. It was Uncle who had made the fatal mistake of bowing to authority. And that mistake had led to Pa's death.

One morning, early in the war, Ah Boon and Uncle had agreed to take Teacher Chia out to Batu. His name had been leaked as someone with strong ties to the war effort back in the Mainland, and the Jipunlang did not take kindly to this. He'd been hiding at the houses of acquaintances in the city, but despite moving regularly, the Jipunlang were always just a few steps behind. Could the kampong help, Teacher Chia had asked in desperation. The kampong could not help. No one wanted to harbor a known target and risk the wrath of the Jipunlang. But Ah Boon himself had suggested—what if Teacher Chia could hide somewhere that no outsider could find? And so it was agreed. For several weeks, Teacher Chia camped on the beach in Batu, sleeping under a tarp strung from the trunks of two large trees, catching fish with a hand line and drinking water brought to him by the villagers. Siok Mei joined Ah Boon, at times, on these trips to bring supplies out to Teacher Chia. They continued their lessons in a haphazard fashion, and grew even closer than before. When finally Teacher Chia decided to come out of hiding and brave the trip up north, Siok Mei cried, clung to his leg. The war had been hard on her. She saw for herself the brutality of the Jipunlang, the very same forces her parents had gone back to the Mainland to face, and with this knowledge, any hope that her mother might still be alive and in hiding somewhere was cruelly extinguished.

In all this time, Ah Boon carefully avoided thinking about Pa. For the most part, the daily business of survival was enough to keep his mind off it. And the family did not talk of Pa, drawing about themselves a shroud of silence that was thick and absolute.

At times, though, in the chilly mornings before the sleep fully cleared from his mind, Ah Boon would wake up, stretch his limbs and call out: "Pa?" To which Pa ought to have grunted from the living room, having already been awake for an hour, finished with his breakfast and impatient to set out to sea. But of course there was no reply, only Ma's soft footsteps, Hia's quiet snores. Then the sleep would clear from his mind, and Ah Boon would remember.

Those were the disappearing years. Homes, belief systems, entire governments, food, people one dearly loved—Ah Boon learned then that all of it could so easily disappear, and unlike the islands, there was no way to find them again.

How did Pa die? On a distant beach, standing in a row of strangers. Perhaps next to a younger man, who cried quietly as the Jipunlang told them to walk to the water's edge. Pa would not be crying. He would not try to swim away as the other men did, only to trip over the chains around their ankles, sputtering and flailing without dignity in the shallow water. While the others wailed around him, Pa would be standing tall and still. Perhaps he found the rhythmic roar of waves comforting in the moments before the bullets entered his back and mangled his spine; perhaps the sand was soft, warm as his knees sank into it, the cry of circling birds overhead welcoming in some way, familiar.

Chapter Fourteen

Inching forward in the dense river of men, the bus lurched and stopped each time someone chose to amble the wrong way. Honking did not work, nor did shouting or cursing out the window. Long had the driver given up, shifting his attention instead to finishing his ashy cigarette down to its dregs.

On the bus, Ah Boon scratched his stubble as he began to worry. "Maybe we should go back," he said to Siok Mei. "So many people."

The huge crowds unsettled him. He did not like it when people walked where they were not supposed to.

But Siok Mei shook her head impatiently. She was craning her neck, peering out the window, trying to catch sight of the Supreme Court. "So slow," she said. "We will never get there."

They were sixteen now, but it would only be this year they would both complete primary school at last. The war had taken from them more than time; theirs was a generation forced into adulthood by the shock of a violence and deprivation so complete that it set something inside them loose, rattling, something that, even as their lives seemed to resume their regular shape, reminded them of all they had lost.

"Mei," Ah Boon said, "shouldn't we—"

"No!" She turned to him, frowning. "We have to go help. You promised. I have to be there when Nadra is freed."

Ah Boon fell silent. He had promised; he knew what it meant to Siok Mei.

Ever since the case had come to light, it had been nothing but Nadra, Nadra, Nadra. The thirteen-year-old Ang Moh girl raised as Muslim in a Malay family in Java, whose Dutch mother had returned after the war to claim her. It was the terms of the adoption that were contested—and the Ang Moh courts, of course, supported not the Malay foster mother, not the child's wishes, but the Dutch mother.

The feeling in their kampong was one of disbelief. Anak angkat—a child given or sold by usually Chinese parents to a Malay family—was common practice. The Ang Mohs claimed that these adoptions, not having taken place formally, were invalid. What was formal, people wanted to know. This was how things were done, how things had always been done. The Ang Mohs wanted papers. Nadra's foster mother had papers— a letter from the Dutch uncle. The Ang Mohs did not judge these to be valid. There was no winning, it seemed; the rules were made according to some invisible, distant logic, and could be changed and reinterpreted at will by the Ang Mohs.

"Heartless," Siok Mei repeated over and over. "Cruel."

The separation of Nadra and her foster mother, Che Aminah, struck some deep place in Siok Mei's heart. The child should be allowed to choose, she thought. Why should childhood render one powerless? If Siok Mei had had power as a child, she always thought, she would not have chosen for her parents to leave her behind. It seemed a luxury to Siok Mei, to have two mothers fighting over oneself, when she herself could not hold on to even one.

After a series of rulings, Nadra had been taken away, weeping, from her foster mother and placed under the guardianship of nuns. Later she had been pictured holding hands with the Reverend Mother, under the headline BERTHA KNELT BEFORE VIRGIN MARY STATUE. It was this—more than anything up till now—that incited unrest. A war between two mothers had become a war of religion, and the rage that had been sparked danced dangerously close to the dry wood of century-old oppressions.

It was why they were on their way to meet Teacher Chia. Ah Boon did not understand exactly how they were meant to help, but Siok Mei had insisted, and with some trepidation, he'd agreed to come.

Siok Mei stood up abruptly. "Come on, Boon." She pushed her way into the aisle—*sorry, sorry, sorry, Auntie*—toward the exit.

"What are you doing?" Ah Boon said.

"Uncle!" Siok Mei cried. "Uncle, can open the door?"

The bus driver did not respond. A puff of smoke billowed from where he sat.

"Uncle!"

"Sit down," he barked. "Not yet reach our stop."

"We are not moving. Why don't you let us off so we can walk?"

"Sit down," he said again. "And stop that!"

Siok Mei would not sit down. She had begun hammering on the bus doors with her fists.

"Let us off!" she cried.

Ah Boon pushed his way apologetically toward her. He seemed to feel everyone staring at them, thinking them ill-mannered, badly brought up. Then, miraculously, the cheer was taken up by the other passengers. "Let us off! Let us off! Let us off!"

There it was, Siok Mei's miraculous ability to shape the will of crowds, which Ah Boon had first witnessed all those years ago in the kampong classroom as she stood down the group of boys making fun of Teacher Chia. Along with his usual pride, Ah Boon felt a pinprick of trepidation.

The power Siok Mei possessed was no longer used to influence children; what would it mean in the new world that was taking shape around them?

With an annoyed hiss, the driver relented. The doors of the bus swung open, letting in the steamy heat and distant chanting.

"Are you sure, Mei?" Ah Boon said again. It was not too late; they could still go home.

But Siok Mei was already halfway down the steps of the bus and did not hear him. The crowd of disembarking passengers was carrying her away; she craned her neck and lifted one arm, as if tossing a colorful ball, and shouted: "Hurry up, Boon!"

And so he followed, as he always did.

At sixteen, Siok Mei still wore her hair in low plaits as she had when she was a girl. Her soft face had sharpened, more crescent than full moon now, and her eyes glittered more brightly than ever before. While Siok Mei remained small, compact, Ah Boon had grown tall, his limbs pulling away from the earth like the thin branches of a well-watered tree. As children they'd stood eye to eye, but now he was a full head taller, and often found himself stooping as if to hear her better, although she spoke loud and clear.

The war had been over for five years. Teacher Chia had returned to the kampong school; Ah Boon and Siok Mei had resumed their educations; the Lees had continued to fish and clean and mend and survive. Life, for all intents and purposes, had resumed its former shape. This had been comforting to Ah Boon in the early years, and he sensed it was the same for them all. After the uncertainty and deprivations of the war, their return to routine, to fuller stomachs and safer streets, the familiar bumbling rule of the Ang Mohs—all of it was a relief. Strange how quickly one could settle back into old rhythms, even with all that had passed before. They mourned the fact that Pa had no grave, that they had never washed his body with their hands or picked the bone fragments from his ashes with chopsticks. But the grief, once a harsh rope that seemed to tighten at every turn, had now softened with time into a delicate thread, woven invisibly into the fabric of their daily lives.

Yet the longer they went on, the more Ah Boon had the feeling that the world he inhabited was false. Though Syonan-To was no longer, the country that stood in its stead felt like a flimsy mirage, an uneasy dream of its former self. The kampong was the kampong and yet it was not, it was temporary, it could not last. The war had shown that to be true. A restlessness plagued him. It had begun in his toes—they could no longer keep still. Then his knees, which drove Ma crazy with all their shaking at the dinner table. It was not nervousness; he was not afraid. An energy was building up in him, a desire for—he knew not what.

And so, although he had not expected this dense river of men, the loud chanting, a noise they were all moving toward, Ah Boon went along with it. Still, an uneasy feeling plagued him, and even as he and Siok Mei allowed themselves to be swept along by the crowd, he asked her again:

"Teacher Chia ask you to meet him here?"

Her voice was unnaturally light when she answered. "Almost there already! Just around the corner."

Here she slipped her arm into his, and his thoughts turned instead to the warmth of her skin, the troublesome tightening it caused in the pit of his belly.

They continued to move down the street. The protesters were nearly all male, mostly Malay, some Indian, Arab, or Javanese. Many wore neat songkoks atop their heads; a few carried and waved large flags bearing the crescent and star. There was an orderly air to the proceedings—everyone seemed to know where to go, no one shoved or ran, from time to time a chant would arise and people would take it up.

Young and Chinese, Ah Boon and Siok Mei stuck out sorely, but nobody paid them any mind. It wasn't them that the crowd was after. Still,

Ah Boon's uneasiness continued to grow; he did not like leaving the kampong, had always found the city with all its shouting vendors and loud motorcars disconcerting. And now this. He couldn't shake the feeling that everyone was looking at them, that they were intruding on a conflict that was not theirs.

"This is where Teacher Chia said to go," Siok Mei said, pulling him into a side street.

They were in a small alleyway between shophouses, where all of a sudden the air seemed cooler. Drops of water landed on Ah Boon's scalp, trickling unpleasantly down his neck. He looked up; it came from the wet laundry strung on a bamboo pole sticking out from the window above him. As he watched, a pale arm drew the pole back in, and the wooden shutters slammed shut.

"Who are you?" said a voice in Malay.

Ah Boon tensed up. He saw now that gathered in the alleyway was a small group of Chinese men and women carrying stacks of paper. The absurd thought that these were reporters delivering freshly printed newspapers entered his mind, before he realized the stacks were pamphlets.

"My name is Mei," Siok Mei said. "And this is my friend, Ah Boon."

Her voice shook a little. For the first time, she sounded uncertain. Ah Boon tried to catch her eye, but she was refusing to look at him. Instead her gaze traveled over the group, as if she was searching for someone.

"We don't know any Mei. Go home, girl, this is not a place for children," the man who'd spoken answered. He'd switched to Hokkien. Tall and thin, he wore baggy trousers held up by a makeshift belt of raffia at the waist, and he had a mean, malnourished look about him.

"I'm not a child," Siok Mei said. "We're here to help."

Ah Boon tugged at her arm. "Let's go, Mei," he said in a low voice. "Come. Go home."

She shook him off. "No, Boon. We want to help."

How could they possibly help? But a stubborn note had entered her voice, a note Ah Boon knew well. Here was the Siok Mei who told off the boys in their class all those years ago, on his first day at school. The Siok Mei who wouldn't be left behind on the beach when the adults went out to the islands. The Siok Mei who, even during the war, always found a way to wheedle an extra cup of white rice out of some provision-shop auntie in the city, and would return to share it with Ah Boon. The chanting out in the main street seemed to grow louder, and Ah Boon was aware of all those people out there, buzzing with heat and rage.

He pulled at her arm again. She ignored him.

"Teacher Chia—we're his students," Siok Mei said. "He—is he here?"

"Teacher Chia?" The man looked about at the group gathered behind him. "There's no Teacher Chia here." He stepped forward. "Who sent you, girl?" His voice seemed full of stones.

"Leave them alone, Kiat," a woman beside him said. "They're just kids."

"Spies," the man said. "You know what the Ang Mohs are like. Of course they use kids."

"Let's go, Mei, please," Ah Boon whispered. He grabbed her elbow and started to inch backward. This time, she seemed uncertain, and allowed herself to be led.

"But Nadra—" she said.

"Nadra doesn't need our help. Look at how many people are here! Let's go home, please," Ah Boon coaxed. Slowly, they made their way toward the main street.

"Eh!" the skinny man shouted. "Never say you can go!"

Ah Boon froze. Two boys, younger than Ah Boon and Siok Mei, ran past them and blocked off the alleyway. They were only a few meters away from the busy road they had come from, and could see the crowds of men still streaming past, flags fluttering in the wind, could hear the buzz of conversation and thrum of footsteps. Yet they were trapped in this quiet, dark alley.

What would they do? Ah Boon had heard of the triads and street gangs in the cities. The two boys were shorter than he was, scrawnier, even. Ah Boon could now lift a small boat almost entirely on his own, had learned, during the war, how to dig a hole deep enough to bury a man. He had come a long way since going limp whenever Hia pinned him down.

But there was only one of him, and many of them. And there was Siok Mei. It would be a different matter if he were alone.

"Don't come any closer," Ah Boon said. The words sounded weak coming from him. That old embarrassment.

"Why you come here? Who tell you to come here?" The mean-faced man spoke again.

"Teacher Chia told me you need help. Where is he?" Siok Mei said.

"'Teacher Chia, Teacher Chia,'" the man said irritably. "Got no Teacher Chia, you understand or not, girl?"

The two boys blocking the way to the main street moved closer to them. Siok Mei always seemed larger than she was; her voice made it so. But here in this darkened alleyway, Ah Boon felt her to be as small as she really was.

"Teacher Chia!" Siok Mei said, her voice ricocheting loudly off the high, wet walls. "Teacher Chia, Teacher Chia, Teacher Chia!"

The two boys moved closer still. One of them reached for Siok Mei, as if to silence her, and without thinking Ah Boon seized the boy's arm and twisted it toward his face. The boy cried out. A sharp twinge at the elbow, the sick feeling of a tendon being stretched the wrong way. Ah Boon knew well this pain; he'd learned the move from having it done to him by Hia countless times. The way out of it was a particular maneuver—the slackening of the trapped arm, twisting toward rather than away from the pain—but the boy in Ah Boon's grip did not know this.

The second boy moved closer. Ah Boon would not be able to hold both of them off. And behind him was a third figure: lanky and tall, looming in the shadows.

"Run, Mei," Ah Boon said.

The tall shadow drew nearer, resolving into a familiar shape. As the man walked toward them, he raised his hand to the bridge of his nose to touch his glasses in an unmistakable gesture.

"Siok Mei?" he said, frowning.

"Teacher Chia, you said the movement needs help, no one wants to help, so I came! Look, Ah Boon is here also!"

"What's the meaning of this, Chin Huat?" the mean-faced man said. His voice had lost its stony edge.

Teacher Chia sighed. "Let him go," he said to Ah Boon, then turned toward the man. "They're from the kampong."

A ripple went through the crowd. Ah Boon realized he was still gripping the boy's arm. He dropped it warily. The mean-faced man cracked a smile. A veil seemed to fall from his face, and suddenly it was as if he had never looked mean at all. He began to laugh. Now the crowd was greeting Teacher Chia, showing him their stacks of paper, joking and milling about as if the whole disturbance with Ah Boon and Siok Mei had never happened.

The mean-faced man—now not so mean-faced after all, it seemed to Ah Boon—slapped Teacher Chia on his back, and they embraced. "Good to see you, Chin Huat. Next time tell us when you send your students, so we don't have to scare them like this," he said, turning to wink at Ah Boon. "Sorry, ah, boy. Okay!" He clapped his hands. "Everybody! Back to work!"

Teacher Chia, it turned out, was not Teacher Chia's real name, but one he went by in the kampong so as to keep a distance from his other activities. Other activities being? When asked this by Ah Boon, Teacher Chia would only purse his lips and lightly push his glasses up his nose.

"Enough for today," he said. "I think it's time the two of you go home."

"But Teacher Chia," Siok Mei said. There it was again, that stubborn note in her voice. "You said I could come. And the judgment will be announced any time now."

"I said, I said, when did I say that?"

"After class on Thursday! When we were talking about Nadra!" Siok Mei said. She switched to Teacher Chia's formal, classroom Mandarin: "It is a fight that concerns all races, all religions, not just the Muslims, and yet we only stand by and watch. How will we ever throw off the tyranny of the Ang Mohs if we do not come together? If fellow citizens do not show up?"

Teacher Chia brought his elegant fingers to his face. But instead of touching them to the bridge of his glasses, he pinched his nose bridge, closing his eyes. Something passed over his face; a strange expression, one that Ah Boon could not read. Then he opened his eyes again, and the look was gone.

"Okay, Mei," he said. "You can stay. But if things get bad—"

"Why get bad? What will get bad?" Ah Boon asked.

"Thank you, Teacher Chia!" Siok Mei grabbed Ah Boon's arm. "See, Boon! You wanted to leave! Maybe we'll even see Nadra!"

"Nadra is not here," Teacher Chia said. "She's at the convent."

Ah Boon knew how Siok Mei's heart dropped, could read in her face the disappointment that she was trying not to let show.

Instead she grabbed a stack of pamphlets. "Let's go," she said, and they went back out to the main street, joining the slow crowd winding its way toward the Supreme Court.

Soon they were standing in front of the white-columned building where the appeal was being heard. Teacher Chia and the others dispersed in the crowd, handing out pamphlets to anyone who would take one.

Ah Boon flipped past the Malay and English pages, to the Chinese. *Develop the fight for Nadra into a true struggle against British Imperialists!* the pamphlets cried. They went on to detail the various injustices perpetuated by the Ang Mohs. It was nothing Ah Boon had not heard before: the food scarcity, the barring of non-English-speakers from jobs, the scams and sleight-of-hand disappearances of military stores and war rehabilitation goods, the exploitative import of opium.

The list went on from the commonly known to the anecdotally alleged: random acts of violence against stallholders and taxi drivers, hushed-up rapes of local women. For a moment, Ah Boon forgot whether he was reading about the Ang Mohs or the Jipunlang, so similar the brutality seemed, and standing there now, with all those chanting people in that large, leafy square in front of the stately Supreme Court building, from which the Ang Mohs would proclaim the fate of young Nadra, Ah Boon, too, felt a knot of anger forming inside him.

He was not angry by nature. Ah Boon had learned from a young age to cut off his anger before it even began, so much so that he was unaware he was capable of any rage at all. Shame, yes, humiliation, yes, soul-rending grief, these were all emotions he knew well. But rage—rage was new. He felt himself now as a cold log whose edges were beginning to glow. After the long years of the war, the confusion of the Malayan Emergency, the vague, unarticulated losses that went beyond Pa, it was deliciously tempting, this desire to catch alight, to allow indignation to course through his veins as a fiery river.

Siok Mei waved at him from where she stood in the crowd. He went to her.

"Just now, you going to punch him or what?" she said.

There was no teasing in her voice; it was a serious question. Ah Boon thought about it.

"I don't know." He shrugged.

"Mmm." She studied the pamphlets in her hands. There was a fierce jut to her chin when she looked up at him again. "I don't need anyone to punch for me."

"I didn't—I wasn't going to—"

"Just don't, okay? Don't try to protect me."

Ah Boon fell silent. A stubborn feeling was welling up in him, and he felt, stupidly, like he might cry. Around them the chanting seemed to grow louder. The crowd was like a single enormous being; it was impatient, it was hungry. Ahead of them the Supreme Court building loomed, bone-white in the late-morning sun. The verdict would be announced any minute. Ah Boon saw clearly that no one would read their pamphlets. The Muslims did not care for the Chinese leftists' manipulations, as much as the latter pushed the vision of some great anticolonial alliance. Nadra did not care for Siok Mei.

Ah Boon handed the pamphlets he held back to Siok Mei.

"What?" she said.

He turned to go. "See you at home," he said.

"Boon! Please—"

"What?" he said. Even as he asked the question his cheeks burned. He heard the pleading in it, hated his need for her.

She set the pamphlets on the ground carefully, then took both his hands. The crowds, the heat, the noise, all of it seemed to disappear.

"It makes me feel weak," she said.

Siok Mei looked down. Her hands were cold and dry. It was all she would say, but Ah Boon felt a weight lift. It was not that she did not want him, then. He understood feeling weak. It was, he saw, a confession that cost her something to make.

He picked up the pamphlets from the ground, carefully dusted them off, then handed half the stack to Siok Mei. They moved through the crowd together, handing the pamphlets out steadily, politely, and it gave Ah Boon pleasure to see the crisp printed sheets in the protesters' hands, even if all they did was leaf through them carelessly or use them to fan the hot air. Most of all, he liked being united in this goal with Siok Mei.

It happened quickly. The hearing lasted a little over five minutes; no longer, Ah Boon thought, than it would take to make a trip to the outhouse. In those five minutes the fate of the girl was decided. She was to leave with her Dutch birth mother.

A mournful roar rose from the crowd. Injustice! Imperialism! Anti-Islamic colonizers! The foster mother emerged from the entrance of the bone-white building, slow and sorrowful. But the protesters that swarmed her would not be restrained. They cried out their fury on her behalf, shouted their grief, stamped their feet. Five minutes. The judgment had never stood a chance to begin with. Five minutes! The crowd swelled and surged, a many-headed, angry beast.

What happened next was unclear. Was it an empty soda bottle that was first thrown, arcing over the crowd to smash at the feet of a Eurasian police officer? A car window that was shattered with the wooden poles from which crescent-and-moon flags flew? An Ang Moh businessman, stepping off a bus at the wrong moment, attacked and set on fire in a storm drain?

Ah Boon and Siok Mei slipped away, but the riots that began that afternoon raged for two full days and nights. Back in the kampong, they listened over the wireless to stories of Ang Mohs being set upon by crowds of hundreds and beaten with sticks, of policemen stepping aside to allow the beatings. Cars and homes set on fire, shops robbed at knife-point, streets filled with broken glass. Left mostly alone were the women and children, Chinese medicinal shop owners, Indian soldiers. The rioters knew who they were after. Pale-skinned ghosts with their soft pink mouths and delicate hands, those who had decided that even the pretense of justice was not worth more than five minutes.

Chapter Fifteen

The month that followed the Nadra riots was one of endless arrests, raids, and curfews, drastic even by the standards of the time. Certain leftist factions had gained the people's admiration for standing up to the Jipunlang when the Ang Mohs had not. At their instigation, unions were formed, clan associations rallied, hartal after hartal called. Bus service ground to a stop, sewers overflowed with excrement, factories emptied of their workers. The smell of revolution was in the air. But the Ang Mohs would not have it. The Ang Mohs would have order, they would rule *their* island as they saw fit.

It was under these circumstances that Ah Boon had been persuaded by Siok Mei to attend middle school.

"When Pa was seventeen he already got his own house," Hia had said when Ah Boon first raised the idea to his family. "So old now still study what?"

True that he was four years older than he should have been. They all were, the war had done that to them. But the war had also made Ah Boon immune to his brother's criticism.

"And who is going to fish?" Hia went on.

"Let your brother be," Ma said, to Ah Boon's surprise.

She worked out a plan where Ah Boon would help fish on weekends, Hia and Uncle on weekdays. And so Ah Boon went.

Middle school was nothing like school in the kampong. Thousands of students across six forms, housed in an elegant building with wide balconies and so many windows it made Ah Boon dizzy to look at. Set up by philanthropists with pockets far deeper than those of the kampong towkay, this school was no stuffy zinc-roofed shack. Its lush tree-filled grounds were larger than the kampong itself, and boasted an artificial lake in which fat spotted koi made lazy circles all day long.

As Ah Boon stepped through the high metal gates onto the front lawn that first day, it was only Siok Mei standing at his side that stopped him from turning around and going back home again. But there she was. She took his arm and they went in together.

It was a heady, inflamed time. Ah Boon quickly learned that school was not about accumulating facts or knowledge; it was about opinions, revolutionary sentiment, and philosophy. His classmates spent more time writing pamphlets attacking the Ang Mohs than they did studying mathematics or geography. It seemed as though everyone was in a study group. It was not the official curriculum they were poring over, but rather Chinese history and Marxist dialectics. There were picnics, overnight camps, mass concerts organized by the Middle School Students' Union, at which fiery speeches were given, bone-shaking cheers taken up.

Ah Boon fell into it as a leaf into a rushing stream, borne along by the strength of his classmates' fervor, the conviction of their beliefs. And how seductive their beliefs were—in his life he had not known to hate anyone, to hold anyone accountable for the difficulties of the day-to-day. Now, as his thinking was corrected, he saw that the towkay was the one keeping the rest of the fishermen down, sitting fat and content in his house of brick while the kampong worked themselves to the bone to pay rent. (When he struggled with this—the towkay, he said to Siok Mei, was surely a kind man; he had not raised their rent, as the towkay in the neighboring kampong had, and forgave their debts when he knew they could not pay—she retorted: "If a wolf decides to spare a rabbit because he is too lazy that one day, does it make him any less a wolf?" He could not argue with that logic.)

What was more indisputable was how the workers in the city suffered. The night-soil collectors, builders, factory assemblymen, bus drivers—he was shown the arduous conditions in which they toiled, the meager meals they could scarce afford, the dilapidated shelters they called home. Meanwhile wealthy English-speaking businessmen and civil servants sipped iced beverages at lunch clubs, rubbing elbows with besuited Ang Mohs.

Ah Boon saw now that though life had never been easy in the kampong, those who lived there, at least, had wide open spaces in which to roam, could always pick fruit or trap crabs should money run out. They had no boss to answer to, no yelling foreman to evade; they were free. He did not voice this thought to his peers, for the only credential he had in this new, fiery world was that of being from a fishing family in the countryside, a trait that bestowed upon him a certain authenticity as one who knew intimately what it was to work.

Siok Mei and Ah Boon were placed in the same student cell, a group of five who did everything together. He had never known there were so many things to fill one's time with. Public swimming pools, full of bare legs glistening in the sun. The Roxy Theatre, where for fifty cents, one could spend two hours in a darkened room watching open-collared P. Ramlee, with his fashionable Western suits and stylish coiled hair, fall in love with the luminous Mariam Baharum and her shy, sweet smile. There were the Worlds amusement parks, where fragrant satay dripped fat over charcoal racks and "taxi girls" clad in colorful cheongsams danced and danced.

All this was nothing new to the other three in their student cell, all older, all of whom had grown up in the city. Two girls—Geok Tin and Ah Mui—and another boy, Eng Soon. They took Siok Mei and Ah Boon around with deadpan world-weariness, but beneath it was a glimmer of amusement, a fondness for these new, strange classmates from the country-side. Sua ku, they were called teasingly, *mountain turtles*.

To Ah Boon the camaraderie between the five of them felt forced, like something they were acting out as part of a performance with no audi-ence. But eventually the studying and the outings did their work, and the others began to feel like distant cousins to Ah Boon, friendly and a little dull, but comfortable in their familiarity. He was especially wary of Eng Soon—a leader in the student unions, a fierce debater, who seemed to have read everything from Lu Xun to Lenin to Charles Dickens—but was slowly won over by the older boy's kindness, the care he took never to embarrass or put Ah Boon on the spot for his lack of learning. Their dynamic was a little like that between Ah Boon and Hia, if Hia had had the patience to take Ah Boon under his wing.

Toward the end of their first year in middle school, news came of an unpleasant incident: a principal at a different school, walking to work one day, had had nitric acid flung on her face by one of her very own students.

"We shouldn't be attacking our own." Siok Mei was on the verge of tears. "Surely that's not the way."

The older students swapped glances, shifting in their seats as if the fact of chemical burns was unfortunate but unavoidable. Eng Soon awk-wardly put an arm around Siok Mei; Geok Tin offered her a tissue. Still no one said anything. Her tears made them uncomfortable, the rest of them having long moved past such sensitivities. They were sorry for the principal, of course they were. No one would wish such violence on another human being. But she ought to have known. Cooperating with the Ang Mohs the way she had—shutting down school dormitories, disbanding political student organizations, informing on her own students—would naturally come with certain consequences.

Years later, Ah Boon would remember this conversation, Siok Mei's tears streaking down her cheek. By then it would no longer occur to her to weep over violence.

Time passed. They were seventeen, eighteen, nineteen. Ah Boon's relationship with Hia grew increasingly strained. Hia still did not see what a fisherman needed with a middle school education, nor did he understand why Ah Boon could not come straight home after school to help with the work, rather than running off to one classmate's house or another to compose meaningless poetry and songs. But Hia's words fell on deaf ears; Ah Boon was moving further and further away from the kampong, returning from school only to eat and sleep.

There was so much work to be done. There were debates to participate in, books to read, discussion groups to run, school picnics to attend. Ah Boon could barely keep up. Threaded through it all was Siok Mei; Siok Mei with her clear, ringing voice, her blunt-cut hair falling heavy and straight as if it held water, her burning eyes that she could turn on you like a spotlight.

Wherever Siok Mei went, he went too, her lanky shadow who did not speak loudly enough to be heard. Neither of them fit neatly into the world of the middle school, where most other students came from the city. It was not that the others were wealthier; Ah Boon's kampong was able to live off the mysterious fishing grounds, even through the lean postwar years when other families were crippled by rocketing inflation and the invalidation of the Jipunlang currency. Yet his classmates, poor as some of them were, were far more worldly. They knew how to weave their sentences in a tight web around their opponents in the midst of some political debate, how to use silence and a fierce gaze to their advantage, how to drink bottle after bottle of beer without showing any signs of inebriation other than a faint red tint to the eyes. The men, especially, were daunting to him; they with their sly jokes about female classmates when the latter were not around, their tales of dance halls and street brawls. At first, Ah Boon and Siok Mei—with their old-fashioned wide-legged pants and hands that smelled of the sea—were looked upon with a certain patronizing kindness. But Siok Mei didn't seem to notice. She barged into any social situation with such oblivious hard-headedness that most found her impossible to ignore.

Part of this was the schooling she'd received from Teacher Chia. When he'd returned to the kampong after the war, his politics had shifted. The Communists, he'd decided now, were the future, the only ones capable of building a Mainland fit for the modern age. And it was the Communists who would lead their own small island into a shiny new independence. From him, Siok Mei borrowed books and pamphlets about struggles in Indonesia, land distribution in Latin America, and early notions of the socialist Afro-Asian vision. She hadn't understood all of it but knew enough to impress the other students.

Her status was cemented when she was forced to divulge her family history. She'd explained it quietly to Geok Tin and Ah Mui, asked that they not tell anyone. But of course the story spread, and Siok Mei was hailed as being the child of true patriots and comrades. Soon she was drawn into the organization of their school's student union, whose ranks numbered in the thousands.

To Ah Boon it did not matter that her concerns were changing, that she seldom laughed and no longer wanted to go to the cinema. It did not matter that she was becoming a minor celebrity at their school, was constantly surrounded by a group of adoring classmates hanging on her every word. When it was time to leave, the others would eventually fall away, until it was just Ah Boon and Siok Mei, and the two of them would go home. The journey from the city to the kampong was a long one, especially late at night, involving a winding bus ride, punctuated by one change or two, depending on where they were, and then a final slow walk from the main road where the bus dropped them off to the kampong itself. On these trips home, everything new that had entered their life seemed to fade. They were their eight-year-old selves once again, walking home from school together.

Ah Boon continued to go with Siok Mei to the various work stoppages, bringing food and cold drinks to the postal workers and nurses and taxi drivers who held strike after strike for fair pay. It was on one such occasion that he found himself in a thick stream of Chinese students marching down a broad tree-lined street toward the Ang Moh governor's residences.

They were protesting mandatory registration for part-time military training for all federal citizens aged eighteen to twenty. Like most of his classmates, Ah Boon, nineteen going on twenty, had not registered. Why train to defend rulers who had actively prevented them from getting jobs within the civil service and other fields, all for their unwillingness to capitulate to their colonial masters' culture and tongue? Did the Ang Mohs plan to send them into the northern jungles to fight the Chinese Communist guerrillas—guerrillas who were their neighbors, cousins, brothers at one point or another? And as for the registration itself, well, the memory of the Jipunlang's "registration" had not faded from their minds. "Only dogs have licenses and numbers!" went the cry made popular by one especially charismatic union leader. Even the local university students had stirred from their comfortable, English-educated world. "Aggression in Asia!" cried a widely circulated newsletter, which denounced Malayans' lot as colonial people being trained to fight Ang Moh wars. "Not fit to rule ourselves," went the editorial's scathing words. "But fit enough to die for other people's interests."

Ah Boon did not like to see Siok Mei on the front lines. Still, he clapped and cheered as she, Eng Soon, and Geok Tin tied themselves to the residence's high metal gates. She had told him years ago that she did not need his protection, his protection made her feel weak. And so he stood by, jostled by the crowd, shouting words of encouragement she could not hear over the noise.

He had allowed himself to be convinced that this was what the future demanded; that it was the future he, like everyone else, believed in. There was no other possibility; any other future meant separation from Siok Mei.

And yet he loved her. Even as he felt her changing, he longed to take her small hand, smooth and brown as an almond, to push the heavy hair from her eyes, press his cold cheek against her warm one. At times he knew she might want this too. All those years ago, on the vanishing island, when she'd made him promise never to leave her. Later, as well, when she argued passionately for why he ought to attend middle school in the first place. Or on nights they walked home together after a study session gone late, and she linked arms with him as they halfheartedly debated some unresolved idea or another. Democratic socialism versus communism or the role of the sultans in a communist Malaya, but all he could think of was how the crooks of their elbows nestled so perfectly. Still, the shapes of what they were to each other had already begun to calcify years before, and the longer he waited, the more difficult it became to shatter them.

As he stood there in the heat and noise, staring at Siok Mei with her wrists chained to the gates, a violent fear struck him. Who knew what could happen in these surging crowds, all these bodies hot with rage? By now he had seen policemen crack the elbows of protesters with their wooden batons, send rows of students tumbling to the ground with the powerful jets of water cannons. What if the unthinkable were to happen—that he should lose Siok Mei?

He pulled himself free from the jostling scrum around him and ran toward the gate.

"Don't worry," Siok Mei said with a laugh when he made it to her. "Are you worrying? Are you here to unchain me?"

"I love you," Ah Boon said.

He felt as if he had shouted it. But everyone was shouting, and no one could hear them.

"Oh" was all she said.

He waited. A small frown settled between her eyebrows. Yells came from behind him, then the crowd surged again. The police had arrived with their rattan shields and were forming a perimeter.

"Oh, and?"

"Boon," Siok Mei said, "why are you doing this?"

"Doing what?"

"This is not the time. I can't."

"Can't love me?" Ah Boon pressed. Police or no police, he had to have an answer. He saw Eng Soon, tied farther down the gate, shoot them an odd glance.

"Boon," Siok Mei said again, more firmly now. "Workers are starving. People are risking their lives up in the jungle. The Ang Mohs want to force us to fight their wars."

"I just want to be with you."

Siok Mei possessed a certain look that Ah Boon loved most, and it was this look she turned upon him now. There was a knowingness to it, as if she could see with utter clarity his weakness, his small, desperate, selfish desires, and yet the look was understanding, the look did not judge. Only she knew him, only she saw him for who he was and held him no higher or lower in her esteem.

"Please," he said. Around them pounded the policemen's boots. "It's so loud here. Let's leave."

"What? Leave for what?"

"Let's go somewhere quiet, somewhere we can talk, you and I."

Siok Mei paused. "I'm not leaving, Boon."

Ah Boon grabbed the chain that bound her wrist and tugged on it pointlessly. The protests, the National Service registration, the Ang Mohs—what did he care for any of it? She had to come with him. They would go home together, just the two of them, as they always did. They would sort it out.

"It's not safe here," he tried again. "People are getting arrested. We have to go."

"People are dying, Boon," Siok Mei said. "People are making sacrifices."

How he hated the lecturing tone of her voice. Not her—he could never hate her—but the voice, yes, the voice he could hate, hate with a burning fury. It was the voice of revolution, of self-righteousness, a pious certainty that filled him with resentment. It bore a strange likeness to Hia's voice, all those years ago, taunting that he would never make a good fisherman. He would never make a good revolutionary either, it seemed. Suddenly he was consumed with a wave of hatred for everyone around him—the classmates, the student unions, Eng Soon, Geok Tin, all of the chanting, stupid masses.

"Siok Mei!" Here he was, Eng Soon, face contorted in worry. A classmate was undoing the chains as quickly as he could, but the metal links were entangled, and it was slow going. "Do her first," Eng Soon commanded. The classmate switched focus to Siok Mei.

Ah Boon was still standing there. His hands hung dumbly, open and empty. Siok Mei was still frowning. The silence between them was swallowed by the roar that rose from the crowds.

"Go home," she said to him.

Her brow softened into a look of pity that Ah Boon felt as a blow to his chest. What good was her pity if he could not have her love? She would truly choose this—the movement, these protests, these people—over him?

Ah Boon threw Siok Mei one last pleading look, but she was busy now with Eng Soon and his chains. On and on they talked, those stupid serious looks on their faces, of police and arrests and who had been taken away. Siok Mei would no longer meet his eyes.

With leaden footsteps Ah Boon left the brawling mass of students. He walked and he walked, down busy streets filled with trishaws and motorcars, into quiet alleyways where chickens pecked and laundry dripped. Past night laborers sleeping in doorways and wooden shophouses with their roofs falling in.

He walked for hours, until he did not know where he was, and the sun had slipped low in the sky, and the edges of buildings were tinged in red. Then he found a bus stop, and for the first time in years, he hailed the bus on his own. He sat down on his own, he steeped in silence on his own. When the bus arrived at the main road outside the kampong, he alighted on his own. And began the long, slow walk back to his house, on his own.

It was dark by the time he got back. Ma was waiting on the steps. She gave him a hard look but didn't say anything, only made him wipe his feet with a wet cloth before coming inside. A bowl of congee waited for him on the dining table. She would heat it up for him, Ma said, whisking the bowl away into the kitchen.

Ah Boon sat down. Around him their old house creaked in the night wind. He could hear Hia tossing in his sleep, Uncle coughing in his bed, Ma stirring the pot of congee in the kitchen. He was safe. He was loved. It should have been enough, and yet it wasn't. *I can't*, Siok Mei had said. *Go home.*

"Boy, don't need to work so hard at school," Ma said later, as he was eating.

Ah Boon knew that Ma didn't approve of everything that he and Siok Mei were involved in, but she held her tongue. He knew she saw him bristling whenever Uncle criticized his attendance at the work stoppages, noticed how he no longer brought Eng Soon, Geok Tin, or Ah Mui around for study groups after the first few times they had visited and Hia had made fun of their soft city hands.

"School is important, but health is important also," Ma went on.

Her eyes implored him. He felt her need, her worry, knew it was only love but could not help the pinprick of irritation. She did not understand.

"People are starving," he said. "People are dying. What we do is important."

"What you do? What are you doing?"

"The Ang Mohs want to force us to fight their wars. Laborers can't afford to feed their families."

"What does that have to do with us?" Ma said.

"You won't understand," he snapped. "Never mind. It's too complicated."

Ma fell silent. He ate his congee. The delicious, silky broth pooled stickily in his mouth. It would have taken hours to make. He could see Ma bent over the fire, hair sticking to her face, stirring the pot, fanning the flames. Too high a heat and the rice would form a blackened crust; too low and each kernel would not yield its soft insides.

Chapter Sixteen

Siok Mei had imagined being arrested many times before. The way it would go was this: Students singing at the tops of their lungs, arms linked, holding a fearless line against the policemen's rattan shields. A classmate's high spirits would get the better of him, and he would find himself shouting insults, spitting, perhaps in an officer's face. This would be the signal for the policemen to move in; for hands and boots to come raining down on the classmate's soft exposed skin, for batons to crack against bone. The classmate would lie on the ground, arms wrapped around his head, cowering pitifully; the policemen would be merciless, laughing, kicking, punching. Siok Mei, seeing the injustice, would rush over and throw her body between the policemen and her classmate.

Imagining this moment always gave her particular pleasure. It was her body that would absorb the blow, it was her spirit that would not break. She longed to be brave, essential. To be the shield for another's suffering. She would protect the classmate at all costs, would feel his warm, trembling form curled beneath her.

In her fantasies, it was here that the faceless classmate, the generalized body, would resolve into Ah Boon. Out of force of habit, she told herself. He was her best friend, after all, and their friendship had always been such that she led and he followed. It was natural that he took a central role in her imaginings, which were about the love of one's nation, the love of a cause, and yes, this was not unrelated to the love of a friend, of one's very best friend. For that was what he was to her, she had believed up till then.

But now it was happening, her hands being put in cuffs by a brusque officer, and nothing was quite right, nothing as she imagined. Now they were led away in a line, her, Eng Soon, dozens of other classmates, the crowd booing loudly at the officers and cheering for their comrades. But even as they passed by all those shining, radiant faces, even as Eng Soon, standing ahead of her in the line as they waited to board the white van that would take them to a holding cell, reached his cuffed hands back to squeeze hers, Siok Mei felt no rush of exhilaration, no joyful defiance at having stood up against the Ang Mohs.

They were in the van. Her hands were cold—were the cuffs cutting off circulation?—and her mouth dry from shouting. A hollow feeling nagged at her.

"Okay, Mei? Got enough space?" Eng Soon, sitting beside her, wriggled away to give her room.

She nodded.

"Don't worry, even if they arrest us, the leaders will get us out," he said.

"Yes," she said. She was not afraid of jail. So many of them had been taken—thirty, forty?—that the prospect of jail seemed to be yet another school sit-in, another mass picnic. As long as they were in a group, they would be safe.

"Tired?" Eng Soon said. He offered his shoulder to her with so much certainty that, without thinking, Siok Mei laid her head on it. The van jolted along the uneven streets; outside, it had begun to rain, and the drops pattered evenly on the metal roof of the vehicle. It was nice to rest. She closed her eyes.

There in the dark, there he was. Ah Boon, watching her with his careful gaze. In many ways he was still the boy from the kampong classroom all those years ago. But he was tall now, his body elongated into a slim, powerful frame. His face had hardened, acquired an inquisitive look, become more cruel, some might say. All this sharpness and power was merely a new structure upon which to hang his caution. For the old fearfulness remained—fear of what? Siok Mei had never considered the question before, but she had always known Ah Boon to be fearful. She considered it now. Failure was the obvious one, rejection the other. And yet he frequently guaranteed rejection by entering each new situation, each group of people, with a wariness that guarded against it—rejecting them before they had the chance to reject him.

For this she loved him. It was the shell he built around himself that revealed his wounded desire. Where others saw standoffishness, she saw fierce, smothered longing, and it made her tender toward him. Perhaps this was why he'd so featured in her imaginings of arrest—she wanted to be the shell that protected him from blows. She wanted him to lower his guard, she wanted him to rest. She wanted him.

The van jolted to a stop. Siok Mei opened her eyes.

"Rise and shine." Eng Soon laughed, a rich, gravelly sound. He gently shook her hand off his elbow.

For a moment she was confused to find Eng Soon and not Ah Boon next to her—it was not Ah Boon's shoulder she'd leaned on, not his arm she had wrapped her fingers around in her drowsing state. Eng Soon was looking at her meaningfully. But now the van doors screeched open; sunlight came in. It was no longer raining, and the crowded street outside had the look of having been washed anew.

"Off! Hurry up!" the policemen shouted.

They banged their batons against the van doors, and the noise was hellish, thunderous. Their classmates left the van one at a time, squinting in the bright sunshine. When it came to her turn, Siok Mei, forgetting her hands were still cuffed, tried to grab a railing to help herself up. But the cuffs made her arms awkward, and she stumbled. The dull clanging of the policemen's batons seemed to grow louder.

The feeling of safety vanished. Siok Mei sat back down. Her hands were bound, a jail cell awaited; her classmates would not protect her. Was this what had happened to her parents, fighting a distant war in a cold, distant land? Had they, too, been picked up by an unmarked van, driven to an anonymous jail cell, left to rot or die? Here it was all of a sudden: the sticky hand of fear, wrapping its fingers around her. Siok Mei's breathing turned short and sharp. The world receded, overtaken by ringing in her ears. She felt as though she were lifting out of her body, floating up and away.

Then a warm palm on her shoulder, tethering her to the earth.

"Siok Mei," Eng Soon said. "Stand up. I'm right behind you."

She felt herself slowly descend. The shouting of policemen, the rattling of motorcars passing them on the street. The scent of fried fish balls from a noodle stand parked next to their van. Siok Mei stood up.

"Okay?" Eng Soon said.

"What's going to happen?" Siok Mei asked.

There would be a prison cell. There would be bare walls and iron bars and a locked gate. Their clothes would be taken from them. The floors would be cement. They would sleep on those floors. Siok Mei tried to tame her thoughts. Fear was shameful. Fear was meaningless in the grand scheme of the cause.

"Don't worry. The union will get us out," Eng Soon said.

They exited the van. The sun was out in full force again, and a humid heat rose from the street. Eng Soon's shadow stretched lazily in front of

Siok Mei, a dark sliver of relief on the hot bright pavement, and impulsively, she stepped into it.

There were forty-eight students in total—including two girls, as the newspapers were careful to specify later, a point of pride for Siok Mei. Their clothes, thankfully, were not taken from them. In groups of ten to a dozen, the boys were put into small, cramped cells with buzzing electric lights. Siok Mei and the other girl were each given a cell to themselves.

The officer who locked her away was Eurasian, with the watery gray eyes of a ghost and shiny red cheeks. "Put me with the boys," Siok Mei said to him.

He shook his head, then grinned, a sloppy sneer so ill-mannered it felt like a slap in the face.

"That's what you hua xiao sheng girls are like, aren't you?" he said in English. "Sorry to disappoint, but this isn't one of your 'group picnics.' You spend the night alone."

Then he left, footsteps echoing down the long hallway. His words lingered like a bad smell. Hua xiao sheng—*Chinese-school students*—she had never heard it said before with such disdain. Of course she knew there were those who looked down on them. The Ang Mohs, the wealthy Peranakans, the middle-class Chinese who went to English schools.

Once, when she was leaving the movie theater late one evening, two boys had trailed her, marching in the stiff-armed, bowlegged way the Communists of their imaginations marched, shouting made-up slogans in poor Mandarin. She'd pretended not to have noticed them, even when they walked so close she could smell the sour liquor on their breath, so close they could have, quite easily, stretched out an arm to grab her shoulders. They followed her with their mocking, suggestive laughs, for what could not have been more than ten minutes or so but felt like eternity, and she continued to ignore them. When they finally got bored and left, she found a doorway, sat down, and did not cry.

Siok Mei had not shared this incident with anyone. Her classmates would have been furious on her behalf, but she could not shake the thought that they would also be disappointed, might view her in a new, reduced light for not having stood up to her harassers. By implication she had failed to stand up for all of them, every Chinese-school student whose broken English was mocked when they applied for government jobs, every union leader detained under Emergency regulations. She ought to have turned around and spat in those boys' faces.

The boys had been Chinese too, might even have ancestors from the same province that hers hailed from, but they'd long since shed their roots, as snakes slide out of old crackling skins. Likely their families had been in Singapore for generations longer than hers; likely they were wealthy businesspeople who owned factories and houses that they rented out to people like her. Somewhere along the way, twenty, fifty, a hundred years ago, their forefathers had decided to send their children to the schools set up by Ang Moh nuns, to learn French, English, how to eat with a fork and knife, the history of Western philosophy.

Siok Mei wondered often about these enterprising forefathers, the decision they made to cut their children off from their own intimate past. Such decisions might have been made out of practicality. Having migrated to a new land, it made sense to want one's children to learn the language of that land. But the Ang Mohs were not of this place—they merely ruled it, had helped themselves to it, trampled upon the rights of the indigenous Malays even as they pandered to them—had those forefathers, deciding to send their children to study in English, realized this? Had they known that this choice would change the fates of generations of offspring for decades to come? How had they felt when their grandchildren were born and given Ang Moh names that they themselves could not pronounce?

Perhaps she was unfair. She could not understand because she had not had children of her own. It was said that when one had a child, the fight for culture and history and society became immaterial. Survival was all that mattered. Siok Mei tried to imagine this, and failed. Culture and history and society would only matter more if she had a child, for they would have to live in the world that she had either succeeded or failed in remaking.

This was why her own parents had left her.

Her cell was narrow but quite deep, and she did not like the shadows gathered in its depths. Siok Mei dragged the one wooden bench so that it was pushed up against the metal gate and lay down on it, legs curled to her chest. The metal bars of the gate were painted a bright, cheerful blue, as if they had been fabricated for a primary school and not a jail. If she pressed her face to them, she could make them disappear, and fool herself, for a moment, that she was out in the brightly lit corridor instead of her dim cell.

The cell across from hers was just as deep, dark, and empty. The groups of students had been placed as far apart as possible, with unoccupied cells between each occupied one. She could hear the indistinct voices of her classmates echoing somewhere farther down the corridor.

"Eng Soon?" she whispered.

Of course, he did not reply. She could shout, he might be able to hear her. But then what? Would she say that she could not bear to look into her small cell? That she felt its emptiness at her back, now, as a terrifying void? Or that the thoughts of her mother—from whom she had not received a letter since before the war—alone and forgotten in a prison somewhere in the Mainland, would not leave her?

No. She could not say any of this in front of her classmates. The Siok

Mei they knew was first to volunteer, loudest to protest, last to back down in any negotiation or debate. The Siok Mei they knew chained herself to gates not unlike this one, chained herself and refused to leave. How different it was, to be chained knowing that one's friend or ally held the key.

She squeezed her eyes shut. To distract herself, she played a game she and Ah Boon had played as children when on some moonless nights, they'd snuck out of their houses to meet by the surf. Sitting side by side on the wet sand, warm waves lapping at their feet, they'd close their eyes and feel the darkness wrap all around them.

The dark was a physical sensation, Ah Boon had always said, as real as the wind in one's hair, the salt on one's tongue. And it was true. The longer she sat there, the more she could feel it. Tickling the tender crease of her elbow, leaning its soft, velvety weight against her back. The dark was friendly, until the dark was not. With their eyes shut long enough, it unsettled them, turned bottomless and elastic. Slowly the dark swallowed everything in the world, one at a time, the trees, the birds, their creaking attap houses. The game was to keep their eyes shut for as long as they could, even as a delicious terror seemed to lap at the edges of their bodies. Often, after a few minutes had passed, one would grab the other's hand, and holding hands like this, they would continue.

Do you feel it? Yes, I do. *It's warm tonight, isn't it? The dark is warm.* It's hot. *We're floating now.* We're lifting off the ground. *There's no more ground.* We're in the air. *Hold my hand?* I'm holding you. *What color is the dark?* Red. I think the dark is red. *More purple, to me.* Are we alone? Is everyone gone? *We're alone.* What should we do now? *Anything.* Where should we go? *We can go anywhere.*

Lying on the wooden prison cell bench with her eyes squeezed shut, Siok Mei tried again to make everything disappear. But the light in the corridor was too bright.

Ah Boon—if only he were here.

She would talk to him as soon as she got out. He might even be waiting at the gates, waiting to see her with his usual anxious look. Siok Mei would apologize for speaking so harshly at the protest. He would say that he was sorry for his poor timing, would reassure her of his commitment to the movement. Never again would he make her choose between it and him. This was their shared future, their shared battle, and they would fight it together. They would hug, then take the bus home together, talking, like always. And then, who knew. Love was not the issue; they had always loved each other. Yet could they shatter the shapes of what they were to one another, to become what Ah Boon wanted? She did not know. But she would try. The thought gave Siok Mei comfort, and even though the lights were still too bright, slowly she began to drift off to sleep.

They were in jail for two days. On the third day, the vans returned and the students were taken to a court, where they were officially charged with obstructing the police in their lawful duties by refusing to disperse. A wealthy businessman at the Chinese Chamber of Commerce, a philanthropist who had helped set up the school, paid their bail. The students were set free.

Never had the sun felt so good on Siok Mei's skin. She looked around in the bright afternoon—families milled about, enamel lunch tiffins filled with steamed buns and other treats clanged cheerfully, a few members from the Chamber of Commerce were herding the students onto two large buses that would take them back to the school. Ah Boon was not there. Classmates grabbed Siok Mei's hands and thumped her on the back, and out of nowhere, a garland of bright orange flowers appeared and was strung around her neck. She was swept up into the festive air; even if they had only been released on bail, and the Ang Mohs had made no concessions about the National Service issue, there was the feeling that they had triumphed. The students would have their voices heard; the Ang Mohs might try to lock them up, but they could not keep them behind bars, together they were stout-hearted enough to overcome any obstacle.

"Mei!" It was Eng Soon, reaching his fingers out to her through the crowd.

He had seen her falter, that first day on the van, yet no doubt or derision flickered across his face now, only the usual warm friendship. She was glad to see him, and grasped his fingers eagerly. Those around them cheered. He pulled her to him, wrapped his arms around her, and planted a kiss on her cheek. The cheering grew louder.

"I'm glad you're okay," he said when he drew back.

"I—thank you" was all she could think to say.

Again! Again! Again! Their classmates whistled and yelled. *Kiss! Kiss! Kiss!*

"No," Siok Mei murmured, pulling back from him.

"Later," he said with a smile. "All right, all right, enough!" he yelled to the cheering crowd.

Siok Mei let him hold her hand as they went up into the bus together, in plain sight of everyone else. She would say later to Ah Boon that she hadn't realized Eng Soon had taken her hand, but the truth was, the feeling of his warm, dry palm against hers was not unpleasant. She found herself stealing a glance at his forearms: coppery from the sun, skin pulled taut over a smooth slab of muscle. Eng Soon was a respected senior and mentor; she could not help but be flattered by his attention. Yet she told herself they were only holding hands. It meant nothing. She and Ah Boon had held hands throughout their childhood, without being anything more than friends to each other. That was what she told herself.

Chapter Seventeen

The next few weeks passed in a blur. The Ang Mohs ordered that their school, being a "hotbed for antigovernment activity," be closed with immediate effect. Outraged students swarmed the campus, occupying classrooms and assembly halls, chaining the gates shut. They would design their own syllabus. What use did they have for the Ang Mohs' government-sanctioned textbooks and recommended course of study, anyway? There was no future for them in this country. The only university on the island catered solely to the English-educated. There were universities in the Mainland, sure, but that was an impossible option for all but the wealthiest of students.

After being released from court, Siok Mei joined her classmates at school, where they slept on blankets in the assembly hall and planned for the weeks to come. The atmosphere was electric; study groups congregated in discussion, open floor debates held, from time to time somebody would break out in song. Siok Mei gave her first school-wide speech from the middle of the broad stage where the principal himself led morning assembly, drawing on her thoughts from those two days in jail. It had become clear to her, she'd said, that given the absolute power that their enemies wielded, the instruments of the state they were willing to turn against students—mere students, who only wanted to learn!—they, too, must harden themselves for the fight. Whoever was not for them was against them. At this point the assembly hall erupted in cheers. All those clapping hands and stomping feet, all of them for her, her words, her ideas. Righteous euphoria burned through her veins.

Still the thought nagged: Ah Boon was not there. Neither at court on the day of the hearing, nor at school in the days that followed. Could it have been that without Siok Mei in the kampong he had not heard of the sleep-in protests? But her uncle would have kept him up to date about the court case; he must have known she had been released.

Or had he somehow found out—here her heart quickened—about Eng Soon? She pushed the thought away. There was nothing to find out, after all. It was true a new closeness had sprung up between them, after what they had been through. True as well that they had been spending almost all their time together in the past few days, poring over lists of demands to present to the Ang Mohs, leading reading groups for junior students, figuring out what food supplies they needed parents to bring. Eng Soon had made his intentions clear on the balcony of the vast assembly hall one evening, as the sky purpled behind them.

"Will you be my girlfriend?" he'd asked, quite plainly.

If she said yes to Eng Soon, things would be simple. They would stand back-to-back at protests, study together, go to the movies on off days, kiss in quiet streets before parting for the night. Eventually they would marry, and a long, worthy life might follow. They were well matched, after all. Both top students in their respective years. Both leaders in the student unions. Both serious-minded, fiercely dedicated to the cause. There was no doubt that she would learn much from him, and together they could do great things.

"No," she'd said to him nonetheless.

Beyond the school, evening birds were sending out their long, mournful cries. The difference between Eng Soon and Ah Boon could be summed up in that simple question. *Will you be my girlfriend?* An actionable request, one that could be answered and therefore risked the piercing disappointment of *no*. Ah Boon would never ask such a thing. Instead, he hoarded his feelings, and then, unable to take it any longer, declared them petulantly, passionately: *I love you*. What could one do with that? How was one to address the vastness of unasked questions behind such a statement?

The strength of Ah Boon's feelings frightened her. More than that, however, was the strength of her own. She could not stop thinking about their unfinished conversation at the protest. His absence was a gnawing wound. The question of whether she loved him, could love him the way he wanted, became clear with his sudden disappearance. Of course she did, of course she could.

Still she hesitated. Long had it been a habit for Siok Mei to resist giving in to love, let alone changing her life for it. To do so, she felt obscurely, would be to admit that her parents had not loved her enough to change theirs. Would choosing to be with Ah Boon weaken her dedication to the cause, as her parents had perhaps feared that staying with their children would weaken theirs?

These thoughts harangued her day and night. In all this time, Ah Boon did not show up. She felt she must see him at all costs. And so with a pang of guilt—feeling she was breaking ranks, even if she intended to return—Siok Mei decided to make a trip home. It would only be for a day, she told Eng Soon, so that she could gather clothes and books.

"Of course," he said. "We'll be waiting for you to get back."

There was no judgment in his voice. Nothing had visibly changed between them since he'd made his proposal to her. He'd been graceful about the rejection, in a way that reminded her of the debate teacher at their school, when Siok Mei declined the opportunity to be the team lead at the national competition. *Be not afraid of growing slowly, be afraid only of standing still*, the teacher had said then. *One day you will be ready.* There was the same quiet confidence about the way Eng Soon received her rejection. It cast a seed of doubt in Siok Mei's resolve, and she wondered if she had made the right choice.

But as soon as she set foot on the bus that would take her back to the kampong, the events of the past weeks began to grow hazy and distant. Outside the bus, the world rumbled by. Here was a construction site, where bent women in their red headscarves hauled baskets of brick slung from wooden poles across their shoulders. Here was a drinks cart, laborers pressing tins of iced coffee against their necks in the midmorning sun. Here was the crumpled body of a tongkang man, passed out on the steps of a carpenter's shop famous for operating an illegal opium den in its dark back room.

How could they hope to change anything at all? They were only students, playing at reading and philosophy and sleep-in protests. Suddenly it all seemed futile and childish to her. Their manifestos and songs and chaining themselves to gates—what had it achieved for the tongkang man who must row his bumboat even in the pouring rain, lest he starve?

And yet, and yet. Siok Mei recalled Eng Soon's words to her at one of their very first study groups: *Education is a privilege. Those who are afforded it must fight for those who are not.* Perhaps it was not the students' aims but their means that were flawed. She was ashamed of the triumphant reception her classmates had given her when she was released from jail. What was two nights in a prison cell compared to the arduous toil of a construction worker? Nothing, nothing, nothing at all. Her parents had made even greater sacrifices for their ideals, leaving safety and family to travel straight into the eye of danger.

It was late morning when Siok Mei arrived in the kampong. She did not go home, but instead went straight to Ah Boon's. She'd tell him about what was happening at school, and they could pack their things at the same time, then leave together.

But when Siok Mei got to his house, only Ah Boon's mother was home. He was out at sea with his brother, she said.

"Sit, girl, have some water, they will come back soon," Ma said. She took the cloth off a bucket in the corner and dipped a small tin cup into it.

Siok Mei gulped the cool water gratefully. The walk from the bus stop had somehow felt longer than usual, and the sun seemed to beat down more fiercely.

"More?"

Siok Mei nodded. Again Ma filled the cup, again Siok Mei drank.

"I saw your uncle the other day. He only seems to get younger! Ask him to tell us his secret."

"Drinking black vinegar, he will say."

"Ah!" Ma made a face.

"I can't drink it either."

"Well, the rest of us will have to be fine with dying."

They chatted like this for a while, and it was pleasant and warm, like it always was when Siok Mei visited the Lees. Cool breeze went through the open windows of the house; outside, the trees moved, birds flinging ropes of songs from one canopy to another. An enjoyable drowsiness began to come over Siok Mei, the feeling of being a child who, having played for too long in the sun, now wanted a nap.

Then Ma asked: "How's things at your school?"

"Okay," Siok Mei said carefully, sitting up a little straighter.

She did not know how much Ma knew, whether she'd heard, for instance, that Siok Mei had been arrested. Her uncle, worried and ashamed, had kept it from most in the kampong.

"Very busy?"

"Yes, school is busy."

"Last time you always come over. Now, never see you anymore. Boon also. Always so busy."

"Don't worry, Auntie. Ah Boon is doing well in school," Siok Mei said. "He's doing good work."

Right away she knew it was a wrong thing to say. The air seemed to change; Ma turned to look out the window. Her chin stiffened.

"I know what happens at that school, girl."

Siok Mei was overcome with awkwardness. How naive to think that Ma would not know about the protests, the police, the arrest. Of course Ma knew; she was the kind of mother who would make it her business to know, even if her son would not tell her. Here Siok Mei suppressed a pang of envy.

"Auntie," she said, "it seems bad, I know. Being arrested, shouting in the streets. But it's—I don't know how to explain—but it is not just for the workers, it is for us all. Our future. Our country. The Ang Mohs—"

"Ang Mohs, Ang Mohs, do you see any Ang Mohs here?" Ma threw one hand out irritably. "No! What does any of it have to do with us, tell me? Will protesting bring in more fish? Will it fix the hole in our roof? Will it find Ah Boon a wife, children, family?"

Siok Mei felt as if she had been slapped. Ma was never irritable or impatient.

"I am sorry, Auntie," Siok Mei said, even though she was not.

It dawned on her that the kampong would never understand. Her own foster family—her uncle, his wife, their children—merely tolerated her out of respect for her father, the older brother who, as a young man, had once supported his siblings with his meager schoolteacher pay. But they did not understand the sacrifices that revolution demanded; did not see that it was, ultimately, their own interests that lay at stake.

"Good that you got out," Ma said. "Prison—aiyo! No place for a girl. Be careful, Mei, be careful. Okay? Promise Auntie."

She knew that Ma was really asking about Ah Boon. She was concerned for Siok Mei, of course, had always treated her with fondness, like a close niece. But it was Ah Boon for whom Ma's heart seized with fear, Ah Boon whose fate Ma would do anything to secure. He had a family who loved him, to whose fold he could return at any point. The movement was not his family, the school was not his family, the classmates were not his family. Not the way they were hers.

She thought of the school, where her classmates would now be having lunch. What would they be eating? Lotus root soup, ladled from an enormous pot.

"Ah Boon won't go school anymore," Ma said. "Now, no school anyway, only trouble, go for what, you tell me?"

"Won't go?"

"No." Ma shook her head. "I ask him not to go anymore. More trouble is coming, more police, more problems. No, no, better he stay here, help his brother fish."

"Is that what he wants to do?" Siok Mei said.

Ma pressed her lips together. "I am his mother."

"Auntie, do you want him to stay here all his life?"

Ma began stroking the harsh jut of her collarbone, just visible beneath her starched white blouse.

"Mei, I know, life has not always been good to you. But your poor brave parents, don't you think they want you to be safe? As a mother—"

"My parents would be proud of me," Siok Mei said calmly.

"Of course they are proud."

"Yes."

"But they also want you to be safe. One day, when you are a mother yourself, you will understand."

Siok Mei stood up from her chair. "Thank you for the water, Auntie."

Ma stood up too, a pained look on her face.

"Mei, Auntie doesn't mean to nag. Aiya. What does Auntie know? I just want the best for all of you."

"Never mind. It was good to see you," Siok Mei said, heading toward the door.

"Going already? You don't want to wait for Boon?"

Siok Mei did not.

"I have to go home to pack," she said politely. "Can you ask him to come see me when he gets back, please?"

Ma paused, then nodded. "I will tell him."

"It's important. Please remember."

"I will, I will. Take care of yourself, girl."

"Goodbye, Auntie."

Siok Mei went back to her uncle's house. Her uncle's house was what she'd called it all these years, never *home*, for home was the wooden house on the crowded lane where she had lived with her parents and siblings before they'd left. Of this she recalled only snatches—the fact that they'd had no ceiling, only a draping of thick canvas to keep out the elements, the jewellike cockroaches struggling in the tide that flooded their living space whenever it rained, the *kok kok* of the noodle seller's bamboo poles knocking against each other, announcing him and his cart. Precious memories, like her mother's soapy hands sliding over Siok Mei's naked skin, the shameless joy of being bathed, as a child, in an open dirt street as neighbors walked by. The lilting song her father would sing her as he put her to bed, a song she would recognize only years later as being one of the many songs of the revolution.

Her parents left when Siok Mei was five, scattering their children among extended family. For a while Siok Mei had bounced from relative to relative, until her uncle in the kampong had taken her in. She had long since fallen out of touch with her sisters. Their respective foster families in the city were busy enough with the daily running of their households, and with an extra mouth to feed all of a sudden, the thought of making sure the siblings kept in touch was hardly on their minds. Siok Mei remembered the early days at her uncle's house—her cousins were teenagers by then, and were not interested in playing with a silent girl. She spent her days indoors, helping her aunt with chores while the others went out to fish. Though kind, her aunt had an air of stern distance, and Siok Mei had the feeling that in front of her, it was inappropriate to cry. And so she would confine her crying to ten- or fifteen-minute breaks snatched in the outhouse, or silently into a pillow at night.

Eventually she learned not to cry at all. She became a serious child who entertained herself by acting out ethical dilemmas in her mind. *Should I save an ant on a leaf if it falls into a bucket of water? If yes, then why not save the fish in the nets that the boats bring back every day?* The fish served a purpose—she concluded, after several days of refusing to eat—and that purpose was to sustain other beings. The accidental death of an ant served no purpose, and should therefore be averted. Slowly she grew to see the loss of her parents not as abandonment but as a source of pride. They had gone to fight a war for their homeland. Siok Mei, too little to fight, could only offer her pain.

As a child she had struggled to understand the idea of homeland. Then she met Ah Boon, and Teacher Chia, and slowly, the kampong became a kind of home. She'd struggled for so long against this—since it would mean her life with her parents was gone—but with Ah Boon as her best friend, that reality finally became one that she could accept. And it was this home she was fighting to protect, even if the kampong couldn't see it. Not the distant lands from which their ancestors had come, but *this*. This beach, this city, this kampong. It was not a game. It was her life, and theirs.

Now they would enter a new phase of life together. Ma's reticence would not matter, Ah Boon would choose for himself. And of course he wanted to be a part of what was happening at the school. He had been a part of it all these years, hadn't he? He loved her, didn't he? All these things were true and would continue to be.

Back at her uncle's house, Siok Mei gathered her things slowly, taking her time to deliberate over this book or that, counting and recounting the pairs of undergarments she would need, taking breaks to chat with her aunt about the latest news of her cousins' children. She offered to sweep the floor and do the dishes, since she'd been away the past few days and unable to help with the chores. Her aunt, thankfully, said nothing about Siok Mei's arrest. In recent years, she'd come to treat Siok Mei as more of a boarder than a relative, and indeed, likely looked forward to the day when her niece would get married and be off their hands for good.

As Siok Mei cleaned and swept and filled her bag with things, the sun slipped slowly across the sky. Soon evening birds began their first tentative calls; the waves grew pink with late-afternoon light.

"Not going yet, girl?" her aunt asked.

Siok Mei shook her head as she repacked her bag for the second time.

"Better go soon, don't take the bus in the dark."

Siok Mei nodded, not trusting herself to speak.

Where was Ah Boon? All the boats would have returned by now, even accounting for a trip to the market, with all the cleaning and selling and idle chitchat. Perhaps he was still packing, she thought, or taking a shower. Or worse—perhaps something had happened. An accident. Siok Mei thought of Ah Tong's second son, who walked with a limp from the time his foot had gotten trapped under the prow of a boat. Or—no, that was not possible, no one had drowned for generations, the last being Ah Boon's grandfather, the gambler who'd passed out in the surf. Of course Ah Boon had not drowned. Still, Siok Mei's heart quickened. She grabbed her things, bade goodbye to her aunt, saying she would be back in a few weeks, and headed for the Lees' house once again.

The evening light was draining from the sky. Shadows gathered beneath the trees, thickening steadily as if egged on by the screech of crickets hiding in their folds. Siok Mei walked quickly. Nothing had happened to Ah Boon, she told herself. There would be a perfectly reasonable explanation for why he'd been delayed. He would apologize for being so slow, get his bag, and they would begin the long walk to the bus stop together. She had so much to tell him—where to begin? With the arrest, the insolent prison guard, her very first speech, the exciting developments at school? Or the answer to his question to her—for she saw now that she had not been fair, comparing him to Eng Soon; the statement *I love you* contained a question that was clear enough.

I love you too. She practiced it in her mind. What was love, if not the fear of loss?

Soon, she glimpsed the Lees' house through the trees. Dusk had fallen; the windows glowed with the warm yellow light of oil lamps. Siok Mei took a shortcut, veering off the main dirt trail to crunch through dried leaves and twigs, blades of lalang tickling her shins. As she drew closer to the house, the dimming evening and the lamps lit inside meant the scene presented itself through the open windows as clearly as if it were a picture.

Her footsteps slowed; then, a few meters away from the house, she stopped in the tall grass. They were all there, seated around the dining table: Ma, Uncle, Hia, and Ah Boon. A wave of relief went through her; Ah Boon was alive and well. She watched the Lees eat. Found herself imagining, over the clicking of chopsticks against bowls, the sound of chewing and peaceful conversation. Like most families, the Lees did not speak much at mealtimes. But the passing of vegetables, the appreciative slurps, the picking out of a piece of choice chicken for one of the boys— all this was speech too.

Ah Boon was alive and well. He had simply chosen not to come.

Siok Mei would bang on the door and demand that he explain himself. But as soon as she had this thought, the sound of laughter came through the window. Hia was holding his nose; Uncle was thumping the table; Ma giggling into cupped hands. Ah Boon leaned back in his seat, his mouth wide open, his sides heaving. The laughter went on and on. How happy they looked, how comfortable together.

When Siok Mei was a girl, one dream had recurred nightly. She had lost her parents, her siblings, and was wandering in a dark wood. Finally she would come upon a house, and in the dream, would realize it was her house, her home. Through a window she would see her family. Her mother would be folding clean clothes, her brothers and sisters playing with some poor insect they had trapped in a jar, her father reading out loud from the newspaper. Full of relief, she would run toward the house. But it had no doors, the windows would not open, and the family inside was deaf to her cries. Forced to keep standing outside the house, the indifferent grass tickling her ankles, she was unable to enter, unable to walk away.

Ah Boon would not come. It dawned on Siok Mei that he did not really care for the cause. Their conversation from the protest came back to her; at the time, she'd felt only impatience for him. He'd simply picked a bad time, she'd naively thought, too overcome with emotion as he had been. She'd been annoyed with him asking her to leave, but had not realized then what it meant. Now she saw that he would always be asking her to leave.

The Lees had stopped laughing and were eating quietly again. Siok

Mei took one long look at Ah Boon. She studied his face as if she would not see him again. Then she walked away.

Still tickled by the sight of Hia spurting soup through his nose, Ah Boon found himself turning toward the window for no particular reason. He'd had the feeling of being watched, but of course, all there was outside were the dark shapes of trees shifting in the moonlight. He turned back to his food.

"What you do today, Ma?" he asked.

Ma paused. She seemed to want to say something, but reached out for some stewed cabbage instead.

"Ma?" Ah Boon said.

"Hmm?"

"What you do today?"

"Nothing, boy. The usual. Work, clean, rest. What else is there for an old woman to do?"

"No visitors?"

"Visitors?" Ma chewed thoughtfully. "Why? Expecting someone?"

Ah Boon was quiet. He'd bumped into Siok Mei's uncle at the market several days ago, and had heard that she'd been released from prison. Each time he'd been to her house, however, she had not been there. *At school,* her aunt had said, *where some big protest was taking place. Aiya, you know that girl.* He did, he knew her well. He'd heard about the protest, of course he had. But he'd put off going in the beginning, when Siok Mei had not been there, and now that she was, he felt guilty about showing up so late. Any day now, he told himself, he would go back to school. But the days of fishing with Hia and Uncle had become an unexpected joy, a physical pleasure. He had not realized how much he'd missed the islands, their clear, shallow lagoons, their high, soaring cliffs.

"No," Ma said. She fixed him in her gaze, as if daring him to say otherwise. "No visitors."

And it was just as well, Ah Boon thought. *This is not the time,* Siok Mei had said. *I can't.* And so he would go on with this life, for now. They carried on eating.

Chapter Eighteen

When, several weeks later, Ah Boon finally returned to school, he was warmly welcomed by his classmates.

"Boon!" Geok Tin grinned, offering him some steamed cakes she had made.

"Come back already!" said Ah Mui, linking arms with him like an affectionate older sister.

There was an overblown argument, they said, between the debate team president and the secretary. It had begun with how they practiced—whether they ought to stand onstage as one would at a competition, or sit at tables informally—and somehow evolved into a personal matter, the secretary feeling as though the president took his work for granted, the president feeling the secretary was always stirring up unnecessary drama, et cetera. Perhaps Ah Boon, with his diplomat's touch, could heal the rift, Geok Tin suggested with a laugh.

That was what his classmates had taken to calling him—the diplomat. It was not that he was especially charismatic or skilled at making people like him, but there was a quietness to Ah Boon that calmed heated tongues. When he was around, people relaxed into themselves, were more inclined to compromise.

And so Ah Boon had been missed. It was a good feeling, to discover that he was well liked, and he in turn was glad to see them all, felt an unexpected rush of warmth upon entering that large assembly hall full of familiar faces. It worried him to hear their stories of arrest and trial; it heartened him to hear that the Ang Mohs might drop the National Service issue after all.

He'd heard it from Siok Mei too. But there had been something measured about the way she related her stories, something summarized in tone. He'd had the feeling that she sped quickly over the details, thinking, perhaps, that he might be bored. It left him with an uneasy feeling. They still had not talked about their last, inconclusive conversation; it sat like a heavy stone between them that neither wanted to lift.

He saw now, and was embarrassed about, how bad his timing had been. The shame that had washed over him when he'd heard about what took place after his confession—arrest, jail, trial—still sat stickily on his skin, as stubborn as the smell of the sea. How small his words seemed in the face of such events! And yet the shame did not cure the wound in his pride. It made him contrite but also petulant; it made him ask about the arrest but left him entirely unable to speak of the state of their love. Siok Mei was busy, he told himself, she had more to worry about than his feelings for her. She would raise the matter if she wanted to.

Instead he allowed himself to be carried along by the electric energy running through the school in those days. The Chinese Chamber of Commerce was willing to write a letter on the students' behalf to the Ang Mohs—many drafts and corrections were circulated, many heated arguments had over the order of demands and precise wording. It was this that Ah Boon had involved himself in when, a few days later, letter draft in hand, he walked in on Siok Mei and Eng Soon reading Lu Xun in an empty classroom.

It was late afternoon. Most students were down by the central

courtyard, kicking an old ball back and forth or chatting in the shade.
The head of the letter-writing committee wanted Eng Soon's thoughts
on the final paragraph, but Eng Soon had been nowhere to be seen.
Someone had seen him up on the third-floor classroom, they'd said, he'd
gone back after lunch to study on his own.

And here Eng Soon was, across a desk from Siok Mei, reading out loud
from a tattered copy of Lu Xun's stories as the classroom furniture sat
mutely around them. The story of a madman who believed he had uncov-
ered a conspiracy in which everyone around him practiced cannibalism,
and that his own family had locked him away in preparation to be eaten.

Siok Mei and Eng Soon were taking turns reading paragraphs out
loud, and sitting on either side of the desk, they looked like nothing more
than classmates studying together. But Ah Boon knew, the moment he
laid eyes on them, that things were different. Was it the way Siok Mei
dropped her gaze when he entered the classroom? The quick shift in her
seat, the tucking of one ankle behind the other? The way Eng Soon had
said *Oh, it's you*, apologetically—as if there was something to apologize
for? Whatever it was, the knowledge hit Ah Boon like a brick wall, and
without saying a word, he walked out the door.

He avoided her for weeks. He attended school less and less, and when
he did, would leave early so that they wouldn't have to go back to the
kampong together. He nodded to Eng Soon in corridors but always
walked swiftly past. Back home he threw himself into helping Hia build
a new boat. His brother would be married soon, and would need a fishing vessel of his own.

Siok Mei tried her best to talk to him, but Ah Boon would not be left
alone with her. On each rare occasion that she did manage to catch him
on his own, she found herself suddenly nervous, and could only ask him

banal questions about homework or student committees. After a few minutes of strained conversation, an ugly mask would drop over his face, and she would become afraid. There was a coldness to Ah Boon that Siok Mei had never seen before, and she was reminded of the frozen lollies they used to get from the drinks-cart man when they were children, of the tiny ice crystals that coated each colorful stick. She'd always had the feeling, licking the ice crystals off to get to the frozen sugary treat beneath, that she was setting something free.

How to set Ah Boon free, when she was the one responsible for his imprisonment?

"I hope you will accept him as a brother," she said at last one day.

They were walking home together for the first time in weeks. Siok Mei had intercepted Ah Boon as he left class early and taken the bus with him back to the kampong. The whole ride they'd exchanged no more than a handful of sentences, speaking only of inconsequential things: the heat, the bus driver's habit of braking whenever he lit a cigarette, the elderly lady who surely wanted to sit down but refused any seat she was offered. It was only when the bus arrived at their stop, when they had alighted and it had rumbled away and they were alone with the trees and distant sea, that Siok Mei felt she was able to speak.

She waited for the mask to fall again. But there was nothing; Ah Boon's face did not change, in fact, he gave no indication of having heard her. There was a long pause, filled by the sound of the dry dirt crunching beneath their feet.

Then: "Are you happy?"

She considered this.

"Yes." Quietly.

Dirt crunching, insects creaking, birds whistling.

"I won't be able to stop—" Ah Boon halted in his tracks. He looked at her at last, and his gaze pierced her with its need. "I still love you."

"I know," Siok Mei said. It took all her willpower to keep her face composed.

"So why?" he said. "Why do this?"

Would it hurt him less to know it was not her love that was in question? That she, too, felt the invisible thread that seemed to bind them, guts to heart, that she felt his pain as if it were her own? Would it be any comfort if she fell into his arms now, only to pull away, go through the lengthy explanation of why she could not be with someone who would force her to choose between him and the work of her life?

She did not love Eng Soon yet, but she knew it would happen eventually. Just yesterday, as they were studying together, he'd reached over and placed the pad of his thumb on the inside of her wrist. *Nothing,* he'd said, when Siok Mei asked what he was doing. Then: *I am feeling your pulse.* He went back to reading. With that simple declaration something inside her loosened, as if a long rope, tightly wound around a rusty nail, were beginning to unravel. How smooth it was, how easy. With Eng Soon she felt none of the painful tenderness she felt toward Ah Boon; none of the strange, raw desire to protect; none of the need, the fierce blood-love. With Eng Soon she felt only deep peace; she was not afraid she might hurt him irrevocably and, in doing so, break something of herself. With Eng Soon she had the space to be calm, reasonable, to do the work that the cause required.

"I love—"

"It will never work with us," Siok Mei said. "You must stop."

She was surprised at the composure in her voice. Feeling like she might cry, knowing that if she did, all would be ruined, she forced herself to look up through the canopy of trees above them, through to the uncluttered field of blue that was their sky.

Ah Boon didn't speak. When Siok Mei looked back down, he was squatting over her feet, moving his hands over them as if to conjure something from the dead. She was shocked, then realized that he was holding in his hands two large dry leaves, using them to wipe the mud from her white shoes.

Tears welled up in her eyes, and before she could brush them away, they fell like tiny raindrops on the back of Ah Boon's head. He did not notice. When he stood up again, Siok Mei's face was dry. They resumed the long walk home.

PART III

Nothing Grows beneath the Banyan Tree

Chapter Nineteen

The Gah Men arrived one bright afternoon exactly nineteen years after Pa died. At twenty-seven, Ah Boon's body had finished its business of elongation and realignment, as if filling a mold that Pa had left behind. Now, when he perched on the wooden steps of their old house, Ma averted her gaze, for the silhouette of his angular form made her ache. It was there Ah Boon sat when he first caught sight of them.

The Gah Men wore white shirts and white pants that glimmered blue in the harsh sun. Their shirts were short-sleeved; they carried ballpoint pens in their chest pockets, wore shiny black shoes on neat, small feet. They arrived on bicycles, foreheads slick, shirts translucent with sweat. Ah Boon watched them unroll large sheets of paper crossed with grids and arching lines, point to invisible demarcations in the earth, shield their eyes as they squinted at the sky.

The sun beat down on oily scalps glistening beneath thin black hair. One of them shrieked as the ground next to him shifted, making a loud splash. His colleagues laughed as it was revealed to be a large mudskipper, primeval in shape, evil in eye. They returned to work soon enough. The Gah Men were industrious; they had no time to waste on the frivolities of the swamp.

Ah Boon's first thought was of Siok Mei. But Siok Mei no longer lived in the kampong; Siok Mei lived in the city with Eng Soon. The Gah Men were no threat to her here.

As he brooded, his nephew came out from the house and squatted beside him. "Who's that, Uncle?" asked little Ah Huat, pointing to the men trampling through the swamp.

The boy would be five this year but seemed older than his age, just as Hia had when he'd been a child. Looking at him, Ah Boon was reminded not of Hia but of the woman his brother had married. The curve of the boy's forehead, the deep folds beneath the eyes, all these were Gek Huay's, and in some distant way, her own father's, Ah Tong's. Hia and Gek Huay had built their house some five minutes from the Lees' family home, and Ah Huat was often left with Ma when Gek Huay had some errand or other to run. Ma grumbled this was no way for a mother to raise a child, but Ah Boon didn't mind. He liked having little Ah Huat around. The boy was content to play quietly in the darkened interior of the house, shredding old newspapers and pressing his face against gaps in the wooden floor to squint at the earth beneath. Sometimes, when Ah Boon was taking his afternoon nap out on the porch, his nephew would come sit with him silently, several meters away, like a cat.

Ah Boon would tell the boy how, when he was just a child himself, he would go out on the boat with his father. He terrified the boy with stories of great shapes lurking beneath the boat, making inexplicable waves near the shore, islands that burst out of the water like volcanoes rising from the seabed. Ah Huat would listen, eyes shining, rationing his questions as if afraid he would not get an answer. Ah Boon embellished gleefully in response, always stretching the truth, except for one time, when Ah Huat said he wished he could go fishing with his ah gong too. "What was Ah Gong like, Uncle?" he asked.

Then Ah Boon told him that his grandfather had been upright and serious, fiercer than both him and Hia put together, but also kinder, braver, wiser than them all. It was why his parents had named little Ah Huat after him; Hia and Gek Huay both hoped that he would grow up to be just like his ah gong.

"What happened to Ah Gong?" Ah Huat asked.

It was only then that Ah Boon fell quiet, and after staring into the horizon for a long while, got up and left.

Now, as little Ah Huat squatted next to him, Ah Boon told him to stop pointing at the Gah Men.

"Go back inside," he said quietly.

Ah Huat's eyes were wide with curiosity. Strangers in the kampong were a rare occurrence, and Ah Boon could see that his nephew wanted nothing less than to go inside the house.

"But who are they?"

"Go," Ah Boon said again, more firmly.

Casting one last look at the men in white, Ah Huat turned and went.

The boy's question was not an easy one to answer. Who were the Gah Men? It depended when and to whom the question was directed. The Gah Men used to mean the Ang Mohs who ruled over the island, for it was from their foreign, unpronounceable, unnecessary word—three clumsy syllables, *gov-ern-ment*, easily shorn of it consonants, shortened to two—that *Gah Men* was born in the first place.

These new Gah Men, with their white shirts and white pants, were different from the Ang Mohs. These Gah Men were Chinese lawyers and Malay journalists, Indian union leaders and Eurasian clerks, Javanese editors and Peranakan economists. Not all had been born on the island, but many had been raised on it and considered themselves local; all had ambitions for what their little country could become. After the war, they'd fought for some measure of self-governance, and while today the Gah Men were elected officials, the island remained a Crown Colony. But the Ang Mohs retained control over military matters and internal security, which gave them the ability to jail any local politician they deemed unfit, and were thus ultimately still in charge.

Wearing all white to signify their purity, the new Gah Men embarked on re-creating the country in their own image. Secret societies were quashed ruthlessly, an end put to their protection rackets, prostitution rings, drug trafficking, gambling networks. Newsstands were cleared of pornography, bars cleared of the women who trawled them. Jukeboxes banned, pinball machines closed down, the radio ordered to stop broadcasting rock and roll. Later it was ruled that the jukeboxes could stay if they stuck to Beethoven and Chopin. Civil servants were mobilized en masse to clean the city's streets, beaches, and parks.

The people welcomed this change. War and revolution were a young person's game. Now they wanted food and jobs, dry homes and safe streets. The Gah Men would provide this, it seemed, and if it required a little brutality to get there, what was the harm? The people were used to brutality by now.

The Gah Men's efforts did not go unnoticed by the rest of the world. *Tieless, coatless puritans!* cried the international newspapers. Everywhere in Asia and Africa the Ang Mohs were being ushered out, and now here was a new generation of leaders who defined themselves in opposition to the colonial masters' nonchalance bred of supreme entitlement. In contrast, the Gah Men planted trees and picked up trash, they built community centers by the dozen, they met their enemies in dark alleyways with knuckledusters. They would set the world to rights if they could, but first they would start with their own little country, their small, precious dominion.

The past decade had been filled with midnight arrests, protesting students tear-gassed and beaten in the streets, important politicians revered one day and indefinitely detained the next. The country was in flux, but for the most part, the country was the city, and the kampong, like many others in the countryside, remained the kampong.

Even so, there were signs things were changing. The brand-new community center under construction near Swee Hong's provision shop, for example, a large brick-and-concrete building with a metal roof that took sixteen weeks and an enormous team of workers to complete. It had caused much disruption, with trucks brought in to pour the concrete and pound the foundation into the wet earth. The noise and dust had been unbearable.

Now the building was complete, as far as Ah Boon could tell, the trucks vanishing down the dirt road from whence they'd come, the teams of construction workers disappearing as quickly as they'd appeared. A banner hung across its gleaming white face, announcing an opening ceremony that would take place in the coming week. The kampong was suspicious of this opening ceremony; most did not intend to go. The Gah Men were not to be trusted, they with their spotless white outfits, their brick buildings that gave the illusion of solidity on what the kampong knew was wet and shifting soil.

Perhaps that was why they were here now, dirtying their shiny black shoes with mangrove mud, shielding their eyes from the glaring sun as they surveyed the strip of twisting, knotted trees. Perhaps they were looking to erect another community center, some other harebrained building that the kampong did not need.

But that made no sense—why choose the swamp they were now

standing in, rather than dry land farther from the sea? No, this was something else, Ah Boon thought. A reflexive distrust reared its head. *Si Gah Men, running dogs of the Ang Mohs*, an old refrain, an instinct honed in the decade following the war, when he, too, had been caught up with Siok Mei's lot. The nets grew slack in his hands as he studied their white forms.

The Gah Men belonged in the city, amid imposing colonial facades and candy-colored shophouse fronts. There they appeared unremarkable, office-bound pencil pushers scurrying about the changing cityscape. They were just another element of a city being rearranged into a sleeker, shinier incarnation of itself: paved roads and multistory buildings with wide glass windows, people in impractical clothes.

As long as the Gah Men remained in the city, the kampong could remain suspended in the gelatinous fluids of their unchanging lives. The radio waves might tremble with the shouts of "Merdeka, Merdeka!"—*freedom!*; the Ang Mohs might busy themselves detaining people left and right; bombs might continue to be detonated, this time from a new threat, a neighboring threat; policemen might fire powerful water cannons into crowds of protesting workers—and still the kampong went on, unchanged.

But here they were. Emissaries from another world, in their blinding white uniforms, with their red plastic clipboards and sheafs of paper on which were written so many words, striding confidently across the same mud flats where Ah Boon and Hia had, in their childhood, spent countless hours trapping tiny crabs in glass jars. What did it mean?

Chapter Twenty

B oy! Eh, help the auntie, please!" Uncle slapped a fish against Ah Boon's forearm playfully, leaving a cold wet mark that would dry sticky.

The boy who usually helped Uncle at the market was sick, and Ah Boon was taking his place. Back when he had been alive, Pa had never liked the mess, the noise, having to swear trustworthiness to pushy, skeptical housewives over and over again. He'd felt it as an affront to his nature in some deep way. Ah Boon had inherited Pa's dislike of the market. He stuck to stacking crates in the back, avoiding the banter and innuendo that flowed freely between stallholders. The air was tinged with rot, a sweet, stifling smell that turned his insides. Everywhere was the frenzy of shouted Bahasa and grubby wet banknotes.

Lately, though, there was more to Ah Boon's habitual dislike of the noise and mess. He'd found himself plagued by the irrational fear that he would run into someone he knew from middle school here, that they would see him in his dirty singlet, wielding the blunt cleaver in his damp, sticky hands.

"So many years in school," Hia had taken to joking good-humoredly. "And here you are, selling my fish!"

Ah Boon helped the housewife pick out the fish she would steam for her grandson tonight. She chose a plump, expensive one. He imagined the strands of cut ginger and red chili, the silver skin steamed soft and paper thin, tender white flesh that flaked open with the nudge of a chopstick.

What did the Gah Men eat, he wondered all of a sudden. Where did they shop? Did their wives visit wet markets? No, they had servants for that, the dignified amahs with their tight buns and satin trousers. He could not imagine the wife of a Gah Man, in her Western attire and broken dialect, setting one expensively shod foot into the market, where the ground shimmered with puddles of gray water and the occasional skim of animal blood.

Ah Boon wrapped the expensive fish in newspaper carefully. As he handed it over to the housewife, he smiled.

"Such a nice boy you are!" she said, and left him the change.

"Wah, got a way with the aunties ah, Boon!" Uncle roared, clapping him on the back. "You should be a politician!"

Ah Boon brushed the comment off. But he returned to it later in the morning, as he cleaned and chopped and wrapped. It was not the first time it had been said. *The diplomat*, they had called him in middle school. Siok Mei herself used to tell him that he underestimated how much people liked him; see how they ask for your opinion when writing letters, she'd say, and Eng Soon would always invite Ah Boon along to the gatherings that senior students held at the Worlds theme parks. This thought made him bitter. Ah Boon did not know how much Siok Mei had told Eng Soon about what had passed between them. And yet—if he cast Eng Soon aside, examined the evidence of his life in the cold light of day, it was true that it was not just the aunties who warmed to him. So had his teachers, classmates in middle school, even the workers in the unions liked to tease him. And was it not true that he was beloved in the kampong, despite the early years of dreadful shyness as a child?

It's true, the Siok Mei in his mind persisted. *You're naturally loved. You could do great things.*

Naturally loved, but not by you, he thought.

She fell silent at that and would say no more. He held these imaginary conversations with her often. Still thought of her as that seventeen-year-old with whom he'd entered the strange new world of middle school for the first time, the Siok Mei who loved to read and sing, in whom enthusiasm bubbled as a bright and overflowing stream, who could win anyone over with an earnest smile. Siok Mei today, a decade on, was different. Only vestiges of the can-do optimism of her youth remained. After years of fighting—first this enemy, then that, then this again—and still feeling no real change to be forthcoming, she had hardened. She was still passionate, but her passion now smoldered behind a sturdy stoicism.

Not the only change, the voice in his head reminded him.

And—he acknowledged, with a pang—she was married.

Today, however, this thought did not trigger the usual tumble into despair. Instead his mind went to the image of the bespectacled, white-shirted Gah Men crossing the swamp. In the midst of the shouted orders and the budding heat of the late morning, Ah Boon seemed to see, for the first time, a crack in his life. An opening.

On the way home from the market, he and Uncle passed the community center. The building was deserted. The new glass slats in the windows still had their protective plastic on them; the front entrance was crossed with orange tape. But the debris that had lain scattered—piles of bricks, spare plants, crumpled tarps—had all been cleared. What was even stranger: the land that surrounded the building, previously a

mixture of wet red earth and sprawling lalang, had been planted with a
neat lawn of grass, little green straws with square edges, as if they had
been manufactured in a factory and trucked here in one smooth sheet.

"Look at that." Uncle snorted. "Not enough to ask us pay tax, now
must build this kind of thing for what? To keep an eye on us?"

Ah Boon nodded along, making noises of vague agreement.

Uncle shook his head. "Taxes. Registration," he said darkly.

"Is not the same, Uncle," Ah Boon said. "The Gah Men are not the
Jipunlang."

"How you know?"

"Aiya," Ah Boon said.

He knew how Uncle saw it. He had heard the things that were said
about the Gah Men, that they would use the Ang Mohs to jail their political opponents, that they lit fires in tenement housing to chase out
stubborn tenants who did not want to be relocated. But it went deeper
than that. Since the war, uniforms filled Uncle with fear. Uniforms
meant organization, power, anonymous cruelty. Such power could pick
you up and crush you in a moment, he believed; such power could de-
stroy your life.

"Just stay away from this Gah Men," Uncle said.

But Ah Boon's attention was on the large sign tacked up on the wall,
next to the banner announcing the official opening ceremony. He hadn't
seen it before; it must have gone up this morning.

HIRING: PASSIONATE INDIVIDUALS FOR COMMUNITY OUTREACH, it
read. The lorry rumbled on. As they drove, Ah Boon stared at the little
white rectangle of the sign in the side mirror until the building disappeared.

When they got home, the swamp was empty, the Gah Men had gone
for the day.

"Boon," Ma called. "Your friends are here."

He left his dirty slippers at the bottom of the steps and went into the house. There was Siok Mei, sitting at the kitchen table. Her hair was in two shiny plaits, trailing over her shoulders like ropes. It was almost a shock to see her in the flesh; he felt caught out somehow, as if she'd been privy to the conversations he found himself having with her in his head. And still, the familiar crackle of pleasure at being in the same room as her, the feeling of waking up from a long, drowsing sleep.

"Boon," she said warmly, rising from her chair.

Ah Boon saw now that she wasn't alone—that was right, Ma had said *friends*—and behind her sat the stolid shape of his former classmate: Eng Soon. He rose as well, came forward and clapped Ah Boon on the shoulder.

"My uncle told us about the Gah Men," Siok Mei said. "Any trouble?"

The Gah Men were now following in the footsteps of the Ang Mohs, she went on, and were seizing any and all books related to Marxism. Having risen to power on the backs of the Chinese union leaders, the Gah Men had now branded the left as Communists, taking up the Ang Mohs' legacy of denouncements and detentions in order to persuade their colonial rulers to grant them full authority. Just two weeks ago a close friend of Siok Mei's had been taken in and questioned for the possession of a single volume of essays.

Ah Boon struggled to focus on what she was saying. There she was, standing in front of the chair she had sat in as a girl, where they had practiced writing together. How could she stand there as if no time at all had passed, when nearly two decades had? How could he still feel this painful pull toward her, the embarrassing desire to brush her cheek, rest his hand on the warm curve of her hip?

"The book was *Imperialism, the Highest Stage of Capitalism*," Siok Mei added. "The irony!"

Was it ironic? He did not know. Ah Boon thought of the white shirts flashing in the sun. The measurements being taken in the swamp, the community center with its recruitment poster.

"Si Gah Men," Eng Soon said, shaking his head.

Eng Soon placed one hand on Siok Mei's back. In the other hand, he held a half-drunk bottle of orange soda, still fizzing for having just been opened. Ah Boon imagined Ma offering it to him, warmly, kindly, making a show of hospitality. The shine of Eng Soon's full lips, the neat coif of his long, gelled hair.

He was his friend, Ah Boon made himself think, a meaningless refrain he'd repeated to himself over the years. He tried to summon up the shared outings, the long afternoons spent reading and debating together, the warmth of camaraderie. It was not Eng Soon's fault that Siok Mei had chosen him.

He became aware that his hands were still sticky from handling fish at the market; his nail beds black with dirt. Ah Boon tugged at his singlet. He noticed now the large rust-colored stain from when he'd been cleaning a fish for a particularly petulant housewife and had squirted its guts on himself.

"I don't think it's anything," Ah Boon said, turning away from Eng Soon, back to Siok Mei. "They just come every day and dig around in the swamp."

"Oh?" she said, and there was something of the old warmth in her voice, as if she and Ah Boon could easily tip back into their familiar dynamic, the pleasure of slowly batting ideas back and forth as they ambled down some coastal path or another.

"Yes," Ah Boon said, the blood rushing to his cheeks. "They—"

"Swamp?" Eng Soon interrupted. "What exactly are they doing?"

How his intensity grated. Eng Soon had always been serious, but over the years, he had grown increasingly somber, losing his easy grin and loose gait, cultivating that particular sanctimoniousness that went along with revolutionary zeal. He'd begun admonishing his peers for learning English, for watching Western films, for adopting Western fashions. Ah Boon did none of these things, and yet when he was around Eng Soon, he frequently felt himself to be on trial, as if whatever he did would fall short of the other man's exacting standards.

"Nothing lah, they look around only," Ah Boon said. "Why must everything be a conspiracy?"

"It's not a conspiracy. You don't read the news anymore?" Eng Soon said.

Ah Boon forced a laugh. "Where got time to read? So much work to do."

"The Gah Men have this idea they're going to build more land," Eng Soon said. They were calling it *land reclamation*, he went on in his lecturing tone; it was a populist vanity project. They would build flats on the new land, a carrot dangled before the eyes of the masses. Why couldn't they build flats on the existing land, was what Eng Soon wanted to know. It was a flexing of power, an imprudent use of taxpayer money. "I don't understand how you haven't heard," he said, ending his speech at last.

Ah Boon flushed. It was true, he did not read the news anymore, he did not know what was going on with the Gah Men or the unions or the fight for Merdeka. He had washed his hands of it all when he gave up Siok Mei.

"Are you visiting your uncle?" he said in the most neutral voice he could muster.

Siok Mei nodded. "My aunt boiled some soup for us—oh!" She looked about, dismayed. "We left it behind."

"I can go get it," Eng Soon said. "No, no, you stay," he went on, as Siok Mei picked up her bag. "No need for us both to go."

A tight feeling spread through Ah Boon's chest as Siok Mei sat down, settling into the old chair as she had so many times before.

"Good to see you, Boon," Eng Soon said. He seemed embarrassed to have gotten carried away with his lecture earlier, and now shook Ah Boon's hand warmly. "I'm glad you are well."

Ah Boon bade him goodbye, and Eng Soon left. Ma was out back hanging laundry, Ah Boon realized, so here they were, he and Siok Mei alone again. They sat in silence, and there was a heaviness to the air that Ah Boon did not understand. Siok Mei scratched a dent in the kitchen table with her index finger, pursed her lips in the way she did when she was troubled.

"Everything okay at work?" he asked.

The question felt unnatural. What did he know of her work? She visited her uncle so rarely, being busy with her life in the city, and Ah Boon was not always around when she came. The last time he'd seen her must have been six, seven months ago, he thought, and even then, only in passing as she rushed off to some union engagement or other.

She nodded. Still she scratched at the dent.

"And Eng Soon?" he went on, willing her to look at him. Something was wrong, he knew, but they were no longer close enough for him to simply ask her.

She looked up. "I'm pregnant," she said.

The words made no sense. She could not be pregnant, he thought, she was a child herself. But of course she wasn't—they were no longer sixteen. He forced himself to smile.

"Congratulations," he said. How many times could his heart break over a single person?

"Eng Soon doesn't know," she said, still with that pursed expression. "I—it was an accident."

"He will be happy. He will be so happy."

"Boon," Siok Mei said, her voice cracking, and he knew something was wrong. "I'm not keeping it."

He was silent. Siok Mei, pregnant. Siok Mei, not keeping it. He veered from shock to despair to relief. And now to guilt, for how could one ever be relieved at such a thing, how could he ever be relieved at Siok Mei's unhappiness, which he could read on her face as clearly as he could read the sky for rain?

"It's impossible," she said in a rush. "The unions, our work. I can't take care of a child. You see what happened with Geok Tin, overrun with her three, she can barely leave the house! No, it's too important, what we're doing. I can't. And me, anyway what do I know about being a mother—"

"You would be a wonderful mother," Ah Boon interrupted.

She paused and softened, and here was a flash of his old friend, her smile easy and free.

"Oh, Boon."

"It's true," he said. "You would make the best mother."

"But I never had one," she said. "My mother was never here. I don't know how to do it. And now with the detentions—what if something happens, I could never forgive myself—"

On and on she went, a torrent of fear and torment streaming out of her like a river breaking free of a dam. She spoke in circles, repeated herself about work, the unions, detentions, her motherlessness, her worry that she simply had no instinct for nurturing, Eng Soon's desire for a child. How long had she kept all this to herself? Ah Boon wondered. He could not bear to see her so unhappy.

"There's no choice," she said. "It just doesn't make sense." She grabbed Ah Boon's hands. Her skin was warm and damp, just as he'd remembered. "You understand, right?"

He gazed into her troubled eyes. It was comfort she was seeking, clarity, absolution. A part of him rejoiced selfishly, that in her moment of crisis, it was still him to whom she turned.

She wanted him to tell her it was fine to do as she planned, that her careful weighing of pros and cons, her cautious considerations, the cataloging of her fears, all of it led to the undeniable conclusion she had come to. And he saw that only he, her old, reliable friend, who had always been there for her in her time of need, had the power to set her soul at ease. She had not told Eng Soon.

How easy it would be to nod and agree, to squeeze her hand and tell her that she was right. And of course he burned with anguish at the thought of Siok Mei giving birth to Eng Soon's child. A child would bind them together in a way that work, friends, even marriage could not. Their blood and lives would be inextricably, forever, threaded together.

And yet. Because he knew Siok Mei intimately, like the lines of his own worn palms, he saw that beneath her fear and turmoil and disbelief, what she wanted deep down—what she was afraid to want, for the terror of another possible loss—was a family of her own.

He gently laid her hands on the table, resisting the urge to brush the hair from her eyes. Once, on an uninhabited island, among the scattered rubber seeds, those same hands had pinned Ah Boon's arms down.

"I understand," he said. "I also believe you can do it."

After Siok Mei had left, Ah Boon went to draw a bucket of water from the well. In the shelter where they washed themselves, he kept his eyes open as he poured the water over his head. The world went blurry and soft; he wished it could stay that way, indistinct, unformed, infinite. But the water soon left his eyes and he could see again. Here was the shabby brick wall, black with mold, crumbling from years of disrepair. Here was the wooden scoop. Here were the scuttling black ants, the slimy film of dark moss creeping over the ground.

There would never come a time when the thought of Siok Mei would not fill him with sharp, painful longing. Her very being, it seemed, was connected to a small and particular place inside him designed to hurt. He felt himself to be standing in quicksand on the shore, she at sea, waving, borne by a boat that would take her farther and farther away. And now he had added wind to the sails of that boat through his very own actions.

After their long, winding conversation, Siok Mei had decided at last to keep the child. Her only request was that he be the godfather. And he had said yes, for how could he not, after all he had said? Still—he was human. There were limits to his endurance.

When the bucket was empty, he didn't leave but stood wet and dripping in the waning evening light. His slippers squelched in the mud; a mosquito buzzed past his ear. He replayed the scene that had passed between him and Siok Mei again and again; he tortured himself with questions of whether her child would be a boy or a girl.

He could not go on this way.

It was dark by the time he stepped out of the shelter, and he had made his decision. He ran one hand across his chest. His skin was smooth and clean, but already the humid air pressed from all sides. By the time he walked back to the house, he would be covered again in a layer of perspiration.

Chapter Twenty-One

When Siok Mei spotted Teacher Chia outside the movie theater, a fist seemed to close around her heart. He had lost even more weight. The detentions had taken their toll on him. The first had been a month long, the second almost a year. Still, Teacher Chia, stubborn as ever, did not let up; still he organized strikes and sit-ins and work stoppages. Freedom from the Ang Mohs, he continued to believe, could not come without freedom for the workers, and only the unions had the workers' best interests in mind.

But Teacher Chia was a man of almost sixty now. In another life, he would be at home, teaching his grandchildren to read, tending to pet songbirds in rattan cages with other old men. Instead he was here. Standing outside the movie theater, the gray wisps on his head barely covering the large bald patches where his hair had fallen out in prison, the loose shirt swallowing his bony frame. Teacher Chia had the look of an old lion whose flashing eyes still spoke of a steely mind but whose body, emaciated and wrung out, could no longer do its bidding.

Siok Mei was seized with hatred for the people who had done this to him. The Ang Mohs, yes, but had the Gah Men stopped them? The Gah Men, having come into power, now distanced themselves from the unions that had made their election possible in the first place. Even though the union heroes had been freed from prison, they'd been sidelined to secretarial roles within the party. Inch by inch the Gah Men were pushing out the left. Inch by inch, proving themselves to be little better than the Ang Mohs, no matter the color of their skin.

And now there was talk of the island merging with the Federation of Malaya, the Ang Mohs relinquishing control over internal security and withdrawing their troops. Full self-governance. Merdeka! But while the Ang Mohs would be ousted at last, the Malayan federal government was even more fiercely against the leftists and would set out on a new spree of political detentions, perhaps more brutal than before. Always, one threat gave way to another, and another. Siok Mei had grown tired of late. But seeing Teacher Chia so small, so scrawny, and still standing tall, still refusing to back down—well, who was she to be tired?

They entered the movie theater. Only when the lights had fallen did Siok Mei allow herself to approach Teacher Chia, careful to sit two seats away. Siok Mei was quite sure she had not been followed, having taken a long and circuitous route to get here, but one never knew. Now that Teacher Chia had been imprisoned several times, a known mark for the Gah Men, it was best not to be seen associating with him publicly. Detentions were swift and arbitrary, and a single meeting with a known revolutionary could be cited as cause for a dreaded late-night arrest, indefinite captivity.

They sat in silence until the movie began. The starring actor was a popular one, but the theater was half-empty—the golden days of local cinema were waning now, with the introduction of newfangled television and a deluge of imported Hollywood movies.

Familiar opening credits appeared, clashing symbols, the name of the illustrious film studio, two curved daggers crossing in an X. In the first scene, a sultan sat on his throne, his court supplicated before him. The actor who played him had a handsome, arrogant face, a tidy mustache and busy eyebrows. He eyed the court as the music trilled ominously, the court trembling at his feet. Something was wrong, the sultan was angry.

"Mei," Teacher Chia whispered. "You are well?"

"Very well," she said. "We are getting good work done."

"Good, good. Young people like you will change everything."

They went on to talk generally about the movement: who had been threatened, who had been jailed, who had turned.

Siok Mei talked and talked, but her heart wasn't in it. For once she wanted to set politics aside, to forget about the Ang Mohs and the Gah Men and the ideological debates and talk openly and intimately with Teacher Chia, as if they were the family she had always felt them to be.

The sultan on-screen ordered a warrior to kill his best friend, the best friend having betrayed the royal family. Siok Mei told Teacher Chia, haltingly, that she was pregnant.

"Oh!" he exclaimed quietly, then paused for a long while.

His demeanor shifted when he turned to Siok Mei again, and it made something inside her sink.

"Don't worry," she said quickly. "I'll still be as involved as ever. Eng Soon and I don't plan on going anywhere."

"It is not that," Teacher Chia said. "But I regret I will not be there to meet your child."

He was going in, he went on. Gently he brought his hand to his face and touched the metal bridge of his glasses.

In being to the jungle in northern Malaya, where the armed insurrection was still being fought by the dregs of the Ma Gong. A fool's mission, many would say. The war was over; the Ang Mohs had won. They'd eliminated large swaths of Ma Gong forces through brutal counterattacks, as well as the forcible relocation and control of kampong populations, thus restricting food and medicine supplies to the guerrilla forces. Still, deep in the jungle, small groups of fighters remained, refusing to admit defeat. It was these last holdouts that Teacher Chia hoped to join. Once in, there was no coming out. The Ma Gong would kill you if you tried to leave; it was the only way they could prevent spies and traitors from infiltrating their already tenuous encampments.

Siok Mei squeezed her eyes shut.

"When do you go?" she said.

"Tomorrow."

Was she destined, forever, to lose the people she loved? Or was it her? Did she choose, deliberately, those who were always drawn away?

"But," she said to Teacher Chia, "your health—"

He raised his hand, stopping her. In that gesture he was her old teacher again, imperious and certain, filled with conviction.

"I am not an old man," he said. By the ghostly light of the screen, his eyes blazed terribly in the dark.

All Siok Mei could see was the loose skin of his neck, the dark smear on his jawline, a bruise that would not heal. The movement was killing him. But what could she say? Not that she wanted him to stay, not that she feared his death.

Instead she kept her tone level. "The Ma Gong have fallen. Why join them now?"

"What is there for me here?" Teacher Chia replied. "More detentions? More squabbling with the Gah Men? More long, fruitless months in prison?"

It was true; now that he had been made a target, they would silence or harass him into submission. But in response to the question of what was left for him here, a part of Siok Mei cried: *Me. My child.* She was still getting used to the idea that she would have a baby. Foolishly, one of the thoughts that had comforted her was of Teacher Chia coaching the child to read and write, as he had once coached her.

"No, better to go where people are still fighting, even with their last breaths," he said.

Siok Mei was silent. Teacher Chia's words pricked her with shame; she was being selfish, she was not thinking of the bigger picture. Still, was it selfish to love?

"How is Ah Boon?" Teacher Chia asked, his voice softened.

"Good." The lump in her throat would not go away.

"Give him my regards. And his mother too."

"He—" The words stuck. "He will be the godfather."

Teacher Chia paused. "Good," he said softly. "He will always take care of you."

Tears welled up in her eyes. Maybe after it was all over, she told him, be it five, ten years, Teacher Chia would be able to meet her child. After the struggle had been won and they could live freely again.

"Yes. Maybe," Teacher Chia said.

They fell silent. On-screen, the two warriors battled, best friends set at each other's throats by a king who believed in his divine right.

Siok Mei's parents had not left her much when they departed: three bags of rice, a framed picture of Sun Yat Sen, and an intricately carved lacquered mirror that could fit into the palm of her hand. The rice, of course, was long gone, the picture of Sun Yat Sen burned during the war, fearful as they were of the Jipunlang finding it. The mirror she kept on her person at all times, slipped into a purse or the pocket of her pants. She liked to think that some fragment of her mother lived in its polished glass.

It was the mirror Siok Mei had always worried about most, should she be taken. The time she'd been arrested at the National Service riots seemed like child's play compared to what was happening now. Back then, the students had had the might of the unions behind them, the support of the press and the people.

But the Gah Men's political detentions were different. There was a ruthless efficiency to the Gah Men that the Ang Mohs had not possessed. Detainees were now stripped of all clothes and belongings; they even had their eyeglasses taken away from them as soon as they arrived in prison. Upon release, things were not often returned.

Now there was to be a child—an entire human child.

It was why she had been convinced she could not do it. Having once been that heartbroken child, she would not even entertain the possibility of inflicting this fate upon her own offspring. Then there was the fear that a child would make her weak. She did not blame her female comrades who left the movement; how could you fault a mother for putting her children before her ideals? Sometimes, in certain moments of weakness, Siok Mei wondered what her own life might have been had her mother chosen differently.

Yet here she was. Ah Boon's words: *I believe you can do it. You are not your mother.* It was he who knew her best, he who saw that all her life she had pushed away the possibility of love because of how she feared the possibility of loss. With a pang, she thought of how he himself had been, years ago, a victim to this impulse of hers. And how generous he was, what a good friend, in spite of how their paths had diverged, to be there for her in her time of need nonetheless.

But even if she had decided to have the child, sitting there with Teacher Chia in the movie theater, she knew that she would never give up her work. She could not give it up. When she'd been younger it had been about justice and ideas, the certainty that they were right, that rightness must prevail. Now it was less clear. Everyone was fighting for whatever they were fighting for; everyone believed in the rightness of their own cause. Perhaps it was she who was delusional.

What had become concrete for her were the people. Teacher Chia, her dear mentor. Eng Soon, loyal, steady, kind. Her colleagues at the union where she worked. The workers, of course. The students, who fought every single day. These were the people she'd be abandoning to the crushing might of the Ang Mohs and the Gah Men. No, she would not do it.

"Know that we're always supporting you," Siok Mei said to Teacher Chia now, even as her heart contracted painfully at the thought that she might not see him again. "You can count on us for anything."

"Thank you," he said. A pause, then: "I'm very proud of you, Siok Mei."

On-screen, the fight had concluded; the warrior had slain his best friend. A tear came to his eye as he held the dying man, but he was firm, he had been loyal to the last. When Teacher Chia then asked Siok Mei to be a messenger in the Ma Gong's network of information in Singapore, a part of her hesitated.

She thought she felt something twitch in her belly and imagined a tiny foot kicking, a plea. Her baby was only a bundle of cells at this point, her baby possessed no feet, was incapable of disagreement. To the baby she said *Shush, Ma knows what she's doing. Ma will take care of you.* To Teacher Chia, she said yes.

Chapter Twenty-Two

A few days after Siok Mei and Eng Soon's visit, Ah Boon went to the community center. He wore his best white shirt, one that he hadn't worn since leaving school. Despite his best attempt to shine the black leather shoes on his feet, they had grown moldy from having been left neglected in a cupboard for so long, and much of the mottled gray appearance remained. Still, he could not justify going into town for a new pair of shoes. He did not need such shoes in his line of work; a fisherman's feet belonged in boots and clogs.

And yet—Ah Boon was standing here, in front of that alien brick building, applying for a job that would require such shoes.

Everyone was so certain about the Gah Men. So convinced the Gah Men were out to get them, in one way or another. It was true, Ah Boon did feel the sting of violation when he saw them tramping all over his family's mangrove swamp. The Lees did not own it, of course, but if it were anyone's, it would certainly be theirs. He felt anger at their audacity, their invasive cameras and spirit levels and the little orange flags they stuck into the ground. And it was true, they had done those things that Siok Mei and the others talked about, locking up union leaders and students whom they'd labeled as dangerous. Ah Boon himself knew some of those who had been put away. Several had been in prison for years now with no trial or release date, an uncertain and cruel punishment.

Still, none of it appeared quite as clear-cut to him as it did to Siok Mei. Would the leftists not do the same, had they the ability? Would they not lock up the Ang Mohs, the Gah Men? They were, after all, not averse to acid attacks and protests turning violent. Then there were the Ma Gong up north, who killed not only Ang Moh soldiers but also civilians they deemed to be traitors and capitalists. In a struggle for power, for survival, whose conscience was spotless?

Perhaps the real question was this: What was he to do with the rest of his life, his hard-won education? Since Siok Mei had become pregnant, Ah Boon could no longer hide from the knowledge that he had lived the past two decades as a shadow closely stitched to hers. Even her marriage, his retreat to the kampong, had not truly changed this. He saw he had been living in a holding pattern, like a bird endlessly circling a bare expanse of water, waiting for land to miraculously appear. Now she would have a new shadow, a living, breathing child. Siok Mei would be bound in blood to Eng Soon, and Ah Boon cut off from her forever. And he'd wanted this for her, he reminded himself. He wanted only for her to be happy. Still, he dwelled on his own selfish desires. What would remain of his inherited beliefs, his half-formed life? Who was he—who could he be—without them?

Ah Boon did not know the answers to any of these questions. What he did know was that over the past week, he often imagined himself in the Gah Men's whites, starched collar scratching his neck, the weight of a ballpoint pen pulling down on his front pocket.

He'd gone fishing that morning and had found the islands very beautiful. The possibility that he might be leaving this life behind cloaked them in tenderness. The low-slung clouds seemed to caress the horizon rather than loom upon it, and the green-gray water took on a precious melancholy. The islands themselves peeked through the dim morning fog, as lush and absolute as they always were. He'd fished around Batu, its high cliffs flushed pink in the morning light, as if they were made of mother-of-pearl and not stone. Though it was his favorite spot, he rarely went there. Now known for its plentiful fish, it was often crowded with boats. He'd taken his chances today and was rewarded with an empty horizon, a sea rippled only by the backs of fish and the occasional frothing crest.

After he threw down the nets, Ah Boon leaned back in the curved clamshell of the boat, turning his body toward the sky. These were the times he felt most strongly that Pa was still with him, the boat bobbing lightly on the waves, the clouds so slow and lumbering that it seemed to be he who was drifting and not they. A decision had already been made, but still, he turned the question over and over in his mind, like a smooth pebble knocking against the riverbed.

When he pulled up the nets, they contained only one kind of fish—black pomfrets, the flat diamonds of their bodies slick in the morning light. This uniformity did not surprise him; over the years, he'd learned that the waters here were temperamental. They could be relied upon for a good catch, but from time to time threw up only prawns or squid, and other times colorful varieties of fish that weren't even supposed to be found in this region. He'd grown to accept the unpredictability, embracing it as a game to be played, like the reading of tea leaves or the grooves of a palm.

The homogeneity of the catch today was striking. There was a conviction about it. Be firm, it seemed to say. There is only one way forward. He allowed himself to believe that it was a message from Pa himself.

And so here he was, standing in front of the community center. The overhead lights buzzed fluorescent, an intense white veering into blue. There was a way the surf would glitter some two hours after dawn, throwing off sparks of morning sun as its loose gray body undulated across the sand, and it was into one of these sparks that Ah Boon felt like he was stepping as he entered the center that morning.

A young Chinese woman got up from the large wooden desk and offered Ah Boon her hand. She wore the pressed whites of the Gah Men, had a pen in her front pocket, and her long black hair in a neat, smooth ponytail. She was around the same age as he and Siok Mei, perhaps, but held herself with a quiet self-assurance that made her feel much older. Unlike Siok Mei, whose face was an open slate for whatever she thought or felt, this woman's face reminded Ah Boon of the inside of a seashell: complete, mysterious.

"Good morning," she said in Mandarin. "My name is Natalie. I'm the regional manager for all CCs in the eastern region. Welcome to CC E14. We're glad to have you with us."

CC. It took Ah Boon a moment to realize that she was referring to the community center. He wiped his hand on the pleats of his pants before shaking Natalie's. Her hand was very warm, and he dropped it quickly.

Natalie didn't seem to notice. "Shall I show you around?"

Ah Boon nodded. Briskly she stepped ahead of him, gesturing at a mural that covered an entire wall near the entrance. A nurse, a construction worker, a teacher, and a policeman, each of a different ethnicity. Only their torsos and heads had been depicted, all facing the windows that lined the wall, as if looking out onto the actual horizon. All had been painted with sparkling eyes, determined mouths, square, straight shoulders.

"Cohesion, progress, multiracialism," Natalie said. "That is the mission of our CC. Of all CCs."

Ah Boon studied the wall. The paint was fresh, the colors vibrant. A chemical smell came off it. He found himself thinking of Pa, Hia, and himself, paintbrushes in hand, crowded around the newly stripped and sanded body of their boat. Cans of yellow paint at their feet, the bright circles of liquid color winking in the sun. Pa had wanted to paint the boat white, but Swee Hong had had the surplus cans of yellow paint sitting in his storeroom and was willing to let them go at half price. That cheerful color had long been stripped from their boat now, with only a few scraps of paint remaining on the otherwise bare wood. In Pa's absence, the Lees had not repainted it.

Next they went down a brightly lit corridor and came into another large room. Two brand-new table tennis tables were arranged in one corner, baskets of paddles and bright orange balls perched on a nearby shelf. The room was dominated by cushy leather sofas, the likes of which Ah Boon had only ever seen in the houses of his wealthiest classmates. And there in front of the sofas, miraculously, was a television set. He stared at the black box with its face of curved gray glass, remembering how, when they'd first started selling them just last year in the department store where Ang Mohs shopped, he had gone with Hia and little Ah Huat to gawk at them through the window, transfixed by moving pictures on the polished glass.

"Our common room," Natalie said.

"Who lives here?" Ah Boon asked. Natalie, perhaps? How strange that she was showing it to him.

A flicker went over her. "No one," she said.

Ah Boon did not understand.

"It's open to the public," she said, her face softening. "It's for everyone. You, your friends, your parents. Anyone in the kampong can use it."

He shook his head, still overtaken by the pristine room, the smell of fresh paint, the silent fans turning swiftly overhead. So this was it, then, the Gah Men's vision for the future. He'd heard much about it on the radio: progress, prosperity, equality, et cetera, but those were empty words

crackling over airwaves. This was different; this was an entire building.
And it was not just the building. He was not that much a country bump-
kin; his middle school, too, had had electric lights (though not as bright
or steady as these) and was built of smooth brick and concrete (though
not painted quite as seamlessly as these walls). No, it was not just this
building, but this building *here*, in the kampong. The whole place felt like
a mirage.

Ah Boon knew what Uncle would say. The Gah Men were
untrustworthy—look how they had treated the union leaders!—and the
place was a lure, a cheap trick meant to dazzle the people. Ah Boon could
see all this was meant to seduce. Everything had been carefully thought
through, from the television set to the arrangement of the sofas to the
attractive shade of blue paint on the walls, meant, perhaps, to mimic the
sea. Everything was planned, premeditated, executed with intention.
The walls would not be yellow here because the yellow paint could be had
at half price.

Si Gah Men, he could hear Uncle saying. And yet, was it so bad, to
have the disorderly parts of the world collected and sorted, put back together again in a form that one could inhabit more comfortably?

That's what we're trying to do, he heard Siok Mei saying. It was true.
The leftists and the Gah Men simply had different visions of the future.
But Ah Boon had tried the way of the revolutionary and failed. He had
tried to be what Siok Mei wanted, and she had found that insufficient.

He walked over to the tables and picked up a paddle.

"Want a game?" he asked Natalie.

A look of surprise crossed her face, and for a moment the strangeness
of the situation threatened to break through. But then she smiled, walked
over to the table, and took the paddle from him. The dream was pre-
served.

Ah Boon let her serve first. It was an easy lob, but he could tell from the way Natalie wielded her paddle that she was a far better player than she was letting on. He returned her shot politely, mimicking her speed and placement. There was pleasure to be had in the little orange ball's tidy flight over the green expanse of the table. They rallied like this for a good few minutes, back and forth. Both careful to place the ball where the other could easily receive it. An agreement was forming between them, one that had to do with the lightness of the ball, the consideration of their strokes.

It was Ah Boon who first introduced a spin into his volleys. Natalie didn't miss a beat and ratcheted up the speed of her returns. The game began to pick up pace. Soon they were playing at their full powers, smashing and slicing with rapid, finely calibrated strokes. Now the little orange ball sped back and forth at near horizontal trajectories, thrilling through the air like a tiny rocket.

Neither could gain an advantage for long, until finally Ah Boon figured out that a certain float of the ball, with a particular spin, directed toward the left foreground of the table, was Natalie's weakness. He sent ball after ball in that direction, and within minutes the game was concluded.

He thrust his fists into the air in a moment of childish joy. He hadn't played table tennis since he'd been in school, where they'd spent many an afternoon challenging one another to games.

"You're a very good player," Natalie observed cheerfully.

Her face was pink with exertion. A slight sheen coated her forehead, a single piece of hair had escaped her ponytail and lay plastered across her left temple. Those loose strands gave Natalie, in her crisp collared shirt and sharp pleated pants, the look of a human being. She appeared newly formed in front of Ah Boon. Suddenly he noticed the rise and fall of her chest, the faint pulse agitating the skin beneath her jawbone, the green veins crisscrossing the backs of her hands.

There came a loud, slow clapping. They turned. A man in the same uniform as Natalie stood in the doorway. He was of Uncle's age, but un-like Uncle had a fleshy jawline and a large, soft middle that strained his white shirt.

Ah Boon realized he still had his hands in the air. Stupidly, he low-ered them.

"Mr. Yik," Natalie said in English. "We weren't expecting you until the afternoon."

She seemed to salute him with her entire body, spine shooting up straight, face wiped rapidly of all spontaneous expression.

"No doubt it's busy at HQ," the man replied. "But this is an impor-tant step in the CC program. I thought I'd come and take a look before the actual ceremony."

Now here was a true Gah Man. The English spoken by the Ang Mohs was full of air, aspirated consonants and round, gentle vowels. The Gah Men's English was like the Ang Mohs' and yet different; it had a certain solidity to it, a hardness, was trimmed at the edges with a clipped preci-sion. Like many of his classmates, Ah Boon had picked up broken En-glish from the Ang Mohs' radio speeches, and more recently by watching American movies, listening to American jazz, but he could in no way speak as the Gah Man did.

Ah Boon felt himself shrinking before this man. He tried to summon the scorn his classmates felt for men and women of this ilk, reciting men-tally the usual slurs—*er mao zi, ang moh sai*—but no indignation arose, no fiery hate to buoy him up.

"This is—" Natalie paused. Ah Boon realized she did not know his name, had not thought to ask it when he first walked in.

"Lee Ah Boon, sir," Ah Boon said to Mr. Yik. The words came out confident enough.

"A member of the community," Natalie said.

"You live here?" Mr. Yik asked, eyeing Ah Boon up and down, as if it could be discerned from his outfit. It was not a critical gaze, per se. Ah Boon found himself stepping forward and offering his hand.

"I live here my whole life," he said.

The English words were like cold marbles in his mouth, and he held them tightly, as if to be careful of them tumbling to the ground. Having little occasion to use or practice it—indeed, there was an active resistance to becoming fluent, for this was seen as treachery—Ah Boon's grasp of the language was slippery, and he felt it now as an inadequacy that burned in his cheeks.

Mr. Yik shook his hand with a cold and calloused palm. It wasn't the hand of a bureaucrat, and yet Mr. Yik was undoubtedly a bureaucrat.

"And you are a—" Mr. Yik paused. "Fisherman, then?"

Ah Boon nodded. He'd taken over from his father just after the war, he said.

"You must have been barely more than a boy then. What a lucky father you have; it's good of you to take care of him."

"My father is dead, sir."

"Ah," Mr. Yik said.

His face retained its stiffness, but he blinked twice, rapidly. Natalie tilted her head ever so slightly, and a thoughtful look came over her. Pity, Ah Boon thought, but then found himself thinking: kindness. Something inside him warmed. The ceiling fans whirled overhead, making smooth and dependable circles in the air. A new life was what he wanted.

Ah Boon cleared his throat. "I came to apply for the job," he said.

"Oh!" Natalie exclaimed.

"Oh?" Mr. Yik said. He seemed to come back to life. He looked Ah Boon up and down again, this time more carefully.

"You want—" Ah Boon paused. The words came slowly. "Passionate Individuals for Community Outreach."

"Indeed. Lots of work to be done," Mr. Yik said.

Ah Boon was not sure what to say; he did not have any experience in the kind of job he imagined would take place in a building like this. He had his schooling, yes, he was very overeducated for his own profession. But he was Chinese-educated, and everyone knew that the Gah Men didn't hire from the vernacular schools. He'd learned the language of revolution, not this language, not the Gah Men's language. He could not chatter away to Ang Mohs as someone like Mr. Yik or Natalie might. On the rare occasion when he'd been confronted with one, forced to speak the foreign tongue, he'd flushed with anger, yet still felt shame, and hated himself for it.

"I know it's not the exact profile we're looking for," Natalie said. "But this could be an important advantage for community outreach. Particularly given the plans."

Mr. Yik looked about the room. "Any other applicants show up?" he asked.

"No, sir," Natalie said.

Again his gaze slid over Ah Boon. Then Mr. Yik gave a barely perceptible nod.

"Okay," he said.

Natalie brightened. "We may hire him?"

"You may *interview* the chap," Mr. Yik corrected. "And following that, make an appropriate decision."

When he left the room, Natalie turned to Ah Boon with a conspiratorial smile.

"Our first employee!" she cried.

"Don't you need to interview me?"

"Don't be silly."

Ah Boon flushed with pleasure. *You have a way with people, boy, you should be a politician.* Natalie's joy was unruly, almost childish, a sharp contrast to the neat pleats of her trousers, the coiffed shine of her hair. It made him wonder what else would please her.

Now there were forms to fill out, so many forms. Name, address, date of birth, prior occupation, education, father's occupation, education, et cetera. Ah Boon filled them in slowly, with small, painstaking handwriting. He had the feeling that to make a mistake would cost him his unexpected good fortune. His pay was to be forty dollars a week, a mind-boggling amount, almost double what fishing brought in even when the islands offered up their bounty. Ah Boon was given an advance against his first weeks' pay to buy himself the clothes he would need for the job. Work would begin the following week.

The precise nature of the job was still unclear to him, but Ah Boon gathered he would be based in the CC, and that his responsibilities included "outreach," which seemed to mean talking to the people in the kampong about the services available to them through the community center. Mostly, he thought, they would be interested in the television, perhaps the table tennis and the badminton court in the back.

Before Ah Boon left, Natalie handed him a slip of paper, on which an address in the city was scrawled.

"Don't be offended," she added quickly. "Many people go to night school now."

It wasn't that his English wasn't good, she said. (An untruth, he knew.) But a little extra help never hurt. She was telling him this as a friend, not a boss. If he wanted to get ahead, this would be a good place to start.

She said this so earnestly, touching Ah Boon's elbow ever so gently, that he could not be offended. And he was not naive. It was true, he knew. Swee Hong himself had sent two sons to night school to learn English and it had paid off—both worked as well-paid clerks in large export companies in the city.

If he wanted to get ahead. Was that what he wanted? Not exactly. He knew only that his old path, intertwined with Siok Mei's, had been cut off. And would he be a fisherman forever, was that why he had gone to school? Something inside him hungered for greater purpose. For so long he had been buffeted by the winds of fate, like a tiny kolek upon the waves. First the brutal might of the Jipunlang, snatching Pa so arbitrarily from life. Then the all-encompassing leftist movement, which had taken Siok Mei from Ah Boon too, and was growing more dangerous for her by the day.

Ah Boon knew this: the Gah Men were strong. Strength was something he wanted, not only for himself but for everyone he loved.

So he thanked Natalie politely and tucked the piece of folded paper into his chest pocket, where it sat like a new layer of protection over his heart.

Chapter Twenty-Three

Here was a thing Hia would never tell anyone: he had grown tired of fishing. He would never tell as it did not matter. One fished because one had to, because it was how one lived. What one was or was not tired of, that was irrelevant.

There were times, though, when Hia remembered how vast the sea had seemed when he'd been a boy, how brave his father for venturing into it. His earliest memory: weaving his first crab trap with Pa, the supple rattan refusing to make the domed shape he'd had in his mind, coming out meager and off-center instead. How proud he'd been when Pa placed the bait tin into his misshapen trap and lowered it into the shallows. How Pa's face had blossomed with genuine delight when they'd pulled up the trap later to find a pair of small crabs scuttling through the lopsided space.

His first crab trap. His first boat trip out with Pa. His first time at the market. His first trip out to those strange islands found by his brother. His first trip out with Uncle, after Pa died. His first boat, after marrying Gek Huay. Soon there would be another first: when little Ah Huat turned six, Hia would take him out on the boat as his own father had once taken him.

Hia still loved it all: the windless afternoons with stale heat hanging over the water; the bright, cloud-lit days, seabirds balancing their slim bodies on round gusts of air; the monsoon rain churning the sea into a muddy soup. And yet he had tired of it, as he had heard some men speak of tiring of beloved wives whom they would never leave. He found himself distracted when out at sea, forgetting how long he'd left nets down, mistaking a strip of gray in the distance for rain and turning back too early, leaving metal hooks out on the porch to rust. The sea had once felt like a vast adventure; now he saw that vastness could be a kind of claustrophobia.

Yet he was protective of his claustrophobia, as men were of their wives, and would defend his way of life against the first detractor. Hia did not think much of Swee Hong's decision to send his sons to work as clerks in the city, though of course he would never say as much to the provision shop owner's face. Neither had he believed in Ah Boon and Siok Mei's foray into that middle school, with all their talk of freedom and city workers and their supposedly difficult lot. A man's lot was his own to improve. Had Pa not overcome it all—the poverty of his youth, the violence of his own father, the ravenous hunger of the brood of sisters—through his own grit and forbearance? And how easy it was for these students with their soft hands to expound and moralize. Unlike Ah Boon, Hia had never had the luxury of going to school, could read and write only with what little he'd learned from Uncle's haphazard lessons. Now that his son was five, however, he felt, for the first time, a pinprick of doubt.

The cause was Gek Huay, who would not stop harping on: Ah Huat must go to school, times were different now, everyone's children went since the Gah Men had made the first six years free. There was much talk about bilingualism—all students were to learn English, along with their "mother tongue," be it Malay, Mandarin, or Tamil. English was to be the language of their new, united nation as they marched toward full independence from the Ang Mohs. It seemed odd to Hia that the country would achieve independence only by aping the Ang Mohs more completely; what kind of independence was that? But he brushed such questions away; these were things argued over in coffee shops by old men with no work to do.

"He can go to the kampong school," Hia had said to his wife.

She wrinkled her nose.

"What?"

"Aiya," she said.

He did not like to fight with her. But he knew what *aiya* meant. It meant the kampong school was not good enough for Ah Huat, just as the secondhand clothes from other mothers were not good enough for Ah Huat, just as brown rice was not good enough for Ah Huat. It disturbed him, Gek Huay's obsession with the child. Other mothers were not like this; other mothers sent their children out to work with a smack on the bottom as soon as they could walk. If not for Gek Huay he would have already taken Ah Huat out on his boat, but the mere suggestion of it made her face darken. It bothered him as well that some days he returned home to find the boy suckling from his mother's breast in the squalid afternoon heat. The two would look at him as he entered the room, as if he were a stranger disturbing their private, unknowable peace, rather than the boy's father. The sight of his wife's nipple—still engorged and purple after all this time—glistening in the boy's mouth made Hia feel strange and dangerous. Yet he could not say anything about this, for to put it into words would make his obscure fears real.

Fears of what? That the all-consuming attachment between his wife and child was abnormal. That some understanding existed between them that

Hia could not breach, that he was becoming an outsider in his own home, necessary for the provision of food and shelter but otherwise irrelevant.

It was on one of these afternoons, Hia sitting out on his porch as his wife and son engaged in another of their oppressive nursing sessions, that Ma came running to their front door in a state of disarray. For one terrible moment the blood drained from Hia's face, as it seemed to him the secret of his wife and son's unnatural closeness had been found out. But then he came to his senses; Ma was saying something about Ah Boon, Ah Boon and Uncle, Ah Boon and the Gah Men.

"Slow down," Hia said. "Do you want some water?"

Gek Huay appeared in the doorway, little Ah Huat clinging to her legs.

"What's wrong, Ma?" Gek Huay asked.

"Boon—Uncle—working at the CC. Aiya. You better come, faster."

Hia went with Ma. Their house was a short walk away, and she told him everything on the way there. Ah Boon had come home with the announcement that he was no longer going to fish; he had found himself a new job at the CC. Doing what? How was Ma supposed to know, it didn't matter, what mattered was Uncle, he knew how Uncle had been with the Gah Men. Anyway, Uncle said something about Ah Boon not understanding, that he was cooperating with the enemy. And Hia knew how his younger brother got. He was proud—weren't they all? Pa had been too, pride would be the downfall of all the Lee men—and in his pride, had said something awful that he did not mean.

"What did he say?" Hia asked.

"He said—" Ma paused. It seemed to pain her to recall. "That Uncle's guilt was not his problem."

"Uncle's guilt?"

"It was not his fault that Uncle went with your pa to the Jipunlang, Ah Boon said, it did not mean they had to hide forever."

They walked in silence.

"Promise me you won't get angry also, Yam," Ma said.

"I won't."

She stopped in her tracks.

"I see you already angry! Angry then don't come, just make things worse."

Ma was blinking rapidly now, as if trying to remove a grain of sand from her eye.

He turned away awkwardly. "Okay. Okay. I won't get angry."

It would be difficult. And yet so unusual was the sight of Ma about to cry—had she cried when Pa died? He did not think so, he could not recall—that by the time they reached the house, Hia had managed to tamp his anger down into a ball of cold clay. Now it was small and dense, like a marble on the deck of a boat, gaining momentum with every minor tilt and dip.

A chair had been knocked over; Uncle sat at the dining table, smoking furiously. He turned a little as Hia and Ma came into the house, light catching the ridges of his scowling face, then turned back again, into the shadow. Ah Boon was nowhere to be seen.

"Uncle," Hia said.

Uncle responded with a nod and grunt. The glowing tip of his cigarette pulsed like a tiny, unreliable sun in the dim of the house.

"Where's Boon?" Ma said.

A sharp exhale from Uncle.

"Leong."

"How I know?"

"Did he leave?"

"He not here, right?"

"Leong."

Silence fell. Ma gave Hia a pleading look.

"Aiya, Uncle," Hia said. "Don't angry already. Boon doesn't mean it. You know what he's like, right."

There was no response.

"If Boon wants to go work for the CC—well, what to do? He's an adult," Hia went on.

He did not believe it. Why he should have to defend Ah Boon, he did not know.

"Adult. Is he not still a son? A nephew?" Uncle said at last.

"He want to make his own life," Hia said weakly. "He's a man now."

"They will pay him forty dollars a week," Ma added.

Uncle's face darkened. "And we so desperate for money? Not enough food to eat, is it?"

"Leong, it is honest work. I am happy as long as my son does good, honest work."

"How is sitting in that building, spying on his neighbors, working for the Gah Men honest work?"

"That's not what he's doing," Ma said.

"Then? Doing what? He got explain?"

Ma fell silent. Hia grew thoughtful. He had not known about the forty dollars a week. Would he give up fishing for forty dollars a week? No, no, he would not, he thought right away. Still, the question lingered in his mind.

"What is he doing?" Hia asked.

Ma shrugged her shoulders. "Don't know. 'Community outreach,' he said."

"Where got money so easy to earn?" Uncle said.

"Maybe the Gah Men are doing something right. Maybe they can see Ah Boon is a good worker."

Uncle snorted dismissively.

"They have been trying to hire someone for so long already," Hia said. "Anyone also they will hire."

"Maybe," Ma said. A stubborn look came over her. "But maybe your brother is capable of more than you think."

"You spoil him." Uncle shook his head. "Let him go to that middle school. I thought he got all that nonsense out of his mind when he came back."

"Middle school was different. Those union people are hooligans, always fighting, always shouting in the streets." Ma shook her head. "The CC—you can see it's not like that."

"How can you not see?" Uncle said. Something cracked in his voice. "How can you—"

"They are not the Jipunlang, Leong," Ma said.

"You don't understand. These kind of men—"

"*I* don't understand?" Ma said.

And it was true, Uncle was not the only one to have lost Pa. He fell silent, a surly look coming over him.

"These kind of men are dangerous," Uncle muttered weakly.

Ma clicked her tongue. "I don't want to argue with you."

"Then don't."

They fell again into a simmering silence. Hia was tired. Having had a long morning out at sea, he had been summoned to mediate this fight whose main subject was not even here. His anger crumbled to dust; all he wanted now was to go home and have his bath. He did not care about the unions, he did not care about the CC and the Gah Men, he did not care about this Merdeka business that the radio and the old men at the provision store were so concerned about.

The three of them turned at the sound of footsteps.

"Boon," Ma said. "Where did you go? Aiyo."

Now that he was faced with his tall, skinny brother slinking into the house with an air of defiance, Hia did not know what to say. Ah Boon had never known how to defend himself.

As children catching small shrimp in the estuary, they had sometimes been ambushed by gangs of older boys from the neighboring kampong with their sticks and slingshots. It would always be up to Hia to fend them off. Once, though, Hia had been pinned to the ground by two older boys, while a third dangled his penis over Hia's face, threatening to pee. The humiliation was unbearable—Hia remembered the first hot drops emerging from the dark tip of the boy's sex, the smell of ammonia hitting his cheek. Then, out of nowhere, a loud scream, a branch descending on his torturer's head. His little brother.

How old had they been then? Hia had been seven or eight, which meant Ah Boon must have been five.

"Got new job ah," Hia said.

Ah Boon nodded. "So? You here to scold me also?"

"As if you will listen," Uncle said.

The tendons of Ah Boon's neck jumped. But again the look of defiance came over him; Hia recognized it as the same look on his five-year-old brother's face all those years ago. Still, he didn't respond to Uncle. Ah Boon was inexplicably holding a bundle of cloth, which he clutched more tightly now.

"Ma, can wash this for me please?" Ah Boon said abruptly, holding out the bundle in his hands.

"What's this?" Ma took it from him and shook out the cloths—a crumpled white shirt, a pair of dark pants with pleats and a belt loop.

"Work clothes," Ah Boon said.

How insolently he said it, *work clothes*, as if the singlet he wore, the rough canvas pants, as if these were not *work clothes*. What were work clothes but clothes in which one worked?

"Wah, work clothes. See, your brother?" Uncle said to Hia. "Big man now."

The way Ah Boon turned to Hia, it was as if he was presenting his face to him for a blow. Hia saw, though, that something had changed. He could not put his finger on it, but it was as if something turbulent and slippery within Ah Boon had frozen. He had made up his own mind, Hia realized. All his life his little brother had lived under the influence of others—Pa, Hia, Siok Mei—and now he had gone and done something inexplicable, perhaps for the reason that the decision belonged to him alone. A familiar grief struck; it was not unlike the time his son had taken his first steps, and Hia realized the boy would no longer need to be carried.

"Yam?" Uncle pressed.

"What?"

"What, what. Not going to say something?"

"No," Hia said. "What's there to say?"

Uncle's face darkened. "You are his brother. You should teach him what's right."

Something like a threat lurked in Uncle's words. And Hia did not like being threatened. Abruptly he turned away from his pale, silent little brother.

"I think it's fine," Hia said.

"What?" The surprise on Uncle's face was matched only by that on Ah Boon's.

"So what? Pays good money. No harm trying for a while."

Hia's tone was even. He did not believe what he was saying. Like most, he was suspicious of the CC. But Uncle had crossed a line. He was not, after all, their father. He would not turn Hia against his own brother.

"You are all crazy," Uncle said. But he seemed deflated now. The danger had passed, the anger gone out of him.

"No one is crazy," Hia said. "It is just a job."

"Right, right," Ma chimed in. "Job only. Aiyo. Get so worked up for what. Fight until like that."

There was silence. They all stared at Ah Boon.

"Anyway. Weekends still can fish, right?" Uncle said at last. It was a reluctant truce, sullenly extended.

Ah Boon wrinkled his nose, wincing a little. It seemed for a moment he would not speak, and the whole fight would repeat itself. Hia caught his eye.

"Boon?" Hia said.

A pause. Then, Ah Boon nodded cautiously. It was enough. Uncle put out his smoldering cigarette. He would go to the provision store, he announced gruffly. He stalked out the front door like a wounded animal. As soon as he was gone, the tension eased, and the wind came whistling through the windows, as if the house itself were releasing its breath. A crisis had been averted, at least for now. Ma took the bundle of clothes to the back of the house to soak in soap and water.

Chapter Twenty-Four

The morning of his first day at the CC, Ah Boon returned to find a hive of activity. Shirtless workers, their backs slicked with sweat, were setting up a platform by the entrance. Men unloaded waxy plants from shiny lorries, hammered poles into the ground, unrolled banners that billowed unruly as they tried to nail them to the walls. Ah Boon watched four workers unfurl an enormous national flag, eight meters across at least, twice the height of a man. With a system of pulleys and cinches, they raised the flag behind the wooden stage, stretching it taut as a giant sail. An expanse of red and white, the slim crescent smile beside a pentagon of stars. The flag had been adopted only a little over a year ago, after the nation's first significant strides toward self-governance, and still felt flimsy, unreal. The little white silhouettes against bright red, like holes cut out of a fiery sky.

Then Natalie appeared, holding a clipboard and pen.

"Ah Boon," she said warmly.

"Can I help? Should I start with the stage?" he said, gesturing at the workers.

A look of confusion came over her. Ah Boon's ears burned. Already he had made a mistake, had failed to grasp some subtlety of CC work.

Then Natalie laughed. It was a miraculous sound, high and clear, without the slightest hint of mockery in it. It was a laugh that included and reassured him.

"With the setup? Of course not. That's what we hired them for." She said *them* with a tilt of the chin. Ah Boon wondered at the *us* implied in that minuscule movement.

"Then how can I help?" he asked.

Natalie and this place made him want to be useful. It was the calm sense of purpose, the feeling of having access to some higher design, some elaborate scheme in which everything had its rationale and place. It was soothing, seductive, easy. To be a whirring cog in an elegant machine struck Ah Boon as a not undesirable fate. This was different from middle school, he felt, this was something he could be good at.

The drinks delivery was meant to be there hours ago, Natalie said now. And still no sign of the supplier. They needed to fill those coolers—she pointed at the crates packed with ice, sitting in the shade—for the lunch reception in two hours. In the middle of this explanation, her attention was diverted by a delivery of potted plants. Shiny palms, delicate ferns, obscene birds of paradise. She began ordering the deliverymen about, telling them where in front of the stage the pots should go. Ah Boon nodded; he would handle the drinks situation. As he left she handed him a stack of flyers to pass out to the kampong.

He headed to the provision store. When he got there, Swee Hong was sitting behind the worn wooden counters as he always was. Leg propped up on his chair, singlet hiked up over his hairy stomach as he fanned himself lazily with a straw fan.

"Eh! Boon!" He stopped. "Wah! Dress so nice. Your ma told us about your new job—big shot now! When you treating me to lunch?"

Ah Boon grinned. He heard the sly admiration behind Swee Hong's ribbing, saw the way his eyebrows shot up as he took in Ah Boon's shiny new shoes and starched white collar.

"Today, actually," he said, handing Swee Hong a flyer. "Today got free buffet lunch at the CC."

"Sure or not." Swee Hong peered at the flyer suspiciously. "Free? Everyone can go?"

"Everyone in the kampong," Ah Boon said. "Opening ceremony."

"Gah Men come here for what? Watching us, is it?"

Ah Boon shrugged. "All I know is got free lunch, you don't come, your loss. Also, I need three coolers of soft drinks delivered. Can or not?"

"Three! Wah, never say earlier." Swee Hong snapped his fingers at the shop assistant, a young boy of Ah Boon's nephew's age stacking boxes in a corner of the shop.

Drinks were among the highest-margin items a provision shop could sell, and three coolers the kind of business they only ever saw at the New Year and other holidays. Swee Hong, who got by selling rice and dried goods to the kampong, came to life now, pulling from shelves packets of chrysanthemum tea and soy milk, bottles of F&N and Coca-Cola, and stacking them in the middle of the floor.

"See you at lunch, okay, Boon!" he said, waving Ah Boon out of the shop without looking at him.

Outside, Ah Boon spotted Auntie Hoon in the distance, the wife of a fisherman who had known Pa well. She was coming down the road, two buckets in hand.

He cupped his hands around his mouth and shouted: "Auntie Hoon!"

She shielded her eyes from the sun, squinting from under the roof of her palm. "Ah Boon! Wah, look at you, wearing shirt and pants. Look so smart. Aiyo, but not hot ah?"

"Auntie Hoon, you like table tennis?"

She laughed as she came up to Ah Boon, and shook her head. "Auntie so old, play what? These games are for you young people."

"Please, I'm sure you can beat me easily. Look at those muscles." Ah Boon tweaked her biceps playfully, setting her off in a giggling fit. He pointed to the flyer in his hands. "Today got tournament at the CC. Free drinks, free food. You come, okay?"

Ah Boon spent the next few hours like this, walking around the kampong, cajoling anyone he saw into coming to the opening ceremony. When he was done, he walked to the kampong next door, going from house to house making small talk and handing out flyers. Eventually he made his way to the other two kampongs as well.

At the opening ceremony were an esteemed officer from the Ministry of Law, rumored to have been the youngest-ever graduate from an important law school in England; a vice chairman of the Chief Building Surveyor's Department, who spent most of the ceremony staring disapprovingly at a stray pile of tools near the stage; and several important people from the Ministry of National Development. All were dressed in white.

Behind the guests of honor were more Gah Men, and Ah Boon recognized several from the group who had been poking around the swamp. Now they carried no tape measures or clipboards, no orange flags or rolled maps, yet somehow they retained their quizzical, assessing manner. They were instruments of the ministries, the eyes and ears, but also the industrious hands, the indefatigable feet.

Behind them were more attendees from the ministries. Dressed in office clothes, these were city people used to working in tidy offices in modern buildings and the discomfort on their faces was clear. There might be newly planted carpet grass beneath their chairs, the building before them might be whitewashed brick, but still the cicadas screeched, still the sun blazed overhead and the dark, cool jungle pressed in from all sides.

Then there were the familiar faces from the kampong and the neighboring villages. Ah Boon spotted Ma, Auntie Hoon and her sons, Swee Hong and his shop boy next to them. Pak Hassan and his daughter Aminah, Sor Hong, Ah Tong, Ghim Huat, many other fishermen. Even Hia was there, and with him, Gek Huay and little Ah Huat. Uncle was nowhere to be seen.

The opening ceremony had thus far been very boring. One of the Gah Men gave a speech in English, Hokkien, and Malay, filled with highflown platitudes about independence, progress, and harmony. A multicultural, nonideological Malaya for all. The message the Gah Men were preaching was, when it came down to it, not so different from that of the union leaders. It was in the details that they differed. Which schools, for example: ministry-approved and English-language or vernacular. How those improved living standards would come about: by accommodating the West or by breaking free entirely. What kind of housing: improving people's existing homes or razing them to make room for blocks of modern flats. Each had their own vision of modernity.

Then the drums came out, and with them, the performers in their resplendent attire. Everywhere silks rustled in the morning sun. The drummers sat cross-legged on the stage, instruments cradled in the boats of their knees.

The performance was slick, the costumes dazzling. This was a far cry from the amateurish entertainments the kampong sometimes put on. A thrill of satisfaction went through Ah Boon when he looked at Ma, Hia, and little Ah Huat, all three of them clapping enthusiastically. And there in the back, whistling in appreciation, was Siok Mei. In spite of all that she and Eng Soon might think of the Gah Men, she had understood that this moment was important for Ah Boon, and she had come. Her brown arms were startling, set against the pale blue of her dress. The dress was cinched at the waist; no sign yet of the child that grew within her.

And as for Uncle not being there—Ah Boon could not live his life pandering to the ghosts Uncle saw around every corner. To equate a job at the CC with cooperating with the Jipunlang made no sense, anyone could see it. Uncle grew more fearful by the day, nursing his pain and guilt at the loss of Pa. Ah Boon was sorry for this, but felt himself growing impatient too. They had all lost Pa, all had to carry on with their lives nonetheless.

When the performance ended, applause rolled through the crowd. Even the ministry people clapped animatedly, the mosquitoes momentarily forgotten. Those from the kampong cheered and stamped their feet. As they craned their necks to look at the audience behind them, the Gah Men's faces gave way to pleasant surprise, as if they had not expected anyone to show up at all.

Afterward, they were all welcomed inside. Everything in the common room was already set up, the paddles neatly laid out, the cold drinks delivered by Swee Hong nestled in red plastic buckets filled with ice. A huge banner was strung across one empty wall. In English, Chinese, Malay, and Tamil it said WELCOME, E14, TO YOUR COMMUNITY CENTER!

When the familiar faces began streaming into the room, Ah Boon offered packets of cold Milo and pulled up chairs for them. He signed Hia up as the first contestant in the Ping-Pong round robin. More people arrived. Ah Boon rushed from person to person, cradling packets of drinks in the crooks of his elbows, scribbling down names for the tournament. Soon all the slots were filled and he was having to turn people away, but no one seemed to mind. Everyone milled about; grandparents took up spots in front of the television set, marveling at the wonder that was the afternoon news. The electric fans whirled busily overhead.

Someone touched the small of his back. It was Natalie, her shirt perfectly crisp, her small nose a little shiny from the heat. He caught a whiff of her soap, a synthetic, powdery scent.

"You did such a wonderful job, Ah Boon," she said.

He flushed at the thought of her delicate fingers on his damp, sweaty shirt. Before he could respond, Siok Mei came up to him, dragging her uncle by the elbow.

"Boon!" she exclaimed. "Uncle, remember Ah Boon?"

"Yes, yes," her uncle said, a smile warming his face. "Wah, Boon! Working for Gah Men these days? Fishing how?"

"Give up for now," Ah Boon said.

"Faster get married and have a son of your own! Then problem solved!" Siok Mei's uncle erupted into laughter.

"I tell him so many times already!" Here was Ma, a packet of iced tea in one hand, Hia by her side.

Ah Boon smiled along. He was used to such teasing; his own relatives were devoted to the conversation topic of when he would finally settle down and produce offspring. He wanted to ask Siok Mei how she was, both wanted and did not want to know how the pregnancy was progressing. He tried to catch her eye, but there were too many people. She was busy chatting with her uncle and did not see. So Ah Boon turned to Ma.

"Everything okay?" Ah Boon asked.

She rubbed his shoulder proudly. "Don't worry about your ma. I see you are busy."

"Nice lunch," Hia said. Little Ah Huat stood by him, chewing on an oily stick of satay. "Very nice!" he echoed.

Natalie was still standing there, her hands patiently clasped behind her back. Siok Mei stretched a hand out to her.

"I'm Siok Mei, Ah Boon's childhood friend," she said.

"A pleasure," Natalie said.

The two women shook hands. They were of similar heights, and from behind might easily have been mistaken for each other.

"Mei! There you are. Here, bandung, your favorite."

Eng Soon approached with a cup of pink bandung in each hand. Siok Mei accepted the drink gratefully, commenting on how warm it was in the CC building—Ah Boon flinched, as if the inadequacy of the over-head fans was his personal responsibility—and gulping down the cold, sweet liquid with her usual appetite. Eng Soon gave Ah Boon a stiff nod.

"Nice party," he said. "Gah Men pay for this?"

The air crackled with awkwardness. A sour taste rose in Ah Boon's throat; the chemical sweetness of the Fanta Orange he'd drunk earlier lingered. But before he could respond, Natalie spoke.

"Not at all," she said pleasantly. "The CCs are run with taxpayers' money, and we take that responsibility very seriously. Every cent we get from the central budget goes toward improving the lives of the residents we serve."

Eng Soon's face darkened. Yet Natalie had addressed him so politely that to ignore her, Gah Woman or otherwise, would make him look like a brute. He nodded again, curtly.

Everywhere, people were talking, smiling, laughing. The lunch was a success. The CC, so empty and sterile the first time Ah Boon had walked into it, was filled with noise and bodies and good cheer. And he had done that; he was responsible for it. He'd walked into the CC's doors and pop-ulated it with all the people who made up his life. Not since the islands had been discovered had they all come together so cheerfully, with such a glowing sense of the future.

And yet Ah Boon was uneasy. He felt the urge to chase them all out. To snatch the Milo packets and Fanta cans from their sweaty palms, to confiscate the table tennis paddles and return them, neatly stacked, to their baskets, to wipe the sand and mud trekked in by his boisterous neighbors from the pristine floors.

Natalie smiled brightly and left the group to mingle with others in the crowd. Her ponytail swayed gently as she walked away, and there it was, announcing itself faintly, unobtrusively: the possibility of a different life.

Chapter Twenty-Five

Aside from Ah Boon and Natalie, the CC had two other employees, both women his mother's age, who treated Ah Boon with the indulgent forbearance of distant aunts. When he called them Madam Kim, Madam Hock, they insisted he call them auntie, and so he did. Neither was from the kampong, or even nearby; instead they commuted an hour daily from their homes in the city. They had been employed at other CCs prior to this one, though he did not quite understand why they had moved.

"Reorganization," Auntie Kim said, enunciating each syllable slowly, as if Ah Boon were an English teacher testing her vocabulary.

"Reorganization," Auntie Hock echoed, nodding sagely.

As far as he could tell, their jobs involved pointing passersby to the modern toilet at the back of the building. They spent much of their days flipping through the collection of newspapers in the reading lounge, dusting the seats in front of the TV, and filing forms that they said Ah Boon need not worry himself with.

Natalie sat at a desk in the farthest corner of their office, half of it taken up by a large flat calendar, the squares containing her elegant cursive protected by a sheet of matte plastic. From time to time, she would flip up the plastic cover to write something down, then carefully smooth it over the paper again when she was done. The other half of the desk was occupied by a typewriter, shiny and black as an expensive car. Natalie used it rarely, only to draft the occasional official-looking documents—Ah Boon learned to call them "memos"—that she diligently reread, folded, and placed into envelopes to be licked and stamped. Ah Boon gathered that these went to Mr. Yik, or some other senior Gah Men interested in the development of CC E14.

Gradually the CC was absorbed into the daily rhythms of kampong life, as a foreign sapling might grow intertwined with resident root systems of an old swamp. It was Ah Boon who made this happen; without him, the building would have stood apart, pristine and sullen, its hallways empty, echoing only with the footsteps of Natalie's shiny leather shoes. But with Ah Boon came the rest of the kampong.

First little Ah Huat after school each day, groups of classmates following close, making playgrounds of the sofas and spinning table tennis paddles on their round heads. Then Auntie Hoon, along with other women of Ma's age who came with small pails to discreetly collect water from the bathroom taps. A rumor, it seemed, was going around that the water piped into the CC was cleaner than that in the kampong standpipe or the wells, given that the Gah Men drank from it themselves. Aminah and other women from the neighboring kampong came with their grandchildren in tow, making themselves comfortable on the cushy leather sofas, arguing over television channels as toddlers clambered over their laps. Soon, Swee Hong, Ah Tong, and Ghim Huat moved their chess games to the common room, bringing with them little tin cans of inky coffee and milky tea that they bought from the street vendor who'd set up shop right outside the CC's doors.

Things could have been said to be going very well indeed, if it were not for the unpleasantness with Uncle. Uncle, who had refused to set foot in the CC. From time to time, he could be seen standing in the shade of the trees some way off from the building, surveilling its exterior as if planning something. But late one morning, he finally crossed its threshold, Hia at his side.

"Uncle, Hia," Ah Boon greeted them with a wide smile.

Perhaps the good-natured ribbing of all his friends had finally convinced Uncle that the CC was nothing to be feared.

"Boon," Uncle said.

He looked around cautiously. Ah Boon saw him take in the overhead electric lights, the brightly painted mural, the clean glass windows.

"Not so bad, right?" Ah Boon said.

Uncle allowed himself a small smile. "Ah Tong and Swee Hong here?" he asked.

"In the common room. That way."

Uncle and Hia barreled down the hallway. Ah Boon could not help but wince at the muddy footprints they left on the smooth cement floor. The order he'd established in the CC, the quiet authority he enjoyed, all of it vanished as soon as Uncle and Hia stepped in. He had hoped for this moment for so long, but their large, unruly presence now made Ah Boon's nerves grow tight.

A raucous round of greetings was taking place in the common room. Backs were slapped, hands shaken. Uncle began to regale Swee Hong and Ah Tong with a story—Ah Boon gathered that a fight had broken out in the market that morning, a certain butcher taking offense at a certain fishmonger for the way he held his knife—and soon expletives were flying, crude jokes about the fishmonger's attractive, much younger wife, bets placed on whether the fight would resume the next day and who would win if it did.

It was a good thing, Ah Boon told himself. Uncle was having a good time with his friends in the CC. Uncle was no longer looking around every corner for invisible enemies out to get him.

Uncle placed one grimy, dirt-encrusted hand on the leather sofa. Hia casually wiped his boots on the leg of a chair.

Ah Boon cleared his throat, and the men turned to him. Once, as a child, his face would have flushed, his hands would have grown cold. Now, though, he merely coughed again, and then, in a calm voice, asked Uncle and Hia if they could please wash their boots at the standpipe outside the building before coming back in.

"Wash? Wash for what?" Uncle said. He had been telling a joke when Ah Boon interrupted, and his face was filled with an odd mix of stalled laughter and irritation.

"Auntie Kim works very hard to keep the floors clean," Ah Boon said. "So we ask that people wipe their shoes outside before coming in."

Auntie Kim did mop the floor perfunctorily every two weeks, but it was Ah Boon who obsessively swept and polished each evening before he went home.

"Huh? What you talking about?" Uncle said.

Ah Boon paused. "Five minutes only. Just go wash, then come back."

The other men were quiet. Finally, Swee Hong spoke. "Aiya, listen to him, faster go, faster come back, Leong!"

Once, Ah Boon thought, Swee Hong would have laughed in his face, treated him like a boy who could be ignored. But here, here in this brightly lit space that smelled of soap and hot coffee, with the television murmuring in the background, the electric fans squeaking overhead, Swee Hong was on his side.

Uncle turned, very slowly, to look at Swee Hong. He looked him up and down, taking in his clean cotton shirt, his bony shins, his large, shiny-palmed hands. They had known each other a long time, but he looked at him now as if they had never met before. Then, slowly, he turned and left. Hia shook his head silently, and went after him.

They were quiet. Ah Boon strained for the sound of running water, but all he could hear was the squeaking of the overhead fan. Uncle was not coming back. A hot shame coursed through him. Why had he insisted? Why not let Uncle do as he wished? Now the rift would never be healed. But the mud on the floor still irked him, and now that Uncle was gone, the CC felt peaceful again, restored to its prior balance.

"Aiya, don't worry about him," Swee Hong said. "Old men, always grumpy. Don't worry, okay, boy?"

Ah Boon forced a smile and a nod, urging them to go back to their game of chess. Then he got the bucket and mop and cleaned the mud from the floors.

Ah Boon's new job, in itself, was not difficult. In the beginning, he mainly oversaw the CC's facilities. In a large brown exercise book, not unlike the notebooks of his childhood, he dated and timed pages; one was allowed to book facilities in forty-five-minute blocks. Ah Boon was proud of the system he had devised. He loved the clean, smooth pages of the notebook, the round regularity of numbers in his own hand. He looked forward to filling those pages with names, creating a record of the comings and goings of the kampong he called home.

But the kampong did not take to the reservation system. The television area was in particularly high demand, and Ah Boon was frequently required to personally break up disagreements between older kampong members as to whose turn it was to sit where, and which of the three channels the set would be tuned to. Those who showed up each day to watch the news either did not remember or did not want to abide by the rule of Ah Boon's reservations book, nodding absently each time he reminded them they were required to sign in and promptly forgetting the next day.

So the book remained empty. He began filling it in himself whenever someone showed up. He marked crosses next to the time slots that were left blank. Life slipped by in forty-five-minute blocks; the passage of time seemed less diffuse, more graspable. The disarrayed world resolved into a gridded clarity.

And outside the kampong, the country was, once again, in disarray. The question of independence via merger with the Federation of Malaya had split the Gah Men in two; the union members, with whom the English-educated had strategically aligned themselves, had been denounced as extreme leftists and expelled from the party in a dramatic vote.

Ah Boon was crossing off the boxes on the page labeled *13 August, 1961*, some months after the opening ceremony, when Siok Mei appeared unexpectedly at the CC.

A furtive electricity seemed to radiate off her body; he saw her gaze dart again and again to the lights overhead, the mural on the wall, Natalie at her desk. There was a shine to her eyes, a quickness to her wrists, as she gestured to Ah Boon to join her in the doorway. It was a look he knew well. She was burning up inside. Something had happened, and whatever it was was knocking about within her, and she had come to Ah Boon to let it out.

"Mei," he said.

He wanted to be formal with her, now that they were in the CC, a realm where he had responsibilities and a small amount of authority— but found that he could not. Why did she come back to him again and again? He reached out and lightly touched her elbow.

"Boon," she said. "You must come."

It was a historic moment, she went on. The union leaders, betrayed by the Gah Men, were starting their own political party to question the terms of the merger and challenge the next election. There was to be a rally at the Happy World Stadium, thousands of people would be there, many of their old classmates and comrades. She knew he'd said he'd given it all up, but wasn't he here—she gestured at the CC all around them—because he wanted to serve his community, serve his people?

Siok Mei's voice was low and urgent. She leaned so close that he could feel her hot, feverish breath on his face. Here it was again, the invisible tide that always drew them back together. And whether or not she was aware of it, Siok Mei felt it too. Her words spoke of the unions and the Gah Men, but Ah Boon could sense, in the force of her gaze, the warm hum of her voice, that more than politics had brought her to him.

As she talked, Ah Boon's gaze drifted over the floor of the CC, which, despite Auntie Hock's best efforts with the broom that was leaning in one corner, was always inexplicably covered in a fine layer of sand. She was convinced it was the children who brought it in, hiding handfuls of it in their pockets to sprinkle when she wasn't looking. Ah Boon watched them closely but never saw any child do this. He'd come upon small heaps of it in unlikely corners: the bathroom far from the entrance, the back of a filing cabinet, the kitchen pantry sink. Each time, he brushed it up with a small dustpan, but before long the heaps would reappear, as mute and inexplicable as the islands themselves.

Natalie was typing a new memo, and suddenly the metallic clack of her typewriter keys became the chatter of a particular type of bird, hidden in the thick canopy of a certain pristine, untouched vegetation. The silence of the CC thickened with sound: the trilling of insects, the rustle of palm fronds, the distant wash of waves. The excited shouts and cries of men making their way through an unknown wilderness. His father, swinging a piece of driftwood in his hand, pointing out a fruit-laden tree here, a bright-billed bird there. He and Siok Mei. A boulder, a rubber seed clasped in the palm.

"I can't go," Ah Boon said.

"What? Why? You want to stay here? Stay here for what?"

"Don't," he said tensely.

"Don't what?"

"You know. You cannot just—" Ah Boon stopped. *Walk in here and ask me to open myself up all over again*, he thought, but did not say.

Siok Mei opened her mouth to protest, but a hard look crossed her face, and she closed it again. A long silence passed.

"But I want you there," she burst out. "I want you to come. It's important."

"For who? Important for who?"

For me, he wanted her to say. And for a moment her mask of calm seemed to slip, a whisper of old emotion flickered over her face. But then her hand went to her hard belly, protectively, as if to defend from the threat of him. The curve, and the sinuous line—so reminiscent of a hill he had once seen, on an island that vanished and reappeared.

"It's important," she repeated. "Will you come?"

"I work here now."

He did not belong in her world, she knew it. And he could not stay forever a fisherman. The country was changing, new lives were possible, why should he not step into one of them?

Siok Mei was shaking her head dismissively.

"Maybe," Ah Boon said, "it's not all bad. The Gah Men are building new homes for the people. They're making schools free. How is that bad?"

Siok Mei clicked her tongue scornfully.

"No, really, tell me," Ah Boon said. "How?"

"The state arises where, when, and insofar as class antagonism cannot be reconciled," Siok Mei replied, an obstinate jut to her chin.

"What?"

"Lenin. Have you forgotten all your reading? Those in power, the petit bourgeois, the Gah Men! They might pretend to be socialists—to be on the side of the people—might pretend that the state is an organ for the reconciliation of classes. But it is not. We know this. It is always an organ of class rule, always an organ for the oppression of one class by another. The creation of 'order,' legalizing and perpetuating oppression by moderating the conflict between classes—"

"Stop. Just—what does Lenin have to do with anything?"

What he wanted to say was: What did Lenin have to do with the two of them?

Ah Boon noticed he still had his hand on her elbow. She pulled away from him, wrapping her arms around herself. The hurt on her face went straight to his heart. Her dark, shiny eyes, deep as pools, made him want to fall into them, as they always did. But he couldn't, he couldn't.

She blinked once, twice, rapidly.

"Okay," she said at last. Then she sighed, long and slow, the sound of it going through him like a cold, hard wind.

Chapter Twenty-Six

Natalie was surprised when a few days later, Ah Boon came to her and asked if she might teach him to type. She would not, of course, for she was not one to fuss over her employees. But the CC would be happy to sponsor his night school fees with a training grant, should he wish.

Ah Boon thanked her. "The grant—can it cover night school for English classes?" he asked hesitantly.

This was even more surprising. Ah Boon, like many other Chinese-educated employees, had made no mention of English classes in the months since her initial suggestion. She had not insisted; he was not her responsibility. Yet the earnest look on his face now suggested he had been mulling over it for a while, perhaps taking time to pluck up the courage to ask.

"I'm sure that can be arranged," she said.

Still he looked troubled.

"Anything else?" she asked.

"I haven't been to school in a long time," Ah Boon said slowly. "Maybe—maybe it's not a good idea."

Natalie looked him up and down. His bony workman's hands were gathered in a nervous knot at his stomach. His leather shoes, as always, were carefully polished, not a speck to be found on them despite the dirt trail she knew he took each day. She wondered if he cleaned them upon getting to the CC every morning. It did not seem unlikely, based on what she knew of the man.

There was a seriousness about Ah Boon, one lacking among the men who courted her at parties thrown by her sisters, the ones who offered her trinkets of jewelry and insisted on walking her home. Ah Boon did not have opinions on the latest movies or glib jokes about mutual acquaintances. He did not drink beer or smoke, did not seem to understand the concept of leisure at all. How different he was from the men she had known in her life. Even her coworkers at the ministry, who, for all the education and privileges of their class, seemed somehow flimsy and insubstantial, as if nothing truly mattered to them. Everything, it felt like, mattered to Ah Boon.

"I think you'll do very well. You're already ahead of most," Natalie said to Ah Boon, as kindly as she could.

Ah Boon clicked his tongue, fending off the compliment. But she saw that he seemed to glow faintly with her approval. Giving a determined nod, he said he would enroll in the class that very afternoon.

Who was Natalie? English-educated, Straits Chinese. Unlike Ah Boon, whose grandparents had come over from the Mainland just decades ago, her family was descended from merchants who settled in the region centuries before, had assimilated with the local community and prospered under the Ang Mohs. Most recently, the daughter of a respectable rubber plantation owner in the north of the island. In some ways, her childhood was not that different from Ah Boon's. She, too, had grown up with the hollow cries of morning birds and spent her early years running barefoot through the trees, touching her fingers to the sunlight captured in drops of dew on waxy leaves. Her father had taught her to tap rubber at the age of five and she'd loved the plantation, felt tender for every manacled red ant, every wet, fertile pile of rotting leaves.

"Does it hurt them?" she'd asked her father the first time she watched him cut into the tree bark. It was some hours before sunrise, and the morning was cool and dark. Natalie held the gas lamp as he worked the hooked knife, stripping the bark back in a clean, diagonal line.

"Not at all," her father said.

"It looks like they're bleeding," she said, watching worriedly as the drops of white sap began to gather, then ooze slowly down the cut made in the bark, into the metal collecting cup. Some latex dribbled down the side of the tree, missing the cup entirely.

"We must be careful not to anthropomorphize," he answered slowly. He reached out and adjusted the cup, correcting the drip.

"Anthropo—" Natalie rubbed her eyes with one hand, the gas lamp swaying in the other.

"To treat everything like it is human," he said, reaching out and taking the lamp from her.

"But why not? 'Do unto others as you would have them do unto you,'" she recited, the oft-repeated words from catechism rolling off her tongue almost involuntarily.

Her father touched one finger to her chin.

"'Then God blessed them,'" he said. "'And God said to them: Be fruitful and multiply; fill the earth and subdue it; have dominion over the fish of the sea, over the birds of the air, and over every living thing that moves on the earth.'"

Natalie considered this. It seemed frightening that human beings should have so much power. Yet was it not true that they routinely organized the trees into rows and columns, stripping their bark for the sap they needed? There was a beauty in this as well, the comforting thought that every being had its place and purpose, and humans were put in charge—by God himself—of it all. Besides, she took whatever her father said to be true, and believed it must be so.

But years later, when the plantation had been lost after a series of wildfires and her father, too old or too unwilling to take up a new trade, descended into a lackadaisical drunkenness, Natalie could not help but wonder if it was the trees' revenge. It pained her especially to see him, whose every word she'd once taken as gospel, turn brooding and unpredictable, roaming the house like an old, hurt dog. She had one brother and five sisters, a large Catholic family that had felt prosperous and rowdy in better days. But after the plantation burned and her father turned to drink, their single-story bungalow out in the quiet of the countryside began to feel oppressive, weighted with her mother's unspoken bitterness, her father's volatility, her siblings' sniping and clamoring for their share of the family's nest egg before it all disappeared.

She began avoiding the plantation, instead spending her afternoons staying late at school, helping the nuns with errands and chores. Gradually Natalie became one of their favorite students, acquiring a reputation for studiousness that had little to do with her actual schoolwork. It was the nuns who pushed her parents to allow Natalie to continue on, studying for the A Levels with a private tutor.

So when her exams were done and she'd landed her job as a junior Gah Woman, Natalie moved out. She took a room in a boardinghouse in the city, an unthinkable move for a young woman from a family like theirs. Her mother went white with fury when she found out, and wouldn't speak to Natalie up till the day she left the house with a satchel containing all her belongings.

"I'll see you this weekend for lunch, Ma," Natalie had said from the door, trying to keep her voice cheery even as the sting of tears threatened.

Her mother did not turn from the kitchen table. As far as she was concerned, daughters did not leave their mothers without being married or impoverished. Natalie was neither. She had been allowed to learn typing and French, and this was where it had gotten them: a daughter who wanted to go live by herself in the city—at a *boardinghouse*, of all places, shut up with all sorts of foreigners and dubious characters—and to work for the Gah Men. Would the Gah Men help her find a respectable husband? Would the Gah Men restore the family's fortune, grow trees anew on the blackened, ashen soil?

Thus her mother did not turn to say goodbye to Natalie as she left. Neither did she speak a word to her when she returned at the weekend for lunch, despite the exhortations of her other children and her drunken, reduced husband. Slowly, Natalie's visits decreased in frequency.

Why had she done it? Broken her mother's heart, insulted her father, abandoned her siblings? There were other options. A job in the uncle's bank, counting money as a teller or taking minutes as a secretary. An assistant in an elegant department store, where the Ang Mohs shopped. Perhaps even a schoolteacher for young children, if she was lucky. The easiest option, of course, would have been to get married; her two eldest sisters had already been paired up with promising young businessmen for not inconsiderable bride prices, and had lives of leisure to look forward to.

It was not that Natalie cared for politics. What the Gah Men were doing, however, she did not see as politics. Swaths of jungle being cleared, wretched housing tenements evacuated, triads and hooligans rounded up and imprisoned, primary education standardized and made free—how was this mere politics? She'd witnessed entire mosquito-infested swamps filled and made useful. She'd seen forests of sparkling new flats that had sprung up all over the island in the past few years. She'd been inside their neat, clean interiors, admired the modern conveniences of running water and electric lights for all. *Fill the earth and subdue it.* It struck her that this new age the Gah Men were ushering in was to be the island's destiny. And it was a destiny she wanted to be a part of.

When Natalie started work as a Gah Woman, she sent money back through her sisters when she met them for coffee, and thus it was in the bustle and steam of the coffee shop next to her gleaming gray office building that she first heard about her mother's sudden illness. Natalie's sisters told her that their mother had taken to bed, complaining of dizziness—nothing to worry about, she'd insisted, as usual—and fallen into a deep sleep, waking, only occasionally, in a confused and disoriented state. She'd mistaken Natalie's second sister for her own mother, her husband for her brother, tried to get up to hide in a wardrobe when she'd heard a knock at the door she was convinced was the Jipunlang, come again to take her away.

Her sisters paused at this point in the story.

"Aiya, you know Ma," her oldest sister said. "She will be okay."

It was clear to all of them that she would not. An awkward silence descended, and Natalie's sisters pursed their lips, seeming to regret having brought up the topic at all.

Natalie's eyes prickled with tears, and she tried to focus on the shopkeeper making coffee behind the counter. A metal cup in each hand, her arms rose and fell, rose and fell. Natalie forced her eyes to follow the dark arc of liquid being pulled between the cups. The conversation moved on to the men her sisters had been most recently seeing. One of them was going out with a colleague of Natalie's, a promising young Gah Man with the smooth face of a shark, who was widely seen as a rising star within the Ministry of National Development. The sister was describing the dress he'd most recently bought her when Natalie interrupted.

"Does she talk about me?" she said.

"Who?"

"Ma." The word pained her to say, not having said it for so long.

Her sisters looked at one another, visibly discomfited. Over the past years, they had continued to mention Ma—her various ailments, opinions, interactions with neighbors—to Natalie as a matter of loyalty. To show Natalie that while they loved her, it did not mean they approved of her behavior or her break with their parents. And it was true that they often expressed envy of her independence, though quickly caveated that they could never leave Pa and Ma in the same way, for who would look after them if they did? The implication being: not Natalie. Regardless, this was never spoken of in the open.

Now a silent rule had been broken. The possibility of a real conversation loomed—the unspoken envy and resentment that had simmered all these years, the fact that yes, every morning since she had fallen ill, Ma had asked for Natalie, and they were forced to lie, to say that she had gone out to the market and would be back in a few hours, just to calm Ma until she forgot again. The sisters looked at one another, examined their nails, then finally met Natalie's gaze.

"No," they said. "She doesn't talk about you."

So it was that Natalie did not rush to her mother's side, but instead waited, and in the waiting, her mother's condition worsened significantly. It was her father, with the hangdog look of a newly sober man, who showed up in the dusty entrance of the boardinghouse some weeks later.

"You better come home," he said.

Curious faces of other boardinghouse residents lined the hallway as she and her father left. Natalie was not known to have a family at all—it was widely believed she was an orphan—and so who was this older man, showing up in the middle of the night, claiming to be a relative? Or if he was indeed her father, come to take her to see an ailing mother, then what kind of daughter was she to have left them behind? The late hour was forgotten, and the residents stayed gossiping in the hallway long after Natalie and her father had left the premises, the round face of the moon staring down upon them through a cracked window.

When Natalie got home, the old house with its painted white bricks appeared to her as a small glowing thing in the moonlight. Without her father's care, the land that had once been their rubber plantation had been left to grow wild, everywhere burned stumps of trees and piles of blackened debris with moss grown over. Their house was like a lighthouse in a wasteland, and now, with Ma on the brink, even that light was weakened and flickering.

Ma was asleep when Natalie entered the room, Pa following close behind her. She noticed absently that Pa had a new, unfamiliar smell: that of spiced soap, a clean smell, a wholesome one. Gone was the metal tang of whiskey on his breath, the wheaty whiff of beer rising from his skin. Ma's illness seemed to have shocked him out of his stupor. The whole night had taken on a dreamlike haze. Her sisters, standing in their nightgowns by the wooden bed where her mother lay. Her father, hands clasped, all minty-fresh breath and clean clothes—who was this man?

And then her mother. Shrunken, small, more the doll of an old lady than the mother she had so loved and resented. Natalie thought of the nights when she had climbed into that very bed as a girl, running from nightmares or sleeplessness or just plain irrational fear. She remembered the warm comfort of her mother's body, and it occurred to her that perhaps Ma would want the same now. So she took her shoes off, peeled back the covers, and got in beside her.

"I'll sleep here tonight," she said, waving away her sisters and father.

They looked uneasy but also relieved, for they had kept vigil the past week and were all exhausted by now. One by one her family disappeared. Natalie put out the gas lamp by the bed and settled back into the pillows, listening to her sisters' familiar footsteps moving through the house. She drew the covers over herself and turned toward Ma. The bed was warm, as it had been the times she'd crawled into it as a child. Ma's breathing was deep and slow, unlabored. Closing her eyes, adult Natalie and girl Natalie merged into one, and she felt that Ma was the one keeping her safe, rather than the other way around. The boundaries between past and present were so porous that one was always leaking into the other, she might be a five-year-old all over again—this was Natalie's last thought before falling into a deep, dreamless sleep.

When she woke in the morning, the bed was cold. Dust motes spun in the weak wash of sun coming in through the curtains. Outside, a koel bird cried, the sharp, mournful sound of it piercing the heavy air in the room. But next to Natalie there was no sound or movement. An unexpected grief surged up inside her. Her own breathing quickened, as if to compensate for the lack of it coming from her mother's still body. She squeezed her eyes and fists shut, counting from one to ten, as her father had taught her to do when waking from a nightmare in the dark.

She squeezed and counted and breathed, yet the mother beside her stayed dead. The mother beside her had never looked upon her face one last time, had never forgiven her for what she had done, told her she loved her nonetheless.

Finally, after what felt like a long time had passed, Natalie opened her eyes again. Her pillow was wet, but her face was now dry. She sat up and looked down at Ma. She appeared exactly as she had the night before, but Natalie knew that if she reached out to touch her face, it would be cold. Wanting to preserve the memory of her mother's warmth, she did not touch her again.

By the time Natalie had attained the position of senior coordinating officer for the assessment and pilot phases of the Great Reclamation Project, she had drained herself of sentimentality, pushed any guilt or resentment deep beneath the topsoil of her soul, where it fossilized, became an artifact that she would, decades later, dig up to examine in the cold light of day. For now, however, as Ah Boon's superior and newly appointed head of the E14 district, her job was to ensure the project go as smoothly as possible.

It was a job she had earned with a decade of dedicated work in various ministries—three years in Trade and Industry as a fresh graduate, three in Law, then the remaining in National Development, where she was now—and one that had the potential to catapult her to the glittering ranks of those earmarked for future leadership. At present she was well regarded, certainly above average for her employment grade, but in the words of her late mother, "nothing to write home about." The reclamation project was her big break. If all went well with the assessment and pilot phases, this would kick-start a ten-year-long plan to reclaim more than a thousand acres along the southeast coast, with a budget of over fifty million dollars.

One of the senior Gah Men's biggest fears for the Great Reclamation Project, she'd learned through the ministry grapevine, was the risk of public backlash. It was a delicate affair, this making of land from sea. It was less controversial than some of the other urban renewal efforts: the relocation of slum residents into flats, for instance, wasn't always easy. Those residents' living conditions were precarious at best, dangerous at worst. Take the fires that often broke out—charcoal stoves being common in the densely packed wood-structure buildings—and were then blamed on the Gah Men as ploys to forcibly resettle thousands. The hearts and minds of the people were at stake; such controversies must be avoided at all costs.

That was the beauty of the reclamation project. No land would have to be acquired, no residents resettled. The people who would be negatively affected were mainly upper-middle-class business owners who had made their homes in luxurious bungalows, losing their seafront views. The risk of fallout, if any, was minimal, and could be easily reframed in a populist light.

With one small snag—the four fishing settlements that had plied the waters of the very coast that would soon be reinforced and extended during the pilot phase. The kampongs had been there for decades. Technically many of the residents could be classed as squatters, for they did not possess the title deeds that official ownership under law demanded. But the Gah Men knew how such technicalities, while legally enforceable, were rarely understood by the people. And it was always better, as an early supervisor of hers had once said, to stroke the mule's mane in the direction that hair grew.

Thus the master plan was drawn up such that the kampongs would be left untouched. They were set far back enough from the shore that the pilot phase of the work could take place without resettling the villagers. This was something that Natalie knew Mr. Yik felt strongly about, concerned as he was about the potential for public backlash. The kampong's livelihood might be strained, as the project would involve the dredging of fertile seabed, intrusive conveyor belts to move rocks and dirt, machinery to drive concrete piles deep underwater and into the sand. Should the project be successful, the new land would be a miracle of technology, testament to the Gah Men's foresight, but it would also leave the kampongs stranded, miles away from the sea that its residents plied as their livelihood. Eventually—once the pilot phase had proven successful and the project was approved to move ahead—they would all have to be resettled. By then the merit of the endeavor would be undeniable, the benefits irrefutable to all.

No document declared it as such, no Gah Man would have gone on record saying so, but it was here that the community centers came in. The CCs were conceived as a way to build national identity and patriotism in a fledgling island state hurtling toward independence, one with disparate racial groups and no clear or unified history to call its own. Officially the centers provided citizens with services such as access to senior Gah Men, information and support on nutrition and hygiene, sports facilities, language classes. Unofficially, the CCs were the Gah Men's strongest tool in their mission of lifting the island out of its wretched state. Particularly in rural areas, such as E14, the CCs were beacons of modernity, harbingers of the bright future.

Any Gah Man or Woman worth their salt knew what the CCs stood for, what they were meant to do. Just as Siok Mei knew what expression she should adopt as she shouted slogans at heated protests (earnest, passionate, eyes up), what questions she should urgently, publicly debate (could democratic socialism ever be an acceptable compromise for true communists?), Natalie knew, without being told, what attitude she should cultivate as she went about her work (one of calm, considered pragmatism), what emotions were appropriate (a certain pious optimism), which causes she should champion (above all, cultivating among the people a trust and loving respect for the Gah Men).

By the time Natalie found herself in charge of CC E14, she had led two different resettlement efforts, one a small slum of zinc and wooden sheds barely held up by rusting nails, the other a group of forty or so squatters, who had lived in dangerously cramped conditions within the subdivided warren of a single shophouse. All had been placed into clean, if basic, one-bedroom flats. These early flats had communal toilets and kitchens but were built of solid brick and cement, were sanitary and safe, kept the monsoon rain out, provided clean running water that would not give one fever or diarrhea. Those resettled were happy. There were complaints, of course; the occasional resident remarking that they missed being able to keep ducks and pigs, or that the flats were too hot and did not let in sufficient wind, or of loneliness. Did they want to go back to their old insecure habitations? When asked, the vast majority of them said no. And the minority that did—well. One couldn't hope to please everyone; it was called the greater good for a reason.

Thus the thought that occurred to Natalie while she was working late one evening at the CC, with only Ah Boon left in the office, was not as unreasonable as it might have seemed. She was reviewing the guidelines she'd drafted for Mr. Yik's approval—guidelines that would be issued to residents of the kampongs when the reclamation work was in progress. Certain trails and footpaths would have to be rerouted, some areas cordoned off entirely. Earplugs would be issued to deal with the noise of heavy machinery working through the night. It was a long document, including annexes and maps that delineated which areas would be blocked off when, which areas were open to foot traffic only, where bicycles were and weren't allowed.

On the whole it would be much easier if the kampongs could be convinced to move.

Natalie looked up and stretched her neck. There Ah Boon sat, bowed over his English homework, pen scratching diligently away. He was an excellent employee. He'd gone about his tasks with the air of a monk devoted to the souls of his flock. How quickly he had come to understand the mission of the CC; how valuable he'd been in advancing its cause. In him Natalie saw how she must have been when she'd first joined the Gah Men: bright-eyed and idealistic, desperate to be shown how to be part of something greater than herself. The inklings of an idea began to kindle in her mind.

Outside, the sun fizzled like an ember, the office cast in its maddening orange glow. Past the receptionist desk and the mural, she could see out through the CC's doorway to where the neat lawn was growing brown and patchy. Beyond it loomed the forest and swamp, and in the distance, a dull sliver of sea.

Chapter Twenty-Seven

The architect-planner had studied in Australia, Ah Boon was told by the man sitting next to him. He was the nation's very first architect-planner.

"CC W5," his neighbor said by way of introduction. "And you?"

"E14," Ah Boon said.

His neighbor's eyebrows lifted; a knowing look came over him, then a kind of envy.

"I've heard all about E14—"

But what his neighbor had heard about their CC, Ah Boon never found out, for at this moment the architect-planner entered the room. A small man, nearly a whole head shorter than Ah Boon, the architect-planner was not technically a Gah Man but walked with the air of one. Quick, purposeful footsteps, leading with his head and shoulders, as if his body could not quite keep up with the ferocity of his ideas.

"Welcome," the architect-planner said. "Welcome!"

The audience shifted awkwardly. Like Ah Boon, all were new CC recruits; like Ah Boon, many were uncertain why they were here. Orientation, they'd been told. Ah Boon himself had already worked at his CC for more than six months now and felt he knew his job quite well. He'd worried, when Natalie had first told him about this day, that he was being sent here because something he'd done had been found lacking. He tended to his duties as best he could—keeping the CC clean and neat, enforcing the rules around booking of facilities, and most recently, overseeing a series of cooking classes that women from the kampong took turns to lead—but worried, often, that the work was too easy. Outside, the fishermen fashioned wire cages and rattan traps, hauled boatloads of fish, went to market and came back again. Theirs was a labor one could see and feel; they harvested, they cleaned, they sold. Their work fed children all over the island.

What did Ah Boon's work achieve? It was true that the CC had become a pleasant fixture in the kampong. The residents had not had such a comfortable place in which to gather before. Often they received slick, colorful posters from "Central," as Natalie called it, that Ah Boon would carefully put up on walls. With bright graphics these posters told of their changing country: free standardized education available to all; the fight against yellow culture (pornography, drugs, and the like; city ills, not anything the kampong was concerned with); the proposed merger with Malaya, which would bring Merdeka at last. Children liked to look at the posters, even if they couldn't always read them. A new feeling had come upon the kampong in the past six months, a strange, humming energy, the sense of being swept up in a powerful tide.

"Speed. Quantity. Quality," the architect-planner said. "This is why we exist. Our colonial predecessors—well intentioned, perhaps, as they might have been—understood little of local needs, lacked ambition in solving problems, and were ultimately, for all their so-called racial superiority, inefficient and inept."

The architect-planner spoke English slowly, enunciating each word, sweeping his gaze over the audience, making eye contact with each and every one of them.

"Fifty thousand flats in five years. That is our goal. An unprecedented plan, some might say, but what we face are unprecedented challenges."

Next to Ah Boon, his neighbor was shaking his knee distractedly. Others in the audience scratched their necks or picked at scabs on their arms. Ah Boon, however, found himself transfixed. He did not understand all that the architect-planner was saying, but each word was pronounced with such thought, such deliberation, that it gave the impression of carefully composed music. Here, again, was that feeling he'd first encountered with Natalie. Here was a person with a plan.

The room dimmed. A metal box, glowing with light, was wheeled in, a transparent sheet placed on its face. Suddenly the blank wall in front of them was transformed; here was a flickering picture of a gleaming white room with ceramic-tiled walls, high painted ceilings, laminate countertops, neat cabinets. In the foreground, miraculously, was a refrigerator. No doubt the kitchen of some rich merchant or Gah Man, Ah Boon thought. Refrigerators had appeared some years before the televisions. He and Ma had attended a demonstration in an expensive department store in the city. Lining up to take their turn, each audience member would have a few seconds to thrust their hand into the refrigerator's lit interior, to marvel at its electric drone. When it had come to his turn, he'd shut his eyes and leaned his face into the miraculous rectangle, savoring the delicious, shocking cold on his hot skin. Then Ma went, jumping with surprise at the cool air. She could not believe it, she said over and over. They talked about the refrigerator all the way home. "Maybe one day you buy me one," she'd teased Ah Boon, both of them knowing it was out of the question. The devices were outrageously expensive, of course, and would work only in a house with electricity. Not even the CC had a refrigerator.

The architect-planner gestured toward the projected kitchen on the wall.

"Earlier versions of our flats relied on communal facilities, with residents sharing kitchen and toilet space. We're proud to say that with our new designs, all one- and two-room flats from now on will have their own kitchen space."

The architect-planner's mouth continued to move, but Ah Boon was no longer listening.

"Piped water, running electricity, dedicated garbage disposal—yes?"

The architect-planner was looking straight at Ah Boon. His hand was in the air. The whole room was looking straight at Ah Boon.

"That is a flat?" he said.

The architect-planner peered at Ah Boon over his dark-rimmed glasses. His lips began to purse in annoyance.

"Yes, my boy," he said. "It is."

"But—" Ah Boon's mind was racing. *How was it possible?* That was his question, but he did not know how to ask it. He stopped. "For who?"

There was a pause. Ah Boon seemed to feel the heat of the entire room's gaze. Who was this sua ku from the countryside, they seemed to think. Added to that was the embarrassment of speaking English in front of a crowd. Despite his night classes, the foreign tongue still felt awkward and unwieldy on his lips. But the gleaming kitchen was impossible. The flats were for workers, those unfortunate inhabitants of the overcrowded warrens of subdivided shophouses in the cities, the fragile structures of zinc and scavenged wood. That they could afford kitchens like this simply made no sense.

A slow smile spread across the architect-planner's face.

"For who?" he pronounced with relish. "For everyone. The demand is already high, naturally, and the wait lists grow longer each day. But eventually, if we manage to reach our building targets, we hope that every Singaporean who wants a flat will be able to have one."

Another voice in the audience piped up. How much did the flats cost to rent, the man wanted to know.

"Twenty dollars a month," said the architect-planner with great satisfaction. "Calculated to be no more than twenty percent of the average wage-earner's monthly pay."

A ripple went through the audience. A mix of exhilaration and uneasiness came over Ah Boon. Was it a hoax? What miraculous world was this? With the architect-planner's announcement came the feeling that, unbeknownst to him, a different kind of life was possible, one in which for twenty dollars a month, anyone could live in a place with a kitchen like that.

Ah Boon reminded himself that he loved his home. The large wooden house with its two bedrooms, the wet, salty breeze that went through it on monsoon evenings. The little red ants that crawled up the walls, the gaps in the wood that let in the morning light.

And then, as if by thinking he had summoned it, the picture on the wall changed to one of an ordinary kitchen not unlike his own, filled with pots and pans, kettles, basins, little tables, a charcoal fire pit. A familiar scene, much like what one would see anywhere in the kampong.

"Instead, these are the conditions of Singaporeans everywhere today. Unsanitary, unsafe. Poor, unhealthy, *dangerous* living conditions. You'll have heard about the recent slum fires. Fifty-four injured, four dead, sixteen thousand homeless."

The architect-planner's calm words came as a slap in the face. Ah Boon felt himself rearing up; this time, he forced his hand down. Their home was not unsanitary or unsafe. They had everything they needed to live, indeed, to thrive. But after the cold disbelief came an uncomfortable shame. He saw that if he spoke, the architect-planner would not believe him. The familiar kitchen scene began to transform before his eyes. He saw the blackened walls from the charcoal fire, the dirt floor, the haphaz-ard towers of old pots and pans. He saw the damp corners of the room, where slimy moss might be found, the dusty ceilings, where lizards scut-tled and left their excrement.

"Charcoal fires," the architect-planner said, aiming his silver pointer at the stove in the picture. "Pit toilets. Oil lamps, water from public standpipes. Where there are electrical circuits, many of them are old and unsafe, prone to short-circuiting."

Each word was a blow. They did not even have electricity in the kampong.

The rest of the presentation passed in a blur. More statistics were shared, a colorful land-use plan with designated zones and their abbre-viations, then pictures of completed flats and happy families moving into them. The lights went back on. The attendees were asked to stand; they would move on to the second part of the tour now.

"Not bad, right?" Ah Boon's neighbor whispered to him as they shuf-fled out of the room. "I heard the waiting list got two thousand people on it now. Fifty new sign-ups each day. Lucky I signed up last month al-ready. The wait just gets longer and longer."

"I don't see what the big deal is," Ah Boon said stiffly. "And how do you know they really look like that? Pictures only."

His neighbor sniffed. "You don't want to sign up, then don't. Shorter wait for me!"

Ah Boon fell into a brooding silence. Still his neighbor continued to stick to his side, chattering on about kitchen and bathroom fixtures as they were ushered through the building, up winding flights of stairs that took them to the sixth floor.

"You have to pay for your own linoleum, if you want," the neighbor said. "Otherwise the floors are just cement. Linoleum is best. Tiles better, but so expensive, who will put in tiles? In the picture, I know they show tiles, but nobody gets tiles."

"This way, this way, spread yourselves out, there's plenty of room," the architect-planner called.

They emerged onto a large, wide balcony. The midday sky curved bright and seamless above their heads, a shocking, empty blue, interrupted only by large rectangular shadows in the distance. After Ah Boon's eyes adjusted to being outside again, he saw that it was these shadows that the architect-planner was pointing at.

"Chup lau," the neighbor whispered into Ah Boon's ear.

"Our brand-new ten-story flats," the architect-planner announced, sweeping an arm out toward them.

The blocks were taller and wider than any Ah Boon had ever seen. Government flats were not new. But those built by the Ang Mohs in the past were ordinary buildings, single-story buildings or squat rows of flats no higher than three or four stories. With their tiled roofs and curved balconies, the old flats had often resembled school buildings or army barracks or even larger versions of the kampong CC.

These new flats—they did not look real. They looked like blown-up versions of the cardboard models that the group had been shown earlier in the presentation, cut out of white paper and decorated with green painted foam on toothpicks for trees. They looked too tall, too long, too thin. As if they might fall down if one were to push on them. Each flat was to have its own kitchen, Ah Boon remembered. Hundreds of gleaming kitchens floating high up in space, close enough to touch the sky. How many thousands, tens of thousands of people might they fit into these vertical cities? At this dizzying thought Ah Boon took hold of the railing.

"And now," the architect-planner said over the oohs and aahs of the crowd, "for the real surprise. The Sultan of Brunei was here just last month and had the pleasure of such a tour. But even he did not view the units up close, since they were unfortunately not quite complete yet. You, on the other hand!"

As the architect-planner rubbed his hands together, his watch glinted in the sun. Ah Boon drew closer, lured by the watch's pearly face, glimmering blue and pink like the inside of rare shells he'd treasured as a child. He saw that in the watch's face was a tiny window in which gears turned; that its strap was a fine, shiny brown leather, its clasp a polished gold.

"Two fifteen," the architect-planner said, pushing his wrist toward Ah Boon's face.

"Oh—I—sorry—"

"No need to apologize. We are running late."

And they were off again, streaming down the same flights of stairs that they'd come up, moving through the headquarters' airy lobby, out onto the street, where large buses awaited.

"The VIP treatment," the architect-planner said. "It's far too hot to walk."

It was ridiculous. The flats could not be more than a ten-minute walk away. Yet no one protested. The crowd moved as if in a daze; they were like children on a school trip. On the bus, housing board representatives handed out cold bottles of soft drinks. Through the window, Ah Boon watched the blocks of flats draw closer. Soon, the group was deposited at the base of one of the blocks.

"Move-in will begin as soon as next week," the architect-planner said.

Here was the broad, open space the architect-planner called the "void deck," where children could play ball and the elderly could sit and chat, shaded from the sun. Here were the green areas—still patches of fresh earth with skinny saplings swaying in the wind, for the grass had not yet arrived, but once it had it would all be much nicer—which provided respite from all the concrete. Here was the covered market, complete with electric fans for ventilation, piped water for cleaning the floors, tiled butcher blocks for vendors. Far more sanitary than the hodgepodge of street vendors that made up a typical market. Surrounding the market was shop space for rent. There would be a medicine shop, a carpenter, several provisions stores, a moneylender. All that one could desire without having to go into the city proper. The beauty of these flats, the architect-planner said, was that they were planned to function as "satellite towns"—self-sustaining communities, where residents would live, work, and play within a five-kilometer radius.

"Like a kampong," Ah Boon blurted.

"Exactly!" The architect-planner beamed. "You understand perfectly. It is that ineffable kampong spirit that we want to preserve."

Ah Boon flushed as the rest of the group turned to look at the one who understood perfectly.

"What is your name, sir?"

It took Ah Boon a second to realize that the architect-planner was speaking to him.

He cleared his throat. "Lee Ah Boon."

"And where do you live?"

"E14, sir."

"E14! Then you'll know exactly what we're talking about. That kampong spirit so prevalent along the coast."

Ah Boon nodded, even if he wasn't sure what spirit the architect-planner was referring to. He wasn't sure if he liked the architect-planner at all. Hadn't he said they lived in unsanitary, unsafe, dangerous conditions? All the while he found he could not stop looking at the architect-planner's handsome wristwatch. How much might a watch like that cost, he wondered. He had little notion of how much things cost, aside from the provisions one might get at Swee Hong's store or the firecrackers one purchased for special occasions like the Lunar New Year. He must have been told what the refrigerators cost when he and Ma had gone for that demonstration, but it was a number so unimaginable that he'd put it entirely out of his mind. Soon he found himself wondering about the architect-planner's fine Western suit as well, his polished brown shoes that were unlike any that Ah Boon had ever seen. The leather gleamed like the surface of a wet boulder worn smooth by generations of waves. And the architect-planner wore that age-old gleam on his feet as if it were something that could be bought. Such wealth was unimaginable power.

He knew what Siok Mei would think about all this. Propaganda, she'd say. Carrots dangled by the Gah Men to distract the people from the bigger picture, the bigger picture being that they were simply taking over the entire mantle of power from the Ang Mohs, complete with all its instruments of suppression and division. Jailing students and union leaders, defunding vernacular schools, and now this: uprooting ethnic communities from their homes, dispersing them into these large, characterless estates. *The state is an organ of class rule; it is the creation of "order,"* he heard her say in his mind. And if there was one thing these massive, uniform blocks with their tidy windows and perfect coats of paint conjured, it was the overwhelming sense of order.

Here it was again, that question that had started as an inconvenient tickle when he'd first begun working for the CC: What was so wrong with order? They could debate ideology all day long, but if he was honest with himself, it came down to a simple feeling of liking it. He had never been at home with the unruly sea, its habit of concealing, with treacherous silt, jagged boulders that could scrape the bottom off a boat. He had always feared the simmering, unpredictable energy of the roiling crowds at the protests that Siok Mei had so loved.

In the CC, Ah Boon had finally found a place where he seemed to fit in seamlessly; where the demands made of him were predictable, where intention flowed from the top of some vast structure down to where he stood, tacking up a new poster on the pristine blue wall of the common room. There was a plan, and he was a part of it. What greater evidence was there of that than these towering blocks before him? The state might be an organ of class rule, but if the order it created was real, if the classes could be coaxed into falling into place, if, indeed, they were *happy* to do so—then who was he to contradict them?

And often, in these times, he thought of Pa, going like a lamb to slaughter all those years ago. Had the Gah Men been in charge then, had Ah Boon been one of them, he thought, perhaps Pa might not have died.

"Big plans for E14," the architect-planner was saying. "Much depends on it."

"You mean the reclamation project, sir," Ah Boon's neighbor chimed in eagerly. "I've read all about it."

"Well, let's not get ahead of ourselves. First the testing and assessment, then the pilot project, and only *then* may begin the first phase of the reclamation. If all goes well, it will be a ten-year-long project, many new flats will be built, many more families housed—a true testament to our new government's will and efficacy."

The neighbor was nodding along so hard that the tendons in his neck strained.

"What will happen to the kampong?" Ah Boon asked.

It had been on his mind ever since Natalie had first mentioned the project. His kampong, along with the three others along the coast, would not be harmed, she'd assured him. There would be no necessity to move. Of course, the villagers were encouraged to take advantage of the priority placement program for new flats, given there might be some disruption to their day-to-day lives.

"We would never force people to move," the architect-planner said. "But surely you see the advantages."

The advantages were emphasized over and over as they continued the tour. Here was the playground, here was the government-funded school. Here was the new polyclinic that would be the first of its kind, envisioned to provide all members of the community with access to modern Western medicine at an affordable cost. "No more relying on quack sinsehs," the architect-planner said, laughing. Here were the brand-new elevators, technology imported straight from Germany, that stopped every three stories. In previous developments they stopped every five stories, the architect-planner pointed out, requiring residents to climb up or down more flights of stairs to get to the floor they wanted.

The tour ended in a show flat, furnished to demonstrate what it might look like occupied by a family. The door was open when they arrived. Inside, the furniture was simple but clean, not unlike that Ah Boon had at home. Knowing the way the Gah Men worked, he knew it was a decision that must have been taken seriously, knew that the desired effect was one of familiarity and comfort even in this strange new environment. And indeed it was. He felt like he was stepping into a superior version of the home he had grown up in. The air was cool and fragrant— as if the molecules themselves had been individually soaped—and the sunlight that came through the windows was softened by their slatted panes of frosted glass. The flat was small, smaller than his home, and yet because of the way the living room gave onto the large kitchen, because of the white paint and the linoleum floors of pale jade, the simplicity of the furniture and ease of its arrangement, the space felt much larger than it was. Now here they were in the kitchen itself. It was like stepping into the picture they'd seen back at the headquarters. Gleaming beige tile, shiny faucets, overhead lights that illuminated every polished corner.

There was no glass in the large kitchen window. "Left open for hanging laundry," his neighbor whispered. Ah Boon stepped toward that rectangle of open air and looked down. A feeling of vertigo came over him; they were on the tenth and highest floor. The tree saplings beneath them appeared again as small as the foam models they'd seen back at the headquarters.

He stepped back from the window. It was too much to take in. Was this what their country would look like ten, twenty years from now? How many of these flats could the Gah Men build? It was terrifying, it was exhilarating.

"Today we are a Third World country," the architect-planner pronounced. "But you see what we are trying to do here. It will catapult us into the First World."

Ah Boon sat down in a chair against the kitchen wall, taking it all in. The whole place felt like a mirage. He thought of the wistful look on Ma's face at that refrigerator demonstration and imagined bringing her here, to this very flat, with his hands over her eyes. On his wrist he would wear a watch not unlike the one that ticked on the architect-planner's wrist. In a corner would be a brand-new refrigerator, mysterious and complete, hoarding its precious cool air.

"You did it," Ma would say, her face glowing with happiness, with pride. "I always knew you would do it one day."

Chapter Twenty-Eight

Gek Huay was newly pregnant again, so for that week's Sunday dinner, Ma would cook her famed black-boned-chicken soup. The two chickens, an expensive variety with silky plumage more like fur than feathers, had been purchased earlier that morning, painstakingly plucked and quartered in the afternoon, and now sat simmering in a large pot over the stove.

Uncle appeared in the doorway. "Need help?"

"No, no," Ma said.

It was the third time he'd asked that afternoon. These days he spent most of his time in the house, knocking about like a bored child. It was all too much for Ma. Her brother had taken to ignoring the fact that Ah Boon worked at the CC entirely. He did not ask about Ah Boon's work, nor did he acknowledge the CC's existence to Ma or any of his friends. This might have been fine except for the fact that Swee Hong and the other men had shifted their weekly coffees and chess games to the CC. Uncle refused to join them, and as a result spent more and more time alone. He'd thrown himself into fishing, tinkering with the boat endlessly, scouring the nets for holes to mend. He pestered Ma with ideas for how to improve their house—perhaps the roof could be replaced a year early, or new framing for the windows put in, or how would little Ah Huat like a raised bed?—to no avail, for Ma had better things to do than come up with recreational projects for her brother.

"Leong," she called as he turned to go.

"What?"

"Be nice to Boon. Please."

A pained look came over Uncle's face. "*I* must be nice?" he said.

"Leong," Ma said again, a plea in her voice. "He is my son."

"And he is my nephew," Uncle said. "You know I just want what's best for him."

"Please, Leong. I don't want to argue again."

Uncle shook his head slowly. "Okay," he said at last, leaving the kitchen.

It seemed the less Ma worried about Ah Boon, the more she worried about Uncle. Her son was growing into a fine young man, had come into his own at last. There might be some who gossiped about his choice to give up fishing. Yet Ma's decision to send Ah Boon to school as a boy had been unconventional too, and although what she'd hoped to achieve back then had been hazy in her mind, she'd always believed Ah Boon's future would be different.

Ma had no illusions about the Gah Men. They were politicians, like any other. She, too, had been skeptical of the CC when it had first been built. She hadn't been convinced by the free luncheons and cooking classes. Everything came at a cost, and that the cost was not apparent kept Ma on her guard. But Uncle's boycott was going too far. He had let events of the past curdle his worldview, becoming bitter and suspicious. Ma did not like the Gah Men by any means, but she did not share Uncle's irrational hate.

And what was undeniable was the Gah Men's effect on Ah Boon. A new confidence animated him, a sense of purpose, the way that fishing had once animated Pa. Even as Ah Boon tried to pretend the English classes were nothing more than a work requirement, even as he asked his uncle about the day's catch, joked around in Hokkien with his brother, Ma sensed change. She saw it in the way he no longer sat with his ankle hooked over his knee as they ate, but instead kept his feet on the floor, knees pressed primly together. She heard it in his voice; even his Hokkien was gentler, the hard consonants rounded with less force, the peaks and troughs of pitch shaven down.

Most of all, his smell had changed. These days, Ah Boon smelled like citrus, a lime-freshness that went deeper than soap or a woman's perfume. Nothing of the ocean remained. Of course, he had smelled different before. When he first went to middle school, he came back smelling like Hia: sweat, salt, the bodies of other people. Then, when he became involved with the student unions, this smell intensified, became a kind of animal odor—not unlike that of poultry out in the yard—with an undertone of chlorine.

Finally, when he left the unions to return to fishing, Ah Boon began to smell most like he had when he was a child: of rain and trees, that particular mustiness of humid swamp air, mixed with the fresh salt of a good day's catch. It was this smell that Ma mourned for when he took up the CC job and developed the citrus scent. It was this smell that reminded Ma of her husband like nothing else did. Yet perhaps it was for the best that Ah Boon did not become the ghost of his father, but instead carved his own path.

However much he changed, Ma still saw beneath it all a little boy who wanted to do good. She could not help but be proud of how he carried himself, his neat, clean uniform, his polite, gentle way of speech. Now that the CC had become a regular fixture in the daily life of the kampong, she saw how respectfully others spoke to Ah Boon, how they asked for his advice on which free primary school was best for their grandchildren and whether they should enroll in night classes themselves. The merger referendum was coming up, it was all anyone would talk about, and at the CC new pamphlets had appeared extolling the virtues of the Gah Men's plans. The kampong, not knowing what to make of it all, went to Ah Boon for explanations. While bringing a tin of freshly brewed soup to Ah Boon for his lunch a few days ago, Ma had stumbled in on one such gathering. There he was, her once-shy son, standing in front of a group of the kampong men—Swee Hong, Ah Tong, even Ghim Huat— and holding forth on the intricacies of each political party's proposal for merger. The other men scratched their chins thoughtfully and did not interrupt, asking occasional questions with an air of attentive respect. What mother would not be proud of such a son?

She could live with the ambivalence of her brother. Uncle and nephew were more similar than they would ever know, for Uncle, too, had been that proud, sensitive boy when he was her playmate as a child. Fiercely devoted as he was, he could not bear a perceived slight, and would dig his heels in for as long as he felt cast aside. But it was no use worrying about all this. There was ginger to chop, red dates to rinse, boiled chestnuts to shell. On the stove the dark-boned chicken grew limp, its ligaments softening, its dense fat rendering.

At first the dinner seemed to go perfectly well. All six of them—Hia, Gek Huay, little Ah Huat, Ah Boon, Uncle, and Ma—sitting around a dining table that was really two tables pushed together, one round and one square. They'd had to get the round table after Hia had married and Ah Huat had been born. Now with Gek Huay expecting again, Uncle joked that they would soon need a third table.

"You leh, Boon? When to get a fourth table?" Uncle elbowed Ah Boon.

Ah Boon nodded good-humoredly, and Ma could tell he was glad for Uncle's joke. Uncle's way with him tonight was cheerful and easy, and for a little while, it was almost as if they had returned to the old days, when as a boy, Ah Boon had been more comfortable with Uncle than with even Pa or Hia. How long ago it had been, when Ah Boon would ride on Uncle's shoulders plucking fruit from trees, or sit by him quietly as the older man read the morning newspaper.

"Still young." Ah Boon laughed back.

"Eh, young what, look, losing hair already!"

"Ah Ma, eat, Gu Gong, eat," little Ah Huat said, grabbing his chopsticks.

Ma ladled the thick, clear broth into their bowls, taking care to give the best parts of the chicken to Gek Huay and Ah Huat. How soothing the sounds of her family's slurps, the quick clicking of chopsticks against bowls, the soft gulps and sighs, the occasional burp. All the petty squabbles and sullen tantrums faded away during a family meal. How like children Uncle and Ah Boon were, Ma thought, how easily distracted with food.

Then Ah Boon cleared his throat. "There's something I want to talk to you about," he said. His tone of voice was stilted, almost formal. "You know the new flats the Gah Men are building?"

"Mmm. Ah Tong's nephew went there after he got married. The wife couldn't stand staying with the parents, so they applied and went," Uncle said.

He was actually trying. Ma could barely believe the easy conversational tone.

"Old Ah Hoon also, right?" Ma chimed in. Her sons had applied, she went on, and they had just gotten the flat. It was somewhere in the west, she thought, very far from the kampong. No one had seen them since they'd gone.

"Ah Kee went along with them when they moved," Uncle said, laughing. "He say everything electric, got their own water inside the house. But very small, you know, and quite stuffy. On the fifth floor also. Ah Hoon don't dare take the lift, she scared stuck inside. So every day she can only go out once, because she don't want to climb so much stairs."

Ma shuddered, clicking her tongue, relishing the shuddering. "Aiyo, so high up," she said. "So scary."

The conversation carried on. Hia said you could choose to live on a lower floor, so you wouldn't have to worry about heights. Uncle said he wouldn't want to die in a house that wasn't really a house, more a concrete box. He liked being able to feel the wind coming through the floorboards and the walls. Ma laughed, she said all he had to do was open a window, but he wouldn't know that because he never did anything around the house himself. Gek Huay said she'd love to have electricity and water, and not have to worry about Ah Huat knocking over a gas lamp and burning them all to death.

"So what if we apply?" Ah Boon said. "Don't even need to go very far. New flats are being built close by."

Uncle laughed, slapped his thigh. The sound of it was like a meaty gunshot, cracking through the house.

"Boy, don't be crazy. We live here so long, your uncle is too old to just change life like that. You youngsters, maybe you can move. But us, what would we do there? And if you go, who's going to take care of us? Your ma living by herself, can you bear it? No, no, forget it."

"Just think about it," Ah Boon said. "Ma won't have to get water from the well every morning. No need to sweep the sand blowing in from outside all the time. Lights we can turn on and off. No more smelly outhouse. They have toilets like the ones at the CC, that you can flush."

The lightness remained in Ah Boon's tone, but from where she sat next to him, Ma noticed he'd begun brushing his heels impatiently against his calves.

"And the fishing how?" Uncle said.

Ah Boon shrugged. "We can't fish forever," he said. "Things are changing."

Uncle's arms were crossed, and worry etched his brow. Ma tapped her little finger against the wooden table nervously. Her brother was sixty-one now, two years younger than Pa would have been. Before Pa's death, Uncle had been the one who took things as they came, who was prone to adventure and risk. Something had changed the day her husband died.

"Your father himself built this house," Uncle said. "When he was younger than you, after his useless father left him with nothing and they were kicked out of their own home. He and your Ma raised you boys in it."

He waved his hand at the house, as if daring Ah Boon to take issue with it. The sagging attap roof, black in places with mold; the wooden walls through which chinks of dying light were visible as the sun set outside; the sparse but dear furniture. Ma felt a squeeze of love for this old, creaking house in which she had raised her boys. Uncle was surely right, her son mistaken. How could they possibly ever leave their home?

"Nothing is wrong with this house," Ah Boon said. Still his left foot moved against his right calf agitatedly. *Sssht, sssht, sssht.* A sound like sweeping sand out the front door.

"We talk about this after dinner, okay? Eat first, talk later," Ma said. She placed more fish onto Ah Boon's plate. "Come, boy, eat, later cold."

Gek Huay stood up to light the gas lamps. Outside the wind was gathering speed. A heavy, fertile damp rose from the earth, and they could smell rain on the air. A tense silence filled the room.

Ma missed her husband desperately. Pa would know what to do; Pa would say either they should move or not, and whatever his decision, it would feel right. Ah Boon's soul would settle. Uncle would defer to Pa's judgment as the head of the household. But there was no Pa. Ma shoveled more food into their bowls.

It was Hia who broke the silence.

"Actually," he said slowly, carefully. "Our place is falling apart. The hole in the roof is only getting worse, and we'll have to replace the whole thing after the next monsoon."

Uncle frowned, rubbing his chin. "No problem," he said. "I will replace it."

"I heard the flats are built near markets and schools. Gek Huay won't have to walk so far, and it will be easier once Ah Huat starts going to school."

"He can go to the kampong school," Uncle said. "The kampong school is right here."

Gek Huay nodded tentatively, looking to Ma. "It will be good for Ah Huat, I think," she said. "He can have his own room. And no more outhouse—wah! Can you imagine!"

Ma looked from Gek Huay to Uncle. He stared at her as if she held his happiness in her hands. A flash of frustration: Why did they put her in this position, being forced to choose between her brother and her son, time and time again?

Ma looked about her old, dear house. Here was the window that would no longer close; here was the scorched patch next to the dining table where she had once knocked over a lamp while preparing dinner. There were the splintered cabinets whose deepest recesses contained things that her husband had owned: a chipped enamel mug he'd always had his morning coffee in, a neatly folded pair of pants that hadn't been worn in twenty years, a small, grainy black-and-white photo of his mother.

She'd never told anyone, but Ah Huat had appeared to her a week after his disappearance. He came one night while she lay crying in bed, unable to sleep for grief. He was a young man again, dressed in the elegant new clothes he'd worn at their wedding all those years ago. As soon as she saw him standing at the foot of her futon, she knew he was dead. Her young husband said nothing, only looked at her with kind, compassionate eyes, in which there was no fear, no pain, only pity. The pity was for her, she knew, for he was gone, but she was still here. Trapped in the fleshy confines of her stubborn, thumping body that would not let her be. The grief she felt was hard and cold, as if a grain of sand had somehow become lodged in one of the tender vessels of her lungs, causing her pain with each breath she drew. She longed to draw breath no longer, but her body persisted.

Still, the sight of him standing there in his fine silk top and pants, gel in his hair, neatly combed back, had eased something in her. He continued to stand there, not saying a thing. She continued to watch him, her sobs softening to a low hiccup. Eventually her eyes grew heavy, and the sleep she fell into was deep and dreamless. He was gone when she awoke, but the lead that bound her insides had loosened, and she felt that she could go on.

Ma had hoped for years that Pa would come back to her. Even in an altered state: a bird, an ant, the black fungus creeping up an old wooden wall. She looked as hard as she could, but never found him again. He was not here.

With all the turmoil in her younger years, she had grown to love the predictable wash of her old age, the comfortable shapes each day took. How would she live in a new place? And yet—her gaze lit upon little Ah Huat's face, that round pale melon of a boy, and something inside her surged up. It wasn't just the electricity, the schools, the markets. It was bigger than that. First the CC, then the land reclamation project, then perhaps merger and full independence. She could smell the change in the air, could feel the ground shifting beneath her feet.

She tried to think calmly, to put Uncle's worried eyes and Ah Boon's restless feet out of her mind. She looked up at the beams that held up their roof, to the corner where years ago, sparrows had once built a small, scraggly nest. No one had discovered it until Ma had been awoken one night by the squeaky chirps of the baby birds hatching. It had been up to her to remove the nest. A ladder was borrowed from Swee Hong; she'd climbed it carefully, and at its top, marveled at how foreign this old house she'd known for so many years looked from up above. It was how she felt now, trying to make a decision.

"Maybe we think about it," she said. "Maybe Boon is right."

Ma lifted her eyes to meet Uncle's gaze. He was staring at her, tense as a cornered animal. She wanted to reach out to him, to stroke his shoulder and soothe him as she had when they were children, and he just a little boy. But she knew if she were to touch him now he would flinch. *I'm sorry*, she tried to say with her eyes. He turned away.

Chapter Twenty-Nine

When it became known that the Lees were applying for a new flat, the rest of the kampong began speculating. There were others who had left—Ah Tong's nephew, Ah Hoon and her sons, Joo Kiat's young widow with the baby—but these were peripheral figures in the fabric of the community. The Lees were different. Everyone knew them, due to the islands whose waters still supported younger generations of kampong families today. But even before the islands, they had known the senior Ah Huat's father, the good-for-nothing gambler who'd drowned in his own vomit on the beach. His mother, whose soft palms stayed free of calluses despite all the laundry work she did, a mark of good nature and virtue, the kampong believed. His sisters, who, though they'd married out and left the kampong, were thought of fondly as sweet, intelligent girls.

Everyone remembered the day Ah Huat married Ah Bee: how they'd whispered about her, this daughter of a rich man with a bungalow by the coast, what was she doing marrying into a fishing family? But as soon as they laid eyes on Ah Bee in her red samfu, her hair simply done, her clear, honest eyes, they saw that she had no airs and graces despite the supposedly wealthy background. It only came out later that she had been born to the rich man by his third wife, whom he treated as a servant, and Ah Bee, less than a servant. By then she'd endeared herself to them with her prawn fritters and steamed cakes, the sly remarks that slipped out from beneath her placid good humor. The kampong still talked about the time, early on, that Swee Poh had gone over to the Lees' house with two of the largest, smelliest fish she could find on her husband's boat, their tails still twitching in the wind. She'd thought to give the new bride a scare, thinking her the type of uppity woman who, not being from a fishing family, would not know how to react. But all Ah Bee did was to calmly take the fish from Swee Poh, saying that if she would like to take a shower before tea—here, wrinkling her nose ever so slightly—she was welcome to use their bathing area.

And when Ah Yam had been born, kicking and screaming, everyone remembered that too, remembered thinking: *Now here was a boy who would grow into a man!* The entire kampong had doted on him, this tanned, rowdy, plump-limbed boy. When Ah Boon came it was clear he was different. Quiet and jaundiced, with large mournful eyes that watched you as you moved about the room. Still, he was beautiful in his own way. Angular and delicate, he seemed even from childhood to be unfit for the life of labor he'd been born into.

So when he'd given up fishing for that CC job, no one had been too surprised. Of course, it was odd. But if anyone were to do something as odd as that, so the thinking went, it would be Ah Boon.

This, though, this was something else. To leave the kampong entirely, go live in concrete blocks that the Gah Men were putting up? Old Ah Huat had always said that even if he were to stop fishing—say, due to injury or old age—he would still go down to the surf each day, just to put his aching body in it. And Ah Boon would leave that behind? The kampong was perplexed, the kampong was discomfited. They liked Ah Boon.

It had been said that the land reclamation project would not affect the kampong, or any of the neighboring kampongs, but there would be "disruption." What this meant was unclear. Noise and machinery, they assumed, perhaps strangers trampling through places that were their own. No one quite understood the scale of the project either. What did it mean, to "reclaim" land? Whose land was it to begin with? What did it mean, a thousand acres? They worried about how far away the sea would be once the Gah Men were done. They'd have to invest in racks and wheels for their boats rather than just carrying them down from their front doors. The Gah Men were very unclear about this. How exactly were they meant to fish? Where would they go once the project began, how would they access the surf?

And now the Lee family was leaving the kampong behind for a modern flat somewhere else. It was perhaps Ah Tong who first said it, or maybe Ah Hoon's cousin, or just someone who had visited one of the flats that a friend had moved to, but whoever it was made the joke that maybe the whole kampong should move. Since Ah Boon, who worked for the Gah Men, wouldn't be moving his family if it weren't something good. After all, the flats were brand new, built of concrete and brick, with running water and lights you could turn on at the flick of a switch.

Resentment began to grow. Why hadn't Ah Boon told them, if he had some kind of inside information, that he thought applying for a flat might be a good thing? It was said that those English night classes he was taking were in preparation for his ascendant career as a Gah Man. He'd forgotten who'd been there for the family when Ah Huat had died—who had sent fruit and rice and clothing for the children, who had chipped in for his school fees, who had helped out on their boat. He'd forgotten how good the kampong had been to him all his life.

And so, by the time Ah Boon put up posters announcing that priority balloting for new flats would be granted to all kampong residents affected by the land reclamation project, he was greeted with some degree of suspicion.

"Save the leftover flats for us, is it?" Ah Tong joked while watching the afternoon news one day.

"Yah, priority means what? You already apply for your family, right!" Ah Kee's son, he of the bad breath and dirty fingernails, who had never liked Ah Boon to begin with.

"Real or not? Or for show only?" Even Swee Hong joined in, though his tone was gentler, for the look of perplexity on Ah Boon's face softened his heart. "What's this all about, boy?"

Natalie watched the conversation from the common room doorway. Poor Ah Boon, she thought, an unknowing victim of his own success. He had come back from the orientation bristling with a nervous, jumpy energy, full of questions. *How many flats had the Gah Men already built to date?* More than ten thousand. *Was it true that anyone who wanted one could have one?* Yes. *But that would mean building far more.* Yes. *But that would be an enormous undertaking.* Yes. *Requiring an unimaginable amount of building materials, workers, money. Where would it come from?* Taxes. Government coffers. It was a big risk, the financial peril was great, but the Gah Men believed it would be worth it. *And the land?* Certain areas would have to be cleared. And of course, the reclamation project.

Here Ah Boon had fallen silent for a long while. Something was bothering him, she could tell. His feet moved restlessly beneath his desk, and she saw him touch the tip of one polished shoe to his clean blue trousers, leaving behind a dusty gray mark. Finally he said what was on his mind.

"Even if the kampong isn't—cleared. If the reclamation project goes ahead, won't the coast be different? Won't the sea be miles away?"

"Yes," Natalie replied evenly. "Not during the pilot phase. But if the pilot is successful, and the project were to go ahead, then yes."

Back and forth his foot went. The gray scuff grew larger. Natalie suppressed the urge to lean over and dust him off. She could tell from the sideways movement of his jaw that he was biting his inner cheek. Something was being worked out inside him. She thought she knew what it was. He was seduced by their vision, she could tell. But there was the question of the coast, the broad, untouched beaches, the gently swaying trees. Ought she to comment? Reassure him, say something about the greater good, the Gah Men's plans for the future of the entire country? It felt better to stay silent.

"And they would build flats here too," he said at last.

She nodded.

"Just like the ones near the headquarters. Ten stories high."

"Fifteen perhaps, maybe even twenty."

"How many?"

"It depends on how much land we get."

"But who would live there?"

She shrugged. "Life in the kampong—it's not bad, Ah Boon," Natalie said gently. "Quite good, in fact. There are others in the city—"

He cut her off. "I know, I know."

Again his jaw was working, more slowly now, thoughtfully, as if the answer were to be found somewhere inside his cheek. His foot came gently to rest on the floor.

The next week he'd announced to her that his family had decided to move. After that, even she'd been surprised by the buzz of interest that arose from the rest of the kampong, first out of nosiness and then from genuine curiosity. Mr. Yik and his superiors had planned for the kampongs to remain. He'd worried about the residents' emotional attachment to the land, or rather, the sea; about an unwillingness to leave the ineffable *kampong spirit* behind. He talked of not wanting to disrupt the kampong dwellers' *long conversation with the land*. But these were the thoughts of someone who had never lived anywhere other than the city, who had never had any kind of conversation with the land. Natalie was fully aware that Mr. Yik was more given to romantic notions than were the villagers themselves. Regardless, he would be pleasantly surprised if this unfolded the way it looked like it was going to.

Those dark, creaking kampong houses had always startled her with how fresh they smelled, despite their appearance of age and decay. The suspension of the house on stilts allowed for significant airflow beneath the floor. Except on the stillest of days, wind was regularly found to be whistling through the gaps in wooden floors and planked walls, tickling the soles of feet as one walked, caressing the insides of ears as one slept. One had the feeling of being outside even as he or she sat down for dinner or lay down for a nap. Natalie's own childhood home, that white-bricked house, was far less porous. It kept the wind out, and with it, all the world.

The boardinghouse where she now stayed did not keep out the world. Its walls were paper thin, and she was often kept up by the elderly woman living in the room below hers, who believed herself haunted by an especially tenacious sitting ghost and had a penchant for wailing prayers late into the night. If it was not the wailing, then it was the younger women sneaking back in after the curfew, their loud whispers and stumbling footsteps clearly audible even if they tried to be quiet. Eventually these women would get booted out of the boardinghouse for breaking the curfew one too many times, but they were inevitably replaced by others who would do the same. Finally, there was the young widow three rooms down from Natalie's, whose baby looked like a red, shrunken plum, its diminished appearance at odds with its healthy, elastic cries that stretched down the hallway.

At first it had frustrated her, all the hubbub of the boardinghouse after the stillness of the home she'd left behind, but eventually Natalie had learned to let the noise flow through her, filling each cell of her body with the outside world. She learned to take her sleep in a half-lucid state, such that—as Ah Boon would learn years later, only after they had been married and had lived together for a considerable amount of time—even in her deepest slumber, if one were to call her name, she would answer in a calm, clear voice untouched by sleep: "Yes?"

"No," Ah Boon said to Ah Tong now. "Of course not. All kampong residents get the same priority, me included."

"Sure or not," Ah Tong jeered. "Big Gah Man like you!"

The men broke out into laughter. Ah Boon forced his lips into an awkward smile. He was taken back to the day he and Pa had led the men to the islands for the first time. Never had he forgotten the sense of violation that came over him when Ah Tong, this loud, brash man, crawled up the untouched beach.

"Yes, I'm sure," Ah Boon said. He turned his back to the men and focused his attention on attaching the informational poster to the wall, smoothing down the curling edges with his thumbnail. The laughter died down.

"Okay lah, Boon, forgive you this time. Next time got good things must tell us, okay!"

Evidently the men felt they had given Ah Boon enough of a hard time, and began asking him questions in earnest. How would the application process work? Where were the new flats, and how new were they, exactly? Could they bring their whole families with them, was there enough room for everyone? Where would they keep their chickens, surely they couldn't be expected to know how to operate the lifts? Was it true the latest flats went all the way to twelve stories high?

At first, Ah Boon was reticent, his pride still stinging from the men's laughter, Ah Tong's derisive words echoing in his head: *Big Gah Man like you!* To have his most secret ambitions stated so crudely, by brutish Ah Tong, of all people, pierced him. Still, the men's questions began to get the better of him. They were like children, curious yet trying hard not to demonstrate their ignorance. And the rumors that had begun to circulate about the Gah Men's flat-building program were at best inaccurate, at worst outlandish. Ah Boon could not resist correcting them—no, there were no indoor pens for chickens and pigs; yes, there were staircases and not only lifts—and soon his monosyllabic answers grew into phrases, phrases into sentences, until he was holding forth on the most detailed specifications of the new flats. They would be able to choose from one- to three-room flats, he said, and with the subsidized rental, it wouldn't cost any more than what they paid the towkay now. Here Swee Hong interrupted proudly. He did not rent from the towkay, he had built his house himself, so it made no sense for him to up and leave, pay rent to the Gah Men.

"Ah," Ah Boon said. "Here's the thing. The Gah Men will *buy* your house from you. The provision shop, your house, everything. They'll pay you for it. Don't you want to retire, Swee Hong?"

Swee Hong fell silent. He had three sons by his deceased wife, all three of them married now, living with their wives in the city. Thanks to the provision shop, Swee Hong had been able to provide each son with a significant bride price when it came to his turn to marry. So their wives were city women from good merchant families, not only deft with a sewing machine but also educated, able to read and write English. Now, with the wife of his eldest son six months pregnant, and the midwife saying that from the angle of her belly it would be a boy, Swee Hong felt that his life, up till now never having been easy, was suddenly arcing smoothly upward.

He did his best to ignore his good fortune, lest he jinx it. He focused on the negatives in his life—his younger son having taken up poker, the dry cough that kept him awake many nights, his wife being dead and him therefore not having companionship to look forward to in his old age.

Yet, most mornings, he walked to his shop as the sky began to fill with pink light, his belly full and warm with the breakfast of half-boiled eggs, the aftertaste of strong coffee lingering at the back of his throat, and he would think of his sons. The salty wind whipping its way up from the sea would fill his chest with a lightness so pleasurable that he'd take a breath deep enough to make his lungs hurt.

Swee Hong was simply, undeniably happy. He starved his joy but it proved resilient, and often came upon him at unexpected times. Sometimes, when business was slow, he'd pull his wooden stool out from behind the counter and drag it to the cement porch, where he'd sit with a cigarette, watching the wind move through the dense canopy of the ancient banyan tree outside.

But happiness was a dangerous thing. Swee Hong felt the eyes of jealous gods and vengeful spirits upon him—a cold breeze like a hand crossing the back of his neck before he went to bed; a treasured porcelain bowl knocked off a table and shattered by something invisible; dust that formed over the countertop in his shop no matter how often he cleaned it.

And his sons were visiting less and less, the kampong being so far from their lives in the city, they said. Swee Hong saw that the wives did not like it, this reminder of where their husbands had come from. Swee Hong's house was bigger than most, and it was his, rather than the towkay's, but it was still built of attap and wood. His house had cement floors rather than wood or dirt, but the wives had grown up in comfortable homes of brick and cement their whole lives, and so were not impressed by this either.

It wasn't just his family. He saw the changes in the city: new buildings springing up between the old tangles of dense wooden structures, the chaotic markets that spilled from street to street. He listened to the wireless—he knew the reclamation project wasn't the only one of its sort. There were also the oil refineries and shipyards the Gah Men were building in the jungled, muddy west, millions of dollars poured into taming the unruly coastal terrain. A friend of his had gone out there in search of a job and said it had been a sight to behold: amid the clay mountains and swampy ground were vast grids of steel, hefty pipes of concrete, barrels used as rafts to cross the straits.

It wasn't the only thing he heard on the wireless. The Gah Men had commenced a series of talks about the controversial merger issue. At first Swee Hong had been skeptical, hostile, even; he himself knew the kind of people the Gah Men had labeled dangerous communists, knew them to be ordinary people making extraordinary sacrifices. And yet—the Gah Man giving the talks did not slander the hardworking union leaders; instead he praised them for their ideals and integrity. The Gah Man talked of the struggle to win their limited freedom from the Ang Mohs, of the riots, the strikes, the boycotts. At the same time he emphasized the inevitability of the merger with the Federation of Malaya—hinting darkly at military coercion or economic collapse down the road should it not take place.

Propaganda, Swee Hong suspected. Still, it was effective. Beneath the Gah Man's calm, measured tones, Swee Hong discerned a steely strength, a propensity for reasoned brutality. While listening to the third of these wireless broadcasts—there were twelve in total—he became certain that the Gah Men would have their way. They would have their way about the merger, about the flats, about their leftist political opponents. The reclamation project, the oil refineries—all of it was just the beginning. In time, the Gah Men would reshape the island in their own likeness, a landscape filled with the architecture of reasoned brutality.

He was just one man, Swee Hong thought, and soon, he would be old. He did want to retire. He did want his sons to visit him, his grandchildren to spend Sundays playing at his feet. If moving to the Gah Men's flats would make that possible, then he would accept the inevitable, and he would go.

Chapter Thirty

It was Natalie who suggested Ah Boon come with her to the meeting with Mr. Yik, since he'd been so instrumental in the latest turn of events. A little more than half the households in the kampong had applied for flats, and it looked like there would be more to come. What this meant, she'd explained to Ah Boon, was that eventually, the Gah Men could mandate that those remaining move as well, since it would only be a small number of people and there would be minimal backlash.

"Backlash," Ah Boon had repeated.

His thoughts went to Uncle.

"The community," Natalie went on, as if Ah Boon didn't understand. "People like your family, your friends. Unhappy that we made them move."

Her face shone with the light of belief; it was a light he'd fallen in love with once before, when he'd been just a child, a long time ago. How good it was to bask in that light again, to know that he was doing something good, something useful.

"They're not unhappy," he said quickly. "They can't wait to move."

In a way it was true. Not since the islands had been discovered had the kampong been so swept up. It was all people could talk about. At all times of day they gathered in the CC common room to scrutinize the shiny posters and colorful floor plans pinned to the walls. The posters told of not only new flats, but new jobs, new policies, new political threats. The merger debate was still going strong, and every CC in the country featured the same exhibits explaining and promoting the Gah Men's stance. The referendum was drawing near.

But the kampong did not care for arguments over the terms of the merger. The dragging on of the latest in a series of political squabbles bored them. Instead, they discussed the height of the new flats, what it meant to live so high up. Someone had heard that a woman emptying dirty dishwater out the window of her tenth-floor flat had killed a man walking by at ground level, water falling from so high having the force of a sledgehammer. Others had heard that the height led to vertigo madness, people finding themselves inexorably drawn to their open windows, climbing up onto the ledges and threatening to fling themselves off.

There were some, notably, who did not participate in these conversations. Uncle was one of them. He had grown quiet again. He remained begrudging whenever Ma came home bristling with excitement at new information on the electrical fittings of modern kitchens, would only grunt and turn away.

"Aiya, you know your uncle," Ma had said to Ah Boon. "He will come around eventually." But he could tell she did not believe it.

Then there was Siok Mei. A distance had come between her and Ah Boon since the day he'd turned down her request to go to the rally. She'd returned to the kampong just once since that evening, the baby in her arms, a purple knot of flesh swaddled in clean white cloth. He'd visited, of course, godfather to the child, together with the other neighbors, bearing gifts of fruit, clothing, and red packets.

There she had sat in her uncle's living room with the sleeping baby in her lap, surrounded by old friends and neighbors. He had braced himself for a new Siok Mei. Motherhood would have changed her in some irrevocable way, he'd assumed, and secretly he hoped it would help him move on at last.

It was true there was a tiredness about her he'd seen in other new parents, that startled look, as if they'd emerged from beneath the earth and were surprised by the fact that it was still there. But she was the same Siok Mei; more herself, not less. It was as if some cloak of politeness, of the necessity to conform, had been pulled from her, channeling oxygen to the fire that had always burned in her eyes. Motherhood did not take away from her, it multiplied and intensified who she was. A fierce protectiveness—a protectiveness she had once directed toward Ah Boon—emanated from her every move. It pained Ah Boon; he saw clearly how it would have been had she borne his child.

He'd gone up to her and handed her his gifts. She'd smiled at him warmly enough, and they'd chatted briefly. She was busy with the new party, having joined as an organizing volunteer; she'd been especially busy with the merger debate. The Gah Men were misrepresenting the leftists' position, she'd said. But enough about politics. How was Ah Boon's family?

They were excited about the move, he'd said, it was very exciting for the entire kampong. A flicker had gone over Siok Mei's face then, but she only nodded and said nothing.

After all, Ah Boon had said, you moved to the city with Eng Soon.

Yes, she'd replied, as the bundle in her arms shifted and whimpered. I did. But it wasn't the same.

After a pause, she thanked Ah Boon. He'd been right, she said, casting a tender look at the tiny baby. She already loved her child more than anyone she'd ever known.

Why would anyone be unhappy about a new home? It's a wonderful opportunity," Ah Boon said to Natalie now, as he watched the trees and houses speed by outside the bus. He tried not to think of Siok Mei.

He told himself that the distance between them had already been there—hadn't he left the unions? Hadn't she had her child? It was only the natural unspooling of time. But he remembered the way she'd spoken to him in the CC that one evening almost a year ago now; her low, urgent voice, the warm caress of her breath. It was Ah Boon she wanted by her side at the leftists' triumphant moment of separation. It would not be complete for her without him.

A flash of pain went through him whenever he thought of this. But it couldn't be helped—things were changing, their lives had moved on.

Ah Boon now spoke English with the clipped, precise enunciation of the newly educated. While his speech was still far from perfect, it was passable, and along with this came a newfound confidence. English was the armor he held up against the world; he didn't stop to think about what this said about either him or the world. With his family and friends he still spoke Hokkien, and if they spoke English to him, he switched back to his old vernacular, dropping propositions and articles, short-circuiting syntax. With Natalie, however, he took every opportunity to practice.

Natalie was a friendly audience; she forgave his mistakes, encouraged his efforts. Now, however, he would be speaking to Mr. Yik. Ah Boon recalled that first day they'd met at the CC, him tongue-tied and sweaty, Mr. Yik imperious, unimpressed. He dared not hope today would go any differently, and yet he *was* different, so perhaps it would.

"Most people dislike change, I suppose," Natalie said.

They had been on the bus now for half an hour, with another half hour to go. Natalie played with a loose thread protruding from one of her shirt buttons, drawing it out again and again. The gesture was uncharacteristically childlike, a crack in her typical poise. Ah Boon realized he knew nothing about Natalie's family; whether her parents were dead or alive, if she had siblings. He did know that she was unmarried, since she had once mentioned the boardinghouse she lived at. He recognized in her the same deliberate isolation that he himself was prone to; he saw all the ways in which she held the world at bay.

"Why did you become a Gah Woman?" Ah Boon asked.

Natalie looked up, smoothing down her shirt with quick, brusque strokes.

"Why does anyone do anything?" she said.

Natalie paused. When she looked at Ah Boon, he could see reflected in her dark pupils the moving world outside the bus window.

"I had nothing to complain about. We never suffered for food to eat, no illnesses befell our family. Even during the war we were lucky, aside from a few unpleasant incidents. Nothing of lasting damage."

Ah Boon thought of Pa. *Lasting damage.* They had never put a name to it, all these years. His family talked about Pa very rarely, and when they did, it was as if he had simply gone away on a long trip and would not be coming back. *After your pa left* was how Ma and Uncle often put it. He became "your pa," rather than her husband or his brother-in-law, or simply Ah Huat. Even his name was co-opted by little Ah Huat, who had been named in honor of him but unwittingly contributed to his erasure. Now the name only brought to mind a living, breathing little boy, rather than the memory of a man long gone. Was that lasting damage?

"I grew up on a rubber plantation. Have you ever been on one?"

Ah Boon shook his head.

"Well, they're large. Lots of land up north. And it's trees, of course, trees everywhere, just like down in the mangrove swamp, or the jungle behind the kampong. But all the trees are in rows."

The bus jolted violently. Natalie's shoulder rammed into Ah Boon's and he put out one arm to steady her. She took it without comment, her slender fingers wrapping around his forearm as if it were the most natural thing in the world. There was a small reddish mole on the flesh between the base of her thumb and her forefinger. It looked like an ant, and Ah Boon felt the urge to reach over and brush it off.

Natalie was still talking. She used to play in the plantation when she was a girl, she said. Once, when she was maybe five, she'd gotten it into her head to see how far the rows of trees went. She took her favorite doll and went off into the plantation, counting the rows as she went.

Ah Boon nodded intently. He tried to keep his gaze on her face as she spoke, but it was difficult not to stare at his forearm, where the warm heel of Natalie's palm rested, fingers curled lightly, so that with each jolt of the bus, they moved a little, brushing his skin in a manner that was not unlike a caress.

"I counted to twenty-six before I lost sight of the house," Natalie said. She described the panic, the endless turning in circles, the realization, at last, that she was completely lost. It was late in the day and most workers had gone home, so there was no one to hear her cries.

"You must have been terrified," Ah Boon said. It would be the perfect time to reach out and cover her hand with his. It would be natural at this point in the story. He swallowed, but did not move.

"Did you know, you have to tap rubber very early? The workers start when it's dark out and the air is still cool, so the sap can flow all morning before the heat sets in and makes it congeal."

Natalie's face had taken on a distant look. Outside the bus, the landscape changed. Thick vegetation gave way to masses of wooden buildings with zinc roofs, crammed and leaning. Wooden poles heavy with laundry were balanced precariously out windows. Children played barefoot in the street. Dogs lingered around drains, sniffing for scraps. Skinny brown chickens pecked rocks outside open doorways, where mothers sat talking as they scrubbed dull pots. Everything was on top of everything else here, pressed together, from the children leaning their warm bodies against one another as they hopscotched to the houses that seemed as if they might fall down without the support of their neighboring structures.

"I was panicking, but I didn't cry," Natalie went on. "I told myself if I kept walking, I would get somewhere eventually, that the plantation did not go on forever. So I kept going until the sun was low in the sky and the shadows of the trees grew long. Still I saw no one. All around me the trees were bleeding, their white sap dripping into the barbaric cups tied around their necks."

And the people, there were so many people. It always made Ah Boon dizzy to look at them. The bus kept going, and still there were more houses, more people, and now there were rickshaws too, pulled by men with the straining, piecemeal muscles of underfed bullocks. In them sat elegant businessmen: Sikhs with neatly wrapped turbans, Chinese in spectacles and Western suits, the occasional red-cheeked Ang Moh. The businessmen sat with briefcases on their laps, pictures of stillness as the rickshaws bumped and rolled over the dirt road. The rickshaw pullers pressed forward with all their weight, arms bent at right angles behind them, shoulders straining as if to pop.

"What happened? How did you get home?" Ah Boon asked.

"Someone found me eventually. A worker on the evening shift. I still remember," Natalie said. "He gave me a milk sweet to chew on as we walked home. It was the best candy I'd ever tasted." She turned to look out the window. "Oh, good. We're almost there."

Now the buildings that rose from the earth were solid brick structures. Some resembled the CC, simply built, with stripped, functional facades, small slatted glass windows, and sturdy metal roofs. Others were more elaborate, with windows as tall as a man, all dressed up with decorative folding and fluted columns. Old Ang Moh buildings, built by the hands of the Indian workers they brought with them on ships, back when they first arrived over a hundred years ago.

"It's not your first time in the city, is it?" Natalie said.

Ah Boon suppressed a smile and shook his head. The question was endearing, in a way. It was what people like Natalie thought of those who lived in the kampong. *Sua ku.* Country bumpkins who never left the confines of their country villages.

"No," he said, weighing up whether to make a joke and deciding against it. "But it always feels like it," he conceded. "It changes so quickly."

Natalie nodded, satisfied. "Yes, a lot of good work has been done. But we still have a long way to go. All those tenement houses, for example—" Here Natalie gestured toward some of the wooden buildings. *Tenement houses,* Ah Boon repeated in his mind, storing the term for future use. "Fire hazards, all of them. Could go up in a blaze within minutes. We need to fix that, and that's why we need all those new flats. That's why we need the land."

Ah Boon wondered who Natalie meant when she said *we.* She said it a lot, evoking some hazy collective, some omniscient authority. He'd always taken it to mean the Gah Men as a whole, or the island, or the people. But perhaps there was a *we* that meant the two of them. She and Ah Boon.

That's why Natalie and Ah Boon need all those new flats. That's why Natalie and Ah Boon need the land.

The bus stopped in front of a large gray building, twice as wide as it was tall, built of cement and peppered with mean square windows.

"Here we are," Natalie said.

She removed her hand from Ah Boon's forearm as if it were nothing, as if their warm skin had not been in contact for the past twenty minutes, as if he had not felt the pulse of her blood through her skin. They got off the bus. Ah Boon realized Natalie hadn't finished her story. He still didn't know why she became a Gah Woman. But they were standing in front of the ministry building; the moment had passed.

Natalie pressed her palms to the sides of her head, smoothing down stray hairs. Her hands shook very slightly.

She hadn't told anyone about that afternoon in the plantation for years. And still, she hadn't told Ah Boon everything. She hadn't told him about how the worker who'd walked her home in the dark told her how she reminded him of his own little girl, who had had long, fine hair just like Natalie's, and had died just a year ago.

How, Natalie had asked sleepily. She felt as though her limbs were wrapped in thick gauze, that they walked in a dream.

She was sick, he said.

Did you call the doctor? Natalie asked.

The worker paused, and then he let out a small, sad laugh.

Anyway, we had not enough food, he said. She would not have survived. It was better this way.

The milk sweet, until now so delicious, turned cloying in Natalie's mouth. The shadows of the trees seemed to elongate in judgment; she had the feeling that they were watching her.

After that night, Natalie no longer enjoyed her food. Every bite she took reminded her of the worker's daughter, too ill, too hungry to survive. She wanted to ask her father how it was possible that their people, who worked long hours in the dark and cold, could not get enough food for their sickly children to eat. But she knew, intuitively, that her father would not approve of such a question. Hierarchies were the natural order of things to him, and her family's place was at the top.

For years afterward, she'd dreamed of that endless walk. The dreams added and subtracted from reality; in them, the walks ended in the lairs of ghost tigers, at the edges of sheer cliffs, by the shores of infinite lakes. In all of them, she was searching for another little girl with long, fine hair just like hers, trying to find her before she starved.

There was another thing she hadn't told Ah Boon, or anyone. The evening the plantation burned down—years after the day she had gotten lost as a girl—Natalie had gone for another walk. She hadn't meant to retrace her footsteps from the nightmare she'd been having all week, but eventually, she was back in the thick of the trees. It was a humid night and the trees were silent. No bird call echoed through their branches, no wind moved their leaves. They looked much smaller than they had in her dream, where they appeared to her again as they had when she was a girl, as towering giants. Now they seemed pitiful things. Scrawny, stripped of bark, corralled into rows like prisoners.

Just before turning to go home, she saw the bobbing light of a kerosene lamp in the distance, weaving in and out of the shadows. Silently she approached it.

She couldn't make out their faces, but from the curved blades at their hips, she recognized the men as workers. There were three of them, she saw, all carrying small metal containers that looked almost like lunch tiffins, from which they sloshed liquid onto the earth. Silently they worked. Finally, one of them struck a match. Flames leaped from pools of oil, painting the trees in a fiery light. The workers ran, disappearing into the dark.

And Natalie—Natalie didn't make a sound. She merely watched it, and had the feeling that she was witnessing some necessary act.

She waited till the crackling noise began, till the smoke stung tears into her eyes. Then she turned, went home, and told no one anything.

Chapter Thirty-One

Mr. Yik's boss had insisted on coming to the meeting, despite Mr. Yik having reassured him that it was merely a routine update.

"Nonsense," the boss had said. "Eighty-five percent of residents have chosen to move voluntarily. I have to meet this—"

"Lee Ah Boon, sir," Mr. Yik said.

"This Lee Ah Boon. Yes."

The boss—ten years younger than Mr. Yik, and already a Deputy Secretary—believed himself something of a champion of the working classes. He himself had, of course, been educated in England, being the scion of an old banking family. Since university the boss had gone by Alexander, though his real name was Chee Guan. He'd relished the experience of picking a new name for himself. Would he be William, or John, or Jacob? Geoffrey or George? Finally he'd settled on Alexander; he liked being associated with greatness.

"I must meet him," he said again. "No doubt this chap has made our work far easier."

Alexander was cursed with a baby face, but his middle age was revealed in his hair; a meager, downy coat that he grew out and brushed with gel so that it formed a severe crust over his scalp. There was something unsettling about his overall appearance. Alexander felt people shrinking from him, and was convinced that they were merely intimidated by his considerable intellect. To mitigate this he smiled widely and frequently, so as to put them at ease. Mostly it only made them more nervous to see his yellowing teeth—Alexander was fond of strong English Breakfast tea and drank cup after cup of it—but all they could do was smile back. It would have been rude to do otherwise.

It was in such a manner that Alexander smiled now. He smiled to disarm Mr. Yik, soften him up, or so he thought, before making the proposition he knew the latter would not approve of.

"And this Lee Ah Boon," he said. "You said he was a fisherman."

"Yes," Mr. Yik said. "Living in the community that CC E14 serves. It was difficult to find the right local representatives, shall we say."

"On the contrary," Alexander said, still smiling. "I think someone like Mr. Lee Ah Boon is precisely who we need."

Mr. Yik's smile was strained. He knew what was coming. Alexander had been going on for weeks about a new working group, one comprised "of the people, for the people," to be involved in the Great Reclamation Project. What their scope of work would be exactly was unclear, but it had something to do with a high-minded notion of "active citizenship." Mr. Yik did not believe in Alexander's working group, but it was not his job, as Alexander's subordinate, to believe in things. And so he said now, in the most ingratiating tone he could muster: "Are you thinking of him for the Citizens' Working Group?"

"You read my mind, Yik," Alexander said.

"With all due respect, sir, I'm not sure Mr. Lee is quite the right fit. I've heard from Natalie that he's a little—rough around the edges. Went to one of those troublesome middle schools, was even briefly on the board of one of the student unions."

Mr. Yik tried to read Alexander's face, but it had sealed itself off.

"One day," Alexander said at last, "when the people are housed and clothed and fed, they are going to turn their gazes from their own small lives to their society, their government. And if only men like us are in power, do you know what they will say? Do you know what they will think and feel?"

Mr. Yik was silent.

"They will say we are out of touch, we ruling elite, we English-educated snobs. They will pick on all the difficult trade-offs we have agonized over, all those master plans we have argued about, and they will find fault in everything we have done. We will be deemed to have scarified too much or too little, been too ruthless or not enough so. But Ah Boon? Someone like him? Scrappy boy from the kampong, plucked from poverty, inducted into the government, given a role to play in his nation's development. Don't you see how powerful that is, Yik?"

A certain fixedness had come over Alexander's features; Mr. Yik had worked with him long enough to know when a matter was decided.

Later, after matters *had* been decided, the meeting would continue to play itself over and over in Ah Boon's mind. He cringed to think about it; how he'd fumbled and dropped his pen as the Deputy Secretary reached out for a handshake, how he'd sat on the wrong side of the table, how Mr. Yik had glared at him for no apparent reason. The room was so grand—high ceilings and huge, wide windows that looked out onto the street—it made him feel even smaller and more out of place than he usually did.

He remembered how he could not take his eyes off the spotless glass in those windows, could not stop marveling at the expense of them. The only buildings in the kampong with glass in their windows were the school, the CC, Swee Hong's shop, and the towkay's house. Those windows were composed of three or four slats, and the rectangles of glass that fit into the metal brackets were small. The glass itself was uneven and the world perceived through it warped with unnatural curves. Small bubbles could be seen trapped within, along with little burrs on the surface that, if one were careless, could scratch a finger or thumb. The glass in the meeting room windows showed no such defects. It was so smooth, so perfect that it was as if the window were nothing but a frame and they were seeing straight out into the street, which had mysteriously fallen silent.

When Ah Boon finally spoke, his voice came out steady and strong. He answered question after question about the kampong: how many people lived there, what their livelihoods were, how far back their families went, the ways in which the community had changed over time. He talked about the tides, the neighboring kampongs, the swamp, the trees. He talked about why he thought people were willing to move—that they, too, sensed the changes afoot in the country, they, too, wanted their children to be closer to schools and other opportunities. He said something about everyone wanting a better life.

He'd believed it up till then. *He* wanted a better life, after all, and so did Gek Huay, so did Ma. And the flats—he found them miraculous. Who would not? Yet as soon as the words left his mouth, he felt himself cringe. What had the architect-planner called their homes? *Unsanitary, unsafe. Poor, unhealthy,* dangerous *living conditions.* It was what the Deputy Secretary and Mr. Yik must think as well.

He did not mention the ones who didn't want to move. He did not mention the Malay fishermen in the neighboring kampong, who had laughed in his face when he gave them informational brochures about the flats. He did not mention Uncle, who spent more and more time alone, smoking mournfully on their porch.

He saw the mangroves where he'd trapped hermit crabs with Hia as a child, morning light glittering off the slippery dark roots emerging from the earth. Pale, untouched shores, lapped by clear, cold waves; the islands where Pa, flush with joy and life, had once taught him to fish. The thick undergrowth, screeching with crickets, through which he'd run hand in hand with Siok Mei. This was all in his head as he spoke as well, cloaked in a painful tenderness.

Ah Boon pushed it away. He focused on the feeling he'd had walking into the show flat, months ago now. Like stepping into a picture. Like stepping into the pristine future.

Just as the Deputy Secretary made his proposition, Ah Boon thought he saw, out of the corner of his eye, a familiar shape out on the street. Stooped back, loping gait, angular cheeks. The soft ache of longing, a bruise being pressed. It was not possible; Pa was dead. There was no going back into the past. The Deputy Secretary repeated his proposition.

"I'm asking you to join the government," he'd said, his strange, serious face crinkled in a way that was both sinister and earnest. "Do you understand what that means?"

The man who looked like Pa disappeared into the crowd, and Ah Boon calmed himself. What was there to be panicked about? What was there to fear?

"I understand," Ah Boon said.

And so it was that a month later, Ah Boon found himself wearing hard hat and vest, standing by an enormous pit gouged into the earth. The pilot phase of the reclamation project having just begun, he was taken to the digging site, a forested piece of land some three kilometers away from the kampong. Jagged stumps of trees adorned the site perimeter, everywhere logs and branches piled haphazardly, waiting to be taken away. The pit itself was a great gash in the ground, revealing orange dirt that in a certain light looked red.

Ah Boon arrived to a strange tableau of frozen steel limbs and wet, viscous earth. It had stormed the night before, and the digging work stopped. From the soil came the humid breath that always followed rain. In a few months' time, Ah Boon would learn to tell the difference between a wheeled trencher and a chained one. He would learn to identify a dragline excavator with its huge bucket, to tell the difference between these and the smaller tracked excavators, which were most prone to failing in wet conditions.

Now the machinery was still mysterious to him, and he was taken more by its scale than its function. Here a truck with a large saw on it, each sharp tooth the size of a dinner plate. There a bulldozer with wheels that came up to Ah Boon's shoulders. And the pit itself: the size of four basketball courts, and only a quarter done so far, he was told. He had never seen anything like it before.

They walked to its edge and peered in. The pit went down a full two stories. It was obscene, the earth being exposed in this way, red rocks glistening in sharp relief under the morning sun, like gallstones in the glare of a surgeon's lamp. Ah Boon felt as though he had been brought here to witness some crime that he would later be asked to testify about.

The men stared at him expectantly. He was the head of the Citizens' Working Group after all, the Deputy Secretary's very own pet project. This whole rigmarole had been put on for him. Now he wore the coveted white uniform; pen clipped to front pocket, clipboard at his side. He was here to observe, assess, make judgments. There was no room for the old feelings of fear and awe at the unknown vastness of all that was around him. A whole new city awaited, one that would be shaped out of this very mud, and he was to be a part of it.

In the depths of the pit were three small excavators halted mid-dig, mechanical arms extended like primeval crabs lounging in the sun. Little rocks tumbled down the pit's jagged walls. A worker's yellow hard hat lay ominously at its deepest point.

"Forgot someone down there," the foreman joked, pointing at the hard hat.

None of the visiting officials laughed.

The smile disappeared from the foreman's face. "Joking only," he said. "Someone probably left it when rushing to get out of the rain."

Ah Boon felt the others in the visiting contingent looking at him. He was the only Gah Man present—the rest were junior officials in the ministry—and yet he felt he might be the least equipped to be there. He thought they must talk about him when he wasn't around, those assigned to work under him, must trade stories of his unfitness, his mannerisms, his awkward English. Never had he been in spaces so uniformly male before, certainly never in the kampong, where the mothers and aunts and wives held such prominent roles in the daily bartering, mending, feeding, fixing. Women might not be allowed on boats, but they were the ones waiting with wheelbarrows on the beach when the fishermen came back in; they sorted and cleaned and salted just as the men did. At the ministry there were only men and more men; at the dig site, even more so.

Once this would have made Ah Boon nervous. But the white uniform had a magic about it, one that rinsed the disdain from the voices of men like these, that straightened their backs and subdued their gazes. In the past month, Ah Boon had felt himself begin to change, and so, when the foreman made the joke about the hard hat left in the pit, he let his features harden.

"Not wearing a helmet on the dig site is a serious safety breach," he said.

He pulled the pen from his pocket, readied the notepad on his clipboard. He felt the eyes of the ministry officials on him. He saw them nod approvingly.

"Ah no, no," the foreman babbled.

He began to make excuses: that wasn't anyone's helmet, that was an extra helmet that had simply been left, that was the helmet of someone who'd been fired.

The sun was out in full force now, and rivulets of sweat were making their way slowly out from Ah Boon's own hard hat. He longed for a drink of water. He had an assistant at the ministry these days, who frequently offered to refill the water jug that sat on his desk. Why had no one here offered him a drink of water? He looked about, allowing himself the pleasure of irritation, as the foreman continued to speak.

"Enough," Ah Boon said. The foreman fell silent. "I will flag this with the relevant division, and you will hear from them."

"Yes, sir," he muttered.

A loud whirring came from behind him. It was then that Ah Boon saw the elaborate system of metal tracks and rubber belts leading away from the pit. The machinery had ground to a start again, and began a rhythmic, ugly clanking that filled Ah Boon with faint dread. It was such a violent sound, and so relentless. Dirt poured from a large metal container fed by the dump trucks, falling onto the narrow metal trench where the rubber conveyor belts did their noisy business, and was slowly borne away. The tracks led into the distance and continued on out of sight.

"Where does that go?" Ah Boon asked.

"The fill site, sir," the foreman said. "By the sea."

Ah Boon realized with a jolt that by *fill site*, the foreman meant the swampy beach by the kampong, the mud flats where he had, as a child, roamed barefoot with Hia while stalking mudskippers. The shallow waters from which they had, for so many decades, launched their boats.

The dimpled shore where he'd collected unusual seashells with the intention of giving them to Siok Mei, but later chickened out. The shifting sand that crumbled beneath his feet as the waves washed in and out, the spot where he had once stepped on a rogue sea urchin and wet his pants from the pain.

All of it was the fill site, all of it would be filled. He watched the conveyor belt do its trundling work of bearing the earth away. An enviably simple task, moving dirt from one place to another. Dig it up, put it back in again. It was elegant in its simplicity, shameless in its daring, as most of the Gah Men's plans were. Squatters? Move them. Communists? Jail them. Housing? Build it. Even the earth itself was deemed malleable, the constraints of geography surmountable. A coastline was identified, a cost-benefit analysis conducted, a decision made. The rest was execution.

PART IV

Fill the Earth and Subdue It

Chapter Thirty-Two

Though windowless and drab, no larger than an outhouse, Ah Boon's new office contained a telephone and a shiny black typewriter of his own. Now, each morning, Natalie went from her city boardinghouse to the kampong CC, and he from his home to the gray building that was the ministry office.

They saw each other less, usually every couple of weeks, when Natalie came in to give her progress update on community matters to Mr. Yik. Then they would go for lunch together, either at the large canteen in the office basement or to a particular noodle cart three blocks away that served Ah Boon's favorite prawn mee soup, where they sat on wobbly wooden stools on the side of the road, spooning hot, sweet broth into their mouths.

The old dynamic between them—Ah Boon shy and deferential, Natalie distant and, at times, imperious—gradually faded, replaced by a hesitant friendship and growing affection. They did not often talk of anything personal, but during one of their lunches, Natalie revealed within the same breath that her mother was dead and that she had never dated seriously. This was said in the context of Ah Boon complaining that his own mother would never leave him in peace until he married and gave her grandchildren. *Gave* her, as if children were property to which one was entitled, to be traded for debt or affection. He'd asked if Natalie's parents felt the same way.

"Ma would, if she were alive," Natalie said. "Pa doesn't care. He drinks so much he can barely tell me apart from my sisters these days. I don't date, anyway. It used to be time, I didn't have it. I was so focused on school, then work, turning men down became a habit. And now—now I'm old, and still single, and it can't be helped."

"You're not old," Ah Boon blurted. He wanted to ask when her mother had died, and how. If she thought of her still, as he did of Pa. But the words stuck in his throat.

Natalie smiled. "Oh, well," she said.

Ah Boon looked at her carefully. She was older than him: thirty-one, perhaps thirty-two. But he had always found it difficult to tell a woman's age. And what was age, really? Other men seemed to agree so instinctively on what made a woman desirable. Small waist, fair skin, large eyes. He'd always felt he was missing this basic instinct. What did the size of a woman's eyes matter if they held no urgent life, no ambitious spark? What good was pale skin if it meant a woman was afraid of work? And surely what mattered more than a small waist was a strong back.

He looked into Natalie's eyes now. Calm, closed, they gave nothing away. Cold was what some would call her, but he saw it was restraint, and restraint, he'd come to believe, was strength. It was the ability to pause, to think, to make decisions that were not immediately popular. He had always been attracted to strength. And there was a predictability about Natalie's strength. It flowed rationally, predetermined, like water through furrows in the hard earth. This was not a strength that would hurt him.

The conversation moved on to their habitual topics, but something had shifted between them. Though the dirty bowls still clattered loudly as the stallholders' young daughter collected them, though the trishaws still rumbled through the streets and the fruit seller still shouted hoarsely the prices of his finely furred rambutans, a quiet had settled between Ah Boon and Natalie. The silence was charged with a new, humming energy, as if someone had touched each and every molecule of air between them, and with a nudge set them off their usual trajectories.

They talked of the usual things, but Natalie found that she could not take her eyes off the large white callus on the heel of Ah Boon's left palm, that she wished to reach out and brush it with the tips of her fingers. Ah Boon, likewise, was distracted by a single stray hair that had fallen to the right of Natalie's nose, lay flat across her lips, and moved as she spoke.

Two weeks later, Ah Boon left work early to catch Natalie at the CC before she went home for the day. He carried in one hand two small tin cans of warm coffee—kopi O from Natalie's favorite coffee shop, thick and tarry—and in the other, a bunch of six pink roses.

As Ah Boon approached the CC, Swee Hong and Ah Tong emerged from the building.

"Boon! Eh, Boon!" Ah Tong called.

Ah Boon forced a smile.

"Wah! What's this? Brought coffee for us?" Swee Hong shouted.

"So nice ah, boy, bring coffee for us—" Ah Tong stopped, eyeing the flowers.

"Ah Tong, Swee Hong," Ah Boon called.

The older men nodded. Swee Hong was doing his best to suppress his smirk, but Ah Tong was openly gawking.

"Who's that for, Boon? Got girlfriend never tell us?"

Ah Boon hated the way his cheeks grew hot, hated how he grew tongue-tied as soon as he stepped back into the kampong. "I—" he said.

"Who is it? Auntie Hock? Auntie Kim?" Swee Hong jabbed one

thumb over his shoulder, toward the CC, grinning impishly. Then the smile fell from his face. "No. That Gah Woman? Natalie?"

"Your girlfriend is the Gah Woman?" Ah Tong said.

Ah Boon cringed. He stared at the CC door, willing Natalie not to come out right now. "Shh. She's not—"

"How serious is it? You going to marry her? Don't give your uncle a shock like this, boy," Ah Tong said.

He and Swee Hong exchanged glances. Of course the whole kampong knew of the rift between Ah Boon and Uncle. Still Uncle wouldn't go to the CC.

"Aiya, leave the young ones alone," Swee Hong said, clapping a hand on Ah Tong's back. "Ah Boon adult already, he knows what to do. Hor, Boon?"

Ah Boon couldn't nod. All he could think about was Natalie coming out of the CC doors, hearing Ah Tong proclaiming that Ah Boon wanted to marry her.

"He knows what to do," Swee Hong repeated.

"That woman," Ah Tong muttered, shaking his head.

The door of the CC swung open. Natalie stepped out, one hand in a salute shielding her eyes from the sun. She tilted her face toward them.

"I talk to you later," Ah Boon said hurriedly, pushing past the two men.

This was not the state of mind he wanted to meet Natalie in. No doubt Ah Tong would stop by their house to tell Uncle and Ma what he had seen. For every hour that Ah Boon did not return home, they would speculate and presume, worry and judge.

"I brought you this," he said stiffly. He handed Natalie her coffee.

"Oh! Thank you," Natalie said.

When she saw the flowers, the corners of her lips twitched up. With the sun setting all around them, the white building behind her was drenched in orange light, and it was hard to tell if this was color reflected onto her face or if she was blushing.

"And this is for you," he mumbled, eyes fixed on the wall behind her as he handed her the roses.

They had not traveled well and were even more wilted now, but Natalie beamed as she received them. She stuck her nose in the flowers and took a deep breath, then exhaled. Ah Boon felt something inside him tighten and expand, as if she were breathing straight into him.

Natalie thanked him calmly for the flowers, as if she had been expecting them, and for this, Ah Boon was grateful. Had she exclaimed in surprise or acted as if anything at all was out of the ordinary, he would surely have flushed, stuttered, wanted to run away. How measured she always was, he thought with admiration, how tactfully she behaved. There was such a calm about her; it always set him at ease. Now he was able to regain his composure, to talk to her normally again. How was her day? Did she see the latest memo about the three new CCs that had been opened? How about the news of the merger referendum that had just been announced? What did she think of the whole thing? And then, casually, he took her by the elbow and said he thought they might go for a walk by the beach.

Natalie nodded as if this, too, was something she expected, and fell in step with Ah Boon so smoothly that he thought of the old fishing boats with their taut sails. They walked side by side. From time to time, he sipped his coffee. It had cooled now, retained only the memory of heat.

The last shadows were being wrung from the trees around them, ocher light flung across the faces of rocks by the dirt path. This hour always filled Ah Boon with melancholy. He could no more stop the sun from setting than he could raise Pa from his watery, unknown grave, or resurrect the two joyful children he and Siok Mei had once been. But instead, he consoled himself, there could be this: Natalie, luminous and beautiful, her every thought and action reverberating with calm purpose.

Soon they were at the beach. It was low tide; the surf pulled back, the wet sand vast and desolate, studded with slick pebbles and mops of bedraggled seaweed.

"You've seen it?" Natalie said.

She lifted her chin to the east, where the beach extended away from the setting sun and gave way to swamp. Ah Boon turned. He'd seen it, of course. Everyone in the kampong had. The fill site wasn't much to look at, not yet, since only the pilot phase had just begun. It certainly did not seem to merit the name it had been given: the Great Reclamation Project. Yet it was only the beginning. Only exploratory work. Forty-eight hectares of land to be conjured out of the sea. And if it went well, a further hundred hectares to follow.

A lone bulldozer stood close to the shore. Behind it, the silhouettes of a few small lorries. Signs and tape cordoning off the area. No heavy machinery like Ah Boon had seen at the dig site; no excavators with their swaying buckets, no saw-toothed trenchers or even large dump trucks. One could almost forget it was a fill site at all, if not for the huge piles of sand, higher than an attap house. Seen from here they appeared like dormant volcanoes risen out of the sea, or the shadow of some ancient, hump-backed creature lying along the beach. Ah Boon counted six piles in total. Just last week, there had been only four.

The sand had been moved there by a two-mile-long conveyor belt, the very same one he'd seen leaving the excavation site. It was more economical, he had been told, to build such a structure than to pay the wages of drivers to move the vast amount of fill material with trucks. Taking seven months to design and three weeks to build in its entirety, it was an ingenious feat of engineering. Two tons of steel and thirty thousand nails, the chief engineer had told him with pride.

The snakelike conveyor belt, the uncompromising mounds of sand, the bulky trucks. Ah Boon was pricked by an uneasy feeling. But he reminded himself of how he'd felt when the CC had first appeared in the kampong. Any change was difficult. Still, it was a wretched thought, that their coast would be destroyed.

Altered, he corrected himself. There would still be a coast. It would simply be different. And different was not bad; different could be better. He thought of all the people who lived in the city, people who were less fortunate than he, who did not have space and fruit trees and the sea for their children to bathe in. He thought again of the soaring, majestic blocks of flats.

"Just think about it. Soon, all this will be land," Natalie said. "And if it works, it's only the beginning. Think how much stronger we'll be if we can make land wherever we need. A little island like our own. First, independence, then, who knows! Why should we not have everything the Ang Mohs do? Why not enjoy the same prosperity that the West does? And here we are, about to take the very first step. You can achieve anything with a hardworking people, a dedicated government—"

Her words always made him feel better. Ah Boon nodded along, allowing himself to be swept away by the gentle fervor of her speech, like a child being rocked to sleep. Yes, it might be sad that the coast would be changed. It was a sacrifice, and sacrifices were necessary. Siok Mei had made sacrifices too—she had sacrificed him.

He marveled at Natalie's mind, her firm ambition and placid objectivity. How reassuring it was, to have such a confident vision of the future. With Natalie he would never feel afraid again.

They had both finished their coffee. First Ah Boon took their empty tin cans and carefully wedged them behind a rock so they wouldn't roll away. Then he took the roses from her and placed them on the wet sand. Finally, he took her face in his hands.

Her lips were soft and warm, her mouth faintly sour from the coffee. Her tongue touching his through his teeth was deliciously obscene. Sweet and a little acrid, her breath was like something secret arising from within her. He breathed it in greedily.

Ah Boon drew back, but when he did, she leaned into him to fill the space that opened up between them. Her face was heavy against his chest, and he felt, finally, that it was really happening. The smell of her skin was one that he was already familiar with, for he had observed it faintly, unconsciously, as they went about their days. He breathed against her scalp, taking in the salty-sweet scent of her. He would be safe now. A different future was possible, one in which the ghost of Pa did not linger around every corner, where his failed love for Siok Mei did not matter, a bright, orderly, prosperous future. And Natalie would take him there.

In the distance, a single bird landed on the metal arm of the lone bulldozer, and the cry of the night insects began to rise from the bushes.

Chapter Thirty-Three

A report on fishing communities had been commissioned by the
Deputy Secretary, a formidable project to gather comprehen-
sive data on demographics, livelihoods, and socioeconomic
makeup of the region. *Before it all changed* was the subtext, before the
coast as they knew it was reshaped forever.

Despite the two junior members of staff who'd been assigned to his
team to assist, Ah Boon decided to conduct the interviews himself. It
meant he could spend his afternoons in the kampong instead of the office, and see Natalie more often. The irony of having made such an attempt to leave, only to make the same attempt to return, was not lost on
him. And yet it gave Ah Boon pleasure to walk the kampong's broad
paths in the middle of the day, to watch the dogs lazily swat flies from
their tails, to let the shrill cry of insects fill his head. Besides, it was not
the same Ah Boon who returned.

Each afternoon he picked a neighbor's door to knock on. Greeted with
smiles and offers of peanuts and soft drinks, he would stay for an hour or
so to chat about the latest goings-on in the kampong. Toward the end of
the hour he might ask them some questions about when and where they
had been born, how they would characterize their livelihoods, whether

they owned or rented the dwelling they lived in, and so on. Often they would tease him as he conducted this official portion of the interview. Little Ah Boon all grown up, wearing the Gah Men's uniform and asking questions with big, important English words!

At first he performed these duties with embarrassment—*you know this is just work, I have to talk like this*—but slowly he came to enjoy these last fifteen minutes of his visits, where he got to take the papers out from his leather briefcase and spread them onto whatever worn kitchen table or floor mat was nearby, to uncap his elegant fountain pen and examine the nib for ink clots, clear his throat and read the official questions from the interview template.

"What are your preferred fishing methods?" he'd ask.

Jaring-hanyut, *drift net*. Panching-mengail, *hand line*. Pelontang, *floated line*. There were also the methods involving multiple households, pukat-tarek, *beach seine*. Twelve to fifteen fishermen standing in the shallows. The large dragnet cast in a billowing arc while the boat moved against the tide. The graceful dance of fishermen jumping overboard, two groups at either end to haul the net in as they approached the shore. There were the kelongs, permanent wooden platforms on nibong trunks built in deeper waters to catch larger fish: ikan tenggiri, parang, selar. Owned by towkays who would engage the services of the likes of Pak Hassan to locate the best fishing grounds, they were expensive structures, costing at times up to sixty thousand dollars.

"After reclamation, how?" the fishermen would ask Ah Boon anxiously at this point in the interview.

"Don't worry so much," he'd say. Smaller methods that involved taking a boat out would likely be fine. One might simply have to go a little farther than before. Ah Boon did not comment on the future of methods that relied on shallow waters; beach seines would be impossible once the works began, and no one knew exactly how the kelongs might be affected.

The interviewees' reactions to this would vary based on whether they had chosen to leave or stay. Those who'd applied for flats were sanguine, perhaps a little wistful, but did not dwell. Those who were undecided or who'd chosen to stay would fall silent, at times staring at Ah Boon as if they had been personally betrayed.

It was natural for them to feel this way. But no one had been personally betrayed, Ah Boon told himself. They would understand once the work was completed. Their little kampong would be the site of a historic undertaking; and while it might be upsetting that old ways of life were altered, surely everyone would be proud to witness their part in the project that would change the trajectory of their country. *From Third World to First*, he thought to himself, recalling the architect-planner's words.

And how he enjoyed translating the English words that the interviewees did not understand, growing accustomed to the undertone of respect that laced their questions. They fussed and they worried, but beneath it all was the grudging shimmer of pride, as if they, by being part of the kampong that had raised the now-important Ah Boon, had a personal hand in his success.

He might conduct two or three interviews in one afternoon. Then, around four o'clock, he'd walk over to the CC. The heat was just beginning to soften, and he'd make a point to walk slowly, staying in the shade of trees. If he was careful, he arrived at the CC with only the slightest sheen of sweat on the back of his neck. Often he stood under the awning of the CC building, just out of sight of the entrance, cooling off before he went in. In these moments he often felt himself caught in a swell of emotion. Not happiness exactly; rather, the feeling that he *would* be happy now, that life might not be as impossible as he had once believed. In the distance, the wind raked the sea, throwing off sparks of light as if in quiet celebration. The sound of someone mending a boat somewhere—the hammering of nails, sawing of wood—might float through the otherwise still afternoon. The CC was far enough away from the fill site that the clanking of the conveyor belt could barely be heard, the occasional roar of trucks no louder than the distant cry of some animal in the forest.

But he did not think of work in these moments. It was the pale curve of Natalie's neck that preoccupied him, the strange triangular mole behind her left earlobe, the surprising coarseness of her thick, glossy hair. Her small, placid mouth, out of which came the powerful words and ideas that would conjure their new city. He liked to dream of her as she sat just meters away, on the other side of the brick wall.

At times, he ventured to imagine himself the Ah Boon of old: that awkward, silent youth so in awe of Natalie when he first arrived at the CC. He remembered his badly fitting shirt, his worn shoes, the way the words had stuck in his throat as he shrank before Mr. Yik. The memory of his past self only made greater the pleasure when he turned his thoughts back to the present. He was better able to savor his current position, secure in the knowledge that in five minutes or so, he would walk into the CC, open the door to the glass office, and press his lips to Natalie's perfect, previously unattainable face.

Rudely the noise began just before lunch, as men tucked into steaming bowls of noodles at the stand outside the CC, unwrapped warm buns from damp cloths, settled at kitchen tables where pickled vegetables were laid out. A dull *thunk*, so loud that some thought that bombshells were falling, that after twenty years the war had returned. Then a pause, in which the seabirds could be heard again, the waves, the insects. Perhaps they had imagined it. But no, here it came, louder now, more insistent—*thunk, thunk, thunk*—reverberating around the kampong and for miles around. This time it did not stop. The piling had begun.

The pilot project had been going for a while, and the kampong had grown accustomed to rising, each morning, to the sounds of the conveyor belt clanking into action. Down the shore scuttled crabs as the jarring noise began. Each night, as faces were washed outside houses, moon reflected in buckets, the conveyor belt clanked and droned. The piles of sand grew higher and more numerous with each week that passed, like enormous anthills with especially industrious inhabitants.

But the noise of the piling was different. Before the seabed could be filled with sand, it had to be reinforced with concrete pillars driven deep into the earth. These were unloaded by enormous ships, ships that looked too large to be docked that close to land. With a complex contraption of pulleys and chains, they lowered the pillars off their metal decks, onto platforms where the pile drivers awaited.

An assault on body as much as mind, this noise entered the ears and trammeled the bones, loosened the fibers holding muscles together. Decades later, people would attribute strokes, heart attacks, pulmonary embolisms to a slow chain reaction the noise set off in their bodies that morning the piling began. One man's eczema, triggered by its scraping force on his already sensitive skin. Another woman's color blindness, a result of brain cells rearranged by violent sound waves. The noise slowed clocks, lengthened hours, caused shadows to pool unnaturally at the bases of trees in ways that they ought not to. Food rotted more quickly than it should, water boiled more slowly. With the noise came aches in knee joints and tenderness in gums, nervousness in sleep, aggression at work.

The people who came to the CC now did not want to play table tennis or weiqi. Even the pleasure of television was ruined, punctuated always by the relentless *thunk, thunk, thunk.*

"Si Gah Men, what are they doing?"

"How you expect us to live like this? Huh?"

"Cannot, aiyo, cannot!"

Auntie Kim and Auntie Hock were dispatched to the front desk in these trying times. In front of them sat two large bowls of foam bits in candy colors—disposable earplugs. Their job was to listen patiently to the complaints, nodding and saying that they understood, that the complainant's message would be relayed, then to hand over a pair of earplugs. They were infinitely patient, their liver-spotted hands clasped at their chests, their crepe-skinned eyes crinkled sympathetically, and yet they could do nothing else but listen.

And so the villagers went to Ah Boon, and the peaceful routine of his interviews was broken. Now no one offered him water or peanuts when he visited; instead, they launched into a tirade of complaints as soon as he set foot in their house.

"What are your preferred fishing methods?" he asked Ghim Huat—a little nervously, as he'd always been intimidated by the headman—one afternoon.

"What fishing, how to fish, cannot eat, cannot sleep! My sons say all the fish scared away by the noise! And the water, so sandy, how to see anything? Fishing not good, not good, Boon, what are you going to do?" Ghim Huat, usually so calm, was full of agitation. He thumped his cane against the floor.

"But the islands," Ah Boon said. "The fishing around the islands is always good."

Ghim Huat squinted at him. His milky brown eyes, clouded with cataracts, had the unnerving look of a cooked fish.

"When you last go to the islands?"

"Don't know." Ah Boon racked his brain. "Maybe—a year ago?"

Not since he had become a Gah Man, certainly. But he was so busy, and besides, there was no need for it. Uncle fished, Hia fished, and even if they did not, Ah Boon made enough money to feed them all.

Ghim Huat shook his head heavily. "You are Ah Huat's son. You have a responsibility to this place."

His words stung. Who was Ghim Huat to lecture him on who he was? What did he know of the reclamation project? Of the work that Ah Boon was doing?

"I know," Ah Boon replied tersely.

Ghim Huat was the head fisherman. Ah Boon would not be rude to him. But how tiresome these people were. First Uncle, now Ghim Huat. All they did was repeat themselves, over and over. Did they not realize things were changing? In a modern country, there were no fishermen. People had jobs in factories and offices. They drove cars and lived in concrete houses. They had kitchens with refrigerators and ceramic tiles.

"Go to the islands, boy. See for yourself."

Ghim Huat was still staring at him with his eyes that had terrified Ah Boon as a boy and still disturbed him now. There was a long pause. A prickling cold seemed to creep over Ah Boon's skin. It was true, he had been so caught up with his new career that he no longer knew what was going on in the kampong, let alone with the islands. The old feeling of possessiveness returned. They were *his* islands, after all. He had found them. Surely he would have heard, or felt, or somehow known if they had been affected in some way. But what if Ghim Huat was right?

"Let's get back to the questions. How did you finance the purchase of your first boat?"

Three months from Ah Boon's interview with Ghim Huat, the report still had not been completed. The Deputy Secretary summoned him for a meeting to discuss the slow progress.

"Are you facing problems?" he asked, baring his yellow teeth.

"No," Ah Boon lied.

The Deputy Secretary made a pyramid of his fingers, on which he perched his chin. "Ah Boon. I am here to help you. What seems to be the problem?"

"It's— I— Nothing, sir. They're just not used to it, that's all," Ah Boon said. "The noise, the dust."

"Then it is good that they will soon be leaving, is it not?"

Ah Boon nodded.

"My dear man, the document you are compiling will be an important record of our time. It will be an archive of what our country looked like before the great changes to come. One day, our descendants will look back and marvel at these accounts of outdoor toilets and hard manual labor. It will allow them to appreciate how far they have come, how many sacrifices have been made. What it takes to claw our way into modernity."

Ah Boon nodded again. He believed the Deputy Secretary, but the gnawing feeling he'd had ever since the interview with Ghim Huat would not go away.

The ministry had just had air-conditioning installed, a change hailed as an incredible luxury. Senior Gah Men believed air-conditioning to be crucial to productivity, and indeed, many were already choosing to eat at their desks over braving the heat to go out for lunch. A new air of crisp efficiency prevailed; everywhere in the building people moved more briskly, ceased lingering in hallways, even found themselves gossiping less. The languid tropical heat had been successfully banished. No more would shirts stick uncomfortably to backs during long meetings, no longer would mosquitoes slide maddeningly in and out of earshot as one tried to write an especially tricky memo. An efficient, climate-controlled future was now possible, and the island had begun its swift march into it.

Ah Boon knew the air-conditioning was meant to be more comfortable, and indeed, in all the ways people talked about, it was. But he found it unsettling. In it, his body—all its heavy, perspiring, itchy weight—seemed to disappear altogether. At times he felt he was floating, a brain held aloft by invisible fluid. It made him forget he was there. And the chilled air itself was strange, suspended, thinned out, as if the water had been drained from it.

He tried to like it. It was a mark of civilization, of advancement. Yet his office, which he'd initially been so proud of, felt like a jail cell. The once-beloved typewriter was now a tyrannical reminder of the work he had not done. Each time he sat down with the intention of going through the transcriptions his assistants had prepared, a deep fatigue overcame him, and his shoulders began to ache. And there were still interviews to be completed, yet he avoided the kampong, since all the residents did was complain about the disruption being caused by the reclamation work. Too loud, too dusty, too few fish. What was he to do about it?

When he told Natalie this, they were having lunch at their usual noodle stand. She lowered the chopsticks from her mouth, placing the fish ball she'd had in their grasp carefully back into her bowl.

"Progress cannot be won without dedication," she said. "Our decisions will not always be popular. We have to make difficult choices that the people cannot make for themselves."

"But—" Ah Boon struggled to articulate what he felt. "How do you know what's right? If people are unhappy?"

"Our job is not to keep people happy. Our job is to do what's best for them, in the long term."

"Right," Ah Boon said. Still his mind raced. What was best for the kampong? What did he want for them? He thought of the war, of Pa kneeling on a distant shore, riots in the streets, Siok Mei handcuffed and taken away.

He wanted them to be safe, he thought. He did not want to lose anyone else.

"In a country, everyone has their role. We are here to serve the people, but that does not always mean agreeing with them. Think about a family. What is best for a family? Is that achieved by a parent giving in to their child?"

The logic of her reasoning was irresistible. But it was he who had decided on this course, he reminded himself, not Natalie, and he must stick to it. His old life was gone. Most of the kampong was leaving. His family, too, would move. And the truth was he did not want to go back to being his old self, the little boy who could not save Pa, who could not keep Siok Mei. The Gah Men had power. Their trenchers and bulldozers advanced with an inexorable might. With them, Ah Boon would never be helpless again. And the kampong would be housed, would have new kitchens and light, would be safe. At this thought the warm glow of certainty was restored to him.

"Where is this going?" Natalie said at last, staring at him with uncharacteristic intensity. "What are we doing together?"

Ah Boon had no answer for her then, or rather, he could not speak what was in his heart. The logical step, of course, was to marry her.

"How's your noodles?" he said instead.

His ears burned. Natalie fell silent, poking with her chopsticks at the slivers of prawn in her soup.

"Good," she said after a long while.

She would not fill the silence, he could tell. She was allowing the awkwardness to hang in the air, to accuse him for his failure. He wanted to marry her. Did he? He did. Still, Ah Boon did not speak.

By the time the stallholder came to clear away the half-full bowls—even if they weren't done, he needed the seats back for the busy lunch hour—the silence had soured and settled into a fact. The day was ruined;

what ought to have been said was unsaid. They kissed perfunctorily and parted ways.

Back in his office, Ah Boon threw himself into the haphazard pile of transcriptions on his desk. The work was slow and tedious, the air-conditioning hummed maddeningly overhead. One of his assistants knocked, wanting to know if he would be going to the kampong to conduct interviews that afternoon. Ah Boon felt a tug of longing; he could see Natalie, put his arms around her, apologize, make up for his earlier silence. But then he would have to face the kampong and their questions about the noise, the dust, the fishing.

Ah Boon looked down at the pile of transcriptions and told the assistant no, he would not be conducting interviews today. The assistant should go instead.

It was Wednesday. Ah Boon did not go to the CC on Thursday or Friday either, ringing Natalie to tell her he thought he should concentrate on getting the report done for the Deputy Secretary. She did not sound upset over the phone, although when Ah Boon thought about it, he had never really heard Natalie get upset, so perhaps it was more the case that he could not tell. He spent the next few days obsessively searching his memories of their interactions for signs of Natalie being upset. How could he claim to know her if he had never seen her sad or unhappy? This led him to think about all he did not know about Natalie. The sisters she would not let him meet, the mysterious aged father whose precise nature of villainy was unclear.

On Saturday, he went to the office again. He worked, he continued to brood.

Natalie knew his family and friends. She spent her days at the CC, often going back and forth between kampongs on the dirt road Ah Boon had taken to school as a little boy. But there were some things she would never know about him. She would never meet Pa, whose absence still made life feel porous to Ah Boon; it was so easy to slip over into non-existence. And there was everything else that had disappeared, that was disappearing. Siok Mei. The fish, the coast.

If he were to tie his life to Natalie's, to remake himself anew, he wanted, also, for something of his old self to be known. The islands, he thought.

Abruptly Ah Boon stood up and went to catch a bus to Natalie's boardinghouse.

The boardinghouse was in an area he was familiar with from his days with the student unions, many of their events having taken place in the clan association buildings there. He passed an old, crowded temple. A long time ago it had been a sea temple, one of the clan elders had told him once, next to where the harbor used to be, so that men could pray to the sea gods before they set sail. Then the Ang Mohs filled in the harbor with sand cut from a nearby hill, pushing the coast out to where it was today. Now the temple was just a regular temple. Ah Boon went in, lit a few joss sticks. He asked that Natalie not leave him, that he would know how to keep her. It occurred to him that Natalie was Catholic. They did not give up their religion easily, he knew, and so if he was to marry her, he would become Catholic as well.

He left the temple and walked to the boardinghouse. It was an old shophouse in the middle of a busy street, above a provisions store not unlike the one that Swee Hong ran in the kampong, but much larger. Large baskets overflowed with chilies, dried mushrooms, and red dates. Housewives sniffed cloves of garlic; store assistants lounged on wooden stools, shouting to girls passing in the street. Next to the provisions store was a medicine shop, next to that, a carpenter, and next to that, a tailor. Bicycles weaved by, trishaws rumbled past. Water dripped from wet laundry that hung from bamboo poles poking out of windows on the upper floors of the shophouses.

Ah Boon had never been there before. How strange that Natalie lived here, amid all these people and all this noise, in a building that she would normally condemn as outdated and unsafe. He climbed the stairs to the second floor, where an elderly woman sat fanning herself behind a counter. A Cantonese drama blared from a Rediffusion radio set in the corner. The woman was plump, her clothing clean and without patches. A gold chain glinted at her neck.

The woman narrowed her eyes at him. From the chain hung a large pendant of fine, pale jade, likely very expensive. From this he guessed her to be the owner of the boardinghouse.

"Low pan leong," Ah Boon said.

He asked for Natalie. His Cantonese was poor, and he stumbled over the words.

"I call her to come down," she said. "No men upstairs."

She shouted to a little girl sitting in the window, playing with a loop of yarn. The girl ran up the stairs.

Ah Boon was left fidgeting in the doorway. He could still hear the shouts of the provision shop assistants coming from downstairs.

Suddenly, he thought of Siok Mei. He remembered now with a jolt that she lived in a shophouse somewhere in this exact neighborhood, and he moved toward the open window to look down into the street, as if she would be right there.

"Boon," a voice called. He turned, certain for a moment it was her.

But there Natalie stood, at the base of the same wooden stairs the little girl had gone up. Instead of being pulled up into its usual ponytail, her hair floated about her face in a soft, silky cloud. She wore not the usual white uniform, but instead a butter-yellow dress that was fitted at the waist and stopped at midcalf. Her feet were propped up by little navy shoes with straps across the fronts and tiny flower shapes cut out of the leather.

Emotion—relief or love, he could not tell—rushed into his chest, making him feel large and buoyant. He was suddenly aware of the tinny Cantonese voices coming from the radio set, the clicking of the boarding-house owner's lacquered nails against the worn wood counter, the roar and trundle of the road downstairs. Natalie came to him, the hem of her dress fluttering in the solid light that streamed in through the window.

"Let's get married," Ah Boon said.

"What?"

"Married," he said again. He took her hand and it was exactly as he remembered, warm in the palm, cool at the wrist. He pressed the face of his thumb against her skin, counting the beats of her pulse.

"I'm not—"

"Don't answer yet," Ah Boon said. He brought her wrist to his mouth. He saw her brows begin to knit. He would not let her say no. "Don't answer now, let me show you something first."

"I really don't think—"

He clapped his hands over his ears. "Can't hear you," he said. "Can't hear anything you're saying."

Slowly her face relaxed into a smile.

"Fine," she mouthed. "Show me."

Chapter Thirty-Four

At four thirty the next morning, Ah Boon waited at the bus stop by the light of a battery-operated flashlight. He had bought it in the city yesterday, along with a tin of lemon cream biscuits and a simple, narrow jade bangle. The biscuits were stowed in the boat that was waiting on the beach, along with a flask of hot, freshly brewed tea. The bangle was in its little silk pouch, nestled in his left pocket.

As he waited, he seemed to hear every insect rubbing its wings together in the undergrowth, could feel every wet, sodden leaf disintegrating into the earth. Hours before, he'd dragged the boat down to the beach in the dark. The particular damp smell of morning, the flash of moon behind gauzy clouds, the slow, dependable crash of waves. He half expected to see Hia and Pa waiting for him.

Ghim Huat's words would not leave him. Each interview he'd done after Ghim Huat's had mentioned the same thing. The fish were gone. He could not bear to ask Uncle, but had raised it casually with Hia the day before.

"You don't know meh?" Hia had said with a surprised look. "Boon, already got no fish for weeks. Ever since they started digging."

"And the islands?" Ah Boon had asked.

"Same thing. Bad, very bad. But we are leaving soon, anyway, so looking for other jobs. Construction is good these days, pays a lot." Hia scrutinized his brother's face. "Why? Uncle giving you a hard time?" he asked.

"No," Ah Boon said. "Hia—" He stopped.

"What?"

He wanted to ask if he was doing the right thing. If joining the Gah Men had been a mistake. If, perhaps, the flats were not the brilliant solution he had thought them to be.

"Are you happy to move?" he asked instead.

"Gek Huay is happy," Hia said, "so I am happy. She will have more to do there. More shops to go to, more friends to meet. Not always at home with Ah Huat."

He paused, then leaned over and patted Ah Boon on the shoulder.

"Not that I like this Gah Men now. But I think the move is good."

Ah Boon's eyes grew unexpectedly hot, so grateful was he for Hia's kindness.

"But people are upset—"

"After they move, they'll forget. Don't worry so much."

"And the fish?"

Hia sighed, cupping a hand over his mouth.

"Boon," he said at last. "Cannot have everything. You made this choice. Now we live with it."

What did it mean to live with something? He had to confront it for himself. He wanted Natalie to see the islands, to know the place so intimately threaded into his past, to understand what was being given up. And so he was here, waiting for her. Light snaked around a bend in the road. Then the sound of the bus, the noise and fumes of it shocking in the quiet, dark morning. It clattered to a stop, and out stepped Natalie.

They murmured greetings without kissing. She touched a cold hand to his. Birds seemed to fall silent on their perches, the insects' roar lowered to a gentle trill. The bus disappeared down the road, taking its light and noise with it.

Back they went down the muddy trail, away from the road and toward the beach. Halfway there she stopped. "Can you turn that off?" she said.

She meant the flashlight, which he'd been keeping pointed a few feet ahead to light her way. He clicked it off, and they were enveloped by the purple dark. Slowly their eyes adjusted. Moonlight fell piecemeal onto the dark path, strained and scattered through the shifting canopy. Above, a hornbill shrieked and flapped its wings.

Natalie threaded her fingers through Ah Boon's and they set off together again. She had no difficulty walking in the dark, moving with sure-footedness, anticipating each tree root and pothole before he did.

Soon they were at the beach. It gave him a pang to see the boat on the shore, mute and alone. He remembered another afternoon, all those years ago, when the entire kampong had gathered to see the islands for the first time. How uncomfortable he'd been to feel so many eyes on him, how afraid of being seen.

He pulled the boat down toward the surf, the water licking his ankles, rising to his knees. The boat's familiar flank bumped his hip. He called to Natalie. When she reached the surf, she paused, as if contemplating whether she could possibly make it to the boat without getting her feet wet. Then, hitching her skirt up, she stepped squarely into the water.

He held the boat still for her as she climbed in, canvas shoes dripping. Ah Boon took his usual spot at the engine. If it were day, the strangeness of the situation would be impossible to bear: Natalie sitting there in her blue dress, its elegant high collar, hand-knotted buttons that crept across her chest. Smooth white hands that had never hauled a net or scrubbed a deck crossed neatly on her lap. And he, in the incongruous outfit he'd put on this morning—ironed shirt and rough fisherman's pants, gel in his hair—sitting at the boat's helm. He was glad for the darkness. He was hoping they would not meet any other boats, that no one from the kampong would see them. *Wah, Gah Man go fishing still must wear uniform*— but it did not matter. He started the engine and with a loud rip, they were off.

"Oh!" Natalie cried as the boat surged forward. Her hands shot down to grab the wooden plank of her seat. Steadying herself, she turned her face to the wind.

He would marry this woman, Ah Boon thought. He would marry her and the rest of his life would be complete. They would apply for a flat of their own. With Natalie's help, he would climb the ranks of the Gah Men, eventually earning enough money for her to leave her own job, to stay at home and raise their children. There would be children, three, perhaps four. As Ma got older, she would come live with them, to help with the children and keep Natalie company.

"What's that?" Natalie said.

A large shape loomed to their right. The waves grew choppy. A loud vibrating noise was coming from it—it was a ship.

Large merchant ships did sometimes pass the fishermen on their way to the harbor, but Ah Boon had never seen one in waters this shallow before. And instead of the usual containers stacked like enormous bricks, the ship seemed to be carrying a small hill, as if a sugar merchant had dispensed with sacks and simply heaped the merchandise on the deck.

"Sand," Natalie said.

The mounds of sand loomed like a slow mountain range. Their little boat rocked in its shadow, and Ah Boon turned the engine off. He had done this, he found himself thinking, he had invited this into the kampong, into their home. But he had not made it happen, he protested.

These changes had been set in motion by a power much greater than himself. And yet he had gone along with it, had cast his lot on this side of history.

What did he hope showing Natalie the islands would do? To him it felt like some great sacrifice, like baring his soul. But they would not have the same significance for her, she who had grown up far from the sea, on solid ground, prosperous land where trees grew in straight, irrigated rows.

The ship passed, it was quiet again. All around them the sea was empty.

"Maybe we should go back," Ah Boon said. "Are you cold? I don't want you to fall sick."

"No," she said. "Let's keep going. We should keep going."

"What?"

"I don't know—I have this feeling."

Natalie turned her head to the left, then to the right, then to the left again. Then, with one swift motion, she threw her arm out, pointing with great conviction into the darkness.

"There," she said. "It sounds crazy, but we have to go there."

Sitting with the warm engine pressed against his thigh, the boat rocking gently in the dark, Ah Boon had the disconcerting feeling that he had become his father, all those years ago when he'd asked his seven-year-old son to find the islands that no one believed existed.

Ah Boon started the engine again. He felt, too, that they were moving toward Batu, and its pull was irresistible. Again he was that little boy who could not take his eyes off the horizon; again he longed to set foot on its sparkling white sands. Within minutes, the dark shapes of cliffs loomed in the distance.

Natalie let out a cry. Ah Boon felt it as a splinter piercing some deep and hidden part of him. He wanted to wrap his arms around her, but also push her away, over the side of the boat, to leave and never come back. He was reminded of the moment Ah Tong had jumped off the boat unbidden and swum to the island's shores. But the other fishermen he'd known all his life. They were of the sea in ways that he himself could never be, and the islands belonged to them too, even if he was the one who'd found them.

Natalie was an outsider. But had she not just found the islands he'd thought only the kampong could find? Perhaps it was a sign. After all, he loved her, he wanted to marry her. It was he who'd brought her here, he who had wanted her to see. And so she would see.

He guided the boat to its usual spot, a short distance away from shore. Scarce moonlight lit the high pale cliffs, the bone-white sand. Dark treetops laced against the purple sky.

"Where are we?" Natalie asked.

"It's hard to explain," Ah Boon said.

"Merlimau, maybe? Seking? Sajahat?" She wrinkled her nose, thinking of the map. "But we traveled maybe twenty minutes. No, we didn't go nearly far enough."

Natalie stared at the island with the same interrogative intensity she had when trying to balance a budget or summarize a particularly difficult piece of information. Ah Boon's hand went to the rudder. It would not be difficult to start the engine and whisk her away, convince Natalie it was some strange hallucination, a common mirage that fishermen encountered in the dead of night. How quickly the island resolved for her into a puzzle, a problem that could be solved with the application of sufficient thought.

"What do you think it is, Boon?" Natalie said.

She turned to him, moonlight spilling across her forehead. In the half-light, she was sculptural. Her small nose porcelain and delicate, her eyes like dark pools, inscrutable as a fox. She was waiting to hear what he thought. Calling to him as an equal, as one who would wield his intellect as sharply as hers, who would rationally participate in the solving of the problem of this landmass where there should have been none.

Ah Boon didn't answer, but instead lowered the nets. Following his lead, Natalie fell silent and turned to contemplate the cliffs rising before them. They waited. Five minutes passed, then ten. There was an unnatural stillness to the water. Ah Boon found himself stroking the side of the boat as was once Pa's habit. Eventually he hauled the nets up. They showed what he already knew from how light they were: a paltry catch, ten, maybe fifteen silvery bodies wriggled in the moonlight. Shaken, he let the net slip from his hands, and the thrashing fish took it down into the dark sea with them.

"What's wrong?" Natalie said.

Her face was so understanding, so earnest, but it brought him no comfort. How could he explain to her what was wrong? To do so he would have to go back twenty years, to the very first day that he, Pa, and Hia had come to this island. He would have to explain what it was to be a child, terrified and in awe, out at sea for the first time. To recount that sultry afternoon when they'd brought the rest of the kampong to the islands, to describe the feeling of walking through the pristine undergrowth with Siok Mei's small, hot hand in his. He had done this. It was his fault.

He gestured lamely at the lost net. "The fish."

"Yes?"

"They're gone," he said, heavy-hearted.

"What do you mean? There were fish in the net, you just let them go," Natalie said.

Her forehead was scrunched up. How straightforward it was to her. There had been fish, she had seen it. There was an island, there must be a rational explanation. No complicated histories, no ghostly vanishings, no mysterious carpets of fish.

His hand went from the rudder to his pocket, where he felt the hard shape of the jade bangle. Was this not what he wanted? A woman who would shine a light into every darkened, cobwebbed corner of his mind, of his life? He might be the head of the Citizens' Working Group. He might even advance within the ministry to a more senior role. He would move from the kampong to a flat, maybe even buy a private apartment or house of his own one day.

Yet he knew this: Thirty, forty years in the future, even if he was a man like Mr. Yik—house in a leafy estate, servants, a car of his own—a sheen of unreality would continue to glisten over the surface of his life, like morning dew on the leaves of trees, too pervasive and innocuous to shake off. But Natalie would live in his house as if he had always owned it, sit next to him in his car as if he had been born to be there. She would speak English to their children and they would grow up knowing nothing different.

A splash came from behind them. Something was turning in the water; every now and then, a slick smooth surface, shiny as if polished with oil, would present itself to the moon. At first, Ah Boon thought it might be the fish, that they had returned after all. But then a snout became visible, a bulky torso, a tail.

He gasped. "Dugongs. Look, Natalie!"

There were four of them, three large and one small, a pup. Their round, meaty heads were almost human, in a way that whales' or dolphins' weren't. Their bodies were cylindrical, their snouts square, as if a walrus had been crossed with a fish. And yet, despite their appearance, they moved with such slow elegance it was impossible not to feel he bore witness to something rare and dignified.

When Ah Boon was a boy, dugongs had been a common sight in the estuaries along the coast. Once, when they were both little, Hia had taken him to see them, borrowing a paddleboat from a friend and rowing with Ah Boon through the swamp to the mouth of the river. He remembered the heady scent of the flowers in the berembang trees, the sound of water lapping the mangrove roots, the tiny fireflies that had dotted the tree branches as the sun began to go down.

It was ten years ago—long before the CC had appeared, long before the words *land reclamation* had even been spoken in these parts—that the dugongs had started to disappear. The seagrass around the coast had been receding for a while by then. The growing number of container vessels discharging their oily fumes as they passed the coast by; the water, once clear and green, now a milky brown. The loss of the seagrass. The disappearance of the hermit crabs. And now even the fish around the islands were gone.

It was true that this had been set in motion long before Ah Boon had joined the Gah Men. The fish were simply the latest to fall victim to the ships, the gambier plantations, the acrid smoke spewing from new naval bases and factories. And long before the Gah Men's thirst for industry and progress, there had been the Ang Mohs, knocking down hills, digging enormous quarries, forcing the Orang Laut up to Johor. Was this not just the latest step in a long history of destruction? Rationally Ah Boon could not be held responsible for it. Not directly, not single-handedly. Still, he felt tight with guilt. So much had been lost, so much disappeared. And the disappearing would go on, every single day.

But here were the dugongs, flaunting their graceful bulk as if nothing had changed. Surely it was a good omen, despite everything. The fish were fewer in number, but they had not vanished entirely. Perhaps the changes were not irreversible, perhaps there was a way for progress and past to coexist.

"See," Natalie said, as if reading his thoughts. "There are fish. There are dugongs. What are you worried about?"

The load on his heart began to lift.

Ah Boon started the engine at its lowest, steering the boat so that they were just meters away from the animals.

Natalie was whispering something he could not hear, her hands clasped beneath her chin. He got up from his place by the engine and went to her, the boat rocking gently beneath his careful steps. She made space for him on the wooden plank, and he squeezed in between her and the boat's side. Her warm, round hip pressed against his through the fabric of their clothes. He could hear her breathing; she smelled of coffee and soap.

Ah Boon drew the bangle from his pocket and slipped it from its pouch. It gleamed in the moonlight, a slender, perfect circle of near-transparent jade. It had cost almost all that he had saved over the past five years.

"Boon," Natalie said. "Why did you do that?"

But she was smiling, and so he took her hand, reached it over the side of the boat, and dipped it into the water. He dipped the bangle in the water too, then pressed the bones of her fingers together and slipped it over her hand. It was a tight fit—the man in the shop had warned him it might be, had in fact recommended this smaller size so as to prevent it coming off once it was on—and he worried he was hurting her, but Natalie didn't wince. When the bangle was on, she lifted her wrist to the sky and admired it.

Ah Boon wrapped his arms around her. The citrus scent of her perfume seemed incongruous out here, with the distant squawking of seabirds, the salty air settling wetly on his skin. The island, familiar and inexplicable, loomed just meters away. And yet she was here, and she was his, almost. A restless feeling came over him.

Ah Boon pulled away. "How good are you at swimming?"

Natalie shook her head. "My parents would take me as a child," she said, "but I haven't swum since—no, no, no."

He was already unbuttoning his shirt. He did it quickly, so he wouldn't have time to change his mind.

"Boon!" Natalie laughed, bringing a hand to her mouth.

Then she stopped laughing. Ah Boon, too, was still. Gently, she placed her hand on the bare skin just above his left hip, where a slim line of muscle marked the boundary between his abdomen and thigh. She brushed her thumb over that line, feeling its protrusion, pressing gently, as if testing the firmness of a plum. Where she touched it, his skin felt tender and hot, as if stricken by infection. Then her fingers, gentle yet insistent, maddening.

She undid the buttons of her dress slowly. Soon the high collar fell open to reveal the white flesh of her collarbone. Still he didn't move. Still she kept going. The dress fell to her waist.

He did not touch her. As she stood, the dress pooled at her feet. The boat rocked, the dugongs splashed. Even then, he permitted himself only to place one hand on her waist, marveling at how naturally the heel of his palm came to rest in the hollow of her back. She brought her face to his. Still the fronts of their bodies did not make contact, as if they were identical poles of a magnet, as if the force keeping them apart grew stronger the closer they drew together.

Natalie pulled away from him and dangled her legs over the side of the boat. Her underclothes were dark beige, a color of skin more tan than hers. Gone was the quality of sculpture; never had he felt so strongly that someone was alive. Blood ran in the veins beneath their skin, blood that was salty and warm should it be spilled. Pieces of interlocking bone made up the shape of her lovely forehead, bone that was delicate, fragile should it be challenged. He felt the vulnerability of her physical form painfully, and it was almost too much to bear. What was love, if not the fear of loss?

Swiftly, and with no more than a tiny splash, Natalie pushed herself off the edge of the boat. The pale skin of her arms gleamed in the moon-light as she began swimming. The dugongs did not seem to mind her presence, and went on with their business of rising and falling in the water. Ah Boon watched her pass within a meter of them. Still she kept going. Soon she would reach the island.

Chapter Thirty-Five

Uncle was chopping garlic clumsily when he heard Ah Boon's voice at the door. Hia had landed a new job, as a foreman on the construction of the new industrial estate out west, and Ma was making his favorite dish to celebrate. Black sauce chicken, stewed with star anise, cinnamon, rock sugar, and sticky dark soy sauce.

It was honest work, Uncle reflected, sweaty and backbreaking. Like fishing, the fruits of one's labor were tangible: a newly constructed building, a fresh catch of fish. It was clear what was being made or sold, unlike in Ah Boon's desk job with the ministry. And it was true that Hia would be making a good deal more than he did fishing, now that the catch was so poor. But there were so many changes, all happening at once, and Uncle did not like the feeling of the ground shifting so rapidly beneath his feet.

Hia went out to greet Ah Boon. They heard his voice, then, inexplicably, a third voice, indistinct. Uncle put the cleaver down, wiping his forehead. Ma had two fires going, one for the rice, the other for meat and vegetables. He would go see who the third voice was, he told her, glad to have an excuse to leave the kitchen.

The breeze in the living room was delicious against his skin. Hia was talking to Ah Boon and someone else in the doorway, but with the sun behind them, all Uncle could see were their shadows.

"Uncle," Ah Boon called.

"Hello, Uncle," the woman said.

At her voice he found himself clenching his jaw. It was the Gah Woman. What was her name again?

"I'm Natalie," she said, offering a hand.

Her Hokkien was polished, careful, almost too correct. He felt it untrustworthy.

Nodding curtly, Uncle turned to Ah Boon.

"Boon, your mother work so hard to cook tonight. How can just bring someone back without telling her?"

"Ma always cooks extra. Worst case, Natalie can eat my share," Ah Boon said.

He reached over to take her hand, grinning at her. The way he did it—as if no one else could see them, as if no one else were there. Uncle felt himself tightening with unreasonable rage. Why did it make him so angry, Ah Boon's relationship with the Gah Woman? Why couldn't he see his nephew's new job, his new life, as a good thing, like his sister did?

Uncle was about to speak when Hia jumped in, asking if Natalie had worked in the Chief Building Surveyor's Department previously. Though she had not, she'd frequently dealt with them in her time at the Ministry of National Development. Ah Boon shared the news of Hia's job—a three-year contract, no more bouncing around from job site to job site to supplement the fishing—and how glad they all were, not least Gek Huay with the new baby. Natalie exclaimed her congratulations, clasping her hands to her mouth in a manner that Uncle could not help but read as contrived. How wonderful, she said. She wanted to meet Gek Huay, she said.

The three of them moved back toward the kitchen, leaving Uncle standing by himself. Soon, he heard Ma's and Gek Huay's voices join theirs, Ah Huat's shouts of delight at seeing Ah Boon. The smell of caramelizing shallots wafted from the kitchen.

Uncle stepped out onto the porch, leaving the noise of the house behind him. His head pounded. Up till now he had pretended that none of it was happening. Ah Boon's job was just a phase, the CC would eventually lose its shine and shut down; even the land reclamation project, with its comical conveyor belt of dirt and piles of sand, seemed like some child's fancy bound eventually to fail. And he saw now that even if he had gone along with it to keep the peace, he had not truly believed that they would move.

But the Gah Woman's presence here—in this house, where his brother-in-law had once lived and breathed and taken him in as a member of his own family—he felt some invisible boundary had been crossed. They were really doing it. The whole kampong would really move. And what would be left here, of their way of life, as beloved as a worn pair of boots that had been through storm and famine alike? Could they really cast off who they were so easily, like the snakes in the undergrowth shedding thin yellow skins?

And the kampong would throw their lots in so readily with these white-shirted Gah Men? They would entrust their lives to them? Had no one else lived through the war; did no one else see what an iron will of this sort could do? He had no doubts Ah Boon's Gah Woman meant well. Surely she had come from a wealthy family to be educated so highly; surely she believed herself the savior of the masses. But it was such people who were swept up in the machinery of power, like gunners on a tank, so focused on the immediate problems of targets and threats that they failed to see the trail of destruction the convoy left in its wake.

Uncle stood there until the clatter of bowls and chopsticks told him the table was being laid.

"Uncle! Eat!" Hia shouted.

He was in a good mood, Uncle could hear it in his voice. Perhaps the Gah Woman had promised him some other job, luring him away as she already had Ah Boon. But Hia was a grown man. Hia had himself, already, chosen to work on the industrial estate in the distant western regions of the island.

Little footsteps pattered up to him. "Gu Gong, come eat!" Ah Huat tugged at his shorts.

He rested a hand on the boy's warm neck and they went in. The two tables were pushed together as always. Ma, Hia, and Gek Huay sat at the square table, Ah Boon and Natalie at the round one. There were two empty seats, one at each table. Uncle paused. He did not want to sit with the Gah Woman, but it would be strange to separate Ah Huat from Gek Huay.

He would behave himself, Uncle thought. He would be polite to the outsider. He would go to Ma in private, tell her what he felt deep in his gut, that they should not move. That all these changes were happening too quickly for them to understand what was being given up, that it might sound irrational, or sentimental, but he had the strong and simple feeling that they needed to stay.

Then he saw that the steaming dish of black sauce chicken had been placed at their table, in front of Ah Boon and Natalie. At Hia's table were the morning glory, lotus roots, and soy-marinated bean sprouts. Clearly Ma had done this to make the Gah Woman feel welcome. It was meant to be Hia's big dinner, but even this had been sidelined for their guest.

"Come sit, Leong," Ma said, gesturing at the empty seat next to Natalie.

Natalie smiled at him, demurely flashing her small white teeth.

Uncle leaned over and picked up the plates containing the lotus root and bean sprouts. These he placed in front of Ah Boon and Natalie. Next he lifted the heavy bowl that held the black sauce chicken. For a brief moment he considered dashing it to the floor. The fragrant, sticky sauce would ooze slowly over the wooden planks, the soft meat—stewed for hours over the fire, carefully tended to by Ma—would lie, wasted, among the broken pieces of the bowl.

Instead he placed the bowl squarely in front of Hia. He observed the tables, satisfied, then sat down.

"Now we can eat," he said.

The table was silent.

Little Ah Huat chirped: "Ah Ma eat! Gu Gong eat! Pa eat, Ma eat, Uncle eat! Auntie Natalie eat!"

Uncle picked up his chopsticks. The rest of the table was still. The Gah Woman, who must have understood the slight, seemed unfazed. Her head was tilted, and she seemed to be waiting for something. Ah Boon's fists rested beside his bowl.

They should start, Ma said with a nervous smile, before it got cold. Slowly, hesitantly, Hia and Gek Huay began. For a moment, it seemed as if the evening might continue.

But even as the others started to eat, Ah Boon didn't move.

"Boon?" Natalie said quietly.

At the sound of her voice, an odd look flashed across Ah Boon's face, and his features relaxed. Surprised, alert, smug, as if he had remembered something, something that meant he had already won, though what the battle was, Uncle could not say.

"Natalie and I are getting married," Ah Boon said calmly.

"Ah!" A wide smile spread across Ma's face.

"Little scoundrel," Hia said, also smiling. "Why never tell us? About time too."

"Congratulations," Gek Huay said.

"Congratulations!" Ah Huat repeated, beating his chopsticks against the side of his bowl like a drum.

"I will look up auspicious dates," Ma said. "Maybe four, five months? But with the move—"

The move was scheduled for the end of the year. The notice had come in the mail just days before, an official envelope bearing the stamp of the Gah Men.

"As soon as possible," Ah Boon said. He went on to say that they would get married before the move, so they could apply for a flat on their own. He took Natalie's hand and squeezed it. Around her wrist was a jade bangle, pale and exquisite.

"Apply for a flat on your own? Now don't even want to live with your ma?" Uncle said.

He saw the look of alarm on Ma's face, but he could not be quiet.

"Leong," Ma said. "Aiya. The flat, we talk about later, okay? Let's just celebrate now. This is a happy moment."

"If I don't say something, who's going to say? First you go work for the CC, I don't say anything. Then go join Gah Men, I also keep quiet. Then you want us to leave the kampong, move to some Gah Men housing project, I still say okay, still don't say anything."

Uncle realized he was on the verge of shouting. Natalie and Ah Boon sat there silent and inscrutable, as if simply waiting for Uncle to exhaust himself. He knew the more he shouted, the more reasonable they seemed to Ma and Hia and Gek Huay. And yet he could not stop.

"Now want to marry her? Leave your ma and I to live by ourselves, move away from our home, for this woman?"

Ah Boon put his chopsticks down, taking care to lean them against his bowl so that they would not slip. "If you're not happy," he said, "you don't have to move. You can stay here. No one is making you do anything."

Uncle turned to Ma. "You hear what he say? Your son. I don't have to move! I can stay here!"

"You don't mean it, boy," Ma said. "Quick, say sorry to Uncle."

But Ah Boon was silent. Flushed, he stood up from the table, sending his stool clattering to the floor.

"Let's go," he said to Natalie. She stood up as well, shooting an apologetic glance at Ma and thanking her. Off they went.

After they were gone, no one said anything for a while. Finally, Ma let out a long, ragged sigh.

"What? You think he's right? You all think he's right," Uncle said, trailing off.

Ma would not meet his eye. Hia, too, was looking at his bowl, as if the cold rice had become endlessly fascinating.

Uncle knew what he sounded like, for the years had curdled it all— his grief, his guilt, his fear—made it a sour, soft thing. He was gripped by helplessness. Yet again he was watching his family walk into another trap, this time more elaborately laid, more carefully adorned with the trimmings of authority. If they moved into those flats, the Gah Men would have complete control over their lives. First they would be dependent on them for housing, then for schools, then who knew what else. And once they were completely dependent, the Gah Men could do whatever they liked.

Uncle had failed to protect the family from a great power once, and it had cost them dearly. If Pa were here, he would talk sense into them all. But it was Uncle's own fault that Pa was not here.

"Hear me out," Uncle said. "Just—"

"Enough for tonight, Leong," Ma said. "Enough. Please."

Uncle fell silent. Gek Huay and Hia started clearing the dishes away.

"Thank you," Ma said softly. She got up from the table and went to her room.

Uncle was alone at the table. But he wasn't; Ah Huat was still there, crouching down in his seat, face buried in knees, curled into a ball. His hands were wrapped over his head, as if to protect himself from blows.

"Boy," Uncle said. "Boy, it's okay. It's okay, Uncle's here."

But Ah Huat would not look up. Finally, when Gek Huay returned, he uncurled, allowing himself to be led away, the whole time avoiding Uncle's gaze.

Chapter Thirty-Six

As the year drew to a close, the Gah Men began a campaign the likes of which the island had never seen before. People were puzzled; were the Gah Men not already in power? Had they not most recently won the referendum on merger, thus cementing their authority? Merdeka seemed inevitable now. Singapore would join the Federation of Malaya, achieving independence from the Ang Mohs at last.

But the Gah Men felt their grip on power to be insecure. The leftists may have lost the referendum, but there was that matter of the miscommunication, of blank votes, of the various obstacles the Gah Men had thrown up in their path to ensure their opponents' loss. It did not mean the leftists had lost the hearts and minds of the people. And indeed, on their campaign trail, the Gah Men encountered boos and cheers in equal measure. It was unclear until they showed up whether they would be heckled, shoved, or garlanded. Tense moments tipped into real, simmering danger, crowds surging forward and threatening to overcome the white-shirted technocrats. The Gah Men showed no fear, the Gah Men did not back down. Tirelessly they carried on with their campaign. Every single constituency would be visited, every kampong preached to, every citizen converted.

The message was simple. Now that Merdeka was on the horizon, the island needed the Gah Men more than ever. They would soon be free of their Ang Moh rulers, and a sure and steady hand would be required to represent the island in the wider federation. Homes had to be built, clinics set up, roads planned, schools run. The people must be taken care of. Had the Gah Men not shown themselves capable of this? Had not the budget's health care expenditure gone up by almost a third, had the public hospitals not welcomed citizens into their spotless halls regardless of their ability to pay? Were the New Towns—housing estates as clean and modern as their names suggested—not marvels to behold? Did the vast industrial and construction projects not provide a wave of new jobs, too many for the people themselves to fill?

The kampong acknowledged these things to be true. But the kampong also woke each morning to the relentless *thunk, thunk, thunk* of the pile driver, the softer background clank of the conveyor belt, the itinerant roars of enormous dump trucks. Every day ground was excavated, sand was shifted, concrete piles hammered deep into the earth. Hardhat-wearing workers swarmed the fill site, scuttling across the sand like the tiny crabs they had chased from the shore.

It was not only the crabs that had grown scarce. The birds, too, had stopped singing, tired of being drowned out by the machines. Then the water itself grew murky, clouded with particles thrown up from the piling. At a certain time of day, a thin slick of grease shimmered on its surface.

It was in these conditions that Ah Boon and Natalie's wedding preparations were to take place. With the report for the Deputy Secretary now complete, as head of the Citizens' Working Group, Ah Boon found him-self back at the CC, fielding complaints about the current living conditions.

"Boon, how can like this?"

"Boon, faster do something, this noise will send me to my grave!"

"Boon, if your pa still alive, you can let him live like that?"

Sleep grew elusive for Ah Boon. Tangled in his sheets he sweated and cursed, slapping mosquitoes away irritably and holding imaginary conver-sations to defend himself. Finally, at three or four in the morning, he would drift off, only to be gently shaken awake by Ma what felt like minutes later.

"Talking again," she would say.

"I'm fine," he'd say, turning away, not wanting to face Ma's search-ing gaze.

He was fine, he told himself. People seemed to blame him personally for what was happening, seemed to think he had full control over the audacious scale of the work taking place. It was unreasonable, it was shortsighted. He knew it made no sense and yet it pained him to have the kampong think so poorly of him.

Finally he went to Natalie. "We have to bring the move-in dates forward."

"I don't know," she said. "There's a lot of demand for flats, and the lat-est inventory—"

"I'll talk to the Deputy Secretary."

He did, and within days, it was arranged. Those who were moving would be able to move out within the week. Ah Boon announced this at the CC with great relief, expecting thanks, perhaps even a cheer, and yet all he heard was a confused muttering.

"Move so fast?"

"Aiyo, not ready."

"Still need to clean, need to pack, and our boats how?"

Finally Ah Boon washed his hands of the matter. The fish had gone, he knew now, and there was no bringing them back. This vast thing he had helped set in motion would only trundle ahead ceaselessly until it reached its final destination. It would do no good to question every decision he had made up till then.

Still, looking at the site filled him with dizziness, a feeling that was almost fear. So easy it was to simply change something that had endured for decades, centuries; so very quick. With the right technology and willing hands, anything could be transformed, into anything at all.

"It's a pain now," Natalie said, "but just imagine when the project's done. A highway linking east to west, new schools, new flats, a whole new coastal park for everyone to enjoy."

He believed in her greater good. And had the kampong not been assigned the flats they wanted? Would they not soon all share in the fruits of the Gah Men's labor?

And so Ah Boon concerned himself wholly with the matter of Natalie, his marriage, the house his father-in-law had promised them. Despite his fears, the encounter with Natalie's family had gone well. He'd dreaded meeting them ever since the fight with Uncle. If his family could not accept her, why would hers accept him? The rubber plantation might be in ruins, but they were still a landowning family, Teochew Catholic, English-educated. He knew what people like them thought of people like him. The old fears returned. To his shame, Ah Boon found himself sniffing his underarms compulsively, checking for the smell of fish, the tinge of the market. Sand was still appearing, inexplicably, wherever he went. He found a thin layer of it under his sleeping mat, sieved into bags of rice in the kitchen, by his desk in the CC. He swept obsessively. He ramped up his English practice, listening to Ang Moh channels on the radio every night, the crisp tones of British and Australian newsreaders crackling over the airwaves.

The night of the dinner, his worst fears seemed to be confirmed when they passed the gates of her family home and the large white-brick house came into view. A motorcar sat before its doors; a servant was weeding the lawn. And yet the old man who greeted them at the door was watery-eyed and smiling. He clasped Ah Boon's hand in both of his, pumping it up and down enthusiastically. Natalie he did not touch, only nodding with restraint, asking after her work. Ah Boon did not notice this, so overwhelmed was he by the grand white staircase that led to the entryway, the electric lights, the fine teak furniture and the paintings hanging on the wall. He had never been in a house like this, in a house as beautiful as this, and in his awe, he said as much.

"Ah, my son," Natalie's father said. "Do you like it? Do you like it very much? If so, I have an offer for you!"

His breath was tinged with the sour scent of beer, but even after the night was done, Natalie's father remembered his offer. There was another, smaller house, one that he'd bought years ago and currently rented out for income. He wanted them to have it as a wedding gift; it was the least he could do.

Natalie did not want the house. Ah Boon knew now that what he'd once thought of as natural independence was in fact a deep-seated guilt. By now he'd heard the stories of her father's plantation workers struggling to buy medicine for their sick children; by now he understood she wanted to do everything she could to distance herself from her family's wealth. The boardinghouse was a kind of penance for being born into unearned privilege, her Gah Woman's crusade a means to give back, set the world to rights.

Yet he persuaded her it might be permissible to accept this one thing, for if they did not take the offer of the house, they would have to apply for a rental flat of their own, and there was no guarantee as to when they would get one. The other option was to move into the flat with Ma and Uncle, but given their last meeting with Uncle, no one wanted this.

And so Natalie agreed to go see the house. It was not too far from the kampong, located in one of the wealthy neighborhoods along the coast. The house was small, smaller even than their wooden dwelling in the kampong. Framed by a small garden teeming with ixora bushes sporting cheerful red flowers, its brick walls were punctured by generous windows from which gauzy curtains fluttered freely in the breeze. The walls were painted a thick cream that reminded Ah Boon of the icing on the welcome cake they'd had at the CC's opening ceremony.

Natalie gave in, won over by Ah Boon's childlike excitement, but insisted that they would pay her father back over the years instead of accepting the gift. Her father agreed, overjoyed at what he saw as a reconciliation after years of distance, and loved Ah Boon all the more for being the one to bring about this thawing.

And so as the Lees prepared for their move, Ah Boon and Natalie prepared for theirs. They did not own very many things between them, and packing was a straightforward business. Hia brought old crates home from Swee Hong's store, in which Ma piled dish cloths and bedsheets, jars of chili pastes, chipped crockery and dented pots. Ah Boon folded shirts into little squares and stacked them neatly in cardboard boxes. Hia took on the job of sorting through Pa's clothes, which had sat in a closet for more than twenty years.

Only Uncle did not lift a finger. An ominous calm had come over him after the fight with Ah Boon.

One afternoon, as he sat out front mending a small hole in their boat, Ah Boon went over to him. The silence was punctuated by the pounding of the pile driver—*thunk, thunk, thunk*—and Ah Boon was glad for it, for once.

"Need help?"

Uncle shook his head and carried on.

"Did Ah Hock agree to buy it?" he tried again.

Uncle's face was impassive. Again he shook his head.

"Aiya, too bad. But I'm sure someone will."

Uncle paused. His hands stilled.

"We are not selling the boat," he said, calmly spitting into the grass beside him.

"What, you think you can bring the boat with you to the flat?" Ah Boon found himself retorting. "Keep in the kitchen?"

Uncle studied the grass. He was in a squat, arms hanging off splayed knees. His hair, thin and streaked with chalky white, shifted gently in the wind. From where Ah Boon stood, looking down at him, he could almost be a different man, a man he had once resembled, who was long gone, whom Ah Boon had not thought of for a very long time.

Finally Uncle looked up. "I'm staying here," he said in a calm voice. "I'm not leaving. Cannot just give up like that."

Ah Boon had overheard Pa's words to Uncle on that fateful night all those years ago, but did not remember them. *How can just—go? Give up like that?* And Uncle's response: *This is bigger than us. Even the Ang Mohs also must surrender.* Still, he felt a chill go through him.

"No one's giving up," Ah Boon said.

"Going to live in a nice house with your Gah Woman? Leaving this, all this—" Uncle swept one arm out, taking in the attap houses, the mangroves, the kampong, the sea. "Making everyone think they need to leave too, go live in these concrete—boxes. Tombs. In the sky, away from all this—" Uncle stopped. *Thunk.* He dropped his arm. *Thunk.* A long, slow sigh went through him. *Thunk.*

"Want to go, just go."

Ah Boon started to walk away. Then he stopped and turned back to Uncle.

"Why do you hate me so much?"

A bolt of surprise broke the sullen mask of Uncle's face. "Nobody hates you, Boon."

"Then why can't you see? I never wanted to go against you. I did this for us. So we can have a better life."

Uncle shook his head sadly. "What is better, boy?"

"I didn't want this to happen to the coast," Ah Boon said.

"But you help them, right? You convince everyone to leave without fighting back. You run their little CC."

"It's not—it wasn't about the CC—"

It was about the vision, about the flats, about the modern future, he wanted to say. But he knew how meaningless these words would be to Uncle.

"This was our home, Boon."

That same tirade. But home was not a place. Home was people, home was family. The family that he was moving, so Ah Huat could go to better schools, Ma could be closer to modern doctors. Uncle was a sentimental old man, railing against a world that was leaving him behind. If he wanted to be left behind, then so be it. But Ah Boon would not change his course for one man.

"Ma and Hia are happy to leave," Ah Boon said.

"Because you—"

"Because I nothing. They want to go. They say so themselves. Gek Huay also."

Uncle was quiet.

"None of the other kampongs are leaving," Uncle said. "Pak Hassan—the Malay fishermen—"

"Yet. They will understand, eventually. The other kampongs will leave too."

"They will not."

"They have no choice; changes are coming. This is bigger than them."

"And bigger means we just give up?"

Ah Boon shook his head in frustration.

Uncle ran his hands over the boat in front of him, as if stroking a horse. "Your Pa would not have gone," he said quietly. "He believed in standing up to authority."

Here it was again, the source of all Uncle's bitterness.

"You have no right," Ah Boon said.

"What?"

Ah Boon took a deep breath. "*You* wanted to go. To the Jipunlang. *You* wanted to register."

Then a mask dropped over Uncle's face. Eyes squeezed shut, mouth open in a silent bellow. It was a look of pain so naked that Ah Boon was filled with a sudden remorse. Uncle did not know how to weep, Ah Boon realized with a shock. Uncle could not shed tears, even if he wanted to.

Ah Boon stepped forward to place his hand on the older man's arm.

"Uncle—"

"Don't touch me." Uncle pulled away.

"Please, Uncle, can we just—"

"Yes. Me, my fault." Uncle's face was tight with grief. "But you? You see what happen and you do the same thing, let the same thing happen again?"

"It's not the same, Uncle," Ah Boon said.

"Always the same. Always."

Ah Boon bit his tongue. "I just want what's best for the family."

Uncle shook his head. "You are blind," he said. "You only want this for yourself."

A cold feeling came over Ah Boon. This was how it would be, then.

"I am going to pack," he said.

Ah Boon took one last, long look at Uncle. Beneath the anger, he felt his heart contract with love. This was the man on whose shoulders Ah Boon had once ridden, with whom he'd plucked fruit from trees and shared its flesh, sticky juices running down their arms. This was the man who had taught him to swim, Pa being too impatient, too frustrated with young Ah Boon's crying. This was the man who had been more like a father to him than his own absent father, with whom he'd shared the work of protecting their family for so long.

But nothing lasted forever, not even the closest of bonds. Uncle no longer understood him; Uncle no longer understood the world. Silently, Ah Boon went back into the house.

Chapter Thirty-Seven

A nd so they went. Ma, Hia, Gek Huay, and little Ah Huat. The crates and boxes and sacks of clothes piled in the back of the same lorry that Uncle and Pa used to drive to the market each day, Hia now at the wheel. Ah Boon and Natalie met them at the flats, bearing tins of soupy noodles from a hawker nearby who was famed for his hand-rolled fish balls.

To their surprise, a representative from the local residents' committee was there to greet them—special treatment, Natalie whispered, because they had heard Ah Boon was the head of the Citizens' Working Group—and personally hand over the keys to Hia and Ma. He shook each of their hands in turn, congratulating them heartily, while the family smiled nervously, unsure exactly what they were being congratulated for.

The representative showed them how the lifts worked, assuring Ma that sensors in the doors made it impossible to get crushed by them, smiling indulgently when little Ah Huat insisted on pressing all the buttons to see them light up, clapping along with him when, sure enough, the lift proceeded to stop every three floors. It began to feel like a game: the family squeezed in together in that little box, the doors sliding open at each new level. The same concrete, same pink-painted walls, yet different somehow: here a carefully tended potted plant, there a child's charcoal scrawl. When the doors opened to reveal two chickens standing incongruously in the electric-lit hallway, they burst out laughing at the same time.

"Some new tenants bring their animals with them," the representative said apologetically. "Even though it's prohibited, for sanitary reasons." He looked over the Lees approvingly. "You don't have any animals, do you? No, I didn't think so."

They felt encouraged by this, as if their inadvertent compliance somehow proved the rightness of their choice, that they were indeed *meant* to be here. For, standing crowded together in that hot, small elevator, going up and down that twelve-story concrete building, they had the feeling of being in a dream.

The block was one of six, closely clustered together, separated by rectangular strips of grass upon which a few trees obediently grew. There was a trim, tidy quality to the vegetation here, one that the Lees were unused to, so different was it from the sprawling, encroaching mangroves, the tree roots that destabilized the foundations of their houses, the slimy moss that crept over everything left outside. Here, the dead leaves were swept up as soon as they dared fall; the grass was permitted to grow only to a certain height. Wildflowers and weeds were rare, springing only occasionally from the wet cracks in the rounded walls of wide storm drains.

They continued their tour through the estate. Banners were hung in the void decks, the serious faces of Gah Men printed on them.

Vote for our own flag! Vote for merger with special rights! Vote for equality for our four languages! Vote for common citizenship!

"Sorry," the representative said. "We'll be taking those down soon.

It's been so busy since the vote, so many people moving in, that we haven't had the chance."

"The referendum," Ah Boon said, mistaking the blankness on Ma's face as confusion. "On the merger with the Federation. We won."

Ma nodded, noticing her son's use of *we*. She knew about the merger and the Gah Men's referendum. It came to her through the chatter of the fishermen who gathered outside Swee Hong's shop to listen to the wireless. The Gah Men wrangling with the Ang Mohs on the precise terms of their dominance, wrangling with the Federation across the straits as to whether or not they were part of them—et cetera, et cetera. It had little to do with what Ma wanted: for little Ah Huat to grow up healthy and strong, go to a good school, and make a life for himself.

"Here's the neighborhood primary school," the representative said, as if reading Ma's mind.

"Look! That's where you'll go," Hia said to Ah Huat.

It was a low-slung blue building with a bright metal gate and a large courtyard filled with children running, climbing, screaming. A single pole stood at the end of the courtyard, upon which hung the nation's red-and-white flag, draped lankly in the windless afternoon. There were tens, hundreds of children, and the noise was considerable. Teachers sat in the shade, marking homework absently on their laps while chatting with one another.

Ma thought of the kampong school that Ah Boon had attended, with its spartan single classroom, its lopsided desks and creaky chairs, its tens of students who kept having to drop out, Teacher Chia's unofficial, scrappy syllabus. Inadvertently she thought of Ah Boon at seven. That serious, proud little boy, his cold hand sweaty in hers on his first day of school. How much she had wanted for him, even if she hadn't admitted it to herself then. Her husband would never have approved of such foolish hope, such greed. Had Ah Boon not fulfilled her secret ambitions? All this—the new flats, the representative kowtowing to them, this school that her grandson would attend—it was all Ah Boon's doing.

"And here is the market," the representative said.

They saw now that the blocks were organized around a kind of central square, in the middle of which was a covered open-air space. Whirring fans and bright lights hung from the ceiling, and tiled blocks were set up in neat rows for vendors to occupy. It being late in the day, the market was now empty except for a few dried-goods vendors, lazily swaying their rattan fans in the heat of the afternoon.

"So clean," Gek Huay said.

And indeed, no dirty water slicked the floor, no baskets of rotting fruit lay strewn about, no piles of rubbish accumulated in the walkways. It was nothing like the market Ma was used to frequenting, a haphazard collection of itinerant fruit, vegetable, and meat vendors gathering in an empty street between shophouses, the shouts and smells trapped in humid pockets within the crowded space.

They passed a playground. A large mosaic dragon rose from a rectangular sandpit, its spine a series of rings that two boys were now climbing through, its tongue a metal slide a little girl slowly slipped down. Its tail was a hook, from which a black tire swing squeaked. The dragon's skin was an orange mosaic tile set in gray cement, creating a geometric pelt. Elsewhere in the playground were a large rotating disk and a set of undulating monkey bars, the shiny metal grips rubbed dull gray by hundreds of little hands. Everywhere, children shrieked and ran, dug holes in the sand, clambered over concrete, and swung from metal.

Ah Huat tugged at Hia's pants. "Can I, Pa? Can I go?"

Hia nodded and the boy took off, racing toward the scrum. Soon he was part of an elaborate catching game that involved four teams and three safe zones, required dexterous scaling of the dragon and leaping over holes. The family watched him, feeling as though it were all of them out there on the sand, climbing, jumping, dodging, narrowly avoiding being caught, emerging victorious at the end.

The year was drawing to a close. After the family moved to their new flats, Ah Boon and Natalie moved into the house that Natalie's father had given them.

Their wedding was a simple affair—a tea ceremony in the morning, a church ceremony in the afternoon. Few from the kampong were there, so busy was everyone with moving out, but Swee Hong showed up, as did Pa's old friends Ah Tong and Ah Kee, men whom old age had turned wiry and copper-hued as the dry wood of a strangler fig. A handful of Ah Boon's friends from the kampong school, though none from middle school or his brief union days. He had not spoken to them in years, and he was not sure that they would want to speak to him, given his new life.

The battle between the Gah Men and the expelled leftists raged on. It had grown especially bitter around the merger referendum, with the Gah Men employing the full apparatus of the state to ensure their victory. They revoked the license of their opponents' printer, denied them permits for mass rallies, purged their supporters from the civil service. Simultaneously the leftists encouraged public employees to strike, and strike they did. One work stoppage involving night-soil collectors, garbagemen, and sewage plant workers had threatened to turn especially nasty, and the army had to be sent in to man public installations. Another situation, an exam boycott by Chinese high school students, teetered on the edge of violence and was defused only by the Gah Men deciding to hold back the police and send in the students' parents instead. There were crackdowns and arrests, detentions and secret threats. Those with more extreme leanings had long since fled abroad.

Such had been the past two years, and so, when Ah Boon invited Siok Mei to the wedding, he had not expected her to come. Sure enough she called him at work, saying that she would try to make it, but that things were "difficult" right now. She had not shown up, and Ah Boon was glad for it. He had not really wanted her to come. In his heart of hearts, a small part of him feared her presence would make him falter.

It was a relief to have only Natalie in his mind on the day of the wedding, to have the church pews filled with minor Gah Men from the ministry, Auntie Kim and Auntie Hock from the CC, Ma and Hia and everyone else. Even Uncle, he noted with a pang, had come, wearing a look of tired calm. He made no comments about the Gah Men or the kampong leaving, only smiled sadly as he accepted tea from Ah Boon and Natalie.

The time for questioning was now past, buried with the self that had worried about not speaking English well enough, about his shirts not being clean enough, about being afraid of the water. The water was harmless; he could see that now. It could be corralled and commanded, directed into trenches, pushed back or removed entirely when it did not serve one's needs. All that was required was the right machinery, willing hands, and a firm resolve.

And the kampong was happy, as far as Ah Boon could tell. Swee Hong had moved into his new flat, and at the wedding, he spoke cheerfully about being closer to his sons and their wives. One of his daughters-in-law came over often, he said, to help him hang the laundry. When asked why he didn't do it on his own, a look of embarrassment had come across his face. He'd said something evasive about his grip being poor, the bamboo poles, heavy with wet clothes, being too heavy for him.

The truth was Swee Hong was afraid of the unobstructed kitchen window. His flat was on the tenth floor, despite his having applied for one lower down. Even when he stood at the sink, some feet away from the open window—as was standard, there was no way to close it, and most residents used tarpaulin sheets to keep out the rain—his hands shook nervously. The faint terror of being so high up never quite left him. There were times he thought longingly of his provision store, now empty and boarded up, or of the patio on solid ground where he'd sit on his wooden stool and enjoy a cigarette. But he did not let himself dwell on these times. It was true the flat was easier to maintain, there were no leaks or rot, he did not have to worry about the monsoons when they came, and his daughters-in-law brought his grandchildren to visit him frequently. The ambient fear he felt when stepping into the kitchen was silly, he told himself, and a small price to pay. It was only a matter of time that he would get used to it.

Ah Tong, too, had settled in. He'd taken up tai chi, he said. There was a group of older men who met regularly in the void deck beneath his flat. What he hadn't realized was how spread out the kampong residents would be, how large the estates and how high the buildings. There was no one from their kampong in his block, and he'd been lonely at first, not knowing what to do without his boat to tend to or his nets to mend. Ah Tong's adult sons supported him now, and so for the first time in his life, he had no need to work. Vast stretches of time went unfilled. It was not always easy. There was an awkward pause when he'd said this. But there was tai chi, he said hurriedly, not wanting, perhaps, to blemish Ah Boon's wedding day. And with it came new friends to go to the coffee shop with.

Ma was happy, Hia was progressing in his new job, Gek Huay had recently had a healthy, screaming baby. Ah Huat loved his new school. This was enough for Ah Boon. He could not be responsible, he told himself, for the entire kampong's worries and complaints. They were adults. They had made the decision themselves, and for the most part, they seemed content.

In the meantime, there was Natalie: the grace of her wrists, the clarity of her mind. Recently she had taken a strong stance against "the Communist threat." The student union leaders he'd known in his youth were dangerous insurgents, bent on wreaking anarchy and causing the breakdown of all civil society. She understood that Ah Boon had "fallen in" with them during his school days, but commended him on having the independence of mind to see them for what they really were, subsequently extricating himself from these dangerous associations. Of course, Ah Boon had left, quite simply, because of Siok Mei, but this he did not say.

"There is the class element," she was always saying. "That is what we have such difficulty accounting for. The Chinese-speaking majority is one we cannot naturally reach, thus leaving them vulnerable to the brainwashing of the Communists."

We being the Gah Men. The pragmatic, the rational, the antiradical, antichauvinist. Unlike the alleged Communists, the Gah Men would never brainwash. The Gah Men merely persuaded by the rightness of their actions, the generosity of their civic contributions. *We* now included Ah Boon. Finally, his union with Natalie, his ministry job, his comfortable terrace house in the wealthy neighborhood—all this gave him what he had wanted for so long, which was to be someone other than himself.

His job paid well, and even while supporting Ma, he and Natalie still set aside a decent amount each month, such that it looked as if they might have a little nest egg before long. To fill their new house, they purchased a handsome set of teak furniture, porcelain plates, a modern gas cooker. He thought they might save up for a motorcar. Sunday mornings were spent in their well-watered garden, sitting on rattan chairs with mugs of milky tea clasped between their palms. Soon, they decided, once all the commotion of moving had died down, they would have a child.

PART V

From Third World to First

Chapter Thirty-Eight

The Gah Men had anticipated any number of things going wrong with the Great Reclamation—sinking, equipment cost, worker deaths, public outcry, international meddling, and so on—but the lack of sand had not been one of them. It was assumed the difficulties of the ambitious project would be in the transporting of sand, the preparation for its receipt, the appropriate settling of it. Never had they thought that there might not be enough.

Preliminary dredging for the pilot site found that they would need two to three times the amount of fill material initially estimated. After the pilot site was filled, the material from the designated excavation site would barely be enough for the first phase of the reclamation project, let alone all four phases planned.

The project was put on hold until other sources of sand could be identified. Existing quarries were inspected island-wide, small hills measured for how much fill they might yield, inland swamps and jungle assessed for their suitability to be turned into reservoirs. And yet, no matter how they did the numbers, they always came up short. There simply was not enough sand to create the amount of land they wanted to.

Other industries that competed for the resource were scrutinized, but the most sand-hungry sector of all was construction, and no one was going to suggest they build factories and roads at a slower pace. Besides, it was a different kind of sand they needed. It was starting to look as if importing was going to be their only option. A large amount already came in on enormous barges to feed the construction industry; it might be possible to increase this. It was, however, a sensitive issue. No neighboring country wanted to feel like it was selling its territory to the fast-growing island state. A high price would be demanded, financial and political.

The Gah Men continued to survey, to assess, to budget. For the time being, the conveyor belt trundled to a stop, the barges returned to their distant harbors, the incessant, bone-shaking noise of the piling machines was halted at last.

What was left of the kampong rejoiced. Most houses were empty now, with official notices on their front doors designating them as Gah Men property, warning off squatters and trespassers. Those who had remained felt these notices to be unnecessary; who, after all, was going to squat or trespass in what was quickly becoming a village of ghosts?

The day the piling stopped, Uncle opened the windows of the house for the first time in months. The wooden shutters, stiff from disuse, squeaked as he unlatched them. Light spilled in, a pale gold liquid that wanted to touch everything: the worn floors, the mildewed roof, the lonely pieces of furniture Ma had left behind.

There had once been a time when the house felt crowded. Hia had been a boy then, Ah Boon a newborn baby. Ma and Pa, harried young parents. Uncle remembered how he tried to make himself useful, helping his sister with the sweeping and cooking, how she would not let him. He remembered the long, weakening illness, the straining visits from the sinseh, the expensive tonics and nourishing meals.

Now the house stood empty. He was still in it, but he did not count. Since the family had gone, he'd felt himself grow insubstantial, as if it were their gaze, their voices, that kept him alive. He went entire days without seeing anyone. Some afternoons he would take his shirt off down at the beach, laying himself on the soft sand that, warmed by the sun, felt like the body of another human being.

He knew it made no sense to stay. He was being stubborn, as Ma said. But where was Ma? At first she came to visit him weekly, then every two weeks. It had now been a whole month since he had last seen her. Hia, Gek Huay, little Ah Huat and the new baby had been back just once. They'd come full of laughter, bearing gifts of fruit and spices. They looked the same, but the change had already begun. Little Ah Huat stood a little differently, Hia had a new kind of gel in his hair, Gek Huay would not stop talking about some stupid Hollywood movie she'd seen. Uncle had not been to the flats. He was putting it off by claiming he'd hurt his hip and could not cycle the thirty minutes that separated them.

And Ah Boon—Ah Boon had not been back at all. Uncle had heard he was now living in a large house of his own, given to him by the father of the woman he'd married. When Ma told him this, her voice full of pride, Uncle had said it seemed strange that with such a big house, her son had not thought to offer her a place to stay. At this Ma fell silent.

The day the piling stopped, the crash of the waves and the cries of insects entered the house once again, but still the relentless *thunk, thunk, thunk* continued on in his mind. He was not so naive as to believe it wouldn't return.

He thought often of his brother-in-law. What had Ah Boon said?

You *wanted to go. To the Jipunlang.* You *wanted to register.* And his nephew had been right. Uncle's fault. And still he was unable to stop his family from making the same mistake again.

Uncle started going to the fill site in the evenings, after the workers had gone home for the day. He followed the curve of the shore as far as he could before he reached the swampy area, which had been cordoned off with orange tape and large wooden signs warning not to enter. Much of the vegetation had been cleared to allow the dredging to take place, and even outside the taped area, many trees had been cut down, shorn to naked stumps.

The machines, so loud and threatening during the day, looked almost pitiful in the dwindling sun, like prehistoric creatures finding themselves suddenly in the wrong place, in the wrong time. Even bathed in pink and gold light, the ugliness of the site remained. The mangroves decimated, the earth turned this way and that to reveal its vivid red insides. Everything was still; no crabs scuttled, no birds hopped, nothing rustled in the undergrowth now that the undergrowth was stripped back. Equipment leaking oil and fumes crowded the waters, barges with piles of sand were tethered to makeshift jetties. The dreaded piling machine was poised midpound, a forest of concrete pillars already driven deep into the seabed.

Uncle studied the scene for movement and spotted, atop a chopped-up tree root, a single mudskipper. It was still, given away only by the occasional hard blink of its close-set eyes. A fish above water, with twinned, protruding eyes and sharp fins it used to drag itself forward across the swampy earth. From where it sat on the tree root it seemed to be surveying the scene, contemplating its place in this now-desolate landscape.

Grief gathered within Uncle. He thought of the monsoon clouds, heavy and patient, that pulled water from the sea for months before releasing it all suddenly, angrily. Uncle began to feel that he would do something terrible, but he did not know yet what that thing was. The graveyard of the swamp, the persistence of the conveyor belt, the steady, unrelenting violence of the pile driver. What was one man in the face of an all-powerful force like the Gah Men? But he had thought that once, and paid for it dearly. No, even if he was just one man, it did not mean he could do nothing.

He began traveling out to the islands again, his boat alone on the water. Just once he saw Pak Hassan on his slim kolek, cutting through the empty waters like a blade. The men nodded at each other grimly from afar, then carried on. The catch had dried up. Ah Boon did not care, the kampong did not care. The kampong had left. Still, there was comfort to be had in these pristine shores. The high white cliffs gleaming like exposed bone, the thick green foliage that moved softly with the wind.

Sometimes Uncle stepped on shore, something he had not done in years. A shiver still went through him when he set foot on that fickle land. He thought often of what they had believed all those decades ago, when the islands had first been found by Ah Boon and Pa: that they were cursed. Later, the kampong was too busy enriching themselves, growing fat and comfortable, and the curse had been conveniently forgotten.

But it was real. The kampong had brought the Gah Men and their machines upon themselves. What was wealth, what was progress? They had lost the ability to see things as they really were; this was the true nature of the curse.

Uncle endured his penance. He lived through the noise and the dust, remained suspended in this hellish loneliness, bore witness to the ravaging of their coast. The storm within him gathered strength each day. Everyone else had averted their gaze, everyone else had somewhere else to be. He would stay, he would watch, and when the time came, he would be ready.

Ah Kee's house caught fire in the middle of the night. He had not lived there in months, of course, having ceded it to the Gah Men after moving to a new flat with his children. Still, he was distraught, rushing to the site the next day to see the damage for himself. According to his son, all that was left were the blackened foundations. He'd dug through the cinders with his bare hands, finding bits of glass, the blades of old knives forgotten in the kitchen drawer, a single charred biscuit tin.

Finally, deep in the disintegrating debris, he found what he was looking for: a scorched block of twisted metal, what had once been the outboard motor of the boat he'd piloted for more than twenty years. He fell upon the chunk of metal as one would the body of a relative, running his hands over its blackened skin, its melted corners, the places where intricate parts had welded into one gnarled tangle.

Like most, Ah Kee had left the boat under his old house when he moved, since there was nowhere to keep it in the new flat. No one could bear to sell their boats, even though they had moved on from their old livelihoods by now and would not return. So the boats gathered dust and mud under the stilts of the empty houses.

Perhaps it was for the best, Ah Kee's son ventured, that the house had burned down. There had been nothing of value left in it, after all, and it solved the problem of what to do with the boat. At this remark, Ah Kee's face filled with such grief that the son concluded he had grown unstable, and would not let him return to the kampong again.

Chapter Thirty-Nine

Two months into her pregnancy, Natalie was prone to sleeplessness, and thus already awake when the phone rang in the middle of the night. Still, the unfamiliar noise was shocking, for
while they had rented the phone when they first moved into the house,
they had yet to use it. The shiny black machine that sat on a little glass
table in the living room was identical to the ones they had at the CC and
at Ah Boon's office in the ministry.

"Natalie? Where's Boon? Can you get Boon?"

Natalie shook Ah Boon awake. It was Ma, calling from a neighbor's
flat. Since Uncle had decided to remain in the kampong, and Ah Boon had
moved in with Natalie, Ma lived with Hia, Gek Huay, Ah Huat, and the
new baby. Like most, they did not have a phone installed, thinking it an
unnecessary expense. Her voice was strained and faraway. She would not
say what the problem was, but continued to insist that Ah Boon come over
then, right then, adding only that he should not bring Natalie but come
alone. Finally, bleary-eyed, he threw on a shirt and got on his bicycle.

When Ah Boon got there, he saw from the ground floor that all the
lights were on in Hia's flat. The rest of the block was dark, illuminated
only by the streetlamps outside. He ran up the stairs two at a time, remembering only when he got to the third floor that he could have taken

the lift. At his knock, Ma opened the door a crack, looked about warily, then closed it, undid the chain, and let Ah Boon in.

"Boon," she whispered. "Good, you're here."

Ma seemed fine, her face its usual soft assemblage of creases and worry. Ah Boon let out a breath he did not realize he had been holding.

"What's wrong? Is it Hia? Ah Huat?"

Ma placed a finger over her mouth. "All sleeping."

Ah Boon looked around the flat. There, too, everything seemed normal, no different from the week before, when he and Natalie had come over for the New Year celebrations. The red cloth was still up over the door. The refrigerator—Ma's proudest possession—hummed quietly in the corner of the living room, next to the wooden dining tables they had brought from the kampong. The festive sweet tray, filled with red melon seeds, kumquats, dried coconut, and candied melon. The plush upholstered sofa he had bought for Hia as a move-in gift, the electric fan standing by it. The tiled floor they'd paid for, at extra expense. A faint smell of food lingered.

Ma gestured toward the kitchen. They went over to the wide doorway together, and there, slumped over the table, was Siok Mei. Her head was resting in her arms, and she appeared to be asleep. Next to her were a glass of water and an untouched bowl of lotus root soup, oil congealing on its surface.

"She came about an hour ago," Ma said. "Aiyo, Boon. Better talk to her."

Siok Mei appeared to have dressed in a hurry, wearing a thin sleeping shirt over a rumpled skirt. Her tan ankles showed the ghostly marks of socks pulled up to different heights. He saw her as she had been twenty years ago: a girl with a strong neck and blunt-cut hair, in their school uniform. His heart leaped, and he felt suddenly as though he were himself an eight-year-old boy, and Siok Mei come knocking to take him on some adventure or another again. Off they would go, with no thought of the years that had passed, free as children dashing through the undergrowth, whispering secrets to each other as they went. A load he had not known himself to be carrying seemed to lift off his chest.

"The child is sleeping in my room, don't talk too loud," Ma said.

The child, of course; there was a child, to whom, nominally at least, he was the godfather. He and Siok Mei were not eight, they were not even eighteen. His own wife was pregnant. Heavily he fell back into the present. He reminded himself of Natalie, his job, his house. Siok Mei, too, had an entire life without him, a family of her own. And he had encouraged her into it. Ah Boon pushed away the pang it caused him. What use were aches and pangs? Merely inconvenient remnants from a long-buried past. They were friends, that was all. She had come seeking help, and he would help her.

Taking a deep breath, he pulled out a chair and sat down. Then, like she had done to him so many years ago in that small classroom in the kampong school, he touched his fingers gently to her back. When she lifted her face from her arms, her eyes were blurry with sleep, her forehead streaked with red imprints from where hair had pressed into skin.

"Boon," she said drowsily, then reached out and gripped his hand.

Slowly, Siok Mei related what had happened. Just hours before, after she and Eng Soon had turned in for the night, a loud pounding had come at their door. Both knew immediately this was nothing good. They had feared this moment for a long time, and yet now that it had come, she could not quite believe it was happening. Siok Mei did as Eng Soon said, waking their sleeping one-year-old, taking the child into her arms and concealing herself and her son in a wardrobe. Eng Soon went to answer the door.

Ma shook her head at this point in the story. Ah Boon knew she was thinking of the war, the Jipunlang raiding households at random hours of the day. Siok Mei went on. She could hear the voices from where she was hiding. In her arms, the baby boy stirred, and she bounced him softly to keep him slumbering. There were several men, three at least, maybe four or five.

"One of them said: 'Oh, it's you.' And then he apologized. My heart sank. Why was he apologizing? What was he going to do?"

They didn't hurt Eng Soon, she said. If they had, if she had heard the slightest hint of violence, a gasp or a grunt or the sound of something falling to the floor, she didn't know what she would have done. Leaped out of the wardrobe, flung her body between the men and Eng Soon? Once, she would have done this, but now she had Yang to think of, Yang to protect.

It took Ah Boon a moment to realize Yang was her son. He'd forgotten the child's name, or perhaps had never cared to find it out. He would grow up to be a man. An entire human being, whose life would be inextricably linked to Siok Mei's and Eng Soon's union. Why was this such a difficult thing to hear? Ah Boon forced himself to focus on the story at hand, reminded himself that he was married to Natalie. He was here in the capacity of no more than an old friend, one who would help Siok Mei in whatever way he could, as any old friend would.

Anyway, Siok Mei went on, they searched the living room. She heard them knocking books off the shelf onto the floor, asking Eng Soon if they were his. He said they were, and asked what the men were doing with them. The books were evidence, they said. Evidence for what? Eng Soon asked, though of course, he already knew.

There had been rumors of a crackdown like this for months, and talks of whether they should flee or not. Some other union leaders had already left to hide at the homes of distant relatives or, in more extreme cases, to "go in," as Teacher Chia had just a couple of years ago. It made no sense. The fight in the jungle was long over. They had not heard from Teacher Chia in months, and feared him dead or captured. She and Eng Soon had made the decision to stay, reasoning that they, after all, were not important in the way that some of these other leaders were. They had always worked to be moderate, to reason first with the Ang Mohs and then the Gah Men, resorting to striking and violence only when all else failed. Here Siok Mei hinted at having been more "involved" than Ah Boon had understood her to be, but she did not elaborate on the nature of that involvement.

It did not matter now, Siok Mei said bitterly. The Gah Men's win at the referendum had emboldened them. They had long wanted to crush the leftists who opposed them. It was clear that the time to strike had been chosen carefully. With the feeling after the referendum that a great decision had been settled and the start of the Lunar New Year, they were betting on the fact that people were in no mood for politics. What people wanted, Siok Mei said, was to drink beer in relatives' living rooms, gossip about neighbors and friends, wager their red-packet money on blackjack and mahjong. And so it was, on the ninth day of the New Year, that they had finally come knocking at Eng Soon and Siok Mei's door.

"Where's your wife?" the men had asked Eng Soon.

"In Johor, visiting relatives," he'd said.

In the wardrobe, Siok Mei's heart was pounding so loudly she felt sure they could hear it. Little Yang snoozed peacefully against her chest. It was for his sake, she thought, that she would remain silent. She breathed as quietly as she could. All it would take was for one of them to come into the bedroom, to see her clothes strewn across the floor, her purse strung up on the back of a chair, her water glass, half filled, on the bedside table. But miraculously, they merely grunted assent and didn't ask anything more. They took Eng Soon and left, not even letting him lock the door behind him.

As soon as they had gone, Siok Mei came out of the wardrobe and went into the living room. It was in a terrible state, she said, books flung open, papers lying everywhere. The men had not bothered taking their shoes off, and the floor was covered in muddy footprints. The door was ajar. Standing there in the middle of that mess, with Yang still sleeping in her arms, she felt a chill come over her.

"I knew I had to leave," she said to Ah Boon.

He found it difficult to concentrate on her story, terrible as it was. Instead all he could think about was her smell, so familiar he felt himself to be not in Hia's flat but back in the kampong. She was gripping his hand, her fingernails digging into his palm.

She'd packed light, Siok Mei went on. A small bag with clothes for herself and Yang, money, all the jewelry she owned. She permitted herself a few nonessential trifles: her and Eng Soon's university diplomas, a single photo from their wedding day.

"Oh," she said, digging around in her bag. "And this."

In her hand lay a rubber seed, smooth and brown as a stone.

"From the kampong. The tree next to your old house."

"Oh." A lump rose in Ah Boon's throat.

When had she picked that seed? As a child? When she left the kampong to live with Eng Soon? When she returned to visit with Yang? Did it matter? He was flooded with a stupid, stupid joy, staring at that little rubber seed. In all her troubles, she thought of him still.

Then Siok Mei looked away and put the seed back into her bag. She paused. Did her lip tremble, or was it his wishful thinking?

When she spoke again, her voice was steady. "These men," she said. "They can do whatever they want. They have the support of the Ang Mohs, the people; who's stopping them from doing whatever they want?"

These men. Her words were a punch in the gut. It was the Gah Men she spoke of. The Gah Men he worked for. He was a Gah Man. And they had hurt her—did that mean he had hurt her?

"Don't worry," he said. "I'm here. I'll fix it."

His mind raced. Even as he rushed to reassure her, he felt himself to be powerless. What could he do, what recourse did he have? Siok Mei muffled a quiet sob. He had never seen her cry, not in all the time he had known her. Cautiously he wrapped his arms around her. The Gah Men were an enormous enterprise, and Ah Boon belonged to the realm of organization, efficiency, and optimization; daylight, public activities. This midnight purging, this creeping secrecy, this was something else altogether.

But is it? a small voice inside him said. Was it not two sides of the same coin? What made the flats possible, the land possible—was it not the same seamless, efficient machinery that plucked political opponents from their beds in the middle of the night and conveyed them to prison?

He held Siok Mei more tightly, as if the force of his grip could ease her pain. Then he thought of Natalie, the only other woman he had ever held this way, but who had never needed him like this. He and Natalie were partners, joined together in their common cause. But Siok Mei reached some deep place inside him that was fierce with need and longing, a place that frightened him, that he had long sealed off.

"Mei," he said, looking into her eyes. "I'll do everything I can to help. I don't know what or how, but I will try. Eng Soon will be all right."

But what could he do? No one at work would sympathize with his plight, let alone help him. Just being with Siok Mei right now was a compromising position for him. But it was Siok Mei. He had to do something.

She wiped her eyes. "I can't go back to the flat," she said. "I thought of going back home for a while, but what if they come looking for me there?"

By *home*, she meant the kampong. Home was the mangroves, the sea, the breezy houses on stilts. The harsh trill of cicadas at sundown, the tiny crabs scrabbling across the surf. The flash of fish, hundreds of fish, straining in a net. Despite her life with Eng Soon, despite the distance that had grown between them, *home* was still their shared past. Then it clicked.

"You can't go home," Ah Boon said. "But I know where you can go."

Hours later, they stood at the door of his childhood house, two large bags at their feet. In one were blankets, an umbrella, Siok Mei's clothes. In the other, bottles of water, tins of biscuits, canned tuna and luncheon meat, a jar of homemade kaya, a loaf of soft white bread. In spite of Siok Mei's protests, Ma had insisted on giving them everything she had in the kitchen that wouldn't spoil.

Ah Boon thrilled to the feeling of Siok Mei's hand on his elbow, small and warm and familiar. She had held him like this many times before, as one would a brother or father, but tonight, something was different. Here they were again, returning as shoals of fish return upstream to where they were born. Everything else had fallen away. Politics, other people, the outside world. No Eng Soon, no Natalie, no leftists, no Gah Men. Years ago Siok Mei had told Ah Boon that she did not need his protection. Yet now she had come to him in need, and the warm, soft part of him—that, at her request, he'd buried for so long—leaped up to meet her call.

Standing on the creaking wooden steps, he thought of the boy he had once been, the boy whose elbow Siok Mei had grasped while walking home from school. Here that boy had stood by the light of a kerosene lamp as Pa showed him his drawings that mapped the islands' movement. There, just past the threshold, was where Hia had dunked that boy's head in a bucket of seawater, to teach him how to open his eyes underwater. Here, in front of the wooden steps, he had first spotted the Gah Men in their spotless uniforms moving like mirages through the swamp. There, by the window, he had talked to Ma about how much the new job at the CC would pay. Here, he had first walked hand in hand with Natalie to their first family dinner together. There, just beyond the old stone well, he and Siok Mei had chased each other with hot rubber seeds. There, on that patch of wet earth, he had lain with his face in the grass, the day that Uncle had come home without Pa.

Now Ah Boon knocked loudly. It occurred to him that Uncle might not hear, for he was a deep sleeper, and the sound of his snoring tended to drown out all else. But soon he heard the sound of someone stirring within the house. The door opened, and there Uncle was. His face was alert, unclouded by sleep. His eyes were red-rimmed, his sparse hair flat and greasy. He seemed to have aged a decade since Ah Boon had last seen him, at the wedding.

"Boon," Uncle said stiffly. Then, a look of surprise. In a softer voice: "Siok Mei. How are you?"

He took the bags at their feet and, without asking anything more, ushered them into the house.

The square table looked forlorn without the rest of the furniture. Uncle poured them mugs of water and they sat down.

"How are things, Uncle? Isn't it very noisy, living here?" Siok Mei said.

"Noisy, noisy. What to do? Still, doesn't mean I have to leave."

"We need the boat," Ah Boon said, as evenly as he could.

He explained what had happened, Siok Mei interjecting from time to time. Uncle listened without interruption. When he finished, Uncle took a sip of water, moistening his lips.

Finally he spoke. "You want to hide Siok Mei there," he said slowly. "Alone, on an island that disappears with the moon."

"I'm not asking for your opinion," Ah Boon said. "I'm asking for the boat."

All the windows were closed. The humid night air pooled in the house like stagnant water. Ah Boon could feel the moisture gathering in the folds of his elbows, the backs of his knees. His neck prickled with heat.

Uncle's lip curled. "Siok Mei, who are the men who took Eng Soon away?"

"I—I don't know. I didn't see their faces," she said.

Still her fingers fussed at the fabric of her blouse, still her arms rocked her absent child. They had left Yang with Ma, his warm, small body curled up on Ma's bed. He had remained, miraculously, in a state of drowsy confusion during the entire ordeal, such that when Siok Mei whispered her goodbyes as she took her leave, he did not protest but merely turned softly on his side and shut his eyes. Ah Boon caught the stricken look on her face, the fear, the reconsidering. The situation was forcing her to do what she had promised her child she would never do: leave, as her own parents had. But she knew it would not be safe for him to come with her. He saw her face change, charged with a resolve he knew well. Here was the Siok Mei who always chose sacrifice over what felt natural or easy. The Siok Mei he'd once fallen in love with, though it was this very trait that had caused her to choose Eng Soon over him.

"Not their names, I mean. But who's responsible for this? Who's locking union people up? Who's been against the leftists all this time?"

Ah Boon sprang up from his seat. "If you don't want to help, just don't help. Come, Siok Mei, this is a waste of time."

"It's the Gah Men!" Uncle cried. "The Gah Men are the ones who took Eng Soon, who want to take you. So why can't our Ah Boon here *do* something about it?"

"I am not the Gah Men," Ah Boon said. "I work for them. I want—"

"What?" Uncle said. "What do you want?"

He wanted to make things better, Ah Boon thought. All he wanted was to have a purpose. But Uncle would not believe this, he knew.

"See?" Uncle said. "I told you it was the same." But there was no satisfaction in his voice, only sadness.

"Stop with this again," Ah Boon said.

"But they are! Taking people from their beds in the middle of the night—what did I say, boy? What did I say? And you want to be one of them? You want to be a Gah Man like that? What would your father think?"

"Let's go, Mei," Ah Boon said.

His hands trembled at his sides. If Siok Mei did not get up, if she did not come with him, he did not know what he would do.

When Siok Mei turned to him—shadows gathering beneath her eyes, face shining like the moon—something inside Ah Boon's chest shifted. An old wound opened once again, the emotion that rushed in.

"Mei," he said again, quieter this time.

He tried to read her face. Did she believe the awful things that Uncle was saying about him? Did she think that was what he was?

Siok Mei uncrossed her arms. When she spoke she did not look at Ah Boon but at Uncle.

"I've known Ah Boon all my life. He's nothing like them."

"He lives in that big house with that woman," Uncle spat. "He speaks English. He's responsible for—this! The noise, the dust, the land!"

Uncle waved his hand angrily at the window. Then he stopped, as if suddenly exhausted. His entire person seemed to sag with the weight of all his protests, all his cares.

"My own nephew," he said. "Our own boy."

"Come on, Mei," Ah Boon said. "Let's go."

Chapter Forty

107 HELD IN DAWN DRIVE.

THE SWOOP BEGAN AT 3 A.M.

44 NAMES ON THE LIST.

The ministry was abuzz with the news when Ah Boon walked in the next morning. It was said that the newspapers were imprecise: the raid had begun at fifteen past two in the morning. Conspiracy was alleged, armed struggle suggested to be imminent, a Communist infiltration assumed. Those taken during the raid were now in a secure facility, being questioned, subject to indefinite imprisonment without trial. In total: thirty-one politicians, forty trade union leaders, eighteen teachers, eleven artists and writers, seven members of rural hawker committees.

A not-insignificant number were still on the run. Rumored to have skipped town, taken clandestine boat rides across the straits, made a break for jungles up north or the vast archipelago east and south. But many, it was said, were hiding with friends and family right under the Gah Men's noses.

The atmosphere was oddly festive; buzzing with a morbid excitement that came with any disruption to the routine workday. People lingered in hallways, by water fountains, outside bathrooms. They hogged sinks in the pantry, crowded newspaper racks, held whispered conferences in private offices. It got around that someone's second cousin had been taken. Another's neighbor. Yet another's middle school teacher.

"Anyone you know?" one colleague asked Ah Boon.

He shook his head and turned away with his cheeks burning. He was sure that the guilt showed on his face, that Siok Mei's image was imprinted on his pupils, and that if anyone were to look into his eyes, they would see it right away.

The thought of her, however, calmed him. Turning back to the colleague who'd asked, he straightened his back and lifted his chin with some disdain.

"Terrible, isn't it?" he said. "Good thing they managed to get so many of them."

He went back to his office and shut the door behind him. There, he placed a fresh piece of the paper in the typewriter, fixed his gaze on it, and began hitting the keys at random. The gibberish that crowded the white space seemed to take on a hidden meaning, and he felt as though he were channeling some secret language, some lost, unknown tongue. The thought soothed him; he kept typing. The smell of ink filled his head.

Ah Boon had not slept all night. After he and Siok Mei had left Uncle, they'd gone and gotten the boat themselves. It was where it always was, nestled in a groove of sandy earth beneath the house. They brought the boat down to the surf, moving by the pale light of the moon, and Ah Boon was reminded of the last time he'd gone out to sea in the dark. Siok Mei's silhouette turned into Natalie's. Ah Boon stopped in his tracks. He thought of his job, his family, the child growing, day by day, in his wife's belly.

"Boon?" Siok Mei's voice came out of the dark like a lullaby.

"Mei," he answered.

"Thank you," she said. "I know—well. It's been such a long time. And we haven't been—"

"No need to thank me," he said quickly. He could not bear to have their past alluded to.

"Okay." She fell quiet.

He could not *not* help her. Besides, this was the safest option possible—no one outside the kampongs knew about the islands. The islands themselves seemed to exist out of time, out of space. If there was one place Siok Mei would be safe, it was there. As long as they could get to the islands, Ah Boon felt, they would be wrapped in their thick magic, sheltered by their vanishing bays. And a part of him, a stupid, foolish part of him, wanted her to be protected by the place he had discovered, the place he had missed as deeply as he had missed her.

"Let's go," he said, and they pushed the boat into the water.

Ah Boon took up his usual place next to the engine, Siok Mei settling at his feet, leaning her back into his bare shins. How warm her skin was beneath her thin shirt. How maddening, even after all these years. Ah Boon tried very hard not to move his legs. There was a small brown dot at the base of her neck—dirt? An ant? Without thinking, he reached out and brushed it with his thumb. She did not jump or turn to look at him, but instead leaned, very gently, into his touch.

"I didn't know you had a mole there," he said.

"I never did. They keep appearing, the older I get. I have them all over now."

Ah Boon started the engine to chase the image of *all over* from his mind. They set off. So many times he had made this same trip, this very boat carving its various paths into this same water, water that parted and then closed in its wake as if it had never been disturbed at all. He was

reminded of yet another trip, saw the small figures of himself and Siok
Mei at the front of the boat, pressed together for that very first time.

When they got to Batu, they disembarked at the same place the villagers had on that very first communal trip. The cliffs shone bone-white
in the dark, the branches of the mangroves forming an intricate black
lace against the purpling sky.

Ah Boon found the spot as if he had been here only yesterday. Here,
where the men had once joked would be perfect to build a house. There,
the same bowed casuarina tree, the same smooth sand studded with
the tiny, spiky husks of fallen fruit. Again Ah Boon had the feeling of
being trapped in time, of acting out, again and again, a part that had
been written for him decades ago. And yet it was different, he reminded
himself; everything was different now.

Old needled leaves littered the ground, forming a soft, springy bed.
Here they spread the blankets and propped up, with sticks and pegs, a
large tarpaulin sheet, adjusting and restringing until they had a satisfac-
tory, if makeshift, shelter. Under this they laid the food and extra
blankets.

When they were done, Ah Boon stood awkwardly, avoiding Siok
Mei's eye.

"I'll come back tomorrow with water and more food," he said. "But I
guess I should go."

"Okay," she said.

"Will you be all right?"

She sat down in the nest they'd made. "I think so," she said in a small
voice.

He heard the need in her voice, did not stop to think what it was born
of—Yang, Eng Soon—but instead sat down next to her, the two of them
looking out toward the moonlit waves.

His heart was already pounding when she laid her head on his shoulder, so that when her hair brushed his neck, he felt his chest might burst. Her smell was everywhere, or was it the sea? He could not tell, but it filled him with both contentment and agitation. The pleasure of her proximity was too much. He wanted to run away and tumble into her all at once; he felt himself balanced on the knife-edge of fear and desire, and knew not which way he would fall.

They sat there for a long while, breathing quietly in unison.

That they were not looking at each other, perhaps, made it finally possible for him to put his arm around her, possible for her to turn her face toward his. The air was still, disturbed only by the occasional chirp of a lonely cricket. Ah Boon pressed his mouth against the place where her hair gave way to her bare forehead, and she did not protest. Ah Boon breathed against her skin, and she did not protest. Her head remained where it was, her breath pulsed warm and damp against his collarbone.

There was nothing, technically, unchaste about this. But every tiny hair on Ah Boon's body stood to attention, every muscle, it seemed, tensed. He dared not, did not, move, until Siok Mei buried her face deep in his neck, until her small hand reached beneath the fabric of his singlet and brushed his hot skin. Even after the situation became unmistakable, Ah Boon continued to hold himself back. Yes, his limbs felt as though they were on fire. Yes, his nerves were cold, hot, shimmering, leaden all at once. Yes, something inside him was breaking. Still he held himself in check; did not move a muscle, did not permit a sound.

How many times had he dreamed of this? How many times had he kicked himself, shamed himself, hated himself for dreaming of this? And now here they were, sand tangled in their hair, salt crisping on their skin, wind nowhere, wind everywhere. Here was Siok Mei's warm mouth, unbearably, terribly, brushing his ear. Here was her talcum-sweet smell, one he knew so well, had craved for so much of his life. Here was the solid length of her body, the firm muscularity of her strong limbs pressing into his.

"Wait," Ah Boon said.

He wanted to look at her. He wanted confirmation. When Siok Mei drew away, her eyes were bright—with desire, tears, he could not tell—and her lips curled in the shape of a question.

"Boon," she said.

In that voice he knew better than his own, he heard her want. He felt a crushing joy. It was true, then; she desired him as he did her. He was not comfort for the lack of Yang or Eng Soon; in fact, it was as if there were no Yang, no Eng Soon, no Natalie. It was not the island that had vanished but all the world, and nothing remained but the two of them again. The years fell away like leaves from an old tree, their love for each other, impossibly, still as deeply rooted as it had been two decades ago.

He pulled her in, let her warm hands roam his body. As they pressed against each other it all came back to him. That first day in school, when Siok Mei had stood up in defense of Teacher Chia. The idyllic afternoons running around the kampong. Her hand steadying his as he practiced his penmanship. Her shin sliding past his as they swam together at the public swimming pool with their study group; their elbows intertwined as thousands of voices rose around them at a union rally. It would take someone inhuman to resist, and in spite of everything that Ah Boon had forced down in himself all these years, something at his core, something soft, and yielding, and wanting to believe, persisted.

He gave himself up. When Siok Mei sighed his name, he held her more tightly than he'd ever held anything before, feeling already the terrible fear of having to give her up again. After, they lay quietly for a long while, his mouth crushed against her ear, her legs tangled tightly with his. The sound of the waves washing in and out, in and out, was the only indication of time passing. A deep peace settled over them.

It was close to six in the morning by the time Ah Boon got home, and he found Natalie soundly asleep in bed. The sheets were twisted around her like a shroud; ever since getting pregnant, she'd begun thrashing her legs in her dreams. As quietly as he could, Ah Boon wiped himself off with a wet towel, then changed into clean clothes. She stirred as he slipped into bed beside her.

"What time is it?" she said, voice hoarse with sleep.

He paused, then, with a cold slick of shame at his back, told his first lie. "Just past four. I wasn't gone long."

"Is your mother okay?"

"Just a little scare. She felt dizzy and was worried she'd faint. I stayed with her till she felt better."

"Mm. Poor thing."

He couldn't tell if Natalie meant Ma or him, but she was already falling back asleep, one hand up by her ear, like a child. Later in the morning, she would not remember this exchange, but the lie he'd told had stuck, and she was certain he'd been gone for only a little under an hour. But for now, Ah Boon shut his eyes, allowing the night to come back to him with all its unbearable pleasures, all its tiny, barbed pains. He lay awake until the sun came up, and then he rose, bathed himself, and went to work.

A knock at the door. "Come in," Ah Boon said.

The Deputy Secretary's assistant peeked in. The Deputy Secretary wanted to speak with him, she said. Could Ah Boon go see him now?

He said yes, he would be right there. When the assistant left, Ah Boon stared at the sheet of paper filled with unreadable text. He knew he should be worried about the Gah Men finding Siok Mei, about Natalie, maybe even about going to prison. But the calm from before remained. Again and again he revisited the night in his head. His time with Siok

Mei felt as far from life as a dream, yet searingly true the way only dreams could be. For this reason he did not feel he had been unfaithful to his wife. Natalie belonged to his waking hours. Natalie was future, Siok Mei past. Being with her was like visiting a lost world, a world in which Pa was still alive, the kampong still intact, Uncle happy and loving, where Siok Mei had not chosen her beliefs over him.

Ah Boon turned these thoughts over in his mind until a second knock came. It was the assistant again—asking if he would please go now. Ah Boon rose from his seat, following her to the Deputy Secretary's office.

"Ah Boon," his boss greeted him.

Ah Boon could detect nothing in the man's face. His expression was as relaxed and friendly as it always was. He leaned back in his swivel chair, hands clasped at his stomach, as if keeping captive a tiny bird that would otherwise fly away.

107 Held in Dawn Drive. The Swoop Began at 3 A.M. 44 Names on the List.

Ah Boon thought, now, of the 107 people. The newspapers had said they were being held in a detention center for questioning, that the Emergency laws passed several years ago allowed for them to be held for as long as necessary, given their threat to national security. He thought of those he had known in school—Geok Tin, Ah Mui, what had happened to them?—with whom he had composed spirited songs, shared post-swimming lunches, gone to the movies and theme parks.

"Alexander," he said hesitantly.

"Bad business," the Deputy Secretary said, gesturing at the paper in front of him.

Ah Boon forced himself to nod, twisting his face into an expression of worry, making a sound of agreement.

"You used to be involved with the student unions, back in your middle school days, didn't you?"

Ah Boon realized his arms were crossed. He uncrossed them. He said yes, indeed he did, but that had been a long time ago. He hadn't kept in touch with any of them.

"Know anyone who was rounded up?"

Siok Mei's face as she had appeared last night, stricken, strange, came into his mind. Ah Boon shook his head. His hands were damp, he realized, turning them to face the back of the room, as if the Deputy Secretary might be able to see the sweat glistening in the lines of his palms.

"No one I've spoken to in years," he said. "A couple of old classmates. Came through the grapevine."

The Deputy Secretary nodded. A look of satisfaction crossed his face.

"There are some who believe that we are defined by our past," he said. "Some who will be all too eager to have their suspicions confirmed."

Ah Boon stared at him.

"Do you remember a Lim Chin Huat?"

It took Ah Boon a few seconds to realize he was asking about Teacher Chia. Yes, he replied, he did remember Teacher Chia. It was he who had taught Ah Boon how to read and write. Last his mother had heard, he'd been killed in a scuffle up north with Ang Moh soldiers during the Emergency.

Again the Deputy Secretary nodded. He brought his fleshy thumbs to his chin.

"I'll be direct with you," he said. "Some people here do not like the trust I have placed in you."

What was the Deputy Secretary getting at? Was he trying to tell Ah Boon that he was one of the forty-four on the list, that he was trying to decide if Ah Boon should be?

"One of your classmates, a certain Tan Eng Soon, was apprehended last night. He named you while trying to get out of trouble. Said you were a childhood friend of his wife's."

Incongruous that it would still sting for Eng Soon to refer to him as *the friend of his wife*.

"He tried to use you as a bargaining chip. Said you might be a Gah Man now, but that you were no different from him or anyone else who had been taken in."

Then the Deputy Secretary unfolded the newspaper on his desk, smoothing it out so it lay flat in front of him. The black-and-white faces stared up at them. Eng Soon was not there, Ah Boon already knew, having scrutinized the paper earlier that morning. The Deputy Secretary was pointing to one of the head shots. A slim man with a boyish face and thick eyebrows. Familiar, somehow, Ah Boon thought. Was this another forgotten acquaintance of his who would prove damning?

"Mr. Yik's brother," the Deputy Secretary said.

There was silence. Ah Boon struggled to understand what he was saying.

"Everyone has someone. Our story—" Here the Deputy Secretary paused, as if this were a practiced speech he'd envisioned giving many times before. "Our story is a tangled one, as all great stories are. I vouched for you, so for now, your ex-classmate's claim will not hold water."

He put the newspaper away. Ah Boon seemed to feel the fear drain out of his body, and yet, where it had been was only emptiness.

"Thank you," he said stiffly.

"You're aware of the issues with the pilot."

It took Ah Boon a second to realize the Deputy Secretary meant the reclamation project. Yes, he said, he was aware of the sand shortage that had stalled its progress. It was too bad, he said, after all the work that had been done.

"Oh, no, no, no. It is not too bad. The work will continue. We will find a way," the Deputy Secretary said. "I am sure of it."

He made a cage with his fingers, resting its peak beneath his chin.

From his perch, he scrutinized Ah Boon's face, pausing, as if he expected something from him. As if Ah Boon knew very well how they could continue.

Ah Boon's mind raced—what did he have to do with the sand shortage?

"If only there were an alternate source," the Deputy Secretary said. "An unpopulated hill, for example."

The understanding came in a flash.

"An empty parcel of land one could dig up, for a reservoir."

The hands of the clock, clicking coldly around its white symmetrical face.

The Deputy Secretary paused, blinked, fixed Ah Boon in his gaze. "A deserted island."

"I—"

How could he know? How could he know?

"Natalie."

The problem of the sand shortage had been plaguing the Deputy Secretary for months now, every report coming in with more bad news, every survey showing further complications. Just a week ago Natalie had walked in through that very door, sat in the very seat that Ah Boon was now sitting in. She'd told him about a mysterious island off the coast that appeared on no maps, was listed in no Gah Men census or survey. It was sizable, four kilometers across, at least, and boasted swaths of sandy beaches, tall cliffs that could be detonated for rock. As far as she knew, no one lived there. No one even knew it existed.

"Natalie had seen it," the Deputy Secretary said. "She claimed she could bring me there."

And so they had set off the very next day. Natalie, the Deputy Secretary, a few cronies from his office. They hired a boatman from the jetty in the city and headed back to where Natalie had said she'd seen the island.

"We circled the area for hours."

But of course, nothing was there. It was almost funny, the image of the serious Deputy Secretary, Natalie, and other less senior Gah Men going around the empty sea in a boat. Funny in the way that when, as an adult, he recalled the fear he'd felt on his first trip out on the fishing boat with Hia and Pa, and had inexplicably found himself laughing.

Natalie's betrayal did not make him angry. It made him very cold, and very calm. He found himself scared by this placidity, felt as though he was a man who could do anything, who was capable of anything.

But of course Natalie had brought the Deputy Secretary to the island. She had seen a solution to a problem, and to solve it was her nature. She did not understand what the islands meant to Ah Boon. Could he blame her, when she knew so little about who he truly was? And who was he, truly? He had the feeling he was only just figuring it out, but the answer lay with Siok Mei on the island, not here, in this bright, whirring room of the Gah Men.

The Deputy Secretary was explaining that they had gone back a second time, a few days later. Still, they found nothing. At this point, Natalie was apologetic, unsure. She thought perhaps she'd been mistaken altogether, that the island Ah Boon had taken her to was merely one of the mapped ones farther south.

"Or perhaps," the Deputy Secretary remarked drily, "she had dreamed the whole thing."

He would have paid the incident no further mind, he said. But when he got back to the office, something made him pull out the kampong census that Ah Boon had recently turned in.

Opening a drawer now, the Deputy Secretary took out that very report. There was a satisfying heft to the bound pages. He had done that, Ah Boon thought. He had gathered those words and put them in the right shape, filled sheet after sheet of empty paper with information. Colorful flags stuck out from certain pages.

"The 'islands' are referred to fourteen times in the oral transcriptions," the Deputy Secretary said. "I began wondering. One woman, fine. But can a whole village be hallucinating?"

He placed the report on the folded newspaper, over the black-and-white faces.

"Natalie says you can show us where they are. And after all we've done for you, Ah Boon, surely this is a thing you can do for us?"

Ah Boon did not speak.

"You don't have to answer now," the Deputy Secretary said. "You have a—*relationship* with the land. I understand that. But think of the future. Ours, yours. Your country's. I simply ask that you think about it."

Gently, the Deputy Secretary placed both hands on the report, as if soothing an animal, then slid it back into the dark mouth of the desk drawer.

Chapter Forty-One

I t was only after the fourth house burned down that the newspapers picked up on it. The fourth house was Swee Hong's old place, which, like Ah Kee's, had been empty. Swee Hong was practical about the whole thing—being a landowner, he'd been paid by the Gah Men for his house. The way he saw it, it was their loss, not his. Still, he had questions. Fires did happen in the kampong, but never more often than every few years or so, set off by kerosene lamps knocked over in the night, carelessly tossed cigarettes, and once, an especially fearsome lightning storm. The recent fires, however, had all taken place in houses that were empty, where there were no thoughtless hands to flick hot ash, no clumsy elbows to tip lamps over.

With no plausible explanation in sight, speculations soon turned toward the supernatural. The land itself, it was said, was displeased. Some said it was the twinkling fireflies that dotted the berembang trees at night, turned to actual flame; others that the houses caught alight spontaneously, with no kindling at all; others still defaulted to that age-old fallback: the ghosts of their ancestors, angry at having been left behind.

The few who remained in the kampong grew nervous. They barred their doors, gave up smoking, sat in darkness at night. The neighboring kampongs were equally fearful, but no fires appeared there. The story spread beyond the kampong, picked up as a strange ancillary tale to the reporting around the sand shortage and stymied land reclamation project. Uncle even gave an interview to a small Chinese newspaper. Now that everyone had moved to flats, he said, those who remained were living in a ghost town. The spirits were angry, he was reported as saying, angry that the kampong had capitulated so quickly to the Gah Men's promises of progress or newness. Or, he hinted darkly, perhaps it wasn't spirits at all.

What was he suggesting? The reporter went on, growing excited.

Oh, he wasn't suggesting anything. He would never dare suggest anything. He was a poor fisherman, he didn't know anything about politics or the ways of the educated, civilized Gah Men.

Was he saying the Gah Men had something to do with it?

No, no, he wasn't saying anything at all. Forget that he had said anything to begin with.

Though the article that was published—FIRES ARE GAH MEN'S RELOCATION CONSPIRACY, SAYS KAMPONG—was not helpful to Ah Boon's life in the ministry, he didn't acknowledge the furor to Uncle. Part of it was not wanting to give Uncle the satisfaction of knowing he had seen the article at all, or that it had gotten under his skin. Ah Boon knew that whenever Uncle complained about the Gah Men, he was really complaining about his nephew. The headline might as well have been FIRES ARE AH BOON'S RELOCATION CONSPIRACY. But the other part of it was practical. Ah Boon couldn't get out to the island every day without arousing suspicion, and so he relied on Uncle to bring food and fresh water to Siok Mei.

A silent truce had sprung up between them. Uncle agreed to help in spite of himself, for he could not bring himself to punish Siok Mei, whom he had known since she was a little girl. Uncle and Ah Boon fished together again now, to catch food for her, and on those trips out it was almost as if Ah Boon were a boy again and nothing had changed at all. In quiet companionship they dropped their nets, fell back into old routines of who would steer and who would sort the fish, made easy conversation about the clouds and whether they contained rain. A lightness came upon Ah Boon in these times, and he thought often of Pa, their first trip out to the islands that dark, wondrous morning. And it soothed him to be fishing with Uncle again, to feel his life settle into the worn grooves of what it once had been.

It was not the same, of course. In the distance loomed the reclamation site, the shorn trees and tilled earth. Then there was Alexander's request, made two weeks ago now. The Deputy Secretary was a busy man, and it was not difficult for Ah Boon to avoid him, but chance encounters with him in hallways were becoming more pointed. Despite Alexander's benevolent exterior, Ah Boon sensed his patience wearing thin.

The water was dark with sediment, and the catch far poorer than it ever had been. Uncle and Ah Boon did not talk of this. He could not forget Uncle's words about him being just like the Gah Men, the Gah Men being just like the Jipunlang. Ah Boon grew paranoid that when he could not get out to the island, Uncle was talking about him behind his back to Siok Mei. This made him sullen on the times that he did manage to get out to see her.

"What's wrong?" she asked. They sat side by side, legs pressed together in the sand.

It was dusk. They'd fallen quickly back into their familiar, childhood ways of affection: holding hands, touching feet, lying with their heads in each other's laps. It felt natural, inevitable. But old actions took on new intimacy now, with the knowledge of each other's bodies, the frisson lingering in the humid air.

Ah Boon was turned away from her. He didn't respond. His hands were buried in rough, warm sand. He remembered the night that Pa had woken him up to tell him his theory about the moon and the confidence Ah Boon had shared in return: that little matchbox containing a few grains of sand, which no longer disappeared once removed from the island. He'd thought this discovery wonderful then, but found it sad now. That something with the power to vanish was made material and fixed by his actions. He had the feeling that he had done this with his entire life.

Ah Boon turned abruptly to Siok Mei. "Do you love me?"

She looked at him with pain. "Yes."

"Do you love Eng Soon?"

"Boon—"

"Do you?"

She turned away. "Do you love Natalie?"

"That's different," he said weakly.

"I have a child with Eng Soon."

"So?"

"How is Yang? Did you give him the shells I found?"

"Yang and Ah Huat are becoming the best of friends," Ah Boon said, breaking into a smile. "They share everything. I even saw them try to split a poor ant the other day."

He had grown fond of Siok Mei's son, and had secretly fallen into the habit of thinking of Yang as *their* son. It was foolish, he knew, but the boy had Siok Mei's wide, curious eyes and uncompromising gaze, and Ah Boon could not help himself.

"Good. Good."

"Remember when we said we'd live here?" he asked.

"Yes." She smiled and took his hand.

He thought about that golden afternoon all those years ago, dashing through the trees toward a red boulder, rubber seed clasped in his hands.

"Do you want more children?"

"Oh, Boon—"

"Do you, though?"

"Maybe," she said. "I think it would be nice to have a daughter."

If they had a daughter, she would look just like Siok Mei, Ah Boon thought. He would teach her to swim as Pa had once taught him; Siok Mei would teach her to read and write and change the world.

"We could raise her right here," he said dreamily. "She'll be like a forest animal."

"And what about school?"

"You can teach her. You were Teacher Chia's pet, after all."

Siok Mei gave him a playful shove. "And I suppose we'd live off fish and guavas for the rest of our lives."

"Sounds like heaven to me."

She fell into a pensive silence.

"What is it?"

"Boon."

"What?"

"You know I can't stay here forever."

Ah Boon took her hand in his, flipped it up toward the sky, and with his little finger began tracing the deep lines in her palm.

"Why not?" he said. "Things are perfect here."

False words, they both knew. Things were perfect, briefly, each time he pulled his boat up the shore of the island and saw her waiting for him in the shade of the casuarina tree. Perfect when they embraced, tumbling sandy-footed into the nest of blankets still warm with the heat of Siok

Mei's body. Perfect, even, after, as they lay watching the sun drop slowly into the sea, pointing at the occasional hornbill in the trees, the curious shapes of clouds floating by. But at the edges of their consciousness loomed everything that was unsaid. Eng Soon, Yang, Natalie. The Gah Men's determination to purge the union leaders. The fact that Siok Mei's picture had appeared in the newspapers as one of the forty-four wanted leftists still on the run.

Natalie's pregnancy was starting to show now. Ah Boon knew he ought not to cause her distress, and yet the day that the Deputy Secretary had talked to him about the islands, he'd slammed their bedroom door so hard it made a chip in the frame. Natalie had stayed calm, but her voice trembled, her hand fluttered over her belly. She'd done it with him in mind, she said. If the islands did prove to be the solution to the sand shortage, and Ah Boon was the one to offer them up, then it would be more than just a feather in his cap. It would cement his importance among the Gah Men; it would make his career. She'd known he'd never have agreed if she'd suggested it to him herself, and so she'd gone directly to the Deputy Secretary, thinking that he could persuade Ah Boon. She'd done it for him, she said, touching her stomach. She'd done it for them. Besides, why did the islands have to be a secret in the first place? The kampong had moved on, no one fished there anymore, no one even lived there anymore.

Ah Boon could not argue with this, not without giving away the secret that was Siok Mei. She hadn't been there yet when the Deputy Secretary and Natalie had set out to find the islands, it still having been several days before the raid. Still, he shivered to think of them circling those empty waters. If they had done so then, they could do so now. All that stood between Siok Mei being found and the both of them being thrown in prison was the island's inconsistency, its seemingly magical refusal to be reliably found by outsiders.

"Tell me again what it's like when the moon grows," he said to Siok Mei now.

"I was trying to talk about—"

"Tell me," he insisted. "We can talk about that later."

"You're like a child," she said.

But she began to tell him. It had been two weeks now since she'd come to the island, long enough for the moon to grow and the island, in theory, to disappear. They'd had a fear of what might happen then. They speculated of ground vanishing beneath her feet, Siok Mei plunging into the cold sea as she slept or disappearing along with the island. Uncle had towed a small old rowboat out to the island in preparation, and it lay next to Siok Mei's shelter now.

When darkness came, the moon swollen to its fattest and brightest, the air turned cold, like the dawn after a long night of rain. The sand beneath her feet stayed solid, but each grain seemed to vibrate very gently, emitting a quiet, high song, and she felt she was dissolving into it. Standing there in the darkness, she had the impression, suddenly, that she could see her life as clearly as if it were laid out on a string in the sand, stretching ahead and behind her. She saw how many other lives were tangled in it—Eng Soon's, Ah Boon's, Yang's, her missing parents', Teacher Chia's—saw how insubstantial each thread was, how easily blown about by the wind and lost among the grains, and yet how real they were, how strong and unbroken.

Then, as she stood there staring at the sand, she became convinced that her parents were standing behind her. She could feel their breath on the back of her neck, sense the disturbance in the air, hear the subtle shifting of the sand. A feeling of deep comfort came over her. She knew that should she turn around, they would disappear. And so she continued to stand there, staring out at the dark sea. The sand singing beneath her feet, the perfect moon so bright it was like a hole of light punched into the velvet sky. Hours passed this way. And in the morning, the sand was quiet, the moon returned to the night, the sea brown and ordinary again.

"I wonder if—" Ah Boon stopped.

"You're thinking about your pa."

"I just wish I could see him again. One more time."

"What would you say to him?"

He thought about it. "I don't know."

"Mm."

"What would you say to your parents?"

"That I was all right. That I lived my life as they would have wanted, and they didn't have to worry. They could go on into the next world with peace."

Was he all right, Ah Boon wondered. Had he lived his life as Pa would have wanted?

"That I had a son," she said quietly. "That I wish they could have met him."

Ah Boon took her hand. There was so much that Pa would never know about him or his life. And yet on the island, Ah Boon felt most strongly that Pa was still here. Not apart from him, as a ghost lurking in the trees, but in his own body and soul. His long fingers were Pa's fingers, his brooding love for the sea was Pa's love.

"I can't stay here alone," Siok Mei said hesitantly. "I think of Yang all the time."

"You're not alone," Ah Boon said. "I'm here."

Siok Mei squeezed his hand, but she kept talking. "Uncle's been in touch with one of my colleagues at the union who got across the border. I think I should go too. With Yang."

"What are you saying?"

"It's a good time, Boon."

"How is it a good time?"

"The Gah Men have their hands full right now. The sand shortage, the raid. All the protests about the unfair referendum. Hammering out the details of citizenship—"

"No, no, what I mean is—" Ah Boon fell silent, a panic coming over him. He could not bear the thought of Siok Mei crossing the border, disappearing into an anonymous subterfuge. He might never see her again.

"What do you mean?"

He stared at Siok Mei, her limbs rosy in the dusk. Why should everything disappear? Pa, the kampong, the land, even Siok Mei? He could not lose her.

"You can't go," Ah Boon said.

"Oh, Boon."

The waning light, the gentle breeze. Siok Mei touched his cheek, and he covered her hand with his. He stared into her face, falling into the shining quickness of her eyes, searching for that elusive thing that sparked within her, the mysterious clarity of her soul.

The gears in his mind were turning, fueled by the sharp fear of losing her.

"What if I can get you free?" he said at last.

She frowned.

"They want the island. They need this—" Ah Boon reached out and grabbed a handful of sand. "And I can give it to them. Under one condition."

The lines between Siok Mei's eyebrows resolved.

"If you run away, you'll always be looking over your shoulder. You'll never be able to come back. Yang would have to grow up with that. Could you do that to him? But if I get you free, we could stay," he said. "Or we could leave. Whatever you want."

"And Natalie?" she said. "Your child?"

Ah Boon looked away. How to explain that he wasn't heartless, that it was the opposite. To stay with Natalie would be to remain trapped within the fortress he had built himself, behind the walls of education, money, status. Did he love Natalie? He struggled to remember. He had believed so, once, not that long ago. And yet where that love had once been was only a blank, smooth space. Was it callousness? Self-delusion? He did not know. All he knew was that Natalie felt spectral, a projection of his imagination, a construction of desire. Did he love her or what she stood for? Did he love Siok Mei? He couldn't answer any of these questions. He only knew what he wanted now, fiercely, and without doubt.

"I want you," he said. "I'll take care of you, you and Yang both."

He hated the ragged edge of his voice, the way it dragged with need.

Siok Mei closed her eyes. He saw that she was thinking. Considering, perhaps, what a life with him might be like. If he would be a good father to her son. Whether he could be trusted.

The waves filled the silence, and the old dread returned. A squirming sensation beneath the arches of his feet, a monstrous flashing swarm of bodies. The fish were gone, he knew, emptied from the sea by the noise and dust and grease. For the first time he wondered *where* they had gone, if they had found some other waters to populate, some other coast to ply. Where did things go when they had been driven away? Where was *away*?

Finally Siok Mei blinked her eyes open, like a sleeping child waking up. Her voice was thick with something Ah Boon didn't understand, something he chose not to understand, that ran counter to the meaning of her words. But he didn't care, because the words she said were: "Okay. Talk to your Gah Men."

Chapter Forty-Two

The days slipped by, the country marched forward. Merdeka shimmered on the horizon: a promise, a belief, a tempestuous god continuing to demand sacrifices. Those locked up wrote letters, issued instructions, filed petitions, but still languished within prison walls. Eventually the remaining leftists marched on city hall to protest their colleagues' ongoing detention, but the march grew heated, and twelve more leaders were arrested. The Ang Mohs were pleased. The Gah Men had delivered. The raid had been a success, smashing the underground Communist networks that the Ang Mohs so worried about, at least in the short term. The merger, scheduled to take place in September 1963, would deal with the threat in the long term. The Ang Mohs would withdraw the velvet hand of their iron rule, and the island would be independent at last.

And so the Gah Men would have their Merdeka. Their terms, their negotiation, their story. They would be the ones to lead the country into its new future, drag it forward if need be, and dazzled, as if by the million flickering lights given off by the forest of concrete blocks magically sprung from the earth, the country would follow.

In the kampong, the sixth house burned down, and then the seventh.

Ah Boon went over that evening and found Uncle sitting on the front steps, mending an old net. Ah Boon watched him from the path that led to their house. Uncle's head was bowed, his knees splayed as he worked the nets between his feet. For an aching moment, he was Pa, and Ah Boon was seven again, running home from school to greet his father. Then Uncle looked up and frowned. The spell was broken.

"I thought you coming tomorrow?" Uncle said.

Threaded through his voice was a skein of defensiveness. Uncle looked down at the nets, as if guilty of something, and began gathering them up in a messy pile.

"I came to see you, not Siok Mei," Ah Boon said. He raised the warm packages he held in each hand: Uncle's favorite char kway teow, fried greasy black and sticky sweet. "Thought we can eat dinner together."

Again, Uncle looked down at the bundle of nets. He nodded, then did something strange: instead of putting them away under one of the tarps beneath the house, as they always did, he gathered them in his arms and brought them inside.

Ah Boon followed him up the steps and into the house. Uncle took the nets into the kitchen, saying that he would get them bowls.

The air in the house was stale; all the windows were shut, Uncle's thin mattress dragged into the living room, next to the dining table, as if he had given up on using all the rooms of the house and now lived only in this small space. Aside from the staleness, something else was different, an atmosphere Ah Boon could not quite identify. He looked around, but aside from the mattress on the floor, the house looked the same as it had the last few months.

Each time it was sad, coming back to the space so familiar to him and yet so different. He always felt to have stepped into the shell of something that should no longer exist, that existed purely to remind him of what had been lost.

Still, there was something else—a smell, an unfamiliar smell.

Uncle returned with bowls and chopsticks. They shook the kway teow out of the oily bags, each ball of noodles landing with a smack in its bowl. The charred sweet scent filled the house, and for the first time in a long while, Uncle smiled.

They began to eat. The silence that descended was comfortable, like an old, forgotten shirt discovered at the back of a wardrobe and slipped over one's skin again. The sounds their chopsticks made clacking against their bowls felt like conversation, and Ah Boon wished it were the only conversation he needed to have. But soon their bowls were empty, containing only the hollow tails of consumed prawns, glazed ceramic slicked with oil and the sticky residue of black sauce.

"Ma's lonely," Ah Boon started. "She wishes you would go see her more."

Uncle grunted.

Ah Boon placed his chopsticks across the chipped rim of his bowl. He cleared his throat.

"I'm sorry, Uncle," he said.

The silence thickened, turned awkward. Uncle was still. Instantly Ah Boon felt what he was doing—approaching a problem head-on, acknowledging it to one's face—to be wrong.

After a long pause, Uncle said quietly: "Nothing to be sorry, boy."

"I know—I—"

Ah Boon fell silent. He wanted to say that with his feelings for Siok Mei had come a longing for the family's old harmony. That he wished things could be the way they had once been. Though he did not quite know what he meant by that—did he want the kampong to move back? Did he want the coast to be restored, to give up his job, to return to the fishing life?

None of this was possible.

Still Ah Boon thought Uncle wrongheaded and bitter. But he no longer wished to settle the score. He would trade the islands for Siok Mei's freedom. Leave Natalie, start his life anew. And perhaps in this new life, he could somehow mend the fissure that had come between him and Uncle. But he did not know how to say these things, so instead, he told Uncle his plan to get Siok Mei free.

"Oh, my boy," Uncle said quietly.

"What?"

"Siok Mei will never be with you."

There was no cruelty in Uncle's voice, but Ah Boon seemed to feel something cold sliding beneath his skin, as if a knife had been slipped into an open seam of his body, its blade so sharp that he hadn't noticed it until now.

"You don't know anything," he said.

Uncle shook his head. "I am an old man," he said. "But I see enough of the world already to know that people don't change."

"You don't know anything," Ah Boon said again. "Siok Mei loves me."

"She does," Uncle said.

Ah Boon fell silent at this.

"She loves you, but she will not leave her Eng Soon. She thinks you will get him free." Uncle shook his head at Ah Boon, as if it were he whose heart was breaking.

"Rubbish."

"She does not want her child to be without his father, just as she was."

It was not true. Uncle could not know. He knew nothing about Ah Boon and Siok Mei, knew nothing about their love.

"You don't understand anything," Ah Boon said.

"Don't I?" Uncle held his gaze calmly.

With a stab Ah Boon thought of all the afternoons he could not get out to the islands to bring Siok Mei supplies, and Uncle had gone instead. What had they talked about? Could it be true, could she have confided in him? Siok Mei had said that Uncle had been in touch with a colleague across the border. What was he doing for her that Ah Boon didn't know about?

The empty bowls clattered to the floor. One of them cracked into three even pieces, the other remained whole. The noise made Ah Boon jump, and he stared in surprise at his hands. He'd done it, he was standing up now with such force that his chair was toppling over behind him, he was pressing his palms against the table and leaning into Uncle's face, so close he could smell the sour tang of his breath, at once familiar and strange, like the memory of a dream he'd had as a young boy.

"You don't know anything," he said. "Look at you!"

He jerked his hand out at the dark house, with the feeling that he was shattering something, some brittle balance that had been in place ever since he decided to work at the CC. *Look at you*, he wanted to say. *You couldn't even protect Pa. I protected us.*

"Stop," Uncle said. "Stop it, Boon."

There was fear in his voice. Ah Boon fell silent. Uncle's breath was pained and slow. When he met Ah Boon's gaze, the fear was gone, sieved into a clarity that made his eyes glint, made his entire being seem as though it were built of stone.

"Come, I show you something," Uncle said calmly.

The feeling of cold had spread to the tips of Ah Boon's fingers, to the tiny follicles in his scalp. Now that he was quiet, he couldn't stop hearing Uncle's words. *She will not leave her Eng Soon.* The house closed in on him; outside, the waves continued to crash on the shore. Wind. The sound was dreadful. He wished for the noise of the pile driver, the clattering of the conveyor belt. He wished for something to prove that life had changed. But it was as if nothing had changed, nothing would ever change.

Uncle was standing up, still beckoning for Ah Boon to follow him into the kitchen. But Ah Boon didn't want to follow Uncle anywhere. He noticed the broken pieces of the bowl he'd knocked to the floor, and slowly, carefully, he gathered them and set them on the table. Then, without looking at Uncle again, he left.

After Ah Boon had gone, Uncle continued to stand, silently, where his nephew had left him. His gaze lit upon first one corner of the room, then another. The dark, moody ceiling, the smooth wooden floors. The shuttered windows, thick with dust. The rocking chair, his thin mattress, worn holes leaking cotton stuffing. The pink towel he used after bathing, hung up carefully to dry.

He looked at each and every object, every dust mote, every cobweb, every trail of slow ants creeping up a wall. Briefly, he considered going outside, to smell the damp air, feel it moving across his skin. Hear the lone hornbill cawing somewhere in the jungle that remained. But that would be too much; then he would have to hear the cicadas, touch the boat beneath the house, press his feet against the wooden step that creaked each time he crossed the threshold. That way he would never be done. There were too many things to say goodbye to; one couldn't possibly say goodbye to them all.

Uncle turned around. His limbs were heavy, as if he were a tree that had grown attached to the ground, as if each step were a painful unrooting. Still, he unrooted himself, again and again, until his feet had borne him into the kitchen. The small room was cluttered with things: old newspapers, bedsheets, ragged towels, clothing, broken furniture, and what Ah Boon had seen Uncle bring in earlier: armfuls of fishing nets. These items lay on shelves that had once sagged with the weight of bags of rice, nets of onions, tins of meat; under the low wooden stool Ma or Gek Huay would sit on while peeling garlic or pounding chilis; against the stove of loose bricks on which so many delicious dinners had been cooked. Resting on one of the bricks was the little green matchbox Ma used to light the fire before each meal.

But they were all gone now—Ma, Gek Huay, Hia, little Ah Huat. His brother-in-law's words returned to him, as they always did, twisted and maddening. *Cannot fight, run, something, anything?* If Pa were around, he would know what to do. He would have put up a real resistance to the Gah Men, he would not have let Ah Boon convince everyone to leave.

Or perhaps not. Perhaps he would have packed up the house, sold the boat, moved to one of those concrete boxes in the sky. Uncle had spent his whole life trying to atone for what he had done to Pa, and it struck him now that he never really knew what Pa would have done in any of the long years that followed, that he was alone in his regrets and guesswork and hypothesizing. The past was over and done with, and there was nothing Uncle could do anymore to change it.

The smell that Ah Boon had noticed came from the open canisters lining the walls of the kitchen. Uncle went over to them now, beginning to slowly, methodically douse the sheets, the nets, the towels with their contents. The gasoline soaked through quickly. He'd used similar methods in the first seven houses, but had found that the best fires were made when enough kindling had been gathered. Old fabric and wood helped the fire burn brighter, and there was plenty of both lying around, now that so many houses had been abandoned.

He'd begun burning the houses out of hope that it would impugn the Gah Men. There were already rumors of such conspiracies—entire blocks of tenement houses catching fire at night, residents forced to re-settle in Gah Men flats. But he'd been too late. Everyone had already gone, and gone of their own free will. Even the most sympathetic news-papers had lost interest in the story. It was futile, he saw; there was no fighting them. The Gah Men would reshape the island to their liking and there was nothing Uncle or anyone else could do about it.

Uncle tipped the next canister over, then the next, the next, until all the canisters were empty.

Finally he picked up the green matchbox that lay on the brick stove, and sat down on Ma's low wooden stool. He hugged his knees to his chest. Theirs would be the eighth, and last, house to burn.

Chapter Forty-Three

B y the time the house caught fire, Ah Boon was halfway to the island. Night had fallen. Slivers of moonlight anointed the slippery dark skin of the sea. The engine puttered, the waves roiled, the house burned. Three-quarters of the way there, a cloud shifted briefly to reveal a thin slice of moon; the kitchen was almost entirely destroyed. When his boat arrived on the island's calm shore, the flames had spread through to the bedrooms. As he walked up the beach, toward Siok Mei, the thick wooden stilts that held up the house finally gave way, and the whole burning structure came crashing to its knees.

Ah Boon could not know this, and would find out only when he returned from the island. Now he was consumed with just one thing: seeing Siok Mei, proving Uncle wrong. Uncle, who, at that moment, lay collapsed where the fire had burned the hottest and brightest, among the cinders of sheets and clothes and fishing nets. But Ah Boon could not know this.

Siok Mei was propped up against the trunk of the casuarina tree, reading a book by flashlight. She waved the light as he approached, sending its bright beam bouncing off trees and rocks, making birds rise from the bushes in which they slept. The dancing light cheered him. The way it cut through the dark reminded him of the dim movie theaters he and Siok Mei had once frequented with their study group members. Buoyed by this memory, he sped up, stumbling over the dunes of sand to get to her. But when he landed on the pile of blankets next to her, he found himself doubting again. Siok Mei was laughing.

"What are you doing here so late?" she said.

He found himself at a loss for an answer, and so he laid his head in her lap. By the light of the flashlight, her face was a smooth moon, a glowing lantern. Her eyes, dark and liquid, flecked in a brown that was almost gold. How to explain his sudden appearance? How to put Uncle's question to her in a way that would elicit the truth?

He could not bear to look at her. Ah Boon reached for the flashlight she held in her hand, felt for the switch, and turned it off.

Now there was only the sound of water meeting sand and rock, the chirp of insects, the wind making its way through the forest at their backs.

"Won't Natalie be wondering where you are?" Siok Mei said.

Her skin smelled of salt and baby powder; fresh water being hard to come by, she'd taken to washing herself in the sea, patting herself down with the floral-scented talcum after. Ah Boon wished he could lie suspended in this moment forever. But the words were already tumbling out of his mouth, already determining the course of the future.

"I spoke to them," he said. "The Gah Men. I told them I would show them the island—this island, all the islands—so they can quarry it. The project can continue."

The lie felt flimsy on his lips. But he went on anyway. He had to know if Uncle was right, if Siok Mei would truly go through with it.

"They agreed to my condition," he said. "You'll go free. Be taken off the list."

Siok Mei fell silent. Ah Boon strained to hear her breathing, but the wind rushed in, and he couldn't tell what came from her and what came from the trees.

"Really?" she said at last. She cupped his cheek with her cool palm. "And Yang?"

"You'll keep him. They'll sign a document promising your freedom," Ah Boon improvised. "I'll only bring them here once I have it."

Ah Boon's heart pounded in his chest. He took her face in his hands.

"We can be together now," he said, the words spilling out of him. "I'll tell Natalie tonight."

Still she didn't speak. Why wasn't she speaking? *Please*, he thought desperately. *Tell me Uncle was wrong. Tell me we can start our life together now.*

"You have been so kind to me," Siok Mei said at last.

No. *Kind* was wrong. He was not *kind* to her; he loved her, he needed her, she was his life.

"But I have one last favor to ask, Boon."

The feeling of cold returned to him; he pictured mercury in a thermometer. He was the thermometer, his veins were the passage through which the silvery liquid ran.

There was no going back for her, Siok Mei went on to say. She had already escaped their net, she had accepted being on the run. In fact, she'd been making plans to join her colleagues across the border for the past week. Ah Boon's bargain with the Gah Men was deftly negotiated, but to trade the islands—she dipped one hand into the warm, rough sand—for her freedom, when she was already free, seemed a waste.

As she spoke, Ah Boon thought of rubber seeds grown hot from being rubbed against cement. He remembered the feel of them, like small burning hearts clasped in the palm of his hand. He wished for one now, to press to the cold skin of Siok Mei's forearm, to shock her, somehow, back into herself. *Remember?*, he would say. *Remember who we are?*

But it was not who they were. The boy and the girl chasing each other in front of his house were long gone. He could not say who had left first, he or she, but what was unmistakable was that they had never come back together, not really.

"You want me to get Eng Soon free," he said.

Through the tears that sprang to his eyes, the movement of Siok Mei's head was unmistakable.

The Lees' house was little more than warm embers now. The stilts that had held up the building for more than three decades were blackened stumps in muddy soil, the attap roof that had shielded them from wind and storm no more than a fine coating of ash.

"Okay," Ah Boon said. "Consider it done."

He would make the arrangements, he said. Once the Gah Men agreed and Eng Soon was released, Ah Boon would come get her. The two of them could head north with Yang, or wherever it was they wanted to go.

Ah Boon said all this in a slow, calm voice. Siok Mei's hand, he realized, was still in his. She squeezed his fingers.

"Close your eyes," she said.

He closed his eyes. A pressure was gathering behind them.

"Do you feel it?" she whispered.

Their old childhood game.

"Yes," he whispered back, fighting the bitterness rising in his throat. "I do."

"It's warm tonight, isn't it?"

"The dark is warm."

"It's hot."

We're floating now. We're lifting off the ground. *There's no more ground.* We're in the air. *Hold my hand?* I'm holding you. *What color is the dark?* Red. I think the dark is red. *More purple, to me.* Are we alone? Is everyone gone? *We're alone.* What should we do now? *Anything.* Where should we go? *We can go anywhere.*

She still loved him, Ah Boon realized. In the end it counted for nothing.

They opened their eyes.

"I have to go now," Ah Boon said, standing up. "Natalie will be waiting."

Siok Mei got to her feet. She wrapped her arms around him, burying her face in his chest. He began to resist, but then softened, allowed himself this one thing.

"Thank you," she murmured.

The vibrations of her words, spoken into his skin, felt like a message from a distant place. The tips of his fingers were cold, and she said so now as he brushed her cheek with them. He took one long, last look at her. Her face was cast in a deep, checkered shadow, features swallowed in pools of obscurity: half a nose, a quarter of an eye, an entire mouth gone missing in the dark.

Chapter Forty-Four

The boat appeared in the glow of the morning, and Siok Mei was surprised it had come so soon. It had been only two days, after all, since she'd seen Ah Boon and he'd promised Eng Soon's freedom. Her heart leaped. Gratitude washed over her for Ah Boon—good, loving, reliable Ah Boon, he was always there for her, would always be there for her—and along with it, a quiet stab of guilt. She understood what she had done. She didn't need to see the hurt in his face when she made her request, didn't need to dwell in his silence to understand the violence she'd inflicted.

Had she manipulated him? Yes. Did she love him, nonetheless, as a brother, a lover, a dear, true friend—why, yes. For so long she had ached for him, as she knew he had for her. For so long she'd wished it had been Ah Boon at her side, at every rally, every speech, every quiet moment of success. She thought often of the life they might have had together, filled with ease and joy and a deep, enduring comfort. She would never love another man as she had loved him.

But the lesson had been waiting within her. From the moment her parents had chosen to leave, she'd understood, on some level, that the people one loved were sacrifices. Ah Boon, she knew, thought she had sacrificed him for Eng Soon, but it was not Eng Soon she cared for. She cared for Eng Soon fondly, as one would a business partner, perhaps as Ah Boon cared for his Gah Woman. No, for Eng Soon she would not have hurt her dearest friend.

But Ah Boon did not yet understand what it was to be utterly bound to the life of another. It was for Yang that she would protect Eng Soon. She was determined that he should have his father. She was determined that he, unlike her, would have his parents, his family. Whole, unbroken, unshakable. For this she would go to all lengths. One day, when he had his own children, his own family, Ah Boon would understand.

At the sound of the engine drawing closer, Siok Mei leaped up from the sand. But as the boat came into view, she crouched down again, heart pounding, pressing her face close to the sand.

It was not a boat she recognized. Expecting the old, splintered wood of Ah Boon's familiar fishing boat, she'd glimpsed instead one that was all sharp corners and metal edges glinting in the sun. From its roof a flagpole emerged, a flag fluttering in the wind. She could not see the flag but had a dreadful feeling about what it was. Red and white, a crescent moon, its attendant stars. Shapes cut out of the sky, commandeered into service.

When she saw the second boat, a short distance behind the first, she felt a stab in her heart. There it was, the familiar white-painted wood, the outboard motor jutting from its rear. Ah Boon's figure perched next to the engine, his knees splayed. His boat stayed idling in the shallows while the first pulled up to the shore.

He had given her up.

Mingled with frantic, futile thoughts of escape—running into the jungle behind her and eluding capture, diving into the sea and swimming as far as she could possibly go—was anger, first at Ah Boon, then at herself. She had done this to him, she saw. She had demanded the same sacrifices from him as she had from herself, and he had declined to make them. He was unwilling to be a martyr, would not let her slip away with Eng Soon and Yang to live her life far away from him. She had asked too much of him, had dealt him a wound too deep. And as angry as she was, she understood his hurt, his fierce, selfish love. A wave of grief washed over her.

Could she blame him? Could he blame her? There was no point to these questions; there was no time for these questions. Ahead of her, the sun was rising, trickling orange into the sea. She seemed to smell something burning. A whiff of ash, a touch of sulfur, but then it was gone, and the uniformed men were coming up the beach, their matching khaki shorts flapping about madly, an army of anonymous flags in the wind.

Chapter Forty-Five

On the day Singapore joined the Federation of Malaysia, thus ending 144 years of British rule, the Gah Men's ban on firecrackers, fireworks, and squibs was lifted for twenty-four hours. Merdeka, at last, and it merited a proper celebration. Still the Gah Men reminded the public to be mindful of where they chose to conduct their celebrations. Hospitals, parliament, public pools, mosques, and recreation centers should be avoided. Nevertheless, for a single day, firecrackers sounded in the streets again. Smoke, ear-popping noise, scraps of red paper that would gust about for weeks to come.

Natalie and Ah Boon went into the city to see the celebratory float procession. String lights swayed in the dimming evening. Everywhere there was the press of sweaty bodies, the whine of mosquitoes, the smell of sweet meats roasting on hawker carts. *Where are the floats?*, children whined, scratching itchy necks and insect-bitten shins, shushed and bribed for silence by adults who pressed boiled sweets and sugared coconut strips into their hands.

Ah Boon kept his arm carefully around Natalie's waist. She wore a billowing maternity dress of fine cotton, shot through with silk to keep her cool during the day and warm at night. Ah Boon had on a new white shirt with matching pants, black leather shoes polished to a high shine. He'd showered in the afternoon, having spent the morning out at the dredging site. His hair, carefully combed through with gel, was slicked back into a neat, hard helmet, so smooth and perfect that one might think it brittle, prone to cracks.

The islands were almost gone now. The dredging had begun shortly after Ah Boon showed the Gah Men where to find them. Because he was the only Gah Man who could reliably locate them, Ah Boon was obliged to return to the site daily, to lead new ships and boats filled with equipment and sand-loading decks back to the elusive spot each day. He watched them dredge the beaches, load the giant buckets of sand onto barges to be taken away. He watched them detonate explosives at the base of the cliffs he had first glimpsed from his father's fishing boat. The cliffs that had made his father gasp, made him place his hand gently on Ah Boon's seven-year-old head. Those cliffs now crumbling like a dry, brittle biscuit. The shore where he had lain with Siok Mei, as if in a dream. That dream now given up.

He watched the islands shrink. A new kind of vanishing.

And so the show went on: The pilot project continued, their little lip of the coast distended and enlarged with the fill material from the vanished islands. The tree-planting stage had begun, the earth-binding roots being the mechanism by which the newly created land would solidify and settle. It was still early days, but all the signs pointed to the pilot being a great success.

The Great Reclamation would commence in earnest now. One thousand, five hundred hectares of land—it was a number Ah Boon couldn't wrap his head around. So much land, waiting to be created from nothing but sand and sea. Twenty-story-high flats, wide-laned highways, shopping centers, carefully designed parks. Their shiny new city awaited.

Ah Boon did not see Siok Mei after she had been detained. The last he'd heard, she was still refusing to renounce any plot to overthrow the state. How could she renounce something that had never existed, she repeated, over and over. Ah Boon did not write to her or ask about her. It was Ma who kept him updated on her life, for she was in touch with Siok Mei's uncle, who was permitted the occasional visit. It was Ma who told him that Siok Mei had lost weight, that her cheeks were sunken, her eyes dull. That even though she answered *fine* when asked how they were treating her inside, her hands trembled and she would not meet her uncle's eye. That the only time she seemed to regain her old energy was when they brought Yang to visit.

Ma herself refrained from pronouncing judgment on what Ah Boon had done, but inevitably ended these pointed updates with the complaint that people from the kampong were shunning her now, because of "what had happened." This was as close as they came to discussing the events of the past year. Ah Boon's response to this was always to direct her attention to some new toy he had brought her: an electric hand mixer, a lamp with an intricate floral shade, a shiny alarm clock. *Never mind all that*, he'd say, and though his insides wrenched, though he could not stop picturing this dull-eyed, sunken-cheeked version of Siok Mei, the smile on his face was unwavering, the patience in his voice eternal.

Saving the land reclamation project had secured Ah Boon a significant raise and promotion. He was looking to buy a newer, larger house. After this child, he and Natalie would have another one, perhaps even one more. They thought it wise to plan for the future. They hoped that Ma would come live with them, especially now. What *now* referred to was the other thing they didn't talk about. Uncle's body was barely recognizable by the time it had been found, crumpled in the burned wreckage of their house. At the funeral, Ma didn't say a word. She didn't cry, she didn't wail, she did nothing at all, only became very, very quiet. After the funeral, no one mentioned Uncle again.

The first float appeared, raising a roar from the crowd. Colorful cardboard cutouts of the people of the Federation in traditional dress—lilac baju kurung for the Malay woman, white kurta for the Sikh man, red cheongsam for the Chinese girl—aboard a platform festooned with bunting and streamers. The flag of the federation flew high above.

Then the second float: a gilded globe, *Majulah* emblazoned and repeated over and over, the same vibrant flags, the same colorful bunting. The third, the fourth, the fifth. The floats were sponsored by industry, religious, and political groups: the Piece Goods and Traders Guild, the Young Women Muslim Association, the Chinese Foodstuffs Importers Group. Flags, lions, people, lights. Each time a new float came into view, the crowd erupted into deafening cheers.

The mood was one of abundant joy. Freedom from the Ang Mohs; an independent, self-ruled federation. The people felt themselves to be part of a sweeping global movement; each day the newspapers reported other empires falling, other nation-states forming anew. The island's Merdeka was merely one of many, a small piece of a greater Merdeka.

What the cheering crowd could not know: A mere two years from this day, they would achieve more freedom than any of them had thought to expect that night, their little country cut loose from a federation rocked by economic strife and violent race riots, set adrift into its own tiny orbit. It would begin its longer life as an island without its hinterland, its heart without its body. That this would not seal its fate but instead make it richer, more prosperous than they could ever imagine, the Gah Men more powerful than ever before. But in other ways, also poorer. Also less prosperous. Either way, the island would transform beyond recognizability; the very streets upon which they stood would vanish, bulldozed in the name of exigency and progress. A forest of cement towers would rise from this rich, fertile earth.

From the sidelines, the Gah Men watched. A row of white shirts, white pants. Garlands of colorful flowers around their necks oozing their fragrance, the hands of photogenic children clasped in their own. As the floats went by one at a time, the Gah Men clapped, enthusiastic but ever controlled, careful, as always, not to get too carried away.

There'd been a moment when Ah Boon had thought himself incapable of doing it. He'd found himself wavering that first morning, when, fueled by bitter resolve, he'd taken the Gah Men out to the islands so the dredging could commence. They still had their hold over him, those lush, vanishing landmasses, those infuriating mysteries, and he still wanted to protect them. He'd almost turned around, shouted his apology to the sleek metal boat cutting through the waves behind him, said that he could not find them after all.

But as the old body of his father's boat thudded over the dull brown waves, the smell of fish pursuing him always, he saw the city, gleaming and spotless, rising as if dormant from the sea. Sparkling buildings of metal and glass, roads of flawless asphalt, bright electric streetlights; and as Natalie so often repeated, it was a beautiful, impossible sight. A beautiful, improbable, unlikely nation. He saw Pa, chained at the ankles with the Jipunlang at his back, kneeling in warm sand as hungry seabirds circled overhead. He saw Siok Mei staring past him in a crowd of rioters, shouting slogans as if her life depended on it. He saw Uncle, alone in a burning house.

He saw himself in his white shirt, white pants, round-rimmed glasses perched delicately on his nose. Clipboard in hand, planting flags in the ground, directing the barges and trucks carrying ton upon ton of freshly dredged sand. Future over past, progress over stagnation.

Fill it up, he would say, pointing to the swamp and sea.

Bury it.

Make it new again.

ACKNOWLEDGMENTS

Thank you to Sarah McGrath, for your deep insight, generous vision, and careful edits. I have learned so much and grown immeasurably as a writer from working with you. Thank you to everyone at Riverhead for all the time, effort, and creativity that has gone into making *The Great Reclamation* a reality.

Huge thanks to Julie Barer for being a tireless reader, editor, and champion of my writing. From our very first conversation when you told me to make the book bigger than it was, I knew my work would be in capable and ambitious hands, and for that I will always be grateful.

This novel could not exist without the scholars who generously shared their time, expertise, and feedback with me. Any mistakes and creative liberties taken are all mine. I am especially grateful to Kwok Kian-Woon for being an early reader, mentor, and supporter of my work. Thank you to Timothy Barnard for historical notes, reading recommendations, and deep knowledge of Singapore's environmental history, to Choo Ruizhi for data on colonial-era fishing industries, to Dan Friess for fascinating information about shifting coastlines and the evolution of Singapore's mangrove forests.

Books that were invaluable to my research and inspiration for this novel include *Singapore: A Biography* by Mark R. Frost and Yu-Mei Bal-asingamchow, *The Politics of Landscapes in Singapore* by Brenda S. A. Yeoh and Lily Kong, *Lee's Lieutenants: Singapore's Old Guard* edited by Lam Peng Er and Kevin YL Tan, *Colonialism, Violence and Muslims in Southeast Asia: The Maria Hertogh Controversy and its Aftermath* by Syed Muhd Khairudin Aljunied, *Nature Contained: Environmental Histories of Singapore* edited by Timothy P. Barnard, *50 Years of Urban Planning in Singapore* edited by Chye Kiang Heng, *Beyond the Blue Gate: Recollections of a Political Prisoner* by Teo Soh Lung, *My Youth in Black & White* by Lim Chin Joo, *Home Is Not Here* by Wang Gungwu, *State of Emergency* by Jeremy Tiang, *My Grandfather's Road* by Neo Kim Seng, *Rawa* by Isa Kamari, and *Unrest* by Yeng Pway Ngon (translated by Jeremy Tiang). Finally, many details of everyday life and the land reclamation work on the East Coast came from *A Report on the Fishermen of Siglap* by the Siglap Community Centre Youth Group, edited by Chou Loke Ming, as well as oral history interviews found in the National Archives of Singapore.

Thank you to everyone at the Michener Center for Writers. Special thanks to my thesis adviser, Elizabeth McCracken, who read countless drafts of this novel, emboldened me to lean into the strange and singular, and never failed to comfort and inspire. Thank you to MCW director Bret Anthony Johnston for advice both sage and practical. Thank you to all the teachers at UT Austin with whom I was fortunate to cross paths, with special thanks to Roger Reeves, Branden Jacobs-Jenkins, and Heather Houser, whose teaching and mentorship have greatly shaped my creative practice.

Thank you to all my Michener classmates. It's been a true privilege to read your poems and books, to watch your plays and films. Special thanks to dear friends and all-around geniuses Tracey Rose, Shangyang

Fang, and Yuki Tanaka. I am inspired by your talent and buoyed by your friendship every single day.

Thank you to my undergraduate thesis adviser, Bruce Robbins, whose teaching on nineteenth-century novels—in particular, Stendhal's *The Red and the Black*, to which *The Great Reclamation* is very much indebted—first ignited my imagination more than a decade ago.

Thank you to teacher, mentor, and friend Nancy Zafris, whom I miss very much.

Thank you to Tan Siyou for reading drafts, sharing ideas and kueh alike.

Sam, Christine, and Vadim—lifelong friends and generous readers—thank you.

To my brother, for plot advice, TV tropes, and the best conversations; to my mother, who told me so many of the stories that make up *The Great Reclamation*: thank you. I wrote this book for you.

To August, thank you for existing. The world is magic with you in it. To Kalle, soul mate, best friend, and first reader in all things, I couldn't do any of it without you, nor would I want to. Thank you for this life of wild possibility. I love you both.

© Juliana Tan

Rachel Heng received her MFA in fiction and playwriting from the Michener Center for Writers. Winner of the New American Voices Award, she has received grants and fellowships from the National Endowment for the Arts, Sewanee Writers' Conference, and the National Arts Council of Singapore, among others. Her short fiction has been published in *The New Yorker* and *McSweeney's*. Born and raised in Singapore, she is currently an assistant professor of English at Wesleyan University.